Strange Things

A blazing diamond of light rose out of the Shadowlander camp. It spun slowly. A core of darkness centered it. From that, blackness pulsed out into the all-spanning web it anchored.

Nobody was looking at the hills when the pinkish light returned. No one noticed until it flared so brilliantly that it rivalled the brightness here at hand.

It burned behind two mounted figures. It cast their hideous shadows upon the night itself. Crow shadows circled them. Two huge ravens perched upon the shoulders of the larger figure.

Nobody breathed for a while. Not even Shadowspinner, I'd bet. And I was sure he had no more idea what was happening than I did.

The pink flare faded. A cable of pink reached toward Dejagore, like a snake probing, stretching. As one end neared us the nether end broke loose. That whipped our way too fast for the eye to follow and in an instant screamed into Shadowspinner's bright diamond. Sun-brilliant flash splashed out of that sorcerous construct's far side like suddenly flung barrels of burning oil.

Immediately the dark web overhead began to shrink back into the remnants of the diamond.

The air vibrated with the Shadowmaster's anger.

Tor Books by Glen Cook

An Ill Fate Marshalling
Reap the East Wind
The Swordbearer
The Tower of Fear

THE BLACK COMPANY
The Black Company (The First Chronicle)
Shadows Linger (The Second Chronicle)
The White Rose (The Third Chronicle)
The Silver Spike
Shadow Games (The First Book of the South)
Dreams of Steel (The Second Book of the South)
Bleak Seasons (Book One of Glittering Stone)

The Sixth Chronicle
of the
Black Company

BLEAK
SEASONS

GLEN COOK

BOOK ONE
OF
GLITTERING STONE

TOR
fantasy ®

A TOM DOHERTY ASSOCIATES BOOK
NEW YORK

This is a work of fiction. All the characters and events portrayed in this novel are either fictitious or are used fictitiously.

BLEAK SEASONS

Copyright © 1996 by Glen Cook

Cover art by Nicholas Jainschigg

A Tor Book
Published by Tom Doherty Associates, Inc.
175 Fifth Avenue
New York, NY 10010

Tor Books on the World Wide Web:
http://www.tor.com

Tor® is a registered trademark of Tom Doherty Associates, Inc.

ISBN: 0-812-55532-5
Library of Congress Card Catalog Number: 95-30051

First edition: April 1996
First mass market edition: January 1997

Printed in the United States of America

0 9 8 7 6 5 4 3 2 1

For Trish and Kim, precious friends
of a decade and more.

BLEAK SEASONS

Incessant wind sweeps the plain. It mutters across grey pavements that sweep from horizon to horizon. It sings around scattered black pillars, a chorus of ghosts. It tumbles leaves and scatters dust come from afar. It teases the hair of a corpse that has lain undisturbed for a generation, mummifying. Impishly, the gale tosses a leaf into the cadaver's silently screaming mouth, tugs it away again. The wind carries the breath of winter.

Lightning leaps from pillar to ebon pillar like a child skittering from base to base in a game of tag. For a moment there is color on that spectral plain.

The pillars might be mistaken for relics of a fallen city. They are not. They are too few and too randomly placed. Nor has a one ever fallen, though many have been gnawed deeply by the teeth of the hungry wind.

1

. . . fragments . . .

    . . . just blackened fragments, crumbling between my fingers.

Browned page corners that reveal half a dozen words in a crabbed hand, their context no longer known.

All that remains of two volumes of the Annals. A thousand hours of labor. Four years of history. Gone forever.

Or are they?

I do not want to go back. I do not want to relive the horror. I do not want to reclaim the pain. There is pain too deep to withstand right here, right now. There is no way to recapture the totality of that awfulness, anyway. The mind and heart, safely over to the farther shore, simply refuse to encompass the enormity of the voyage.

And there is no time. There is a war on.

Always there is a war on.

Uncle Doj wants something. Just as well to stop now. Teardrops make the ink run.

He is going to make me drink some strange philtre.

Fragments . . .

. . . all around, fragments of my work, my life, my love and my pain, scattered in this bleak season. . . .

And in the darkness, shards of time.

2

Hey, there! Welcome to the city of the dead. Don't mind those guys staring. Ghosts don't see a lot of strangers—at least of a friendly persuasion. You're right. They do look hungry. That happens during these siege things.

Try not to look too much like a lamb roast.

Think that's a joke? Stay away from the Nar.

Welcome to Dejagore, what the Taglians call this deathtrap. The teeny brown Shadowlanders the Black Company grabbed it from call it Stormgard. People who actually live here always called it Jaicur—even when that was a crime. And who knows what the Nyueng Bao call it. And who cares, eh? They aren't talking and they aren't part of the equation anyway.

That's one of them. That rascal there, no meat on him and

a skull face. Everybody around here is some shade of brown but theirs is different. It has a grey cast to it. Almost deathly. You won't mistake a Nyueng Bao for anything else.

Their eyes are like polished coal no fire will ever warm.

That noise?

Sounds like Mogaba, the Nar and the First Legion rooting out Shadowlanders again. Some get inside almost every night. They are like field mice. You just can't get rid of them all.

Found some the other day that had been in hiding since the Company took the city.

How about that smell out there? It was worse before the Shadowlanders started burying the bodies. Maybe a shovel was a little too complicated a machine.

Those long mounds that radiate from the city like spokes have corpses stacked like cordwood inside. Sometimes they didn't pile the dirt on deep enough and the gasses of corruption burst the mounds open. That's when you hope the wind is blowing their way.

You see how positively they are thinking, all the not-yet-filled-trenches they are digging. A lot of the dirt goes into the ramps.

The elephants are the worst. They take forever to rot. They tried burning them once, but all that did was irritate the buzzards. So where they could they just dragged the bodies over and incorporated them into their ramps.

Who? The ugly little guy with the uglier hat? That is One-Eye. You must have been warned about him.

How come One-Eye? On account of the eye patch. Clever, huh?

The other runt is Goblin. You should have been warned about him, too. No? Well, stay out of their way. All the time is best, but especially if they are arguing, and most particularly if they have been drinking. As wizards go they are no earthshakers but they are more than you will be able to handle.

Puny as they are, they are the main reason the Shadowlanders have stayed out there in the country roughing it, leaving

the wallowable luxuries of the city to the Taglian troops and
Black Company.

No, now pay attention. Goblin is the white one. All right,
you're right, he is overdue for his annual bath. Goblin is the one
who looks like a toad. One-Eye is the one with the hat and the
patch.

The guys in the once-upon-a-time-they-were-white tunics
are Taglian soldiers. Every day now every one of them asks himself what damned fool notion made him enroll in the legions.

The folks wearing the colored sheets and unhappy expres-
sions are locals. Jaicuri.

Fancy this. When the Company and the legions swooped
down from the north and surprised Stormshadow they hailed
the newcomers as liberators. They strew the streets with rose
petals and favorite daughters.

Now the only reason they don't stab their liberators in the
back is that the alternative is worse. Now they are alive enough
to starve and be abused.

Shadowspinner is not famous for kindness and kissing babies.

The kids all over? Those almost happy and fat urchins?
Nyueng Bao. All Nyueng Bao.

The Jaicuri nearly stopped making babies after the Shadowmasters came. Most of the few that were born failed to survive the hard times since. The handful still breathing are protected more fiercely than any treasure. You won't find them
running naked through the streets, squealing and totally ignoring strangers.

Who are the Nyueng Bao? You never heard of them?

It is a good question. And a hard one to answer.

The Nyueng Bao don't talk to outsiders except through
their Speaker but the word is that they are religious pilgrims who
were on the homeward leg of a once-in-a-generation hadj who
got trapped by circumstance. The Taglian soldiers say they hail
from vast river delta swamps west of Taglios. They are a prim-

itive, minuscule minority abhorred by the majority Gunni, Vehdna, and Shadar religions.

The whole Nyueng Bao people makes the pilgrimage. And the whole people got caught right in the deep shit here in Dejagore.

They need to work on their timing. Or they should sharpen their skills at appeasing their gods.

The Black Company cut a deal with the Nyueng Bao. Goblin and their Speaker gobbled for half an hour and it was settled. The Nyueng Bao would ignore the Black Company and Taglians for whom the Company is responsible. The Nyueng Bao would be ignored in turn.

It works. Mostly.

Their men are a sort you don't want to upset. They don't take shit from anybody.

They never start anything—except, according to the Taglians, by being too damned stubborn to do what they are told.

Sounds like One-Eye style reasoning at work there.

Just kick those crows. They're getting too goddamn bold! Think they own the place. . . . Hey! You got one. Grab it! They aren't good eating but they are a sight better than no eating at all.

Shit. Got away. Hell, that happens. Head for the citadel. You get your best look at the layout from up there.

3

Those guys? They are Company. Never guess, huh? White guys down here? The one with the wild hair is Big Bucket. He turned into a pretty fair sergeant. He is just crazy enough. With him are Otto and Hagop. They have been around longer than anybody but Goblin and One-Eye. Those two have been

Old Crew for generations. One-Eye ought to be sneaking up on two hundred.

That bunch is Company, too. Shirking work. The antique lunger is Wheezer. Not much good for anything. How he got through the big brawl no one knows. They say he busted heads with the best of them.

The other two black guys are the Geek and the Freak. No telling why. Nothing wrong with them. Look like a couple of rubbed ebony statues, don't they?

You think these names just come out of a hat? They earn them the hard way. Usually they come out from under One-Eye's hat, really. Yeah, they probably have real names. But they have been called by nicknames so long even they have trouble remembering.

Goblin and One-Eye are the main ones not to forget. And to remember not to put behind you. They do not deal well with temptation.

This is Glimmers Like Dewdrops Street. Nobody knows why. A real mouthful, right? You ought to hear it in Jaicuri. A jawbreaker. This is the route the Company took coming in to snatch the tower. Maybe they will rename it Runs With Blood Street.

Yeah, the Company charged through here in the heart of the night, killing anything that moved, and jammed in there before they had any idea what was happening. With Shapeshifter's help they roared on up the tower where they let him help finish off Stormshadow before they tagged him.

It was an old Company grudge. They owed Shifter from another generation, when Shifter, helping Soulcatcher break the city's resistance, murdered One-Eye's brother Tom-Tom when the Company was in service to the Syndic of Beryl. Croaker, One-Eye and Goblin, Otto and Hagop are the only guys left from those days. Hell, Croaker is gone now. Isn't he? History-worshipping slob is buried out there in one of those mounds. Fertilizing the plain. Mogaba is the Old Man now. Sort of, in his own mind.

Those who form it come and go but the Company is forever. Every brother, great or small, is a snack just not yet snapped up by the devouring maw of time.

Those big black monster men watching the gate are the Nar. They are descendants of the Black Company of centuries ago. Scary beasts, aren't they? Mogaba and a whole herd of his pals joined the Company quest at Gea-Xle. The Old Crew have had no pleasure of them.

You mix the whole crowd up and squeeze them dry, you could not come up with two ounces of sense of humor.

There used to be a lot more of them than there are now but they keep getting themselves killed. They are bone crazy, the whole lot. For them the Company is a religion. Only their Company is not the Black Company of the Old Crew. That becomes more apparent almost by the hour.

All Nar stand more than six feet tall. All Nar run like the wind and leap like gazelles. Mogaba chose only the most athletic and warriorly to join the quest for Khatovar. All the Nar are quick as cats and strong as gorillas. All the Nar use their weapons like they were born with them in their hands.

The rest? The ones who call themselves the Old Crew? Yeah. It is true. The Company is more than a job. If it was just a job, just selling swords to whoever would pay, the Black Company would not be in this part of the world. There was work a-plenty in the north. The world never lacks for potentates who want to bully their subjects or neighbors.

The Company is family for those who belong. The Company is home. The Company is a nation of outcasts, alone and defying the whole world.

Now the Company is trying to complete its cycle of life. It is on a quest in search of its birthplace, fabled Khatovar. But all the world seems determined that Khatovar shall be unattainable, a virgin forever hidden behind a veil of shadow.

The Company is home, sure, but Croaker was the only one who ever went completely misty-eyed over that damned angle.

For him the Black Company was a mystery cult—though he never went as far as Mogaba and made it a holy calling.

Watch your step. They still don't have all the mess cleaned out from the last attack. If you couldn't tell by the smell. The Jaicuri don't help much anymore. Maybe it is lack of civic pride.

The Nyueng Bao? They are just here. They stay out of the way. They have this notion that they can stay neutral. They will learn. Shadowspinner is going to teach them. Nobody stays neutral in this world. The best you can do is choose your spot to jump in.

Little out of shape? You will come around. A few weeks running hither and yon, blunting Shadowspinner's probes and hustling out on Mogaba's spoiling raids, will get you as sharp as a Nyueng Bao sword.

You thought sieges were all just laying around relaxing and waiting the other guy out?

Man, this other guy is a foamy-mouth lunatic.

And not just nuts. He is a sorcerer. A major player, though he hasn't shown much here. Before the Old Man got himself offed in the big slugfest that trapped everyone here he hurt Spinner real bad. The old devil just hasn't been himself since. Poor baby.

This is it. Top of the tower. And there is the whole stinking burg, laid out like it is on one of those sand tables Lady always liked.

Oh, yeah. Those rumors have made it here, too. They started with some Shadowlander prisoners. Maybe that *was* Kina up north. Or something. But it could not have been Lady. She died right out there. Fifty guys saw her taken down. Half of them got killed trying to rescue her.

How can you say that? You can't be sure? How many eyewitnesses does it take? She is dead. The Old Man is dead. They're all dead, them what did not get inside before Mogaba sealed the gates.

The whole mob is dead. All but the crowd in here. And they

are caught between lunatics. It's a tossup who is crazier, Mogaba or Shadowspinner.

You see it all? That is it. Dejagore enduring the siege of the Shadowmasters. Not real impressive, is it? But every one of those burned areas memorializes a ferocious hand to hand, house to house negotiation with the Shadowlanders.

Fires start easily in Dejagore.

Hell is supposed to be hot, isn't it?

4

. . . who I am, on the improbably remote chance that my scribblings do survive. I am Murgen, Standardbearer of the Black Company, though I bear the shame of having lost the standard in battle. I am keeping unofficial Annals because Croaker is dead, One-Eye won't, and hardly anyone else can read or write. I was the heir Croaker trained. I will do it even without official sanction.

I will be your guide for a few months or weeks or days, however long it takes the Shadowlanders to force our present predicament to its inevitable end.

Nobody inside these walls is going to get out of this. There are too many of them and too few of us. Our sole advantage is that our commander is as mad as theirs. That makes us unpredictable. Don't add much hope, though.

Mogaba will not give up as long as he personally is capable of hanging onto something with one hand while he throws rocks with the other.

I expect my writings to blow away on a dark wind, never to be touched by another eye. Or they might become the tinder Shadowspinner uses to light the pyre under the last man he murders after taking Dejagore.

If anyone does find this, brother, we begin. This is the Book of Murgen, last of the Annals of the Black Company.

The long tale winds down.

I will die lost and frightened in a world so alien I cannot understand a tenth of it when I focus all my soul. It is so *old*.

Times lies heavily here. Two thousand-year-old traditions underpin incredible absurdities taken completely for granted. Dozens of races and cultures and religions exist in a mix that should be volatile but has persisted so long that conflicts are just reflexive twitches in an ancient body mostly too tired to bother anymore.

Taglios is only one large principality. There are scores more, mostly now in the Shadowlands, all pretty similar.

The major peoples are the Gunni, the Shadar, and the Vehdna, names which which define religion, race and culture all at once. The Gunni are the most numerous and widespread. Gunni temples, to a bewilderingly broad pantheon, are so numerous you're seldom out of sight of one.

Physically, Gunni are small and dark but not black like the Nar. Gunni men wear toga-like robes, weather permitting. Their bright mix of colors declare caste, cult, and professional alliances. Women, too, dress brightly, but in several layers of wraparound cloth. They veil their faces if unmarried, though marriages are made early. They wear their dowries as jewelry. Before they go out they illustrate their foreheads with the caste/cult/professional markings of both their husbands and their fathers. I will never decipher those hieroglyphs.

Shadar are paler, like heavily tanned whites from the north. They are big, usually over six feet. They do not shave or pluck their beard, unlike the Gunni. Some sects never cut their hair. Bathing is not forbidden but it is a vice seldom indulged. Shadar all dress in grey and wear turbans to define their status. They eat meat. Gunni do not. I have never seen a Shadar woman. Maybe they find their babies under cabbage leaves.

The Vehdna are the least numerous of the major Taglian ethnic groups. They are as light as the Shadar but smaller, more lightly built, with ferocious features. They share none of the Shadar's spartan values. Their religion forbids almost everything, rules honored in the breach quite often. They like a little color in their costume, though not bright like the Gunni. They wear pantaloons and real shoes. Even the poorest conceal their bodies and wear something atop their heads. Low-caste Gunni wear nothing but loincloths. Married Vehdna women wear only black. You can see nothing but their eyes. Unmarried Vehdna women you don't see at all.

Only the Vehdna believe in an afterlife. And that only for men except for a few female warrior saints and daughters of prophets who had balls big enough to be honorary men.

Nyueng Bao, rarely seen, usually wear loose-fitting long-sleeve pullover shirts and baggy lightweight pants, generally black, men and women alike. Children go naked.

Any city down here is glorious chaos.

It is always a holy day for somebody.

5

From the citadel tower it is obvious that Dejagore is a complete contrivance. Of course, most walled cities are shaped by the probability that, part of the time, neighboring states will be managed by thugs. Your own city's masters will never be worse than benevolent despots, of course, and their worst ambition will be to heighten the hometown glory.

Until the appearance of the Shadowmasters one short generation ago war was an alien concept throughout this part of the world. It had seen neither armies nor soldiers in all the centuries since the Black Company's departure.

Into this improbable paradise came the Shadowmasters, lords of darkness from the far reaches of the earth who brought with them all the wolves of the old nightmare. Soon inept armies were about. They stalked unprepared kingdoms like great cruel behemoths even the gods could not stay. The dark tide spread. Cities crumbled. A lucky few the Shadowmasters chose to rebuild. The peoples of the newly-founded Shadowlands were given their options: obedience or death.

Jaicur was reborn as Stormgard, seat of the Shadowmaster Stormshadow, she who could bring the winds and thunder howling and bellowing in the darkness. She who had borne the name Stormbringer in another age and place.

First Stormshadow raised a mound forty feet high on top of the ruins of captured Jaicur, at the heart of a plain she had flattened absolutely by slaves and prisoners of war. Earth for the mound came from the ring of hills completely surrounding the plain. With the mound complete and faced on its outer sides with several layers of imported stone, Stormshadow built her new city up top. And that she surrounded with walls another forty feet high. She did not overlook the latest theories about towers for enfilading fire and barbicans to protect her elevated gates.

All the Shadowmasters seemed driven by a paranoid need to make themselves safe in their home places.

Never once in her planning, though, did she take into account the possibility that she might have to resist the onslaught of the Black Company.

I wish we were half as wicked as I talk.

Dejagore has four gates. Each stands at one point of the compass rose. Each is at the end of a paved highway running straight in from the hills. Only the road from the south carries any traffic these days.

Mogaba has sealed three gates, leaving only sally ports which are guarded by his Nar at all times. Mogaba is determined to fight. He is just as determined that not one of our raggedy-ass Taglian legionnaires will run off and not go down with him.

None of us, be we Black Company Old Crew, Nar, Jaicuri, Taglian, Nyueng Bao, or someone else who had the bad luck to get caught here, is going to get out alive. Not unless Shadowspinner and his gang get so bored they go looking for someone else to bully. Right. You've got the eight and ten of swords and to go down you're going to bet your ass on pulling the nine.

Your chances of pulling that nine are better than ours of getting out of here.

The fortified encampment of the Shadowlanders stands south of the city. It is so close we can reach it with our heavy artillery. You can see charred timbers where we tried to burn them out the day of the big battle. We have raided them a few times since then, too, but no longer have the strength to risk.

We can't seem to discourage Shadowspinner, though.

Like most warlords he doesn't let reality get in the way of his doing whatever he wants to do.

The artillery gives them a wake-up five nights out of five, pick a random time. That keeps them cranky and tired and a lot less effective whenever they attack. Trouble is, so much effort keeps us tired and cranky, too. And we have other projects going as well.

Shadowspinner is a puzzle. He is not the first of his kind in Company experience. The heavyweight killers in our past, though, when faced with a situation like this, would have stomped on Dejagore like jumping on an anthill before looking for a real challenge. But here lightweights Goblin and One-Eye can slide around quickly and treacherously enough to parry Spinner's every feeble thrust.

His weakness is a mystery.

Makes you nervous when an enemy doesn't do everything you think he can. And a Shadowspinner doesn't become a top badass being gentle.

One-Eye sees everything in its wickedest light. He says Spinner is slacking because Longshadow has a hold on him and is weakening him deliberately. Your basic old-time power politics with the Company in the middle.

Before we came along the Shadowmasters did find their biggest challenges in fighting one another.

On principle Goblin seldom agrees with One-Eye about anything. He claims Shadowspinner is lulling us while he recovers from wounds that were more serious than we suspected.

My guess is, six of one, half a dozen of the other.

Crows circle the Shadowlander camp. Always they circle. Some come, some go, but a baker's dozen minimum are there all the time. Others haunt us day and night. Wherever I go, whenever, a crow is nearby. Except inside. They don't get inside. We don't let them inside. Those that try end up in somebody's pot.

Croaker had a thing about crows. I think I understand it now. But the bats bother me more.

We don't see the bats as often. The crows get most of them. (These crows are not ashamed to come out at night.) And those that the crows don't get we do, most of the time. Inevitably, though, a few get away. And that isn't good.

They spy for the Shadowmasters. They are the far-ranging eyes of wickedness out here where our enemies cannot always manipulate the living darkness.

Only two Shadowmasters remain. Spinner has problems. They do not have the reach or control they showed back when they could and did run the shadows into the very heart of the Taglian Territories.

They are fading from the stage.

One dreams.

Dreams too easily become nightmares.

6

When you look down from the citadel you have to wonder how the Jaicuri manage, all jammed inside Dejagore's walls. Truth is, they don't and never did.

At one time the hills surrounding the plain were covered with farms and orchards and vineyards. After the shadow came enterprises gradually disappeared as the peasant families abandoned the land. And then the anti-shadow, the Black Company, came, ever so hungry after the long sprint south from the victory at Ghoja Ford. And then came the Shadowlander armies which battered us.

Now the hills bear little but memories of what once was. Vultures never picked bones much cleaner than those hills have been gleaned.

The wisest peasants were those who fled early. Their children will repopulate the land.

Later the stupid ones ran here, inside the false safety of Dejagore's walls. When Mogaba is particularly cranky he drives a few hundred out the gate. They are just mouths crying to be filled. Food must be husbanded for those willing to die defending the walls.

Locals who fail to contribute, or who demonstrate a weakness for getting sick or seriously injured, go out the gate right behind the peasants.

Shadowspinner won't take any in but those willing to help raise his earthworks and dig his burial trenches. The former means laboring under falls of missiles directed by old friends inside, while the latter means making the bed where you will lie as soon as you are useful no longer.

Hard choices.

Mogaba cannot fathom why his military genius isn't universally hailed.

He doesn't mess with the Nyueng Bao. Not yet. They haven't contributed much to Dejagore's defense but they don't sap resources, either. Their babies are getting fat while the rest of us tighten our belts.

You don't see many dogs or cats now. Horses manage only because they are militarily protected, and then only a handful of them. We're going to eat hearty when the last fodder is gone.

Small game like rats and pigeons are becoming scarce. Sometimes you hear the outraged protest of a crow taken by surprise.

The Nyueng Bao are survivors.

They are a race possessed of a single impassive face.

Mogaba does not bother them mainly because when any-body does the whole bunch gets pissed off. And they consider fighting a really serious, holy business.

They stay out of the way when they can but they aren't paci-fists. A couple of times the Shadowlanders have regretted try-ing to push through their part of town.

The Nyueng Bao generated an amazing amount of carnage both times.

Rumor among the Jaicuri says they eat their enemies.

It is true, human bones showing evidence of butchery and cookery have been found. Jaicuri are mainly of the Gunni reli-gion. Gunni are vegetarians.

I do not believe the Nyueng Bao are responsible, but Ky Dam refuses to deny even the blackest allegation against his peo-ple.

Maybe he will accept any canard that makes the Nyueng Bao seem more dangerous. Maybe he wants that kind of talk so fear will build.

Survivors grasp the tools at hand.

I wish they would talk. I'd bet they could tell stories that would curl your toes and straighten your hair.

Ah! Dejagore! Those halcyon days, slouching through hell with a smile on.

How long before all the fun goes out of the town?

7

Bone tired, just as I had been every night for as long as I could remember, I went to take my turn on the wall. I had no am-bition at all and even less energy. Seated in a crenel, I heaped aspersions on the ancestors of all my bitty Shadowlander bud-dies. I am afraid I lacked creativity but I made up for that with virulence. They were up to something out there. You could hear rattlings and mutterings and see torches moving around.

There were all the harbingers of a night without sleep. Couldn't these people be normal and handle their business during regular hours?

It didn't sound like they were more enthusiastic than me. I caught the occasional sharp remark about me or my foredaddies, like this mess was all my fault. I guess they were motivated mainly by their sure knowledge that they would never go home if they didn't recapture Stormgard.

Maybe nobody on either side would get out of this one alive.

A crow called, mocking us all. I didn't bother throwing a rock at it.

It was misty out. A half-hearted drizzle came and went. Lightning stalked beyond the hills to the south. It had been hot and humid all day, then had turned viciously stormy toward evening. Lakes of water stood in the streets. Stormshadow's engineers had not made good drainage a high priority, despite the natural advantages available.

It would not be a good night for attacking tall walls. And not much easier for anyone defending them.

Still, I almost felt sorry for the little buggers down below.

Candles and Red Rudy finished the long climb from the street, groaning. Each carried a heavy leather sack. Candles grumbled, "I'm too old for this shit."

"If it works out we'll all get to get old."

Both men leaned on merlons while they caught their wind. Then they dumped their sacks into the darkness. Somebody down there swore in a Shadowlander dialect. "Serves you right, asshole," Rudy growled back. "Go home. Let me sleep."

All of the Old Crew invested time hauling dirt.

"I know," Candles told me. "I know. But what good is alive if you're too damned tired to give a shit?"

If you read the Annals you know our brothers have said the same thing since the beginning. I shrugged. I could come up with nothing inspirational. Mostly you don't try to justify or motivate, you just go on.

Candles grumbled, "Goblin wants you. We'll cover you here."

In battered Shadowlander Rudy shouted downward, "Yeah, I know your turkey gobble. Fuck you."

I grunted. It was my watch but I could leave if I wanted. Mogaba didn't even pretend to try to control the Old Crew anymore. We did our part. We held our ground. We just would not conform to his ideas of what the Black Company ought to be.

But there was going to be one hell of a showdown if the Shadowmaster and his circus ever hit the road.

"Where is he?"

"Down Three." That he signed in finger speech. We use deaf speech frequently if we talk business out in the open. Bats and crows can't read it. Neither can any of Mogaba's faction.

I grunted again. "Be back."

"Sure."

I descended the steep, slippery stair, muscles aching, anticipating the weight of the sack I would be carrying when I came back.

What could Goblin want? Probably a decision on something trivial. That runt and his monocular sidekick religiously avoid taking on any responsibility.

I run the Old Crew, most of the time, because nobody else wants to bother.

We have established ourselves in an area of tall brick tenements close to the wall, southwest of the north gate, which is the only gate still fully functional. From the first hour of the siege we have been improving our position.

Mogaba thinks in terms of attack. He does not believe a war can be won from behind stone walls. He wants to meet the Shadowlanders on the wall, to throw them back, then to charge outside and stomp them. He launches spoiling raids and nuisance attacks to keep them wobbly. He won't prepare for the possibility that they might get inside the city in significant numbers, although almost every attack puts Shadowlanders on our side of the wall before we can concentrate enough to push them back.

Someday, sometime, things won't go Mogaba's way. Someday Shadowspinner's people are going to grab a gate. Someday we are going to see full scale city war.

That is inevitable.

The Old Crew is ready, Mogaba. Are you?

We will become invisible, Your Arrogance. We have played this game before. We read the Annals. We will be the ghosts who kill.

We hope.

Shadows are the question. Shadows are the problem. What do they know? What will they be able to find?

Those villains have not been called Shadowmasters just be- cause they love the darkness.

8

With the exceptions of three hidden doors, all entrances to the Company's quarters have been bricked up. Likewise every window opening below third-floor levels. Alleys and breezeways are now a maze of deathtraps. The three usable entrances can be reached only by climbing outside stairways subject to missile fire their entire rise. Where we could manage we have fireproofed.

For the Black Company there is no inactivity during the days of siege. Even One-Eye works. When I can find him.

Every man stays too damned busy and too damned tired to dwell upon our situation.

After entering a concealed entrance known only to the brothers of the Old Crew, the crows and bats, the shadows, the Nyueng Bao watchers down the street and any Nar who care to keep track from the north barbican, I trundled down flight after flight of steps. I reached a basement where Big Bucket dozed beside a lonely, fitful little candle. Quiet though I was, he cracked an eyelid. He wasted no breath on a challenge. A ramshackle, twisted wardrobe tilted against the wall behind him, its door hanging crookedly on one damaged hinge. I pulled the door gently and eased inside.

Any outsider force reaching the cellar would find the wardrobe stuffed with desperately meager food stores.

The cabinet fronts a tunnel. Tunnels join all our buildings. Mogaba and anyone else interested might expect as much. If they got down into our cellars a little work would show them what they hoped to find.

That ought to satisfy them.

The tunnel entered another cellar. Several men were asleep there, amidst tremendous clutter and a smell like a bear's den. I moved slowly until recognized.

Had I been an intruder I would not have been the first never to return from the underworld.

Now I entered the real secret places.

New Stormgard rose atop old Jaicur. Little effort was made to demolish the old town. Many of the earlier structures had been in excellent condition.

We have a bewildering maze dug out down where no one ought to think to look. It gets a tad bigger whenever a sack of earth goes to the wall or into one of our other projects. It is no cozy warren, though. It takes willpower to go down into those dank, dark places where the air hardly moves, candles never come wholly to life, and there is at least a chance that any shadow may harbor a screaming death.

And me, I have a thing about being buried alive.

It gets no easier with practice.

Hagop and Otto, Goblin and One-Eye and I went through this before, on the Plain of Fear, where for about five thousand years we lived like badgers in the ground.

"Cletus. Where's Goblin?" Cletus is one of three brothers who serve as our engineers and master artillerymen.

"Around the corner. Next cellar."

Cletus, Loftus and Longinus are geniuses. They figured out how to bring fresh air down the chimneys of existing structures up top, then into the deep tunnels, let it flow slowly through the complex, then send it up other chimneys. Plain engineering, but it seemed like sorcery to me. A flow of breathable air, though slow and never pure, serves us well enough.

It does nothing to lessen the damp and the smell.

I found Goblin. He was holding a candle for Longinus while the latter slapped wet mortar onto freshly scrubbed stonework about eye level. "What's the problem, Goblin?"

"Rained like a bastard up there, eh?"

"Gods swiped a river somewhere and dropped it here. Why?"

"We've got a thousand leaks down here."

"Big problem?"

"Could be later on. There's no drainage. We're as low as we can go unless the Twelve tunnel goes good."

"Sounds like an engineering problem to me."

"It is," Longinus said, smoothing the mortar. "And Clete did anticipate it. We've waterproofed from the start. Trouble is, you can't tell how you're doing until you get a really nasty rain. We're lucky it didn't go on the way it does during the rainy season. Three days of that, we might've gotten flooded out."

"Still sounds like an engineering problem. You can handle it, right?"

Longinus shrugged. "We'll work on it. That's all we can do, Croaker."

Little dig there. Like telling me, let everybody do their own worrying.

"That's why you wanted me?" It seemed a little weak, even for Goblin.

"No. Longo, you don't hear anything." The toad-faced man made a complex gesture with three fingers of his left hand as he said that. Some half-hinted glimmer trailed behind his fingers momentarily. Longinus went back to work like he was deaf.

"It so important you need to cut him out?"

"He talks. He don't mean no harm but he can't help repeating everything he hears."

"And makes it better when he tells it. I know. All right. Tell me."

"Something has happened with the Shadowmaster. He's changed. Me and One-Eye only decided for sure about an hour ago but we think it's been going on for a while. He's just kept us from seeing it."

"What?"

Goblin leaned closer, as though Longinus might yet eavesdrop. "He's gotten well, Murgen. He's just about back to normal. He's been getting his feet under him before he comes down on us with them both at once. We also decided that he is hiding the change more from his buddy Longshadow than he is from us. We don't scare him that much."

I stiffened, recalling strange behavior on the encircling plain, going on right now. "Oh, shit!"

"What?"

"He's going to come tonight. Real soon. They were moving into position when I came down. I thought it was just the usual. . . . We'd better go full alert." I headed out of there with what energy I had, announcing the alert wherever I saw anybody.

9

Shadowspinner did not hurry. The Company took its positions on the wall. The Taglian rabble we led got as ready as they ever get. I sent warning to Mogaba and Speaker Ky Dam. Mogaba is a jerk and a lunatic but not a complete fool. He believes he keeps the job separate from personalities. If Goblin claimed we were in big trouble he would listen.

Alarms sounded everywhere. Shouts of anger at being anticipated rose outside the wall.

The civilian population began to respond. Fear swept the darkened streets. This felt bigger than usual. As always, the old-timers among the Jaicuri recalled the first coming of the Shadowmasters. Back then the enemy first wave consisted of deadly flickers of darkness.

"One-Eye. Any shadows out there?"

"Won't be any of those, Murgen. They have to come up from Shadowcatch. Longshadow would have to be in on it."

"Good." I've seen what the shadows can do, on a small scale. The Jaicuri were right to be scared.

"I promise you some sorcery, though. It's already gathering."

"I love how you can always cheer me up, runt." I surveyed the walls beyond our section. Hard to see much but it looked like any assault would meet a ready defense.

Which meant nothing if Spinner was in good form.

"Murgen!"

"What?"

"Behind you."

I looked.

Ky Dam, Speaker of the Nyueng Bao, accompanied by a son and some grandsons, by gesture asked if he could come up to the battlements. Only the son was armed. He was a squat, emotionless man rumored to be some kind of master swordsman. I nodded. "Welcome aboard."

The Speaker looked like he was about a thousand years older than One-Eye but was spry enough to climb without help. He didn't have a lot of himself to move around. His hair was evenly distributed around his head and face but very little of it remained. It consisted of white wisps. He was covered with liver spots. His skin color had faded. He was more pallid than some of us northerners.

He bowed slightly.

I responded in kind, trying to match his bow exactly. That would indicate an honor between equals, which ought to earn me some good guy points because, although junior in years, I was senior here because he was on Company ground and I was Company top dog.

Clever me, I make every effort to be polite to the Speaker. And I keep reminding the guys to be respectful and protective of all Nyueng Bao, even if provoked. I am trying to encourage the taking of a longer view than is usual with ordinary people.

We have no friends anywhere in these strange lands.

Ky Dam faced the darkened plain. His presence was strong. Many Jaicuri believe he is a sorcerer. Goblin and One-Eye say he *can* be called a wizard in the word's most archaic sense, of wise man.

The old boy drew a breath that seemed to enhance his aura of strength. "It will be different tonight." He spoke mainstream Taglian with no accent.

"Their master has recovered his powers."

The Speaker glanced at me sharply, then at Goblin and One-Eye. "Ah. So."

"Exactly." I've always wanted to do that when some old fart made cryptic noises. I couldn't help myself when the perfect opportunity arrived.

I eyeballed the Speaker's escort. The swordmaster seemed too squat and bulky for his reputation. Such as it was. Not a lot crosses the cultural boundary.

The grandsons looked like most Nyueng Bao men in their prime. Like if they smiled, or showed any emotion whatsoever, they would forfeit their souls. Like they had cactus plugs up their butts, in Goblin's words.

I went on with my work while Ky Dam considered the night. His escort stayed out of my way.

Big Bucket checked in. "All set, boss."

And the Shadowmaster's men sounded like *they* were ready to play. Their horns began calling like bulls in rut. I grumbled, "It won't be long." They could put it off for another twenty years, though. I wouldn't mind. I was in no hurry.

A Taglian messenger stumbled up from the street, fought for

breath, croaked out word that Mogaba wanted me.

"On my way. Less than five minutes," I told him. I scanned the darkness. "Hold the fort, Bucket."

"Just what this outfit needs. Another comedian."

"Oh, I'll slay them."

Ky Dam said something. The swordmaster squinted at the night. For half a heartbeat there was a ghostly flicker in the hills. Star? Reflection of a star? No. The night was cool, wet and overcast.

The Speaker said, "There may be more happening than is immediately apparent, Bone Warrior."

"Perhaps." Bone Warrior? "But, unlike Nyueng Bao, we are not warriors. We are soldiers."

The old man got his mind around that quickly. "As you will, Stone Soldier. All may not be as it seems." Was he making these up as he went?

He did not seem pleased by his speculation. He turned, hastened down the stair. His grandsons had trouble keeping up.

"What was that about?" Bucket asked.

"I don't have a clue. I've been summoned by His Holiness, the Prince of the Company." As I stepped to the stair I glanced at One-Eye. The little wizard was staring toward the hills, about where Ky Dam had done the same. He seemed both puzzled and unhappy.

I didn't have time to ask. Nor did I have much inclination. I had had bad news enough already.

10

Mogaba stands six feet five. Any fat on him has to be between his ears because there isn't an ounce anywhere else. All bone and muscle, he moves like a cat, his slightest twitch pure liquid grace. He works hard to stay hard but not to become overly muscled. He is very dark but a deep mahogany more than an ebony. He glows with conviction, an unshakable inner strength.

He has a ready wit but never smiles. When he does show humor it is entirely surface, for effect, an illusion spun for his audience. He doesn't feel it and probably doesn't understand it. He is as focused as any human being who ever lived. And that focus is the creation and maintenance of Mogaba, greatest warrior who ever lived.

He is almost as good as he wants to be. He might be as good as he thinks he is. I never saw anyone who could match his individual skills.

The other Nar are almost as good, almost as arrogantly self-confident.

Mogaba's self-opinion is his big weakness but I don't think anyone could get him to believe that. He and his reputation stand squarely at the center of his every consideration.

Sadly, self-indulgence and self-admiration aren't always traits that will inspire soldiers to win battles.

There is no love lost between Mogaba and the rest of us. His rigidity split the Company into Old Crew and Nar factions. Mogaba envisions the Black Company as an ages-old holy crusade. Us Old Crew guys see it as a big unhappy family trying to survive in a world that really is out to get us.

The debate would be much more bitter were Shadowspinner not around to snap up the mantle of bigger common enemy.

Many of Mogaba's own people are less than thrilled with the way his mind is working these days.

Something Croaker harped about, from the moment he first set quill to paper, is what might be called matters of form. It is not good form to bicker with your superiors, however wrong they may be and however one-sided their determination of their superiority is. I try to maintain good form.

Croaker quickly elevated Mogaba to third in the Company, after himself and Lady, because of his exceptional talents. But that did not automatically entitle Mogaba to assume command if Croaker and Lady were gone. New Captains are supposed to be elected. In a situation like the one here in Dejagore the custom is to poll the soldiers to see if they think an immediate election is necessary. If they think the old Captain has become mad, senile, dead, incompetent, or otherwise in need of permanent replacement then a election will be held.

I cannot recall any instance in the Annals when the senior candidate was rejected by the soldiers, but if an election were held today a precedent might be set. In a secret ballot even many of the Nar might declare no confidence in Mogaba.

There will be no vote while we are besieged. I will oppose any effort to hold one. Mogaba may be mad and I may not be able to go along with him in areas he considers religious, but only he has the will to control thousands of skittish Taglian legionnaires while keeping the Jaicuri in line. If he should fall his assistant Sindawe would step up, then Ochiba, and only then, maybe, if I can't hide fast enough, me.

Soldiers and civilians both fear Mogaba more than they respect him after all this time besieged. And that troubles me. The Annals demonstrate over and over that fear is the most fertile soil for treachery.

11

Mogaba holds staff conferences in the citadel. There is a war room there, once the toy of the sorceress Stormshadow. Mogaba considers meeting there a great concession to the distances us underlings must hike. He does not like leaving his own part of the action. For that reason I could count on this being short.

He was polite enough, though it was a strained courtesy obvious to all. He said, "I received your message. It was not entirely clear."

"I garbled it intentionally. I didn't want the messenger telling everybody on his way to see you."

"It is not good news, then, I assume." He spoke the Jewel Cities dialect the Company picked up when it was in service to the Syndic of Beryl. Most of us used it only when we did not want the natives to understand what we were saying. Mogaba used it because he did not yet have enough Taglian to get by without interpreters. Even his Jewel Cities dialect was badly accented.

"Definitely not good news," I said. Mogaba's friend Sindawe translated for the Taglian officers present. I continued, "Goblin and One-Eye tell me Shadowspinner is completely healthy again and means tonight to be his big comeback show. So tonight won't be just another raid, it will be a big punchout for the whole works."

A dozen pairs of eyes stared, praying I was making the sort of bad joke Goblin and One-Eye would find hilarious. Mogaba's own eyes were icy. He wanted to make me recant by sheer weight of his gaze.

Mogaba has no use for One-Eye or Goblin. They are one of the big sources of contention between him and the Old Crew. He is sure that real wizards, however puny, have no place among real warriors, who are supposed to rely on their strength, their wit, their will, and even maybe their superior steel—if they have it.

Goblin and One-Eye, besides being wizards, besides being sloppy and undisciplined and rowdy, worst of all fail to agree that Mogaba is the best thing that could have happened to the Black Company.

Mogaba hates Shadowspinner in part because he knows the Shadowmaster will never meet him in a trial by combat that can be sung about down through the ages.

Mogaba wants his place in the Annals. He *lusts* after a major place in the Annals. And he is going to get that, but not the way he wants.

"Do you have a suggestion about how to deal with this

threat?" Mogaba showed no emotion, though Shadowspinner getting well meant the date of our executions had been advanced.

I considered suggesting prayer but it was obvious Mogaba was not in the mood. "Afraid not."

"There is nothing in your books?"

He meant the Annals. Croaker tried hard to get him to study them. Croaker was big on looking for, and deferring to, precedent—mainly because he lacked much confidence in his mastery of strategy and leadership. On the other hand, Mogaba lacked no confidence whatsoever. He always had an excuse not to study Company history. Only recently had it occurred to me that he might not read or write. Those are skills considered unmanly in some places. Maybe that was true among the Nar of Gea-Xle, despite the fact that keeping the Annals was a holy duty of our Black Company forebrethren.

The Nar say very little about their beliefs. The rest of us are aware that they consider us heretics, though.

"Very little. The time-honored tactic is to attract the wizard's attention to a secondary target where he will do less damage than he wants. You hold his attention there till he gets tired or until you sneak up and cut his throat. Sneakups aren't practical here. This time Spinner will protect himself better. He might not even come out of his camp if we don't make him."

Mogaba nodded, unsurprised. "Sindawe?"

Sindawe is Mogaba's oldest and closest friend. They go back to early childhood. Sindawe is now Mogaba's second in command and leader of the Taglian First Legion, which is the best of the Taglian formations. And the oldest. Croaker put Mogaba in charge of training when first we arrived in Laglios and the First is the juggernaut Mogaba built.

Sindawe can pass as Mogaba's brother. Sometimes he acts like Mogaba's conscience. Mogaba values his good opinion possibly more than he should.

Sindawe said, "We could try to outrun them. . . . Whoa, Ga! I'm joking."

Mogaba didn't get it. Or if he did he failed to see the humor.

I offered, "Use artillery to distract him, wherever he is. And if we do catch him in range we can hope we get lucky."

We did that during the big battle that ended with us trapped. And it worked. We even got lucky, some, which was why we were alive to be in deep shit now. But we did not come near eliminating Shadowspinner.

"We will include motion in everything," Mogaba decided. "Our artillerymen will shoot and run. Wherever the Shadowmaster attacks directly we will fade away instantly. We will cover with enfilading fire till his attention is drawn elsewhere. We will not look him in the eye."

Mogaba looked me in the eye. He wanted help from Goblin and One-Eye but his pride would not let him ask. He is on record as saying he cannot abide sorcery, that sorcery has no place in the Black Company. It is wicked, dishonorable, the alternative of rogues. The man just cannot lay off the flattery. He spreads that stuff all over those two clowns every time he sees them, too. He has made them some big offers intended to get them to retire from "his" Company.

Help? Ain't it funny how flexible you get when absolute destruction looks you right in the eye?

Sort of flexible. Mogaba never addressed the matter directly.

I did not twist his tail. I never do. And I hope that drives him crazy. I said, "We will all exercise all our talents to their limit. If we don't get through this, our differences don't mean shit."

Mogaba winced. Among the many things a Nar warrior does not do is employ colorful language. Whatever language he uses.

Good thing we were using the Beryl dialect. Our discussion had gone on long enough that the Taglian officers were beginning to doubt Sindawe's bland translations. We tried to show the outside world a single face. It was especially important to deceive our employers. In the tradition of these things they are,

likely, already figuring out how to screw us as soon as we save
their royal butts.

Counting sworn brothers taken in since our advent in this
forsaken end of the world, the Nar and Old Crew factions together total sixty-nine men. Dejagore's main defenders are ten
thousand inadequately trained Taglian legionaires, some willing but ineffective former Shadowlander slaves, and some even
less effective Jaicuri. Each day snaps our numbers. Old wounds
and current diseases thin our ranks as swiftly as enemy attacks.
Croaker tried to teach good field hygiene but it has not stuck
anywhere outside the Company proper.

Mogaba awarded me a small bow, the way honors are paid
in these parts. He would not thank me outright.

Sindawe and Ochiba now had their heads together over
some unit reports that had just come in. Sindawe announced,
"No time left for talk. They are about to attack." He spoke
Taglian. Unlike Mogaba, he made a grand effort to get beyond
pidgin. He strove to understand the culture and thinking of the
several Taglian peoples—weird though they are.

Mogaba said, "Then let's go to our posts. We don't want to
disappoint Shadowspinner." You could see the edge on the man.
He was eager. His excitement was almost unreasonable. He reviewed the tactics he wanted used to reduce friendly casualties.

I left without a word. Without being dismissed.

Mogaba knew I did not consider him Captain. We discuss
it occasionally. I will not acknowledge him without a formal
vote. He does not want an election yet, either, I suspect because
he fears his popularity is not what a Captain's should be.

I will not force the issue. I might get elected by the Old Crew
faction. And I don't want the job. I am not qualified.

I know my limitations. I am no leader. Hell, I don't even
handle these Annals very well. I don't see how Croaker kept
them up and did all the other stuff he had to do at the same time.

I ran all the way to my section of wall.

12

Something hit me like a small, silent cyclone of darkness that dropped out of the night and nowhere. It devoured me, unseen by anyone around. It grabbed hold of my soul and yanked. I went into the darkness thinking, Boy, the Shadowmaster came back in a *huge* way, didn't he?

This was unlike anything I had encountered ever before.

But why come after me? There were few players less significant than I was.

13

I was summoned. I could not resist. I fought, but soon I realized that a strong part of me did not want to win.

I was confused. I had no idea what was happening. I was sleepy. . . . Was all this just because I wasn't getting enough sleep?

A voice called my name. The voice seemed vaguely familiar. "Murgen! Come home, Murgen!" I felt violent motion, probably due to a blow I didn't feel. "Come on, Murgen! You have to fight it."

What?

"He's coming. He's coming back!"

I groaned. A major accomplishment, apparently, because it generated more excitement.

I groaned again. Now I knew who I was but not where I was or why, or who that voice belonged to. "I'm getting up!" I tried to say. Must be some kind of training. "I'm getting up, goddamnit!" And I tried. But my muscles would not lift me.

They were rigid.

Hands pulled on my arms.

A new voice said, "Stand him up. Get him walking."

The original voice said, "We've got to find a way to head these seizures off before they happen."

"I'm open to suggestion."

"You're the doctor."

"It's not a disease, Goblin. You're the sorcerer."

"It ain't sorcery, either, Chief."

"Then what the hell is it?"

"Anyway, it isn't any sorcery like any I ever seen or heard of."

They had me upright now. My knees would not cooperate but these guys would not let me fall down.

I opened an eye. I saw Goblin and the Old Man. But the Old Man was dead. . . . I tried my tongue. "I think I'm back." This time I had it. This time my words were slurred but understandable.

"He is back," Goblin said.

"Keep him moving."

"He ain't drunk, Croaker. He's back. He's aware. He can hang on here. You can hang on here now, can't you, Murgen?"

"Yeah. I'm here. I won't drift away as long as I'm awake." Where was here? I looked around. Oh. There. Again.

"What happened?" the Old Man asked.

"I got pulled into the past again."

"Dejagore?"

"It's always Dejagore. This was the day you came back. The day I met Sarie."

Croaker grunted.

"It hurts less each time. This trip wasn't bad. But you lose a lot besides the pain. I didn't see half the horror I know was there."

"Maybe that's good. Maybe if you can shed all of that you can break out of this."

"I'm not crazy, Croaker. I'm not doing this to myself."

Goblin said, "It's getting harder to pull him back, not easier. This time he wouldn't have made it without us."

My turn to grunt. I could get caught in a cycle of reliving the nadir of my life, over and over.

Goblin had not guessed the worst. I was not back yet. They had dragged me up out of the deeps of yesterday but I was not home. This was my past, too, only this time I was aware of my dislocation. And I knew what evils lurked in my future.

"What was it like?" Goblin stared like that every time. Like some facial tic of mine might be the one clue he needs to unravel the puzzle and rescue me. Croaker leaned against the wall, the way he does, satisfied now that I was talking.

"Same as every other time. Just less painful. Although this time when I started out I wasn't really me. That was different. I was just a disembodied voice, just a viewpoint giving a guide's sort of speech to a faceless visitor."

"Also disembodied?" Croaker asked. This variation had him interested.

"No. There was somebody there. A complete person but he had no face."

Goblin and Croaker exchanged troubled looks. At that time Otto and Hagop were still away. "What sex?" Croaker asked.

"Wasn't clear. It wasn't the Faceless Man, though. I don't think it was anybody from our past. Might just have been something out of my own head. I might have separated me into pieces so I wouldn't have to deal with so much pain in such big blasts."

Goblin shook his head, not buying that. "It ain't you, Murgen. Something is doing this. Besides who, we want to know why and why you. Did you catch any clues? How did it go? Try for specifics. It's teeny details that will give us our handle."

"I was detached completely when it started. I went down into it gradually. Then I *was* the Murgen back then, living it all over again, trying to get it all down in the Annals, unaware of the future at all. You remember going swimming when you were a kid? When somebody would come up out of the water behind you to dunk you? He would jump in the air and put his hand on top of your head, then let his weight push you under? If you were in deep water instead of just going straight down you would sort of curve through the water and lay out flat? This whole thing went like that. Only once I was out flat I couldn't float to the top. I forgot that I have done it all before, almost always the same way, who knows how many times? Maybe if I could remember the future back then I could change the way things went, or maybe at least I could make extra copies of my books so they don't get. . . ."

"What?" Croaker was alert now. Mention the Annals and you have his undivided attention. "What was that?"

Did he realize that I was remembering the future? In this time my volumes of the Annals are still safe.

The fear and the pain swarmed in on me, then. The despair followed. Because despite all those plunges back there, and despite the visits here, I cannot stop anything from happening. No amount of willpower can divert the river from the horrors.

For a moment I could not talk because I had so much to say. Then, obliquely, I managed, "You came here about the Grove of Doom. Right?" I knew this night. I have been through this country often enough to know its terrain well. Here the landscape varies slightly from visit to visit but afterward time becomes the same relentless river.

If I squinted I could almost see the ghosts of other versions playing out alternate dialogs.

Croaker was surprised. "The grove?"

"You want me to take the Company out to the Grove of Doom. Right? It's time for some Deceiver festival. You think Narayan Singh himself might show up for this one. You think there's a good chance to catch him—or to catch *somebody* who knows where he has your baby hidden. Worst chance, you think we'll get the opportunity to kill lots of them and make them hurt more than they already do."

Croaker has been implacable in his resolve to exterminate the Deceivers. More so even than Lady has been, I think, and she was the more deeply insulted of the two. Once upon a time he wanted his legacy to be the completion of the Black Company's historical cycle. He wanted to be captain when the Company returned to Khatovar. He has the dream still but a nightmare shoved it aside. The nightmare demands satisfaction. Until its gossamer thread of terror, pain, cruelty and revenge has been spun, Khatovar is going to remain nothing but an excuse, not a destination.

Croaker eyed me uncertainly. "How could you know about the grove?"

"I came back knowing." Which was true. But the two of us would not give the same meaning to "back."

"You'll take the men out there?"

"I can't not."

Goblin eyed me weirdly, too, now.

I would do it. And I knew how it would go but I could not tell them that. There were two minds inside my head. The one doing this thinking wasn't the one heaving on the running lines and reefing the sails.

"I'm all right now," I told them. And, "I think there is a way to keep me from falling back. At least, to keep me from going so far back. But I can't get it out." I would have shared gladly. I did not want to keep stumbling off the edge of time to fall back into those too-real dark dreams of Dejagores past. Not even if I tumbled into a viewpoint almost blind to the horror and cruelty everywhere then.

Croaker started to say something.

I interrupted. "I'll be down for the staff meeting in ten minutes."

I could not tell them anything directly but maybe I could get something out sideways.

But I knew nothing would change. The worst of all horrors was waiting up ahead and I was powerless to avert it.

I'd still do my best in the grove. Just in case this time that would come out differently. If I could remember the future well enough to make the right moves.

You. Whoever you are. Whatever you are. You keep dragging me to the wellsprings of pain. Why do you do that? What do you want? Who are you? What are you?

As always, you give me no answers.

14

The goddamned wind had teeth. We huddled in our blankets, shivering, as unmotivated as guys get without hanging it up. Weren't many of us wanted to be in that haunted grove in the first place.

Yet something I could not quite catch, some elusive emotion deep inside me, told me this was critical, that this had to be done just right. That more than I could imagine hinged upon that.

Unseen trees creaked and cracked. The wind groaned and whined. It was easy to let your imagination get away and brood on the fact that thousands had been tortured and murdered there. You might hear their moans inside the wind, their pleas for mercy ignored even now. You might expect to see broken corpses rising up to demand vengeance on the living.

I faked being a hero. I could not stop shaking, though. I pulled my blanket tighter. That did not help, either.

"Candyass!" One-Eye sneered. Like the little shit wasn't about to have a seizure himself. "That bonehead Goblin don't quit farting around and get his dead ass back here I'm gonna go strip him barebutt and nail him to a chunk of ice."

"That's creative."

"Don't be no wiseass, Kid. I'll . . ."

An especially exuberant gust took off with what he would.

It wasn't just the cold making us shake, though nobody would admit that. It was the place and the mission and the fact that heavy cloud cover robbed us of even the meager comradeship of starlight.

It was goddamned dark. And these Stranglers might now be friends with the man who ran shadows. A little bird said. Actually, a big black bird said.

"We spend too much time in town," I grumbled. One-Eye didn't respond. Thai Dei did, though, with a grunt. But that was a speech for this particular Nyueng Bao.

The wind brought the creak of a stealthy footfall. One-Eye barked, "Goddamnit, Goblin! Quit stomping around. You want the whole damned world to know we're here?" Never mind that Goblin could not be heard five feet away, dancing. One-Eye refuses to be constrained by mundane reason or consistency.

Goblin drifted into place in front of me, squatted. His little yellow teeth chattered. "All set," he murmured. "Whenever you're ready."

"We'd better do it, then. Before I break out in a case of common sense." I grunted as I rose. My knees crackled. My muscles did not want to stretch any more. I swore. I was getting too damned old for this shit, though at thirty-four I was the baby of the bunch. "Move out," I said, loudly enough to be heard by most everyone. You couldn't use hand signals in that darkness.

We were downwind and Goblin had done his stuff. Noise was not a worry.

The men drifted away, mostly so quietly that I had trouble believing I was alone suddenly except for my bodyguard. We moved, too. Thai Dei covered my back. The night didn't bother him. Maybe he has eyes like a cat.

I had plenty of mixed feelings. This was the first time I had run a raid. I was not sure I was over Dejagore enough to handle it. I shied at shadows and remained crazy suspicious of everybody outside the Company, for no reason I could understand. But Croaker insisted, so here I was sneaking around in a dark and evil forest with icicles hanging off my butt, directing the first purely Company op in years. Only it wasn't so purely Company when you considered the fact that all my guys had bodyguards with them.

I got over the self-confidence hurdle just by getting myself moving. Hell, it was too late to stop anything.

I stopped worrying about me and went to work worrying about how we would look after the raid was over. If we blew it we could not blame that on Taglian treachery or factionalism or incompetence, the usual sand in the machine.

I reached the crest of a low ridge. My hands were frozen but my body was wet inside my clothing. Light wavered ahead. The Deceivers, those lucky bastards, had a bonfire to keep them warm. I paused to listen. I heard nothing.

How did the Old Man know the leaders of the Strangler bands would gather for this particular festival? It was downright spooky the way he knew stuff sometimes. Maybe Lady was rubbing off. Maybe he had some magical talent he never mentioned.

I observed, "We're about to find out if Goblin still has that talent."

Thai Dei did not spend a precious grunt. Silence was comment enough.

There were supposed to be thirty to forty top Deceivers over there. We hunt them relentlessly and have done so since Narayan snatched Lady and Croaker's baby. The Old Man has eliminated mercy from the Company vocabulary. And that fits Deceiver philosophy perfectly, though I would bet those guys up ahead would not think that way in a minute.

Goblin still had the knack. The sentries were napping. Still, inevitably, all did not go as planned.

I was fifty feet from the bonfire, sneaking along beside this especially big, ugly shelter when somebody went heeling and toeing out its end like all the devils in Hell were after him. He bent under the weight of a big bundle. That bundle wriggled and whimpered.

"Narayan Singh!" I knew him instantly. "Stop!"

Right, Murgen. Freeze him with your voice.

The rest of the guys recognized him too. A yell went up. We could not believe our luck, though I had been warned that the big prize might be there to grab. Singh was the number one Deceiver, the villain Lady and the Captain want to spend long years killing, an inch at a time.

The bundle had to be their daughter.

I yelled orders. Instead of responding the men did whatever they thought of. Mostly they went after Singh. The racket wakened the rest of the Deceivers. The quickest tried to run.

Luckily, some of the guys stayed on the job.

"You warm now?" Goblin asked. I puffed heartily as I watched Thai Dei shove a skinny blade into the eye of a sleep-befuddled Strangler. Thai Dei doesn't cut throats. He doesn't like the mess.

It was over. "How many did we get? How many got away?" I stared the direction Singh had fled. The silence there was not promising. The guys would have raised a real hoorah had they caught him.

Damn! I was excited for a while there. If only I could have dragged him back to Taglios. . . . If wishes were fishes. "Keep some alive. We'll want somebody to tell us bedtime stories. One-Eye. How the hell did Singh all of a sudden know we were here?"

The runt shrugged. "I don't know. Maybe his goddess goosed him and told him to haul ass."

"Give me a break. Kina didn't have anything to do with it." But I wasn't that sure. Sometimes it is hard to disbelieve.

Thai Dei gestured.

"Right," I said. "Just what I was thinking myself."

One-Eye looked puzzled. Goblin grumbled, "What?" My wizards. Right on top of everything.

"Sometimes I wonder if you guys could find your dicks without a map. The shelter, old-timers. The shelter. Don't it seem like that's an awful lot of shack for one runt killer and a kid barely tall enough to bite you on the kneecap? A bit big even for a living saint and the daughter of a goddess?"

One-Eye developed a nasty grin. "Nobody else came out, did they? Yeah. You want I should start a fire?"

Before I could answer him Goblin squealed. I whirled. A shapeless darkness, visible only because of the bonfire, reared out of the shelter entrance—then I slammed into the ground, felled by Thai Dei. Fire blasted over my head. Lights crackled. Balls of flame darted in from all around.

The killing darkness took on a moth-eaten look. Then it came apart.

That darkness was why so many of us had been shivering before the attack. But we won this round.

I sat up, crooked a finger. "Let's see what we've caught. It ought to be interesting." My guys knocked the shelter apart. Sure enough, they turned up a half dozen wrinkled little old men, brown as chestnuts. "Shadowweavers. Running with the Stranglers. Now isn't that interesting?"

The geezers gobbled their willingness to surrender.

We had run into their kind before. They never were big on personal heroics.

A soldier called Wishbone said, "These Shadowlanders are getting good at this 'I surrender' stuff." He sneered. "Everybody down there must be practicing their handy Taglian phrases."

"Except Longshadow," I reminded. I told Thai Dei, "Thanks."

He shrugged, a gesture foreign to the Nyueng Bao. The world did touch him occasionally. "Sahra would expect it."

And that was very Nyueng Bao. He would blame his actions on his sister's expectations rather than on any notion of duty or obligation or even friendship.

"What are we supposed to do with these guys?" Wishbone asked. "We got any use for them?"

"Save a couple. The oldest and one other. Goblin. You never said how many got away."

"Three. That counts Singh but not the kid. But we're going to get one of them three back on account of he's hiding in the bushes right over there."

"Collect him. I'll give him to the Old Man."

Sarky One-Eye cracked, "Give them a little authority, they

turn into field marshals. I remember this kid when he was so green he still had sheep shit between his toes. He didn't know what shoes were for." But the humor wasn't in his eye. Every move I made he watched like a hawk. Like a crow, in fact, although we had no crows hanging around tonight. Whatever experiment Goblin and One-Eye had going in that area was a complete success during this outing.

Goblin suggested, "Ease up, Murgen. We'll get the job done. How about some of you lazy asses toss a couple logs on the fire?" He began to circle the hidden Deceiver in the direction opposite that taken by One-Eye.

They were right. I get too serious under stress. I was a thousand years old already. Surviving Dejagore had not been easy. But all the rest of these guys had come through that, too. They had seen Mogaba's slaughters of innocents. They had suffered the pestilences and plagues. They had seen the cannibalism and human sacrifices, the treacheries and betrayals and all the rest. And they had come away without letting the nightmares rule them.

I have to get a handle on it. I have to get some emotional distance and perspective. But there is something going on inside me that is beyond my control or understanding. Sometimes I feel like there are several of me in there, all mixed up, sometimes sitting behind the real me watching, watching. There may be no chance for me to recover complete sanity and stability.

Goblin came strutting back. He and One-Eye accompanied a man who was not much more than skin and bones. Few Deceivers are in good shape these days. They have no friends anywhere. They are hunted like vermin. Huge bounties ride on their shoulders.

Goblin flashed his toadlike grin. "We've got us a red-hand man here, Murgen. A genuine black rumel guy with the red palm. What do you think of that?"

The thought lightened my heart. The prisoner was truly a top Strangler. The red hand meant that he had been there when Narayan Singh tricked Lady into thinking she was being inducted into the Strangler cult when in fact the Deceivers were really consecrating her unborn child as daughter of their goddess Kina.

But Lady had employed a trick of her own, marking every Strangler there with the red hand that could not be denied later. Nothing they tried would take the color away, short of amputation. And a one-handed Strangler could not manage the rumel, the strangling scarf, that was the tool of the Deceivers' holy trade.

"The Old Man will be pleased." A red-hand man would know what was going on inside his cult.

I crowded closer to the fire. Thai Dei, done helping dispose of redundant shadowweavers, eased in beside me. How much had Dejagore changed him? I could not imagine him ever being anything but dour, taciturn, remorseless and pitiless, even as a toddler.

Goblin, I noted, was doing that thing he did lately where he watched me from the corner of his eye while pretending to do something else. What were he and One-Eye looking for?

The runt held his hands out. "Fire feels good."

15

Paranoia has become our way of life. We have become the new Nyueng Bao. We trust no one. We let no one outside the Black Company know what we are doing until we are sure what the response will be. In particular we prefer keeping the Prahbrindrah Drah and his sister, the Radisha Drah, our employers, way back there in the deep dark shadows.

They are not to be trusted at all, ever, except to serve their own closest interests.

I smuggled my prisoners into the city and hid them in a warehouse near the river, a Company-friendly Shadar fish place possessed of a very distinctive air. My men scattered to their families or someplace where they could drink beer. I was satisfied. With one quick, nasty stab we had decimated the surviving Deceiver leadership. We almost got that fiend Narayan Singh. I got within spitting distance of Croaker's baby. In all honesty I could report that she seemed all right.

Thai Dei knocked the prisoners to their knees, wrinkled his nose.

"You're right," I agreed. "But this place don't stink half as bad as your swamp does." Taglios claims the river delta but the Nyueng Bao disagree.

Thai Dei grunted. He could take a joke as well as the next guy.

He does not look like much. He is a foot shorter than I am. I outweigh him by eighty pounds. And I am far prettier. He has crudely cropped black hair that sticks out in unkempt spikes. Skinny, lantern-jawed, taciturn and surly, Thai Dei is entirely unappetizing. But he does his job.

A Shadar fishmonger brought the Captain to us. Croaker *was* getting old. We were going to have to call him Boss or Chief or something. You cannot call the Captain the Old Man once he's really old, can you?

He was dressed like a Shadar cavalryman, all turban, beard and plain grey clothing. He eyed Thai Dei coolly. He did not have a Nyueng Bao bodyguard himself. He loathed the idea despite his having to disguise himself whenever he wanted to walk the streets alone. Bodyguards are not traditional. Croaker is stubborn about Company traditions.

Hell, the Shadowmaster's officers all employ bodyguards. Some have several. They could not survive without them.

Thai Dei reflected Croaker's gaze impassively, unimpressed by the presence of the great dictator. He might say, "He is one man. I am one man. We begin even."

Croaker examined my prizes. "Tell it."

I told it. "But I missed Narayan. I was this close. That bastard has a guardian angel. There's no way he should have slipped

Goblin's sleep spell. We chased him for two days but even Goblin and One-Eye couldn't hang onto his track forever."

"He had help. Maybe from his guardian demon. Maybe from his new buddy the Shadowmaster, too."

"How come they went back to the grove? How did you know they would be there?"

I thought he would say a big black bird told him.

They are less numerous these days but the crows still follow him everywhere. He talks to them. Sometimes they talk to him, too. So he says.

"They had to come someday, Murgen. They are slaves to their religion."

But why *this* particular Festival of Lights? How did you know?

I did not press. You don't press Croaker. He has grown cranky and secretive in his old age. In his own Annals he did not always tell the whole truth about personal things, his age especially.

He kicked the shadowweaver. "One of Longshadow's pet spook doctors. You'd think he wouldn't have enough left to waste them anymore."

"I don't reckon he expected us to jump them."

Croaker tried to smile. He produced a nasty, sarcastic sneer instead. "He's got lots of surprises coming." He kicked the Deceiver. "Let's don't hide them. Let's take them to the Palace. What's the matter?"

Ice had blasted my back, like I was out on the wind of the Grove of Doom again. I didn't know why but I had a grim sense of foreboding.

"I don't know. You're the boss. Anything special you want in the Annals?"

"You're the Annalist now, Murgen. You write what you have to write. I can always bitch." Unlikely. I send everything over but I don't think much gets read. He asked, "What was special about the raid?"

"It was colder than a well-digger's ass out there."

"And that walking sack of camel snot Narayan Singh got away from us again. So that's what you write. Him and his kind are going to get back into our story before we're done. When we're roasting him, I hope. Did you see her? Was she all right?"

"All I saw really was a bundle that Singh carried. I think it was her."

"Had to be. He never lets her out of his sight." He pretended he did not care. "Bring them to the Palace." That chill hit me again. "I'll make sure the guards know you're coming."

Thai Dei and I exchanged looks. This might get tough. People in the streets would recognize the prisoners. And the prisoners might have friends. And for sure they did have enemies by the thousand. They might not survive the trip. Or we might not.

The Old Man said, "Tell your wife I said hello and I hope she likes the new apartment."

"Sure." I shivered. Thai Dei frowned at me.

Croaker produced a sheaf of papers rolled into a tube. "This came in from Lady while you were gone. It's for the Annals."

"Someone must have died."

He grinned. "Bang it around and fit it in. But don't polish it so much she gets all righteous again. I can't stand it when she flays me with my own arguments."

"I learned the first time."

"One-Eye says he thinks he knows where he left his papers from when he thought he was going to have to keep the Annals."

"I've heard that one before."

Croaker grinned again, then ducked out.

16

Four hundred men and five elephants swarmed around an incomplete stockade. The nearest friendly outpost lay a hard day's march northward. Shovels gnawed the earth. Hammers pounded. Elephants swung timbers off wagons and helped set them upright. Only the oxen stood around, lazing in their harnesses.

This nameless post was barely a day old, the newest point in the relentless Taglian leapfrog into the Shadowlands. Only its watchtower was complete. The lookout there scanned the southern horizon intently. There was an electric urgency in the air, a heaviness like the smell of old death, a premonition.

The soldiers were all veterans. Not a one considered fleeing his nerves. Each had developed the habit and expectation of victory.

The sentinel began to gaze fixedly. "Captain!"

A man distinct for his coloring dropped a shovel, looked up. His true name was Cato Dahlia. The Black Company called him Big Bucket. Wanted for common theft in his home city, he had become advisor-commander of a battalion of Taglian border rangers. He was a hardass leader with a reputation for getting his jobs done and bringing his people back alive.

Bucket scrambled onto the observation platform, puffing. "What have you got?"

The lookout pointed. Bucket squinted. "Help me out here, son. These eyes ain't what they used to be." He could see nothing but the low humped backs of the Loghra Hills. Scattered clouds hung above those.

"Watch."

Bucket trusted his soldiers. He selected them carefully. He watched.

One small cloud hung lower than the others, dragging a slanting shadow. This rogue thunderhead did not travel the same direction as the rest of its family.

"Headed right for us?"

"Looks like it, sir."

Bucket relied on his intuition. It had served him well during this war without major battles. And intuition told him that cloud was dangerous.

He descended, spread word to expect an attack. The men

of the construction company, although not combat soldiers, did not want to withdraw. Sometimes Bucket's reputation worked against him. His rangers had prospered, freebooting across the frontier. Others wanted a share.

Bucket compromised. He sent one platoon north with the animals, which were too valuable to risk. The other workers stayed. They overturned their wagons in the gaps in the stockade.

The cloud advanced steadily. Nothing could be seen inside its shadow and tail of falling rain. A chill ran before it. The Taglian soldiers shivered and pranced to keep warm.

Two hundred yards beyond the ditch, teams of two men shivered in covered, concealed pits lighted by special candles. One man maintained a watch.

Rain and darkness arrived. Behind the initial few yards of downpour the rain slackened to a drizzle. Men appeared. They looked old and sad, ragged and pale, vacant and hopeless, hunched against the chill. They looked as though they had spent their entire lives in the rain. They bore their rusting weapons without spirit. They could have been an army raised from the dead.

Their line passed the pits. Behind them came horsemen of the same sort, advancing like zombies. Next came massed infantry. Then came the elephants.

The men in the pits spied the elephants. They used crossbows to speed poisoned shafts. The elephants wore no belly armor. The poison caused intense pain. The maddened beasts rampaged through their own formations. The Shadowlanders had no idea why the animals were enraged.

Little shadows found the pits. They tried to slither inside. Candlelight drove them back. They left a deeper chill and a smell of death behind.

The shadows found a pit where rain had gotten to the candle. They left shrieking, grimacing death in a grave already dug.

Lady encountered the northbound laborers. She questioned them, considered the cloud in the distance. "This may be what we're after," she told her companions. "Ride!" She urged her stallion to a gallop. Foaled in sorcerous stables when she was empress of the north, that giant black outdistanced the rest of her party quickly.

Lady studied the cloud as she galloped. Three similar clouds had been reported near sites where ranger companies had been overrun. This was exactly what she had come to investigate.

It took only minutes to fathom how the raids were managed. Lines of dark power had been laid down long before the Shadowlanders withdrew from this region. The attackers were controlled through those. They would fight without wills of their own while run by those lines.

She could scramble the lines easily now that she sensed them but chose not to do so. Let the attack proceed. These things cost the Shadowlanders more dearly than they cost Taglios.

Longshadow must realize that. So why did he find the exchange worthwhile?

She entered the ranger encampment by leaping her mount over an upturned wagon. She dismounted as an amazed Bucket ran to meet her. He looked like a condemned man granted a last-minute reprieve. "It's the Howler, I think," he said.

"Why?" Lady dragged her gear down from behind her saddle, started changing right there. "What can he hope to accomplish?"

"I think it ain't what they're doing but who they're doing it to that matters, Lieutenant." Though she commanded armies, Lady's Company title remained Lieutenant.

"Who they're doing it to? Yes! Of course." Every unit lost had been led by Company men. Seven brothers had fallen. "They're picking us off." The belief that the Company is invincible is the backbone of Taglian military morale and the black beast of Taglian politics. "That's crafty. Must be Howler's idea. He does love to blindside you."

Bucket helped her with her armor. That was gothically ornate, black and shiny, too pretty to be much use in close combat. But her job was to fight sorcery, not soldiers. Her armor was surfaced by layer upon layer of protective spells.

Rain began to fall as she donned her helmet. Threads of fire snaked along channels etched into the surface of her armor. She followed Bucket up the watchtower.

Rain roared down. Sounds of combat grew louder, nearer. Lady ignored those, extended sorcerous senses in a search for the sorcerer known as the Howler. That ancient and evil being did not betray himself but he was out there somewhere. She could smell him.

Was it possible he had learned to control his screaming?

"I'll catch up with you, you little bastard. Meantime. . . ." She reached down. A fog formed, became dense, slithered between the raindrops, gained color. Pastels swirled, deepened, darkened. Soon the entire storm glowed as though some mad artist had splash-painted it with watercolors.

There were screams inside the storm.

The weather stopped moving. The shrieks of lost soldiers peaked, faded. The Shadowmaster's lines of power, twisting and mutating, had turned lethal.

Lady resumed searching for the Howler. She discovered him stealing southward, flying low and timidly, fleeing the pastel death that had begun eating its way back along the lines of power. She flung a hastily concocted killing spell. It failed. Howler's lead was too great. But he did abandon stealth to run hard. Lady cursed like any line trooper frustrated.

The rain faded away. The Taglian survivors appeared one by one, at first awed by the carnage, then grumbling about all the graves that needed digging. Few Shadowlander survivors were found.

Lady told Bucket, "Tell them to look at the bright side. There will be prize money for the captured animals." The Shadowlander animals, excepting the elephants, had not suffered badly.

Lady glared southward, unforgiving. "Next time, old friend."

17

. . . falling . . . again. . . .

Trying to hang on. So tired. When I get tired the present gets slippery.

Fragments.

Not even fragments of today.

The past. Not so long ago.

Freezing my ass off. Failing to catch the great villain Narayan.

Lady at play down south.

Fish stench.

The sleeping man. The screaming Deceiver. Dead men.

Only memories but happier than tonight. There is too much pain here.

It is my apocalypse.

Slipping.

Can't keep my eyes from closing. The summons is too damned powerful.

The pillars might be mistaken for relics of a fallen city. They are not. They are too few and too randomly placed. Nor has a one ever fallen, though many have been gnawed deeply by the teeth of the hungry winds.

In the lightning flares, or in the dawns and sunsets when light steals beneath the edges of the sky, tiny golden characters blaze upon the faces of the columns.

It is immortality of a sort.

After dark the wind dies. After dark silence rules the glittering stone.

18

. . . sliding away. . . .

A vast whirlpool pulling me down.

Perhaps a force pushing. Was that a lying promise of an end to pain?

I cannot resist.

All lies. Endless lies.

Brown pages, torn pages stiff with blood. Agony. Hard to ride that anchor through the storm.

19

There you are! Were you lost? Welcome back. Come! Come! The great adventure is about to begin. The players are all in place. The engines are wound tight. The spells are collected and ready, in arsenal number. Oh, it will be a grand night of doom.

Look there! Look there. Remember them? Goblin and One-Eye, the wizards? But is that really them? There are two more just like them right over there. And see this. And that. And there. One, two, three Murgens.

No. Definitely not. You can't teach those two to suck eggs. They have been in the fooled-you business since your granny's greatgranny was a stinky little surprise for your however-many-greats grandpa. They have set glamors all over this part of the city. If you are a Shadowlander soldier you won't be able to tell the figments from the real thing till one of them sticks a knife in you.

Look there! Raven and Silent. They have been gone for years. And there. That is the old Captain, dead since Juniper. No, they won't scare any Shadowlanders with who they might be. Not right away. The southerners never heard of them.

What?

You are right. Absolutely right. Nobody here but Otto and Hagop will know them, either. But that doesn't matter. What matters is they can be seen and hardly anyone will know which ones are dangerous and which are illusions.

This is a first trial. A big experiment, saved up special for the night of Shadowspinner's big attack.

Yes. Yes. He did hit hard not that long ago. But he wasn't really going for a knockout then. He would have taken it, but that was really a reconnaissance in force, meant to support planning for this attack.

It is going to be a grand show.

Oh, no, there isn't one ghost anywhere else in Dejagore. Mogaba wouldn't have it. He has no grasp of illusion as a weapon. He has no idea how the Company really worked. He clings to his grand notion of chivalrous warfare, the great deadly game, all honor and set rules. He would settled this mess in a trial by combat between him and any champion the Shadowlanders care to send out.

Oh! Look! That one is interesting. That ugly sucker is Toadkiller Dog. He was a real nasty devil dog. And the Limper! Oh, yes. Brilliant. If the man behind Shadowspinner's mask is anyone the Company has faced before those illusions are provocations he will have to test. He will betray himself.

No, of course the Shadowmasters would not risk an entire kingdom on the outcome of a fight between two men. Their champion might lose.

Yes. Mogaba is naive about some things. He is an arrogant, cruel, unsympathetic general, too.

Ooh. Hear those trumpets. The Company has its own personal bunch of bad guys down front. Let's go to the ramparts and watch from close up.

No. They aren't really bright. Well, you *could* say that if they were bright they wouldn't be in that army in the first place but that wouldn't be fair. Not many of those guys had a choice about signing up. Their only real motivation is their fear of the Shadowmasters.

Sure. No argument. That makes them no less deadly. Hell, a rock can fall out of the sky and kill you.

Yes, this definitely is the big one. Shadowspinner is set to send every man. Maybe shadows have come up from Overlook to help.

Bats! Ha. And crows. Which is chasing which? Duck! Almost got you. They are all over. Never been this many around before.

What is that racket? Oh. Bucket yelling at one of the Murgens to get behind something because he don't want to carry no bodies down no goddamn stairs.

And here comes the first barrage. And if that racket across town means anything the Shadowlanders are hitting hard about where the third and fourth cohorts of the First Legion are stationed. Those are good regiments. They will put up a fight.

20

Like a regular hailstorm, isn't it? Makes you wonder where they got all the goddamned arrows and javelins for their engines. Just stay under the mantlet, you'll be fine. They aren't good at laying plunging fire onto elevated targets.

If they let up before they attack the Jaicuri will come out and collect the missiles and bring them to the soldiers. The Shadowlanders will get them back business end first.

No, the Jaicuri do not love Mogaba. They don't love the Taglians or the Black Company, either. They wish the whole mob was gone. But they have some dark suspicions about what will happen if Shadowspinner recaptures this burg. So they sort of try to help, but not much. Not yet.

They help some, they figure maybe Mogaba might be less likely to kick them out next time he is in one of his moods.

The sky? Dark as the inside of a priest's heart, isn't it? Oh. Yes. You're right. It isn't an auspicious sort of night. Never is when they attack without benefit of a full moon. It's devil's work for sure, then. Usually it means the Shadowmasters want the darkness so they can run their pets to their best advantage. Or they want everybody terrified that there are shadows to come.

Look at them scurry! Those Jaicuri are motivated tonight. If they become involved in actually fighting it could be closer than Mogaba or Shadowspinner expect.

Whoa! What was that?

Look at that. What the hell is it? That rosy light over the hills.

Here they come. Going to take their whack at breaking the Company.

You don't think so? Maybe you are right. This could be meant to keep the Company pinned while Spinner concentrates somewhere softer.

Look at them down there, though. Like maggots. And no covering fire now.

You're right. The engines will be moving to support the main attack now.

Check that light. It keeps getting brighter. No. Now it's going away. And it doesn't seem like anyone else noticed. That is a little too weird.

Oh. Right again. Must have been a signal to the Shadowlander officers. The racket is getting louder, now you mention it.

No, I don't like the sound of it either. The attack had become generalized.

Ho! Look over there! Now we have it there, too. What? The light. Don't you see it? There behind the ramparts?

Yes. I see. You're right again. It is different. This is kind of like the cold light of a full moon tinged with a little blue, isn't it. Yeah. It's kind of misty, too. Sort of like we are seeing it through an autumn haze. There. Now it's so bright you can make out the fighting on the far wall.

Right. Fighting. That means they have a foothold there already. And Mogaba don't have any reserves to send up.

Guess we can bend over and kiss our butts goodbye, friend.

21

Damn! The shit is about to start flying but I just realized that when I started putting these notes together I missed doing the famous formula Croaker always used to open a new volume. So here goes:

In those days the Company was in service to the Prabrindrah Drah of Taglios, a prince whose domains spanned territories more vast than those of many empires. We were participating in the occupation and protection of the recently captured city Dejagore.

And I hope princie and his skag sister the Radisha choke on our memory.

22

The shitstorm arrived. Every man defending our section of wall stayed busy returning some of it to the southerners. The illusory doppelgangers appeared to be hard at work, too. Funny how they could wander around never getting hurt.

"One-Eye! Goblin!" I yelled. "Where the hell are you peckerheads? What the frack is going on over there?" I watched a feeble arrow pass through a Murgen a dozen yards away. "What's that weird light?" Whatever it was, it gave me the feeling that things could get worse than they looked already.

I got no response whatsoever from my favorite wizards.

"Rudy. Flip a flare ball out there. Let's see what's sneaking around." Until recently my now less than favorite wizards had provided spot illumination. "Bucket! Where the hell are Goblin and One-Eye?" Ten minutes ago I had three pairs underfoot, all of them squabbling. Now they were gone and the Shadowlanders were quieter than mice below.

Red Rudy yelled at Loftus and Cletus. One of their engines thumped. A blazing ball arced outward, its only purpose to betray what the enemy was doing in the darkness.

Sparkle piped, "I seen them headed downstairs."

Suckass. "Why?" This was for sure not the time to wander away.

"Uh. . . . They went to talk to Pirmhi and some of them guys from the Horse Brigade."

I shook my head. I would choke them myself. In the middle of a goddamned battle. . . .

The fireball revealed that the Shadowlanders had pulled back from the wall. Spending our missiles was a waste. The southerners were setting up engines capable of throwing grapnels in clusters. That was a stupid way to do business against an eighty-foot wall with veteran soldiers on top, but if they wanted to play it that way we would accommodate them. I was confident that, no matter how many ropes they threw up, we could cut or dislodge their lines before they could climb that high, then, with lungs ready to fall out and arms too heavy to lift, get busy defending their bridgehead while other equally dim types made the same climb carrying a half ton of equipment apiece.

"Goblin!" Goddamnit, I wanted to know what that light was over there.

The Shadowlanders had not scaled the wall there. They had attacked off of earthen ramps. Not a surprise. They had been building the ramps from the beginning. That was just basic siegework, employed since the dawn of time and one reason your thoughtful modern prince builds his stronghold on a crag or headland or island. Naturally, the besieger spans the last dozen feet with a bridge he can yank back if a dangerous counterattack develops.

The flareball smashed down four hundred yards out. It continued to provide light until the southerners buried it with sand originally intended to extinguish firebombs if we used them. "One-Eye! I'm going to have your wrinkled balls for breakfast!"

I snarled, "Cletus, keep throwing them fireballs. Who's got messenger duty? Feet? Go find Goblin and One-Eye. . . . Never mind. One of them brain-damaged runts just turned up."

One-Eye said, "You rang, milord?"

"Are you sober? Are you ready to get to work now?" He stared at that nasty light across town without me coaching him. I asked, "What is that?" The light seemed more sinister now.

One-Eye raised a hand. "Kid, why not take this gods given opportunity to exercise your least well-honed talent?"

"What?"

"Be patient, dickhead."

The mist or haze or dust started getting thicker. The light grew brighter. Neither happening buoyed my confidence. "Talk to me, old man. This ain't the time for any of your bullshit."

"That haze, that ain't no mist, Murgen. The light ain't shining off it. It's making the light." And the mist and light were drifting toward the city.

"Horse puckey. You can see where there's a light burning in their camp."

"That's something else. There's two things going on at once, Murgen."

"Three things, halfwit." Goblin had arrived, beer breath and all. Presumably all was well at the secret brewery, the arrangements with the cavalry were secure, and he and One-Eye could take time off to help the Black Company defend Dejagore.

Heaven help them if Mogaba discovered what they were doing with grain supposedly set aside for the horses. I wouldn't have a prayer of saving their butts—nor would I offer one.

"What?" One-Eye barked. "Murgen, the man is a walking provocation."

"Watch, bonehead," Goblin countered. "It's already happening."

One-Eye gasped, suddenly astonished, then frightened. Ignorant in the dark arts, it took me longer to catch it.

Shadows snaked through that blazing dust cloud, thin things little more than suggestions but with something flitting back and forth amongst them. I thought both of a weaver's shuttle and of spiders. Whichever, web or net, something was forming inside the blazing dust.

They did call him Shadowspinner.

The glimmering cloud grew larger and brighter. The web grew with it.

"Shit," Goblin muttered. "Now what do we do about this?"

"Exactly what I've been trying to get out of you two clowns for the last five minutes!" I bellowed.

"Well!"

"Maybe you could pay attention over here if you can't do anything about that!" Bucket yelled. "Murgen, those fools have gotten so many ropes up that we can't. . . . Shit!" Another barrage of grapnels fell amongst us. In moments they showed the strain that meant some moron was trying to climb them.

So much for my belief that there was no chance the southerners could scale my wall.

Guys were hard at work with knives and swords and axes. Imaginary people stood around looking fierce. I heard a man grumble that if he had half a brain he would have sharpened his knives. Rudy reminded him, "If you kept your pecker in your pants more you'd have time."

Some Jaicuri women, naturally, inevitably, did what they had to do to survive.

Doing my part, I hacked on ropes but kept turning to check that light and the webs forming inside it.

Goblin howled, creased by a nearly-spent arrow. The cut,

on his cheek, was trivial. Arrows have little energy by the time they reach us. He was outraged because fate dared show him the back of her hand at all.

He danced around. Words of power virtually dripped from his mouth in pastel colors. He waved his arms. He foamed at the mouth. He jumped up and down, shrieked, flapped his arms.

His doppelgängers all did the same. It was quite a show.

In all likelihood the gymnastics and yelling had nothing to do with results eventually achieved but I don't mind showmanship as long as he produces. Croaker was right. Showmanship is the biggest part of the game.

Everything hemp within three hundred yards burst into flame. That was a happy eventuality where our relationship with our attackers was concerned but not something likely to wring cries of joy from anyone else, either. Temporary defense works began to fall apart. Our artillery pieces flared and died. They had included lots of rope. Some guys use rope for belts. Some wear sandals made of rope. Hemp is a commonplace everywhere. Some fools like One-Eye even smoke it.

Cletus bellowed, "Goddamn you, Goblin, I'm gonna chop your ass into cat food." The rest of us just pulled our pants up and amused ourselves by dropping masonry bits mined from our cellars onto the cursing tangle of limbs wriggling at the foot of the wall.

One-Eye ignored all that, though he took a moment to smirk at the side effects embarrassing Goblin. Then he began to stare at the glow rising from the enemy camp. And began to stutter.

"Come on, shithead," I growled. "You've played with this stuff for ages. What have we got here?" Not that I wanted to know. That web of shadow woven into the light was now obvious to all but the blind.

"Maybe we might ought to head for the cellar," One-Eye suggested. "I promise you, me and the runt ain't gonna do nothing with that. Bet you even Longshadow would be bugeyed if he was here to see it. The man put a lot of work in, getting that ready. It's going to get real unhealthy around here real soon."

Without investing a quarter of the study time Goblin agreed. "If we seal the doors and use the white candles we can hold out till sunrise."

"This some kind of shadow magic, then?"

"Some kind," Goblin agreed. "Don't ask me to look so close I catch its attention."

"Heaven forbid you should actually take a risk. Can either of you come up with a more practical suggestion?"

"More practical?" One-Eye sputtered.

"We're fighting a battle here."

Goblin said, "We could retire from the soldiering racket. Or we could surrender. Or we could offer to change sides."

"Maybe we could offer up a half-pint human sacrifice to one of Geek and Freak's bloodthirsty gods."

"You know what I really miss about Croaker, Murgen?"

"I'm sure you're going to tell me whether I want to hear it or not."

"Damned straight you are. I miss his sense of humor."

"Wait a minute. His sense of humor? Are you shitting me? What sense of humor? The man . . ."

"He knew none of us were going to get out of this world alive, Murgen. He never took himself completely serious."

"Are you talking about the guy who used to be the Old Man? Croaker? Company Annalist and chief bonesetter in his spare time? Some kind of comedian?"

While we bickered the rest of the world bustled along with its business. Which meant our situation deteriorated by the minute. A human weakness, as old as time, arguing while the house burns down around you.

One-Eye interjected, "You gents go ahead and debate if you want. I'm going to invite the boys downstairs, treat them to a beer and take a turn or two at tonk." He stabbed a crooked black finger earthward.

The gleaming dust with cruel web inside began to arc up over the city. It just might grow enough to net us all.

A vast stillness set in.

Inside the city and out, friend and foe, people of a dozen races and religions all focused upon that shadow web.

Shadowspinner, of course, was totally involved in creating his deadly artifact.

The Shadowlander assault lost impetus as the Shadowmaster's soldiers decided to hunker down and let their boss make their jobs easier.

23

The web of darkness would span all Dejagore soon. "One-Eye. Goblin. You guys have any new ideas?"

"Get religion?" Goblin suggested. "Since you won't let us go den up?"

One-Eye mused, "You might amble over and see if Mogaba will change his mind about letting us operate his engines." The Taglian crews were ineffective. "We might be able to distract Spinner."

"You did take shadows into account when you spelled the entrances to the underground?" I knew. They had. That was always our biggest concern. But I had to reassure myself. You keep checking on Goblin and One-Eye.

Small groups were returning after long, dangerous journeys through the night, searching for rope that had survived.

"Yeah. For what that's worth. You ready to go down and start starving yet?"

Bad signs followed ill omens. The situation was grim indeed if One-Eye and Goblin could spare no time to quarrel.

A sudden susurrus swept the city and the plain beyond.

A blazing diamond of light rose out of the Shadowlander camp. It spun slowly. A core of darkness centered it. From that, blackness pulsed out into the all-spanning web it anchored.

Nobody was looking at the hills when the pinkish light returned. No one noticed until it flared so brilliantly that it rivalled the brightness here at hand.

It burned behind two bizarre mounted figures. It cast their hideous shadows upon the night itself. Crow shadows circled them. Two huge ravens perched upon the shoulders of the larger figure.

Nobody breathed for a while. Not even Shadowspinner, I'd bet. And I was sure he had no more idea what was happening than I did.

The pink flare faded. A cable of pink reached toward Dejagore, like a snake probing, stretching. As one end neared us the nether end broke loose. That whipped our way too fast for the eye to follow and in an instant screamed into Shadowspinner's bright diamond. Sun-brilliant flash splashed out of that sorcerous construct's far side like suddenly-flung barrels of burning oil.

Immediately the dark web overhead began to shrink back into the remnants of the diamond.

The air vibrated with the Shadowmaster's anger.

"Goblin! One-Eye! Talk to me, boys. Tell me what the hell just happened."

Goblin couldn't talk. One-Eye burbled, "I ain't got the faintest fucking idea, Kid. But we're downwind of one seriously pissed-off Shadowmaster who's probably going to blame you and me for his ulcers."

A tremor disturbed the night, more psychic than physical. I am magically deaf and dumb and blind, except for perceived effects, but I felt it.

One-Eye was right.

The pink light was gone. I saw no more sign of those bizarre riders. Who were they? What? How?

I didn't get a chance to ask.

Little brown fellows carrying torches so they could see where they were running burst out of the Shadowlander camp. That could not bode well for me, my pals, or anyone else inside the wall.

"Poor Spinner," I cracked. "You got to feel for the man."

"Huh?" Sparkle was the only man close enough to hear.

"Don't you hate it when some no-brain vandalizes a work of art?"

Sparkle didn't get it. He shook his head, grabbed a javelin and threw it down at a short person with a torch.

He missed.

Around where those Shadowlanders had gained a foothold on the wall, and on the earthen approach ramps, a big racket began to develop. The Shadowmaster, piqued, had told his boys to get back to work. And don't be so damned gentle anymore.

"Hey, Bubba-do," I shouted at a soldier, "who's got tonight in the pool?"

There is the Black Company for you. We've got a pool on what night the city will fall. I guess the winner gets to die with a smile on his ugly mug.

24

Goblin and One-Eye had chosen to stay close to me. The real Goblin and One-Eye. I checked every few minutes to make sure. Their attention was on the hills, not the excitement across town or any of their own schemes. Strange lights moved out there.

A band of southerners sent out earlier returned at a gallop, half their number missing. They flew as though devils worse than their boss were after them. They dared ride the way they did only because Stormshadow had been obsessive when she leveled the plain and because there was light from the city.

Fires were burning. Only a few so far, but fires.

Sparkle told me, "They're pulling out down below."

I leaned over and looked. Nobody tried to pick me off. Maybe they thought I was another ghost.

Sure enough, the Shadowlanders were going, leaving us all

those wonderful grapnels without ropes, for us to dump on our "maybe we can use these someday" pile.

One-Eye said, "Guess we can put up our swords and go back to our tonk games now."

Overlooking the fact that Dejagore was being invaded elsewhere, I observed, "This is the second time you've come out with that silliness. What moron is going to play with you? Can't be anybody that dumb still alive." One-Eye cheats at cards. And he cheats badly. He gets caught every time. Nobody will play with him.

"Hey, Murgen. Listen. I've reformed. Really. Never again will I dishonor my talent to. . . ."

Why listen? He's said it all before, countless times. The first thing we do after we swear a recruit into the Company is warn him not to play cards with One-Eye.

A party of Shadowlanders withdrawn from my sector headed for the hills. They all had torches. It looked like the Shadowmaster himself might be driving them.

"Cletus! Longinus! You guys far enough along that you can drop a barrage on that crowd?" The brothers were repairing their engines as fast as they could. Two were ready, cocked and loaded. Not much of a barrage.

One-Eye asked, "Why do that?"

"Why not? We might get lucky. And can we piss off Shadowspinner more than he already is? He's already vowed to kill us all."

The ballistas thumped. The shafts they hurled did not hit the Shadowmaster. Distractedly, he replied with a spear of energy that dissolved several cubic yards of wall far from any of my guys.

The racket from across town kept getting louder. Some seemed closer than the far wall.

"They're inside," Sparkle said.

"A lot of them," Bucket agreed. "This could get to be a big cleanup job." I liked that positive thinking.

I shrugged. Mogaba liked to keep the cleanups for himself and the Nar and their Taglians.

Fine with me. Mogaba can eat all the pain he can swallow.

I really wanted to take a nap. This long day just kept getting longer. Oh, well. Soon enough I would get to sleep forever.

A short while later I got word that small groups of southerners were in the streets murdering anybody they could catch.

"Sir?"

"Sleepy. What's up, youngster?" Sleepy was a Taglian Shadar we swore into the Company just before I decided to take up this pen. He always looked like he was having trouble keeping his eyes open. He also looked like he was about fourteen years old, which was possible. He was paranoid in the extreme, apparently for good reason. He was a good-looking youth. And pretty boys are fair game amongst Taglian men of all three major religious groups. The Stranglers use their more attractive sons to lure victims to their deaths.

Different land, different customs. You may not like them but you do have to live with them. Sleepy liked our ways better than his own.

"Sir," he said, "the Nar aren't trying to keep the southerners from heading this way. They don't bother them at all anymore after they get through and off the wall as long as they don't head into Mogaba's barracks area."

"Is that deliberate?" Bucket asked.

Someone muttered, "Now ask a stupid question."

"What do you think?" One-Eye snapped. "This is the last straw. If that bigheaded, self-important dick shows his face around here . . ."

"Save it, One-Eye." This was hard to accept. But I could see Mogaba being capable of channeling the enemy our way so as to resolve questions of precedence inside the Company. His morality would allow him to picture it as a brilliant solution to several problems. "Instead of standing around bitching about it how about we do some thinking? Best way to fix Mogaba would be to shove his plan up his ass, no grease."

While the others tried to manage that difficult exercise—thinking—I questioned Sleepy more closely. Unfortunately, he could not add much but the general routes the southerners were using to push deeper into the city.

You couldn't blame the Shadowlanders. Most soldiers of most times jump at the chance to go where resistance is weakest.

Maybe we could use that to pull some into some sort of killing pocket.

I even got a chuckle out of my predicament. "I bet Croaker would have seen this coming a month ago, as paranoid as he was about supposed friends and allies."

A nearby crow squawked agreement.

I should have considered the possibility. I really should have. Far-fetched is not the same as impossible. I should have had something planned.

One-Eye became as serious as ever he gets. "You know what this means? If the kid is right?"

"The Company is at war with itself?"

The little guy waved that off like it was just another annoying gnat of reality. "Suppose Mogaba is giving them a golden bridge so they can get rid of us for him? They still have to get through the pilgrims to reach us."

I didn't need to think long to see what he meant. "That asshole. He going to *make* them kill Shadowlanders in self-defense. He's going to use them up killing his enemies for him."

"Maybe he's a bigger snake than anybody thought," Bucket growled. "It's for sure he's changed a lot since Gea-Xle."

"This ain't right," I muttered, although swords would enter the fight on our side—whether or not they wanted to. Other than a few small skirmishes with lost invaders during past attacks the worst that had happened to the Nyueng Bao was that their pilgrimage had gotten them trapped in the middle of somebody else's war. From the first clash of steel they had worked hard to maintain their neutrality.

Shadowspinner has his spies in the city. He would know the

Nyueng Bao had no interest in antagonizing him.

"What do you think they'll do?" Goblin asked. "The Nyueng Bao, I mean." His voice sounded odd. How much beer had he put away?

"How the hell would I know? Depends on how they see things. If they think Mogaba dragged them into it on purpose it might get unhealthy to belong to the Company. Mogaba could see this as a chance to squish us into a crack between a rock and a hard place. I'd better go see their Speaker and let him know what's happening. Bucket. Make up a twenty-man patrol and go looking for southerners. See if Sleepy is right. One-Eye, go with him. Spot for him and cover our guys. Sparkle, you watch things here. Send Sleepy after me if it gets too much to handle."

Nobody argued. When things get tight the guys do become less fractious.

I descended the stairway to the street.

25

I played the game the way I thought the Nyueng Bao would want. Ever since childhood I have suspected you get along better if you respect people's ways and wishes regardless of your apparent relative strengths.

That doesn't mean you let people walk on you. It doesn't mean you eat their pain for them. You need to demand respect for yourself, too.

Dejagore's byways are close and fetid. Typical of a fortified city. I went to an obscure intersection where—under normal circumstances—I could expect to be seen by Nyueng Bao watchers. They are a cautious people. They watch all the time. I announced, "I would see the Speaker. Harm is headed his way. I would have him know what I know."

I didn't see anybody. I didn't hear anybody. I expected nothing else. Someone who strolled into my territory would see and hear nothing, either, but death would be nearby.

The only sounds came from fighting several blocks away.

I waited.

Suddenly, in that instant when my attention finally wandered, Ky Dam's son materialized. He made no more noise than a tiptoeing moth. He was a wide, short man of indeterminate age. He carried an unusually long sword but it remained sheathed across his back. He stared at me hard. I stared back. It cost me nothing. He grunted, indicated that I should follow.

We walked no more than eighty yards. He indicated a doorway. "Keep smiling," I told him. I couldn't resist. He was always around somewhere, watching. I never saw him smile. I pushed the door inward.

Curtains hung two feet inside. Very weak light slipped through a rent. I closed the door carefully once I understood that I would be entering alone, before I parted the curtains. Wouldn't do to let light splash into the street.

The place turned out to be about as pleasant as you can get in a city.

The Speaker sat on a mat on a dirty floor near the one candle offering light. There were about a dozen people visible, of all ages and sexes. I saw four children, all small, six adults of an age to be their parents, and one old woman of granny age who glowered like she had a special bunk in Hell reserved for me even though she'd never seen me before. I saw nobody who could pass as her husband. Maybe he was the guy outside. Then there was a woman as old as Ky Dam, a fragile flower time-diminished to little more than skin-covered sticks, though an agile intelligence still burned in her eyes. You would get nothing past this woman.

Of material things I saw little but the clothing the people wore, a few ragged blankets, a couple of clay cups and a pot maybe used for cooking. And more swords nearly as long and fine as that carried by the Speaker's son.

In the darkness beyond the candlelight someone groaned. It was the sound of someone delirious.

"Sit," Ky Dam invited. A second mat lay unrolled beside the candle. In the weak light the old man seemed more frail than when he visited the wall.

I sat. Though I wasn't used to it and my tendons weren't supple enough, I tried to cross my legs.

I waited.

Ky Dam would invite me to speak when it was time.

I tried to concentrate on the old man, not the people staring at me, nor the smell of too many folks living in too small a space, of their strange foods, nor even the odor of sickness.

A woman brought tea. How she made it I don't know. I never saw any fire. I didn't think about that at the moment, though, so startled was I. She was beautiful. Even in dirt and rags, incredibly beautiful. I brought the hot tea to my lips and scalded them to shock myself back to business.

I felt sorrow instantly. This one would pay dearly when the southerners took the town.

A small smile touched Ky Dam's lips. I noticed amusement on the face of the old woman, too, and recognized there a similar beauty only externally betrayed by time. They were used to my initial reaction. Maybe it was some kind of test, bringing her out of the shadows. Almost too softly to be heard, the old man said, "She is indeed." Louder, he added, "You are wise beyond your years, Soldier of Darkness."

What was this Soldier of Darkness crap? Every time he addressed me he stuck me with another name.

I tried a formal head bow of acknowledgment. "Thank you for that compliment, Speaker." I hoped he would realize that I was incapable of keeping up with the subtleties of proper manners amongst the Nyueng Bao.

"I sense in you a great anxiety held in check only by chains of will." He sipped tea calmly but eyed me in a way that told me hastiness would be tolerated if I thought it really necessary.

I said, "Great evils stalk the night, Speaker. Unexpected monsters have slipped their leashes."

"So I surmised when you were kind enough to permit me atop your section of wall."

"There is a new beast loose. One I never expected to see." In retrospect I realize we were speaking of two different things. "One I do not know how to handle." I strove to keep my Taglian pronunciations clear. Men conversing in a tongue native to neither sorely tempt the devils of misunderstanding.

He seemed puzzled. "I do not understand you."

I glanced around. Did all his people live like this all the time? They were packed in way tighter than we were. Of course, we could enforce our claims to space with our swords. "Do you know about the Black Company? Do you know our recent history?" Rather than await an answer I sketched our immediate past.

Ky Dam was one of those rare people who listened with every ounce of his being.

I finished. The old man said, "Time has, perhaps, made of you shadows of the Soldiers of Darkness. You have been gone so long and have journeyed so far that you have strayed from your Way completely. Nor are the followers of the warrior prince Mogaba hewing any nearer the true path."

I did not hide my thoughts well. Ky Dam and his woman found me amusing again. "But I am not one of you, Standardbearer. My knowledge has drifted far from the truth as well. Perhaps there is no real truth today because there is no one who knows it anymore."

I didn't have a clue what the hell he was talking about.

"You have wandered long and far, Standardbearer. But you may yet come home again." His expression darkened momentarily. "Though you wish that you had not. Where is your standard, Standardbearer?"

"I don't know. It vanished during the big battle on the plain outside. I jammed its butt into the earth when I decided to put on my Captain's armor in order to pretend that he had not fallen, so the troops would rally, but. . . ."

The old man raised a hand. "I think it may be very close tonight."

I hate this obscurity crap old people and wizards like to perpetrate. I am convinced that they do it only because it gives them a feeling of power. Screw the missing standard. It was not germane, now, tonight. I said, "The Nar chieftain wants to be Captain of the Black Company. He does not approve of the ways of those of us from the far north."

I paused but the old man had dried up. He waited.

I said, "Mogaba is flawless as a warrior but he has shortcomings in some areas of leadership."

Ky Dam then proved to be less than the totally inscrutable and eternally patient old-timer you are led to expect in these situations.

"You came to warn me that he has chosen to lessen his problems by letting southerners do his knifework, Standard-bearer?"

"Huh?"

"One of my grandsons was in a position to overhear while Mogaba debated tonight's actions with his lieutenants Ochiba, Sindawe, Ranjalpirindi and Chal Ghanda Ghan. Because Taglian conspirators were present the Nar failed to squabble in their native tongue—though Mogaba showed limited facility with the Taglian."

"Excuse me? Sir?"

"What your honor compels you to report to me, although you only harbor suspicions now, is far worse than you fear. Over-ruling strong objections by his Nar lieutenants, Mogaba set forth a plan for tonight which will allow southerners who reach the ramparts and do not dally there to have their ways behind the wall. Taglian legionnaires will discourage them from attacking any direction but through our quarter into yours."

"You knew already? That what you're saying? Before I got here you had an actual witness?"

"Thai Dei."

A young man rose. He was an unpleasant-looking skinny little guy who held a toddler in his arms.

Ky Dam said, "He does not speak Taglian well but he understands it good enough. He overheard the plot being hatched. He overheard the arguments of those who found it dishonorable. He saw an angry Mogaba go so far as to continue during the visit of a man believed to be an instrument of the Shadowmasters."

That hit me. It meant that, as of that moment, there existed a tacit agreement between Mogaba and Shadowspinner good until me and mine had been obliterated.

"This is cruel treachery indeed, Speaker."

Ky Dam nodded. Then he told me, "There is more, Stone Soldier. Both Ranjalpirindi and Ghanda Ghan are intimates of the Prahbrindrah Drah. Speaking with the Prince's voice they assured Mogaba that, once the siege has been broken and your band has been eliminated, the Prince will announce his personal support of Mogaba's captaincy of your company. In exchange Mogaba will abandon your previous Captain's quest to become chief warlord of Taglios. With all powers necessary to prosecute the war against the Shadowlands."

"Man, that was some job of eavesdropping." Thai Dei almost smiled.

"And some job of treachery put together by Brother Mogaba."

I could see why Ochiba and Sindawe would argue against it. It was a betrayal almost beyond comprehension.

Mogaba had, indeed, gone through some dark changes since Gea-Xle.

I asked, "What does he have against you people?"

"Nothing. Politically he should be indifferent to us. We have never been a factor in Taglian affairs. But we mean nothing to him in any other way, either. He is eager to spend us like found coin. If the southerners attack you after fighting his forces, then us, huge numbers of his enemies *and* us resource-gulping undesirables will have been eliminated."

"Once I admired this man greatly, Speaker."

"Men change, Standardbearer. And this one more than most. He is an actor and but one wicked purpose impels all his acting."

"Speaker?"

"This Mogaba is the center of, and the reason for, everything that Mogaba does. Mogaba will sacrifice his best friend upon an altar to himself, though probably not even a god could convince the friend that that possibility exists. Mogaba's every wicked order draws another veil off the black blotch devouring his soul. He has changed as the most perfect pomegranate will change when the mold gets inside its skin."

Here we go, talking old-timer sideways again.

"Standardbearer! Though I know of the black danger to my people already I am honored that you believed us worthy of a warning, however pressing your other concerns. That was an act of generosity and friendship. We do not forget those who have extended their hands."

"Thank you. I am pleased by your response." You'd better believe. "And if Mogaba allows you to be attacked . . ."

"The problem is upon us already, Stone Soldier. Southerners are dying right now, only yards away. Once it became evident that we were trapped here we all learned every nuance of the ground upon which we might fight. This is not our swamp but the principles of battle remain the same. We have been prepared for this night for many weeks. It remained to be seen only who would chose to become our enemy."

"Huh?" I could be stupid as a stone when I ran into something cold.

"You should rejoin those who look to you for leadership. Do so secure in the knowledge that you have the friendship of the Nyueng Bao."

"An honor."

"Or curse." The old man chuckled.

"Does that mean your people will actually talk to mine?"

"That might be a little too much." He chuckled again. His wife smiled, too. What a wild joker he was! The man was a laugh riot. He said, "Thai Dei. Go with this man. You may speak if spoken to, but only as my mouth. Bone Warrior. This is my grandson. He will understand you. Send him to me if you have a need to communicate. Do not be frivolous."

"I understand." I tried to get up, embarrassed myself by failing to get my legs untangled. One of the kids laughed. I dared glance around for a reaction from the dream woman who brought the tea, sure I was not fooling Ky Dam. A baby slept in her lap. A toddler dozed under her left arm. She was awake, watching. She looked tired, frightened, confused and determined. About like the rest of us. Whenever that moaning came from the darkness she winced and looked that way. The pain was a part of her.

I bowed myself out. The Nyueng Bao Thai Dei led me back to familiar territory.

26

I don't know," I told Goblin when he asked about my Nyueng Bao shadow. "He don't talk much." I had not gotten a word out of him yet. "His all-purpose vocabulary seems to be the noncommittal grunt. Anyway, the visit wasn't necessary. The Nyueng Bao know more about the coming shit rain than we do. The old man admits it's all Mogaba's fault and says we're off the hook."

Goblin made as though to look over his shoulder like he was trying to check his own behind.

"Yeah," I agreed. "Strap on your chastity belt. What's happening?" I didn't see Bucket or Sparkle.

"Not much yet. Spinner and his bunch just got to the hills."

And all kinds of excitement broke out out there. A strong pink light cast silhouettes on the night again. Goblin said, "They look exactly like the Lifetaker and Widowmaker costumes Lady made for her and Croaker. Hey! How come you look like you got bit on the ass by a ghost?"

"Because maybe I did. They do look exactly like what you say. Only if you remember I took the Widowmaker armor off Croaker after that arrow got him. I put it on and pretended to be him. And failed because I started too late."

"So?"

"So last week somebody stole the Widowmaker armor. Right out of my quarters while I was laying there asleep. I thought I had it hidden where nobody but me could ever find it. But somebody came in, stepped over me, got it dug out, and got out of there with the load and I never saw or heard a thing. And neither did anybody else." And that was definitely scary.

"Is that why you were asking all those weird questions the other day?" Goblin squeaked. He could sound like a stomped mouse when he was distressed.

"Yeah."

"How come you never said anything?"

"Because whoever took the armor had to use sorcery to get past me. I figured it was one of you guys and I wanted to find out which one so I could cut him off at the ankles before he knew it was coming."

One-Eye came puffing up the stairs. Not bad for a guy two hundred years old. "What gives? How come the grim faces?"

Goblin filled him in.

The little black wizard grumped, "You should have told us, Murgen. We might have picked up a hot trail."

Not likely. The only evidence I had found was one small white feather and a glob of what looked like bird shit. "It don't matter now. I know where the armor is. Out there." I pointed at the hills, which lay beneath what looked like a premature pink dawn. "What did you do?"

"We killed off a bunch of goddamned southerners, that's what we did. Mogaba must be selling them tickets over there. The little suckers are thicker than lice. Anyway, we got out before we used up our luck. Them Nyueng Bao are really going bug fuck." He gave Thai Dei the fish-eye. "Looks like they're trying to make the Shadowlanders want to go chomp on Mogaba's rear. Serve the asshole right, he gets ate up by his own plot. What the hell is going on out there?" He meant the pink-soaked hills.

Goblin replied, "That's something we weren't looking for."

A gout of darkness reared against the pink. Human figures tumbled within it. They flared, burned like bright, brief-lived stars. Moments later an earth tremor rocked the city. I lost my footing briefly.

One-Eye observed, "For once you're right, runt. There's a player in the game we didn't know about."

A pair of crows a few yards off went into hysterics. They jumped into the darkness, kept laughing as they flapped away.

"Surprise, surprise," I muttered. "What with all that booming and crashing and crap in those hills. Come on, guys! Tell me who. The rest even a dummy like me can figure out. So just tell me who."

"We're gonna work on that," One-Eye promised. "Maybe we'd even start now if you went away and left us alone. Come on, runt."

While him and his frog-faced buddy got to work I turned my attention to the excitement still festering inside Dejagore.

Possibly thousands of Shadowlanders had crossed the wall now. A lot of fires were burning. I asked Ky Dam's grandson, "Will the light be trouble for your people?"

He shrugged.

This fellow was no gossip.

27

There was no night now. Fires burned everywhere. They burned in the Shadowlander camp, set by Mogaba's beleaguered artillerymen. They burned in the city, set by the Shadowmaster's soldiers. Conflagrations blazed in the hills, hinting of surprise volcanos or powers of a magnitude unseen since the Company went up against the dark lords of Lady's empire. It was too much light for the middle of the night. "How long till dawn? Anybody know?"

"Too long," Bucket grumbled. "You really think anybody is actually worrying about keeping time tonight?"

Way back, centuries earlier in the evening, One-Eye or Goblin or somebody expressed dawn as a goal too remote for hope. The general level of optimism remained that low.

Reports came in, none of them good. Innumerable southern soldiers were inside the city. They had orders to drive toward us, wipe us out, then continue on around inside and atop the wall, the long way, till they got back where they had started. But the Nyueng Bao were not cooperating. Neither were my guys. So the invaders were blundering around doing any damage they could till somebody killed them.

Against the Jaicuri, cowering in their homes hoping to be overlooked despite all their experience with the Shadowmasters, the southerners enjoyed some success.

You could not fault them for not going all out after us. They did not want to get killed either. And Mogaba should not have been surprised when some of the villains he let through turned on him.

Our guys held their positions. The doppelgängers and illusions drove the southerners crazy. They never knew which threat was real. But the big reason our side held up well was that there was no choice. We had nowhere to run.

Shadowspinner was no help to his people. He was out in

those hills intent on undoing that mystery personally. Clearly he regretted having made the choice.

Once again a band of riders came flying back, silhouetted by pink light. The Shadowmaster did not appear to be with them. "Goblin! One-Eye! Where the hell are you now, you little shits? Has something happened to Shadowspinner?"

Goblin materialized, his breath heavy with the smell of beer. He and One-Eye had a few gallons stashed somewhere nearby, then. He dashed my hopes. "The Shadowmaster is alive, Murgen. But maybe he's messed his drawers."

He giggled.

"Oh, shit," I muttered. The little toad had gotten *deep* into the home brew. If One-Eye had, too, I might have one truly interesting rest of the night. It was possible those two would forget everything and pick up the feud they have had going for a hundred years. Last time they got drunk and went after each other they tore up a whole city block in Taglios.

All the while the Speaker's grandson hung back in the shadows and watched like one of those goddamned crows. There were a lot more of those around now.

Old Wheezer came puffing up from the street. He had to take a break before he got to the top. He hacked and coughed and spat blood. He was from the same part of the world as One-Eye. They have nothing else in common except a taste for beer. Wheezer had been to the barrel a few times, too.

He came on up top as I surveyed the city and tried to guess how bad things really were. We were getting very little pressure right then.

Wheezer hacked and wheezed and spat.

A new generation of pink lights erupted at the feet of the hills. They cast two shadows against the sky. There was no doubt they were shadows of Widowmaker and Lifetaker, the dread alter egos Lady created for herself and Croaker so they could scare shit out of Shadowlanders.

"This isn't possible," I told my tame wizards. One-Eye was back. He used one hand to support Wheezer, who seemed to be suffering an asthma attack along with the effects of his tuberculosis. In his other hand One-Eye clutched something polelike wrapped in rags. I continued, "That can't be Croaker and Lady because I saw them go down with my own eyes."

A handful of horsemen drifted toward town. Among them was a blob of darkness that had to be Shadowspinner. He was staying busy. Pink fireflies swarmed around him. He had trouble fending them off.

As though they realized their boss would be in a foul temper when he got back, the southerners' attack suddenly picked up.

"I'm not sure," Goblin mused. He sounded like he had been scared sober. "I can't get *any* sense of the one in the Lifetaker armor. There's a shitload of power there, though."

"Lady had no power left," I reminded him.

"The other one does feel like Croaker."

Couldn't be.

Wheezer finally gasped, "Mogaba . . ."

Several men spat at mention of the name. Everybody had an opinion about our fearless war chief. Listening to them you might have concluded that Mogaba was the most lusted after man in town.

A writhing pink thread reached for Shadowspinner's party. The Shadowmaster batted it away from himself but it slew half his party. Parts of bodies flew in all directions.

"Shee-it!" somebody said, pretty much capturing the popular feeling.

Wheezer barked, "Mogaba . . . wants to know . . . if we can free up . . . a few hundred men to . . . counterattack the enemy who . . . are inside the city."

"How stupid does that bastard think we are?" Sparkle grumbled.

Goblin asked, "Don't that camel's wife know we're on to him?"

"Why should he think we might suspect him? He's got such a tall opinion of his own brain. . . ."

"I think it's funny," Bucket crowed. "He tried to screw us and only ended up with his own ass in a sling. Even better, maybe the only way he can pry it out is to have us do it for him."

I asked Goblin, "What's One-Eye up to?" One-Eye looked like he was praying over one of the ballistas with Loftus. Rags lay scattered around their feet. A gruesome black spear lay in the engine's trough.

"I don't know."

I checked the nearest gate. The Nar there could see us. Mogaba would know I was lying if I claimed we were too beat up to send help. I asked, "Anybody think of a reason we should help Mogaba?" To hold my sector, besides the Old Crew itself, I had six hundred Taglian survivors from Lady's division and an uncertain and changeable number of liberated slaves, former prisoners of war and ambitious Jaicuri.

Everyone replied in the negative. Nobody wanted to help Mogaba. As I approached the engines I asked, "How about if we do it just to save our own butts? If we let Mogaba get stomped we could end up facing the rest of the Shadowlander mob by ourselves." I glanced at the gate. "And those people over there can see everything we do."

Goblin looked, too. He shook his head to lessen the beer buzz. "We'll have to think about that."

"What are you doing, One-Eye?" I was beside him now.

One-Eye indicated the spear proudly. "Little something I've been working on in my spare time."

"It's ugly enough." Nice to know he could do something useful without being told.

He had begun with a black wooden pole and had worked it for a lot of hours. It was covered with incredibly ugly miniature scenes along with writing in an unfamiliar alphabet. Its head was as black as its shaft, darkened iron finely traced with silver runes. There was some color on the shaft, too, although so fine as to be almost invisible.

"Very nice."

"Nice? Sigh. You heathen." He pointed. Loftus looked. So did I.

Shadowspinner's party, sadly depleted, surrounded by swarms of pink sparkles and mocking crows, was getting close.

One-Eye snickered. "This here is my Shadowmaster blaster, bastar'!" He howled. He must have put away a lot of that beer. "Nothing he couldn't stop on a lazy afternoon, but this ain't no lazy afternoon, is it? Loftus shoots, this stick won't be in the air five seconds. That's all the time he'll have to figure out what's coming and what to do to unravel the spells that are there to keep him from turning it. And look how busy that asshole is already. Loftus, my man, get ready to carve you a big victory notch on this thing."

As anybody with any sense does, Loftus ignored One-Eye. He laid his weapon with an artist's care.

One-Eye babbled, "Most of the spells are designed to penetrate his personal protection, counting on him not having time to do anything actively. Because I wanted to concentrate on piercing one point in a passive . . ."

I shut him out. "Goblin. Any chance this will work? The runt's not exactly a heavyweight."

"It's workable, tactically. If he really worked that hard on it. Say One-Eye is an order of magnitude weaker than Shadowspinner. That really only means that it takes him ten times as long to get the same work done."

"An order of magnitude?" So that was One-Eye's problem.

"More like two orders really, probably."

He lost me. And I didn't have time to wring an explanation out of him.

Loftus was satisfied he was leading his target perfectly, he had the range, whatever. "Time," he said.

28

L oose," I suggested.

The ballista offered its distinctive thump. Silence spread along the wall. The black shaft darted across the night. The occasional spark floated behind it. One-Eye said five seconds of flight. The truth was more like four but they took forever.

There was ample firelight to illuminate the Shadowmaster. Shortly he would disappear behind one of the enfilading towers. He stared back at the hills as he rode. Those bizarre riders out there were on the plain now, daring someone, anyone, to answer their challenge.

I gasped.

Widowmaker carried the Lance. The standard itself was not apparent but that was the lance on which it had ridden from the day the Black Company left Khatovar. Every single Annalist has kept close track—although the reason for doing so has been forgotten.

I focused on Shadowspinner in time to see One-Eye's treasure arrive.

Later Goblin told me Spinner sensed the threat as the missile hit the peak of its arc. Whatever he did then, it was the right thing. Or he was lucky. Or a higher power decreed that this was not his night to die.

The spear changed course by scant inches. Instead of striking Shadowspinner it hit his mount's shoulder. And ripped through the beast as though it was no more substantial than air. The wound glowed red, flickered. The red spread. Shadowspinner bellowed in rage as the animal threw him. He fell in a heap, lay there twitching long enough for One-Eye to start nagging Loftus about hitting him with a barrage of regular shafts, then he scuttled off like a crab to escape the stallion's pounding hooves.

I recognized that animal then. It was one of those magically bred monster horses Lady brought south with the Company, out of her old empire. They vanished during the battle.

The horse screamed and screamed.

A normal animal would have perished in moments.

I stared at those two riders out there. They walked toward the city slowly, offering their challenge. Now I could see that they, too, were mounted on Lady's stallions. I told Goblin, "But I saw them killed."

One-Eye grumbled, "We got to check this boy's eyes."

Goblin said, "I told you before, that's not Lady. You look real close, you can see differences in the armor."

The troops were seeing that. There was a stir among the Taglians.

"And you don't know about the other one? What're they talking about over there?"

"No. It could be the Old Man."

Sparkle went to see why the Taglians were excited.

Shadowspinner's horse collapsed but continued screaming and kicking. Wisps of greenish steam rose from its wound. That continued to grow. The beast's death was a long time coming.

The sorcerer would have died more slowly and gruesomely still had One-Eye's shaft struck home.

Sparkle came to say, "They're all excited because that armor is an exact match for some goddess named Kina in her battle avatar. That's the way she's always portrayed in paintings about her war with the demons."

I had no idea what he was talking about, only that Kina was some sort of death goddess in these parts.

I wondered when the Shadowmaster would snipe back at One-Eye.

"He won't," Goblin assured me. "The moment he gave it attention enough to be effective those two out there would cut his legs off."

I watched Shadowspinner limp out of sight.

His embarrassment spurred his soldiers to increase their efforts again. Somebody would pay for his indignity in pain. Understandably they preferred that we pick up that tab.

Some of them seemed to recognize the Lifetaker armor, too. I heard the name Kina shouted more than once below the wall.

"Thai Dei. Time for a message to your grandfather. I want to bring part of my force through his area so I can help drive the southerners out of the city."

The Nyueng Bao stepped out of the shadows just long enough to listen. He stared at those riders, troubled. Then he grunted, descended to the street and trotted off into the night.

"Listen up, people. We're going to go save our fearless dick-head leader. Bucket . . ."

29

I stepped into a dark alleyway, planning to set up shop behind a southern company with Goblin to do his hoodoo on them. And it was like I stepped off the edge of the world, into an abyss without bottom. Like some great psychic flyswatter slapped me down into the void. Goblin barked something in the instant it took to go but I did not understand him.

I had that moment to feel seasick, to be bewildered, to wonder who had ambushed me with what sorcery, and why it seemed to twist me like a wet rag being wrung out.

Had Mogaba taken his treachery to another level?

30

Something had hold of me. It pulled so virulently there was no resisting it. I lost track of who I was and where. I knew only that I was asleep and did not want to wake up.

"Murgen!" a far voice called. The pull strengthened. "Murgen, come on! Come home! Fight it, Kid! Fight it!" I fought.

But it was that voice I fought. It wanted me to come somewhere that much of me did not want to go. Pain awaited me there.

The pull redoubled as the force dragged at me with inescapable power.

"That did it!" somebody shouted. "We have him back now."

I knew that voice. . . .

It was like coming out of a coma except that I remembered where I had been in every detail. Dejagore. Every little ache, every horror, every fear. But already the sharp edges were going dull. The ties were slipping. I was *here* now.

Here? Which when and where was here? I tried opening my eyes. My lips would not respond. I tried to move. My limbs refused to be troubled.

"He's all here."

"Pull that curtain." I heard heavy cloth being moved. "Will it keep getting harder? I thought we were supposed to be over the worst. That he couldn't recede so far that we would have this much trouble bringing him home."

Oh! That voice belonged to Croaker. The Old Man. Only the Old Man is dead, because I saw him killed. . . . Or did I? Didn't I just leave Widowmaker, alive long past his time?

"Well, he didn't listen. But it can't do anything but get better now. We're around the corner. Over the hump. Unless he *wants* to stay lost."

I got an eye open.

I was in a dark place. I'd never seen it before but it had to be in the Palace at Trogo Taglios. Home. Never have I seen that kind of stone used anywhere else. And there was nothing astonishing about not being able to recognize parts of the Palace. The princes of Taglios all add on a bit during their reigns. Supposedly only the old royal wizard Smoke ever knew his way around the whole place. And Smoke isn't with us anymore. I don't know what happened to him afterward but several years ago he got torn up when a supernatural creature he disagreed with tried to eat him. Handy, because about then was when we discovered that he had been seduced by Longshadow and had gone over to the Shadowmasters.

I was amazed at me. Although I had a headache like the mother of all hangovers my mind, suddenly, was crystal clear.

"He's got an eye open, chief."

"Can you hear me, Murgen?"

I tried my tongue, blurted fluent gibberish.

"You had another one of your spells. We've been trying to bring you back for two days." Croaker sounded put out. Like I was inconveniencing him on purpose? "All right. You know the drill. Let's get him up and walking."

I remembered doing this part several times before. I was less confused now, more able to grasp quickly the distinction between past and present.

They got my feet under me. Goblin got under my right armpit. Croaker wrapped his arm around me from the left, lifted.

I said, "I remember what to do."

They did not understand. Goblin asked, "You got a grip on when you are, Murgen? Ain't going to drift off into the past on us again?"

I nodded. I could communicate that way. Maybe I could use the deaf and dumb speech.

"Dejagore again?" Croaker asked.

I had the connections all made inside. Even plenty I didn't want made. I tried talking again. "Same night. Again. Later on."

"Set him down. He'll be all right now," Croaker said. "Murgen. You get any clues this time? Anything we can latch onto to break you out of this cycle? I need you here. I need you full time."

"Not one damned thing." I paused to catch my breath. I was adapting faster this time. "I don't even know when it hit me. I was just there, suddenly, like a poltergeist or something, with no thoughts of any future at all. Then after a while I was just Murgen with no awareness, no anomalies like I get now."

"Anomalies?"

Startled, I turned. One-Eye had materialized from somewhere. I saw that curtain still stirring. It closed off half the room.

"Huh?"

"What do you mean by anomalies?"

When I concentrated I really didn't know what I meant. I shook my head. "I don't know. It's gotten away from me. When am I?"

Croaker and the wizards dealt a hand of significant looks between them. Croaker asked, "Do you remember the Grove of Doom?"

"Sure. I'm still shivering." A chill did touch me. Then I recalled the key thing. I had no memories of having visited this room before but I should have had them. Because I was still in my yesterdays. I just wasn't as far away as I had been at Dejagore, which was years ago.

Then I tried to remember the future.

I remembered too much. I whimpered.

"Do we need to get him up again?" Goblin asked.

I shook my head. "I'm solid. Let's think. How long between this spell and the last one? How long since we got back from the grove?"

Croaker said, "You got back three days ago. I told you to bring your prisoners to the Palace. You tried. You lost the shadowweaver along the way, in circumstances so questionable I issued orders for all Company people to stay especially alert."

"He was old. He just died of fright," One-Eye said. "Ain't nothing mysterious about that."

My headache was not improving. I had vague recollections of those events but they were not as clear as my memories of other events immediately before previous seizures. "I don't recall much of it."

"The red-hand Deceiver got here all right. We meant to start questioning him that night. But you went back to your apartment, supposedly just walked through the doorway and collapsed. Your mother-in-law, uncle, wife and brother-in-law all agree. Probably the first, last and only time that will happen."

"Probably. The old lady is like One-Eye. She disagrees just to be disagreeable."

"Hey! Kid. . . ."

"Quiet," Croaker told him. "So you just fell down and went rigid. Your wife got hysterical. Your brother-in-law came for me. We took you out of there to ease the stress on your family."

Ease the stress? Those people never heard of the word. Besides, Sarie was the only one of them I considered family.

Goblin said, "Open your mouth, Murgen." He turned my face to the best light and stared down my throat. "No damage in here."

I knew what they thought. Epilepsy. I had considered that myself. I had asked about it of anyone who would listen. But no epileptic I ever heard of got bounced into the past from a seizure. Into a past that was never exactly like the past I had lived already.

"I told you it isn't a disease," Croaker growled. "When you find the answer it will be right there inside your own field and you'll probably feel stupid about not having seen it earlier."

"If there's anything to be found we'll find it," One-Eye promised. Which left me wondering what he had up his sleeve. Then I knew that I had to know already because they were going to tell me pretty soon. But I could not recall that future clearly enough to grasp it.

Sometimes it was spooky being me.

"Was that headless character there again?" Croaker asked.

After figuring out what he meant I said, "Yes. But he was faceless, boss. Not headless. He had a head."

"Might represent the source of the problem," One-Eye suggested. "You ever remember any features, anything at all, tell somebody. Or get it written down right away."

Croaker told me, "I don't want this to happen to anybody else. Can you imagine managing a campaign when your people can fade out on you any minute, for days at a time?"

I felt confident that that would not happen. But I didn't say so because they would press me on it and I did not feel like being poked and prodded. "I need something for a headache. Please. A hangover kind of headache."

"Did you have this headache the other times?" Croaker demanded. "You never mentioned it."

"It was there but not this bad. Just a minor discomfort. A four-beer hangover kind of headache, if it was beer brewed by Willow Swan and Cordy Mather. That mean anything?"

Croaker smiled at the reference to the world's second worst beer. "Between me and Goblin we watched you almost every minute since you got back from the Grove of Doom. It seemed likely that this would keep happening. I didn't want us to miss anything."

And that keyed a serious question. Since while I am in this time I can remember the future occasionally how come I never remember the trips to the past that I am going to make?

And how could they watch me that closely? I never noticed them. And I try to stay alert. You never know when a Deceiver might pop out of a shadow swinging his strangling scarf.

"So what did you get?"

"We didn't see a thing."

"I am on the job now, though," One-Eye said, preening.

"Now that really inspires me with confidence."

"Everybody's got to be a wiseass anymore," One-Eye complained. "I remember when young people respected their elders."

"That was in the days when they didn't get a chance to know the old folks very well."

"I have work to do," Croaker said. "One-Eye, stick with Murgen when you can. Keep talking about Dejagore and what's been happening to him. There'll be clues there somewhere. Maybe we don't recognize them yet. If we keep at it something will pop." He left before I could say anything.

Something had passed between Croaker and One-Eye about and beyond me. And maybe we all had cause to be concerned. This time I could not remember much about where I was. Things seemed to be new, first time, yet some shaking, terrified little creature way back in the night warrens of my mind insisted I was still reliving yesterdays and the worst of those were yet to come.

One-Eye said, "I think we'll just take you home now, Kid. Your wife will have the cure for what ails you."

She might. She was a miracle. Even One-Eye, who seems incapable of offering respect to anyone, treated her and spoke to and of her, as though he considered her an honored lady.

She is, of course. But it is nice to have others confirm that.

"Now that's the first thing you've said that I wanted to hear. Lead on, brother." I didn't know the way.

I cast a backward glance at Smoke and the covered Deceiver. What in the hell?

31

My in-laws make very little effort to improve anyone's opinion of Nyueng Bao. Mother Gota, in particular, is a major pain in the ass. The old battleaxe barely tolerates even me and that only because the alternative is to lose her daughter entirely. She is very nasty toward the Old Man.

Still, Sarie and I rated enough for Croaker to insist we swap quarters when her folks showed up last month, in town slumming from their glamorous swamps. But they won't make it back to paradise if Mother Gota doesn't control her lip in the street.

The Old Man never reacts to her constant complaints. He told me, "I've had thirty years of Goblin and One-Eye. One crabby old woman hurting from gout and arthritis is nothing. You did say she's only here for a few weeks, didn't you?"

Right. I did say that. I wondered how those words would taste with soy sauce. Or maybe a lot of curry.

Now that Lady is in the south most of the time, emptying her cornucopia of rage onto the Shadowlands, Croaker has no need for a large apartment. Our old space was little more than a monk's cell. There is just room enough for him, Lady when she visits, and a cradle that was given to Lady by a man named Ram who later died trying to protect her and her baby from Narayan Singh. Ram made that cradle himself. Most likely he died because, like almost every man who spends much time around Lady, he fell for the wrong woman.

Croaker gave me his apartment, all right, but it came with limitations. I could not turn it into the new home of the Nyueng Bao. Sahra and Thai Dei belonged. Mother Gota and Uncle Doj were welcome for visits. And not one freeloading cousin or nephew more.

People who accuse the Captain of using his position to feather his nest ought to take a close look at the nest. The Liberator, Mr. By Golly Military Despot of all the Taglians and their many conquests and dependencies, lives just the way he did back when he was only the Company physician and Annalist.

Also, he moved me to provide me adequate work space. He sets great store by these Annals.

My books are not coming out so good. I don't always get stuff down the best way. In his time, when he was on the mark, Croaker was really good. I can't help comparing my stuff to his.

When he tried to be Captain and Annalist at the same time his work suffered. And Lady's writing strikes me as too direct, too curt, and sometimes mildly self-indulgent. Neither was honest all the time and neither considered trying to be consistent with the other, with their predecessors, or even with their own earlier selves. If you read either one closely and you spot some of their slips, neither will admit any screwup. If Croaker says that it is eight hundred miles from Taglios to Shadowcatch and Lady calls it four hundred, who is correct? Both say they are. Lady says the discrepancy is because they grew up in different places and times where different weights and measures were in use.

What about character? They for sure see with different eyes there. You will never catch Croaker portraying a Willow Swan

who is not bitching about something. Lady makes Swan energetic and rattle-mouthed and a lot more mellow. And the difference could be that both Croaker and Lady know Swan's interest in Lady is not brotherly.

And consider how they saw Smoke. You wouldn't think
they they were writing about the same animal, they looked at
that traitor so differently. Then there is Mogaba. And Blade.
Both blackhearted traitors, too. There is nothing in Croaker's
Annals because he was no longer writing when Blade deserted
but in daily life, constantly, he shows you that he hates Blade
with a blue-assed passion, on no rational basis. Meantime, he
seems almost willing to forgive Mogaba. Lady sees those two the
other way around. She would broil Mogaba right in the same
pot with Narayan and probably let Blade go.

Blade was another case like Ram and Swan.

I guess you don't need to agree on everything to be lovers.

They wrote differently, too. Croaker mostly kept his Annals
as he went along, then went back later to fill in after he heard
from other sources. He tended to fictionalize his secondary view-
points, too, so his Annals are not always absolutely straightforward history.

Lady wrote her entire book after the fact, from memory,
while she was laid up waiting to have her baby. Her alternate
viewpoint material is mainly secondhand hearsay. I am replac-
ing her more dubious stuff with material I consider more accu-
rate while I am in the process of putting all the confused stuff
into a uniform format.

Lady is not always pleased with my efforts, he understated.

My major fault is getting trapped in elaborate digressions. I
have trouble leaving things out. I spent some time with the official historians at Taglios's royal library and those guys assured
me that the real keys to history are the details. Like the entire
course of history can veer sharply because one man gets dinged
by a random arrow during a minor skirmish.

My writing room is fifteen feet by twenty-two. That gives
me space for all my references, for copies of the old Annals, and

for a large trestle table where I work on several projects at once.
And there is an acre of floor space left for Thai Dei and Uncle
Doj.

While I write and study and revise he and Thai Dei clack
away with wooden practice swords or squeal and kick and
bounce off the walls. Whenever one of them lands in my space
I toss him back. They are amazingly good at what they do—they
ought to be with all that practice—but I think they are more
likely to hurt each other than any seriously large person, like
our Old Crew guys.

I like this job. It beats hell out of being standardbearer—
though I am stuck with that, too, still. The standardbearer is always the first guy into a scrape and he always has one hand tied
up keeping a bigass pole from falling over.

I worry about not catching details the way Croaker did.
And I envy him his naturally sardonic tone. He claims he did
good only because he had the time. In those days the Black
Company was just a raggedyass gang sneaking around the edge
of things and there wasn't much going on. Nowadays we are in
the deep shit all the time. I don't like that. Neither does the
Captain.

I cannot imagine a man less pleased about having the power
that has fallen into his lap, mostly by default. He keeps it and
uses it only because he doesn't believe anyone else will take the
Company where he is convinced that it has to go.

I managed to get along for several hours without falling
down a well into the past. I wasn't feeling badly. Sarie was in
an excellent mood despite all her mother could do to ruin our
day. I was lost in my work, as comfortable with existence as ever
I get.

Somebody came to the door.

Sarie showed the Captain into the apartment. Uncle Doj
and Thai Dei continued clacking away. Croaker watched for a
minute. "Unusual," he said. He did not sound impressed.

"It's not military," I told him. "It's fencing for loners. Nyueng
Bao are big on lone-wolf heroes." Not so the Old Man. His be-

lief that you need brothers to guard your back amounts to a religious conviction.

Nyueng Bao fencing technique consists of brief but intense flurries of attack and defense separated by inactive periods during which the fighters freeze in odd stances, shifting almost imperceptibly as they try to anticipate one another.

Uncle Doj is *very* good.

"I'll grant you, they're graceful, Murgen. Almost like hutsch dancers."

By marrying into Sarie's clan I bought into Nyueng Bao fighting styles. No choice, really. Uncle Doj insisted. I am not terribly interested but I go along to keep the peace. And it is good exercise. "It's all stylized, Captain. Every stance and stroke has its name." Which I consider a weakness. Any fighter that set in his ways ought to be easy meat for an innovator.

On the other hand, I did see Uncle Doj deal with real enemies at Dejagore.

I changed languages. "Uncle, will you permit my Captain to meet Ash Wand?" They had taken the measure of one another long enough.

Ash Wand is Uncle Doj's sword. He calls it his soul. He treats it better than he would any mistress.

Uncle Doj disengaged from Thai Dei, bowed slightly, departed. In moments he was back with a monster sword. It was three feet long. He drew it carefully, presented it to Croaker lying along his left forearm, where the steel would not contact moist or oily skin. He bowed slightly as he did so.

He wanted us to believe he spoke no Taglian. A vain pretense. I knew him back when he was fluent.

Croaker knew something about Nyueng Bao customs. He accepted Ash Wand with proper care and courtesy, as though deeply honored.

Uncle Doj ate that up.

Croaker grasped the two-hand hilt clumsily. On purpose, I suspect. Uncle Doj darted in to demonstrate the proper grip, the way he does with me during every training session. That old boy is spry. He has ten years on Croaker but moves more easily than I do. And he possesses remarkable patience.

"Fine balance," the Captain said in Taglian. It would not surprise me to learn that he had picked up Nyueng Bao, though. He has an easy way with languages. "But this had better be superior steel." Because the blade was thin and narrow.

I told him, "He says it's four hundred years old and will cut plate armor. I guarantee it cuts people just fine. I saw him use it more than once."

"During the siege." Croaker studied the blade near the sword's hilt.

"Yes."

"Hallmark of Dinh Luc Doc."

Eyes suddenly narrow, usually stolid expression shoved aside by surprise, Uncle Doj reclaimed his lover quickly. That Croaker might know something about Nyueng Bao swordsmiths apparently troubled him. Croaker might not be nearly as stupid as foreigners were supposed to be.

Uncle Doj harvested one of his feeble crops of hair, drew it across Ash Wand's edge with predictable results. Croaker observed, "A man could get cut and never know it."

"It happens," I told him. "You wanted something?"

Sarie brought tea. The Old Man accepted even though he doesn't like tea. He watched me watch her, amused. Whenever Sahra is in a room I have trouble paying attention to anything else. She gets more beautiful every time I see her. I cannot believe my luck. I keep being scared that I will wake up.

Cold shivers.

"You have a definite prize there, Murgen." Croaker had told me so before. He approved of Sarie. It was her family that troubled him. "How come you married the whole kaboodle?" For that he shifted to Forsberger. None of the others spoke that northern tongue.

"You had to be there." Which is really all you can say about Dejagore. The Nyueng Bao and Old Crew became alloyed by the living nightmare.

Mother Gota materialized. All four feet ten inches of bile. She glared at the Captain. "Aha! The great man himself!" Her Taglian is an abomination but she refuses to believe that. Those who fail to understand her do so on purpose, to mock her.

She circled Croaker, walking her bowlegged walk. Nearly as wide as she is tall, without being really fat, ugly, waddling that waddle, she looked like a miniature troll. And her own people call her The Troll behind her back. And she has the personality. She could test the patience of a stone.

Thai Dei and Sahra were very late children. I pray my wife will not come to resemble her mother later, in character or physically. Like her grandmother would be fine, though.

Cold in here.

"Why so hard you push my Sahra's man, ho, Mr. So High and Mighty Liberator?" She hawked and spat to one side, the meaning of that no different to Nyueng Bao than anyone else. She rattled faster and faster. The faster she yakked the faster she waddled. "You think maybe he slave be? Warrior not? No time for grandmother to make of me, him always away to do for you?" She hawked and blank spat again.

She was a grandmother all right. But none were mine and none were alive anymore. I didn't remind her. No need attracting her attention.

An hour earlier she had climbed all over me because I was a no good bonehead lackwit layabout who wasted all his time reading and writing. Hardly the sort of thing a grown man does with his time.

Nothing ever satisfies Mother Gota.

Croaker says that is because she hurts all the time.

He pretended he could not fathom her broken Taglian. "Yes, it really is lovely weather. For this time of year. The agricultural specialists tell me we will make two crops this year. Do you think you'll be able to double harvest your rice?"

Hawk and spit, then a lapse into ferocious Nyueng Bao liberally spiced with imaginative epithets, not all of them native to her birth tongue. Mother Gota hates being humored or ignored more than she hates everything else.

Somebody pounded on my door. Sarie was busy doing something somewhere that kept her from being close enough to her mother to become embarrassed. I went. I found One-Eye stinking up the hallway. The little wizard asked, "How you doing, Kid? Here." He shoved a smelly, ragged, grubby bundle of papers into my hands. "The Old Man here?"

"What kind of sorcerer are you if you don't know the answer to that?"

"A lazy sorcerer."

I stepped aside. "What's this mess?" I lifted the bundle.

"Them papers you been after me about. My notes and Annals." He ambled over to the Captain.

I stared down at the mess in my hands. Some of the papers were moldy. Some were waterstained. That was One-Eye. Four years late. I hoped the little rat did not hang around. He would shed lice and fleas. He takes a bath only if he gets drunk and falls in a canal. And that damned hat . . . I am going to burn it someday.

One-Eye whispered to the Captain. The Captain whispered back. Mother Gota tried to eavesdrop. They changed to a language she did not know. She sucked in a bushel of air and went to work.

One-Eye stopped talking and stared at her. This was their first encounter, close up and personal.

He grinned.

She did not faze him. He was two hundred years old. He had had obnoxious down to a fine art generations before Mother Gota was born. He gave her a thumbs up, sidled over to me grinning like a kid who had stubbed his toe on the pot at the end of the rainbow. In Taglian he asked, "Want to make a formal introduction here, Kid? I love her! She's great! Everything I've ever heard. She's perfect. Give us a kiss here, lover."

Maybe it was because Mother Gota was the only woman in Taglios shorter than him.

That was the only time I ever saw my mother-in-law at a loss for words.

Thai Dei and Uncle Doj seemed taken aback, too.

One-Eye stalked Mother Gota around the room. Finally, she fled.

"Perfect!" One-Eye crowed. "She's absolutely perfect! The woman of my dreams. Are you ready, Captain?"

Was he high on something?

"Yeah." Croaker separated himself from his barely tasted tea. "Murgen, I want you to come with us. It's time to teach you some new tricks."

I started to shake my head. I don't know why. Sarie slipped her arm around me. She was back now, avoiding her mother by being where I was. She felt my reluctance, squeezed my arm. She looked up at me with those gorgeous almond eyes, asking why I was troubled.

"I don't know." I figured we were going to interrogate the red-hand Deceiver. That was not work I would enjoy.

Uncle Doj astonished me by asking, "May I accompany you, husband of my niece?"

"Why?" I blurted.

"I wish to inform my curiosity about what it is you people do." He spoke to me slowly, as though to an idiot. I do suffer from a severe birth defect, by his thinking. I was not born Nyueng Bao.

At least he does not call me Bone Warrior and Stone Soldier anymore.

I never did figure that out.

I translated for the Old Man. He didn't bat an eye. "Sure, Morgen. Why not? But let's get going before we all die of old age."

What the hell? This was the guy who was sure the Nyueng Bao were up to no good.

I looked at the mass of paper One-Eye passed off on me. It smelled of mildew. I would try to make something of it later. If anything could be made of it. Knowing One-Eye it could well be written in a language he no longer remembered.

32

One-Eye's Annals were as terrible as I expected. And then some. Water, mold, vermin and criminal neglect had left most of his recollections irretrievable. One recent memoir, though, did survive except for a page in the middle which was just plain missing. It will serve to illustrate what One-Eye considers to be an adequate chronicle.

He made up the spellings of most of the place names. I corrected to standard where I could, from the maps, figure out where he had been.

In the fall of our third year in Taglios the Captain decided to send the Khusavir Regiment to Prehbehlbed, where the Prahbrindrah Drah was campaigning against a bevy of minor Shadowlander princes. Me and several Company comrades were told to go along to give the new regiment backbone. The traitor Blade was in the region.

The regiment proceeded through Ranji and Ghoja, Jaicur and Cantile, then Bhakur, Danjil and other recently captured towns until, after two months, we overtook the Prince at Praiphurbed. There half the regiment split off to escort prisoners of war and booty back to the north. The rest of us went west to Asharan, where Blade caught us by surprise and we had to barricade the gates and throw a lot of the natives off the wall because they might be spies. With my talent we were able to hold out even though the green troops were terrified.

In Asharan we found a large store of wine and whiled away the hours of the siege.

After a few weeks Blade's men began to desert because of the cold and hunger and he decided to go away.

It was a very cold winter. We suffered a great deal and often had to threaten the natives to get enough food and firewood. The Prince kept us moving, mostly far from the heavy fighting, because the regiment was not experienced.

In Meldermhai three men and I got drunk and missed marching when the regiment moved out. We had to travel almost a hundred miles counting only upon ourselves in order to catch up. Once we took four horses from a local lord after we stayed over the night in his manor. We took his brandy, too. The noble complained to the Prince and we had to give the horses back.

We spent a week at Forngaw, then the Prince ordered us south to High Nangel, where we were supposed to join the Fourth Horse in trying to drive Blade's bandits into the Ruderal canyon, but when we got there we found only one old woman in the whole territory and nothing to eat but rotting cabbages, most of which the peasants had buried in the earth before they fled.

Then we went up to Silure by way of Balichore and in the forest there we found a tavern almost like those in the north. While we were drunk an enemy witch sent an attack of poisonous toads against us.

Next day we had to walk several miles through swamps and melting snow and cold mud in a low place where warm water runs out of the earth and keeps everything from freezing. After a few leagues we came to the fortress of Tracil, where a regiment recruited from former Shadowlander soldiers were besieging their Tracili cousins. They had been there a long time so it was difficult to find provisions anywhere nearby, even when we offered to pay.

I worked three days in the field hospital there, where, because of the cold, they treated many cases of frostbite. The cold killed more soldiers than did the enemy.

From Tracil we marched up to Melopil with the Prince's own guards and laid siege to the local king's fortress, which stands on an island in the middle of a lake. The lake was frozen. It was very cold and the ice was very thick and every time we tried to go forward against the enemy their missiles came bouncing over the ice. . . .

* * *

. . . Shadowlanders were slaughtered with great vigor along with our men by engines atop the walls until the garrison inside got the gates closed. Then the Howler came up from Shadowcatch on his flying carpet and the magicks flew around like lightning in a thunderstorm and we had to run away. Many were captured by the enemy.

After two weeks passed orders came to march to join the siege at Rani Orthal. On the way we found some wine and that ended in disaster, for the natives stole our packs while we slept.

Forces gathered from all over, on both sides, and I began to fear a major battle. That would draw the Howler to Rani Orthal.

After the city was surrounded the enemy made several attacks on our breastworks and trenches, which resulted in heavy losses for them. After two weeks, when it was starting to show spring, we launched a surprise attack at night which carried the outer works right up to the stone wall. The soldiers killed everybody, so angry were they, and so frightened to be fighting at night. When they reached the top of the wall they threw down everyone, even the women and children.

Then the Howler came up from Shadowcatch and with him a small swarm of shadows and we had to abandon everything we had captured.

The Howler and shadows went away when the sun rose and the Prahbrindrah Drah himself went forward to tell the enemy we were going to attack come evening and this time no mercy would be shown, but the attack never took place because the enemy king decided to throw in his lot with Taglios. The city gates were opened and the town given over to the soldiers for one night but the men were allowed no weapons except their daggers.

The soil in those parts is very poor. The crops are not of a delicate nature. They eat much cabbage and roots, and rye is the common grain.

When we were in garrison at Thruthelwar for a month I befriended the landlord's son, a boy of about eleven, and found him intelligent but ignorant of both religion and of reading and writing. His father reported that the Shadowmasters have banned all religious practice and all education throughout their empire and there were rewards out for books, especially older books, which were burned as soon as they were turned in, and likewise there were rewards for priests who tried to serve their faith, who were also burned as soon as they were turned in. This rule must have pleased Blade very much.

After a month in garrison orders came for the regiment to return to Jaicur, where Lady was gathering an army for a summer campaign in the east. At Jaicur I left the regiment and travelled north to Taglios, where I was received with great joy by my old companions of the Black Company.

The record of that campaign appears to be One-Eye's most careful and detailed. The remaining fragments suggest stories much less coherent.

33

The captive red-hand Deceiver awaited us in a room guaranteed proof against sorcerous espionage. One-Eye swore he had woven the spells so well even Lady in her heyday could not have picked through them to eavesdrop.

Croaker grumbled, "What Lady could do back when doesn't concern me. I'm worried about the Shadowmaster now. I'm worried about Soulcatcher now. She's lying low but she is out there and she does want to know everything about everything. I'm worried about the Howler now. He wants a big bite of the Company."

"It's all right," One-Eye insisted. "The Dominator himself couldn't bust in here."

"What do you want to bet that's exactly what Smoke thought about *his* spyproof room?"

I shuddered. So did One-Eye. I had not witnessed Smoke's destruction by the monster that got into his hidden place through a pinhole in his protection, but I had heard. "Whatever became of Smoke?" I asked. The monster had not killed him.

Croaker lifted a finger to his lips. "Right around the corner."

I thought we were going back to the room where Goblin, One-Eye and the Old Man wakened me from my last seizure. I just assumed they had the red-hand Strangler there, behind that curtain. Not so. We arrived at what seemed to be a different place entirely.

And the Deceiver was not alone.

The Radisha Drah, sister of the ruling Prince, the Prahbrindrah Drah, leaned against a wall and stared at the prisoner in a way that suggested she enjoyed a conviction that the Liberator was soft on villains. Small and dark and wrinkled, like most Taglian women who make it past thirty, she was one hard woman, and too bright besides. They say the only time she ever lost her composure was the night Lady killed all the senior members of Taglios's various priesthoods, ending religious resistance to her participation in the war effort as a key player.

There has been a lot less intrigue since that demonstration. Our allies and employers now seem inclined to leave our destruction to us.

If you polled the Taglian nobilities and priesthoods you would find that most of the upper classes believe the Radisha makes the princely decisions. Which is near the truth. Her brother is stronger than is commonly supposed but he prefers to be off soldiering.

Behind the Radisha stood a table. Upon the table lay a man. "Smoke?" I asked.

My question was answered. Smoke was still alive. And still in a coma. He had all the muscle tone of a bowl of lard.

Behind him was the other side of a curtain identical to the one I saw when I awakened. Then this *was* the same room, approached from a different direction.

Strange.

"Smoke," Croaker agreed, and I realized I was being made privy to a major secret.

"But . . ."

"This character said anything interesting?" Croaker asked the Radisha, cutting me off. She must have been amusing herself with the prisoner. And there must be some reason the Captain did not want her paying too much attention to Smoke.

"No. But he will."

The Strangler faked a sneer. A brave man but a fool. He, of all people, would know what torture could do.

Once again I got that spine chill.

"I know. Let's do it, One-Eye. Murgen kept us waiting long enough."

The Annals. He held it off just so I could get it into the Annals.

He did not have to bother. I am not a big torture enthusiast.

One-Eye started humming. He patted the prisoner's cheek. "You're going to have to help me out here, sweetheart. I'll be as kind as you let me. What's this thing you Stranglers got going here in Taglios?" One-Eye looked to the Captain. "When's Goblin coming back, Chief?"

"Get on with it."

One-Eye did something. The Strangler spasmed against his bonds, his scream not much more than a breathless squeak. One-Eye said, "But I found him the perfect woman, Boss. Ain't that right, Kid?" He leered evilly, bent over the Deceiver. That brown raisin of a man wore nothing but a filthy loincloth.

So that was why One-Eye was so excited about Mother Gota. He wanted to use her as a practical joke on Goblin. I should have been angry, I guess, maybe for Sahra's sake, but I could work up no indignation.

That woman begged for abuse.

One-Eye crooned, "You understand your position here, sweetheart? You were with Narayan Singh when we caught you. You have the red hand. Those things tell me you're one of those very special Deceivers that the Captain *really* wants." He indicated Croaker. The word for Captain he used was *jamadar*, which has strong religious connotations to the Deceivers.

Lady got taken in by them but she fixed them by marking their top men permanently with the red hand. That made them stand out in the crowd these days.

One-Eye sucked spit between the stumps of his teeth. Somebody who did not know him might have believed he was thinking. He said, "But I'm a swell guy who hates to see people hurting so I'm gonna give you a chance not to end up like this cockroach over here." He jerked a thumb at Smoke. Fire crackled between the fingers of his other hand. The Strangler screamed the kind of scream that rips your nerves out raw and salts their ends. "You can make this last forever or you can get it over quick. All up to you. Talk to me about what the Deceivers are up to here in Taglios." He leaned closer, whispered, "I can even fix it so you can get away."

The prisoner gaped for a moment. Sweat ran into his eyes, stung him. He tried to shake it away.

"I bet that she'd think that Goblin is just as cute as a bug," One-Eye said. "What do you think, Kid?"

"I think you'd better get on with it," Croaker snapped. He was not happy dealing in torture and had no patience left for the games Goblin and One-Eye play with one another.

"Oh, keep your damned pants on, Chief. This guy ain't going nowhere."

"But his friends are up to something."

I glanced at Uncle Doj to see what the thought of the bickering. His face was stone. Maybe he didn't understand Taglian anymore.

One-Eye barked, "You don't like the way I do my job, fire me and do it yourself." He prodded the prisoner. The Deceiver tensed in anticipation. "You. What's up here in Taglios? Where are Narayan and the Daughter of Night? Help me out here."

I tensed up myself. I felt a big chill. What was it?

The prisoner gulped air. Sweat covered his entire body. He could not win. If he knew anything and talked—as he must eventually—his own kind would show him no mercy later.

"Sufficient unto the day the evil thereof," Croaker told him, sensing his thoughts.

My sympathies all lay with the Old Man. Even if he ever does get his daughter back he won't find what he is looking for. She has been a Deceiver from the day she was born, raised to be the Daughter of Night who will bring on Kina's Year of the Skulls. Hell, they consecrated her to Kina while she was still in the womb. She would be what they wanted her to be. And that would be a darkness to break her parents' hearts.

"Talk to me, sweetheart. Tell me what I need to know." One-Eye tried to keep it one on one, just him and his client. He gave the Strangler a moment to reflect. The rest of us watched without expression, maybe a thimbleful of pity among us. This was a black rumel man. In Strangler terms, generally, that meant he was guilty of more than thirty murders, without remorse—unless he strangled a black rumel man and thus gained acclaim by the most direct route.

Kina is the ultimate Deceiver. She enjoys betraying her own on occasion.

An argument One-Eye did not think to present to our pet Deceiver.

The Strangler screamed again, tried to gurgle something.

"You'll have to speak up," One-Eye told him.

"I can't tell you. I don't know where they are."

I believed him. Narayan Singh was not staying alive by announcing his itineraries in a world where everybody really is out to get him.

"Pity. So just tell us why we have Deceivers here in Taglios, after all this time."

I wondered why he kept going back to that. The Stranglers had not dared to operate in the city for years.

One-Eye and the Old Man must know something. But how?

The prisoner screamed.

The Radisha observed, "The ones we catch are always ignorant."

"Don't matter," Croaker said. "I know exactly where Singh is. Or at least where he'll be when he stops running. As long as he doesn't realize that, I know he'll always be right where I want him."

Uncle Doj's eyebrow twitched. Must be getting exciting for him.

The Radisha glared, frowned, stared. She liked to believe that hers was the only working brain in the Palace. Us Black Company types are just supposed to be hired muscle. You could almost hear the creaks and groans as her mind turned over. How could Croaker know something like that? "Where is he?"

"Right now he's busting his butt trying to join up with Mogaba. Since we can't stop him—because he's moving as fast as any message we could send after him—let's forget him."

I considered offering a word of suggestion about crows. Croaker talks to crows. And crows fly faster than even a Deceiver can run. . . . I was not paid to think and I was not there to talk.

"Forget him?" The Radisha seemed startled.

"Just for the moment. Let's find out what his cronies are up to here."

One-Eye resumed work. I glanced at Uncle Doj, who had stayed out of the way and quiet longer than I had thought possible. He noticed my glance. In Nyueng Bao he asked, "May I question the man?"

"Why?"

"I would test his belief."

"You don't speak Taglian well enough." Little dig there.

"Then translate."

Just for fun, or maybe to nudge Uncle Doj, Croaker said, "I don't mind if he does, Morgen. He can't do any damage." His remark demonstrated clearly his familiarity with Nyueng Bao dialect. There had to be a message in that, meant for Uncle

Doj—particularly when taken with his earlier observation about Ash Wand's provenance.

What the hell? I was confused. And getting more than a little paranoid myself. Had I come back to my own world after my most recent seizure?

In Taglian as passable as I recalled him having, Uncle Doj shot quick, amiable questions at the Deceiver. They were questions of the sort most people answer without thought. We learned that the man had a family but his wife had died in childbirth. Then he realized he was being manipulated and controlled his tongue.

Uncle Doj stamped around like a merry troll, chattering, and winkled out much of the prisoner's past but not once did he get any closer to the facts of any new Strangler interest in Taglios the city. Croaker, I noticed, paid more attention to Uncle Doj than he did the prisoner. The Captain, of course, lives in the eye of a tornado of paranoia.

Croaker leaned close to me. In a midnight whisper he said, "You stay when the others leave." He did not tell me why. He went on to say something to One-Eye in a tongue even I did not understand.

He spoke at least twenty languages, he had been with the Company so long. One-Eye probably spoke a bunch more but shared them with nobody but Goblin. One-Eye nodded and continued about his business.

Pretty soon the runt wizard began edging Uncle Doj and the Radisha toward the door. He did it so gently and smoothly that they never complained. Uncle Doj was a guest to begin with and the Radisha did have pressing business elsewhere and One-Eye went about it so unlike his usual abrasive self that he had them thinking it was their own idea. In any event, they left.

Croaker went with them, which helped, but he was back in five minutes. I told him, "Now I've seen everything. There are no wonders left. I can get out of this chicken outfit and go ahead with my plan to start a turnip ranch." Which was only halfway a jest. Whenever the Company stops moving guys begin developing plans. Human nature, I guess.

The turnip is unknown here but I have seen vast tracts of land perfect for cultivating turnips, parsnips and sugar beets. And Otto and Hagop are not far away so seed should be available soon. Maybe they will even bring some potatoes. Maybe they will even bring some potatoes.

Croaker grinned, told One-Eye, "This weasel isn't going to tell us anything we can use."

"You know what it is, Chief? I'll bet you. He's stalling. He's got something he's trying to hold onto just a little while longer. That's what goes through his head every time I hurt him. He thinks he will endure it just one more time. And then just one more time."

"Let him get thirsty for a while." Croaker shoved the Deceiver's chair over against a wall, tossed a piece of ragged linen over him as though he was discarded furniture. "Murgen, listen up. Time is getting tight. Things are going to start happening. I need you in the first rank, healed or not."

"I don't like the sound of that."

He didn't feel like joking. "We've discovered some interesting things about Smoke." Suddenly he was speaking the Jewel Cities dialect, unknown outside the Company here, unless Mogaba was lurking around. "We stalled because of your lapses and what they might signify, but we have to move on. It's time to take chances. There are some new tricks you need to learn, old dog."

"You trying to scare me?"

"No. This is important. Pay attention. I don't have time to work Smoke anymore. Neither does One-Eye. The arsenal is eating up all his time. And I don't trust anybody else but you to help with this."

"Huh? You're going too fast for me."

"Pay attention. And by that I mean keep your ears and eyes open and your mouth shut. We may not get much time. The Radisha could decide to come back and torment the Deceiver again. She likes that sort of thing." He told One-Eye, "Remind me to see if we can't get Cordy Mather assigned here permanently. She doesn't get underfoot when he's around."

"He's supposed to be back in town soon. If he's not here already."

"That there is my intelligence chief," Croaker told me, pointing at One-Eye and shaking his head. "Blind in one eye and can't see out the other."

I glanced at the cloth-covered villain. He had begun snoring. A good soldier seizing his rest when it was available.

34

Hours passed. Croaker left, then returned. Now he slapped me on the back. "See how easy it is, Murgen? Ever seen such a big trick that was this simple?"

"Nothing to it," I agreed. "Like falling off a log." Or like falling into a bottomless pit, maybe, which I have had enough involuntary practice doing.

Nothing is ever as simple as somebody tells you it is going to be. I knew this would be no exception when I tried it myself, amazing as it was. "At least now I understand how you got so damned spooky, knowing things you shouldn't."

Croaker laughed. "Go ahead." Showing off his astonishing discovery had put him into a grand mood. "Try it."

I gave him a look he chose to interpret as my not really understanding what he meant. Nothing to it. Like falling off a log. Maybe. Only One-Eye is not a very good teacher.

"Do what One-Eye showed you. Decide what you want to see. Tell Smoke. But be damned careful how you do that. You have to be precise. Precision is everything. Ambiguity is deadly."

"That's the way the magic goes in every story I ever heard, Captain. The ambiguities screw you every time."

"You think so? You might be right." I must have touched a

nerve. He became thoughtful suddenly. "Go ahead."

I was reluctant. "This whole thing is too much like what keeps happening to me when I fall down the rabbit hole to Dejagore. Could Smoke be doing that to me somehow?"

Croaker shook his head. "No way. It's not the same. Go ahead. I insist. You're wasting time. Go look at something you always wanted to know about for the Annals. We'll be right here to cover you."

"How about I go look for Otto and Hagop?"

"I know where they are. They just passed the First Cataract. They'll be here in a few days. Try something else." Hagop and Otto had spent the last three years travelling back north with a Taglian delegation and letters from Lady to those she had left behind. Their mission was to learn anything possibly known there about the Shadowmaster, Longshadow. One of the dead Shadowmasters, Stormshadow, had turned out to be a refugee from Lady's old empire, Stormbringer, previously thought dead. And two other big and nasty sorcerers long believed perished also have turned up and remain burrs under our saddles, the Howler and Lady's mad sister, Soulcatcher. And there was Shapeshifter, too, but we took care of him.

That Otto and Hagop managed to survive so incredible a journey was, to me, a major miracle. But Otto and Hagop are blessed.

"I expect they'll have whole new collections of scars to talk about."

Croaker nodded. He seemed a little grim now. I little anxious. Time to get on with my training.

An unexplained tragedy of the past caught my imagination. There had been some grotesque, horrible, senseless killings in a village called Bond that never got connected with anyone or anything, to my recollection. I was sure they had to be important somehow and was baffled that, even today, the slaughter remained unsolved and unresolved.

I gripped Smoke's hand, blanked my mind, spoke careful instructions in a whisper. And away I went, out of my body, so suddenly I almost panicked. For a moment I thought I recalled doing all this before. But I could not remember what was going to happen.

The Old Man was right. This was not the same as my un-wanted plunges into my own past. In this nightmare I was aware and in control. I was a disembodied vision racing toward Bond but my mission remained clear in my mind. That was a big distinction. When I floated over Dejagore I lacked identity and control till I merged with my self of the past. Then I forgot the future.

Bond is a hamlet on the south bank of the River Main, facing the Vehdna-Bota ford. For centuries the Main has been the traditional boundary of the Taglian heartland. The peoples who live below the river share the languages and religions of Taglios but are considered only tributary cousins by the Taglians themselves.

The nonagrarian part of Bond's economy revolved around a small remount station for the military courier post. A minimal garrison of Shadar cavalrymen managed the station and kept watch on ford traffic. Bond was the kind of duty soldiers dream about. There were no officers and very little work. The river was low enough to ford only about three months a year. But the garrison got paid all year round.

Smoke's soul slipped back to that long-ago disaster. I stayed with him, carrying a load of fear despite all of Croaker's reassurances.

It was very dark that night in that Bond gone by. Horror stalked out of the night and those nightmares where men are more often prey than predator. A monster padded through the hamlet, headed toward the army stable. I watched from a place where I could offer no warning.

One solitary soldier had the watch. He was nodding. Neither he nor the horses sensed their danger,

The latch rose inside the stable door. No animal mind knew enough to pull a string. The soldier started awake just in time to see a dark shape with scarlet eyes hurtling toward him.

The monster fed, then padded into the night. It killed again. Screams wakened the garrison. The soldiers seized their arms. The monster, like an oversize black panther, loped to the river, swam to the northern shore.

I knew something now. The killer was a shapeshifter, the acolyte of the sorcerer Shapeshifter, whom we had destroyed the night we captured Dejagore. She got away, trapped in the animal shape.

Why just this one incident in more than four years?

I wanted to follow the panther, to discover what had become of it, but Smoke could not be coaxed to go. The comatose wizard had no will or ego I could detect but, apparently, he did have limits or constraints.

Funny, though. I felt no real emotion until I returned to the reality of the Palace. Then it hit me in a wave, hard, leaving me breathless. I asked, "Is whatever I see out there true?"

"We haven't seen any evidence otherwise." Croaker's caution meant he had reservations. Always suspicious, our Captain. "You look bad. You see something nasty?"

"Very." One-Eye was gone. And the Strangler had fouled himself. I wrinkled my nose. "I can use Smoke to look anywhere?"

"Almost. Some places he can't or won't go. And he can't go back to any time before he went into the coma. You can catch the Annals up now, eyewitness style, if you will. But always remember to be careful about pointing him right."

"Wow." The implications had begun to sink in. "This is worth more than a veteran legion." Now I knew how we had pulled off some really startling coups lately. If you can perch on your enemy's shoulder nothing is going to go his way.

"It's worth a lot more. And that's why you're going to keep your mouth shut even around your dearly beloved."

"Does the Radisha know?"

"No. You, me and One-Eye. Maybe Goblin if One-Eye just had to share it with somebody. And that's the limit. One-Eye found it by accident when he was trying to pull Smoke out of his coma. Smoke has been to Overlook. He's walked around inside. He's actually met Longshadow. We wanted to ask him some questions. We decided they could wait. You don't tell anybody. Understand?"

"There you go being suspicious of my in-laws again."

"I'd cut your throat."

"I get the message, boss. Don't brag it up to my Deceiver drinking buddies. Shit. This could win us the war."

"It won't hurt. As long as it's secret. I have business with the Radisha. Practice using him. Don't worry about working him too hard. You can't." He squeezed my shoulder, left the room with a stride that seemed both determined and fatalistic. Must be facing another budgetary conference. Depending on whether you were the Liberator or the Radisha the military either never had enough or always wanted too much.

So. There was just me and one halfway-dead wizard and one stinky Strangler under a linen rag. I considered using Smoke to find out what Stinky's buddies were up to in Taglios but reasoned that the Captain would not have had him interrogated if Smoke had been able to provide useful answers. Maybe you not only had to be precise in your instructions, you had to have some idea what you were seeking. You could not find your own elbow if you could not guess what directions to give to get you there.

The point? Old Smoke was a miracle but he had major limitations. And most of those would exist right inside our own heads. We would become the beneficiaries or victims of our own imaginations.

What should I go see, then?

I was excited now. I was up for an adventure. So, what the hell? Why not go straight for the biggie? How about taking a peek at the Shadowmaster himself, Longshadow, number one boy on the Black Company shit list?

35

Longshadow could have pranced right out of my fantasies. He was a deadly freak. He was tall and thin and twitchy, given to flights of rage and subject to sudden spells resembling malarial shakes. He wore a sort of loose black floor-length chemise that concealed a deathly gauntness. He ate infrequently and then only picked. He could have been a famine victim.

Threads of silver and gold and glistening black, embroidered or woven into his robe, protected him with dozens of static sorceries. At first blush he seemed a hundred times more paranoid than Croaker. But he did have reason. There was just a whole world full of folks who wanted to roast his skinny ass and he had no friends closer than Mogaba and Blade.

The Howler was not a friend. He was an ally.

One of Longshadow's obsessions was the Black Company. I did not understand. The kind of enemies we were should not have troubled him at all. We were no world-killers.

His face, which he kept masked except when he was alone, was skull-like. His waxy, pallid features were frozen in a permanent expression of fear. There was no guessing his birth race. His eyes were a washed-out grey with splotches of pink around the edges but I don't think he was an albino. I exploited Smoke's ability, fluttered about through time to find out all the interesting stuff fast. I did not catch Longshadow completely out of costume once. The man did not bathe. He did not change clothing. He wore gloves all the time.

The last of the four Shadowmasters, now *the* Shadowmaster, he was the unquestioned tyrant of the city Shadowcatch and a demigod within his fortress Overlook. His slightest whim could set a hundred terrors and ten thousand men scrambling to appease him. And still he was a prisoner doing life without hope of parole.

Overlook is, but for one, the southernmost work of Man. I

tried pushing past that fortress. Somewhere in the mists beyond Overlook is Khatovar, toward which we have marched for years. Just a glimpse would be marvelous.

Smoke refused to go any farther south.

Smoke had been crazy about Khatovar while he was still healthy. Khatovar was the reason he deserted the Radisha and Prahbrindrah Drah, years ago. His fear of Khatovar must have impressed itself upon his very flesh and soul.

Longshadow's fortress was gargantuan. Overlook dwarfed every human construction I have ever seen, including the Lady's monstrous tower at Charm. Already two decades in the building, Overlook's construction had become the main industry of Shadowcatch—the city that was called Kiaulune before the coming of the Shadowmasters. Kiaulune meant Shadow Gate in the local dialect.

The builders worked day and night. They knew no holidays. Longshadow was determined that his fortress be complete before his enemies overtook him. If he won that race he believed he would become master of the world. No power of heaven or hell or earth ought to be able to reach him inside a finished Overlook. Not even the darkness that brushed him every night with its terror.

Overlook's outer walls reared a hundred or more feet high. Where are you going to find a ladder that tall?

Brass and silver and gold characters shone on the steel plates that sheathed the rude stone of the wall face. Battalions of workmen did nothing but keep those runes polished and gleaming.

I could not read them but I knew they anchored massive defensive spells. Longshadow's spellwork overlaid everything that was part of Overlook, layer upon layer. If he was allowed enough time every exterior surface of the fortress would be hidden beneath and behind impenetrable tangles of sorceries.

Once the sun went down Overlook became a conflagration of light. Bright crystal chambers topped every tower, making the place seem a forest of lighthouses. The crystal domes were places whence Longshadow could observe safe from his terrors. The overpowering lights left no places for shadows to hide.

He feared that which he mastered far more than anything else in the world. Even the Black Company, for him, was a buzzing mosquito of a nuisance.

Even unfinished Overlook daunted me thoroughly. What sort of hubris-driven madmen were we to chart a course that must run through and beyond that stronghold?

But Longshadow had enemies not as easily daunted as I. For some of those no earthly fortress, nor even time itself, meant much. They would devour him now or later, the moment his guard fell.

He had chosen to play for the ultimate stakes in a game where the risks were as grim as the potential winnings were great. It was too late to get out. He would be victor or victim.

Longshadow lived inside the crystal chamber that topped Overlook's tallest central tower. He slept seldom, for fear of the night. He spent hours and hours just staring southward at a plain of glittering stone.

A screech ripped the air over the grim city. The people of Shadowcatch ignored it. If they thought about their master's strange ally at all it was, probably, to hope that a fate would catch up and rob Longshadow of this potent weapon. The inhabitants of Kiaulune were a broken people, spiritless, without hope, worse even than the Jaicuri at their lowest ebb during the siege of Dejagore.

Almost all of them were too young to recall a time when there was not a Shadowmaster there exercising more power over their lives than had their lost gods.

Even Longshadow could not extirpate rumor. Even at the heart of his empire some people had to travel and travelers always carry tales. Some stories are even true. The people of Shadowcatch knew that a doom from the north was coming.

The name of the Black Company lay at the heart of every rumor. That made no one happy. Longshadow was a very devil but many of his people feared his fall would be but the precursor to a far bleaker season.

Man, woman and child, the people of Shadowcatch were privy to the one true secret of the universe: there is always a darker shadow lurking beyond the one whose face you can see.

Longshadow reached out and inflicted pain and fear because he himself was the victim of a thousand terrors.

It was ugly out there. So ugly I wanted to go back somewhere where it was warm and there was someone to hold me and tell me that the dark was not always the lurking place of terror. I wanted my Sarie, my light in the night that rules the world. "Smoke, take me home."

36

Croaker did warn me. Be precise, he said. He warned me several times, in fact.

I was ripped this way and dragged that, to and through the place of blood and burning, papers browning, blackening, curling in such slow motion. Blood pooled deep where I lay in my own vomit. The slap of running feet was like the slow booming footfalls of giants.

I heard screams that had no end.

Croaker warned me. I was thoughtless. What he did not tell me, or maybe he did not understand, was that the concept "home" could in one man's mind become defined by emotional pain.

Torn. Shredded. Smoke took me to Taglios only for that minute in the real now that is like the end of all time. I reeled and flung away from there with such revulsion that I threw myself and the hateful shreds and a disoriented Smoke all the way to Hell.

He had no will and no identity so he could not and did not laugh as I floated down into the lake of pain.

Hell has a name. Its name is Dejagore. But Dejagore is only Hell's lesser face.

From the greater Hell I escaped. One more time.

No identity and no will.

The wind blows but nothing moves in the place of glittering stone. Night falls. The wind dies. The plain yields up its heat as shadows waken. Moonlight settles upon the silence of stone.

The plain runs east and west, north and south, without discernible bounds, viewed from within. Though its ends be uncertain it has a definite center. That is an epic structure built of the same stone as the pillars and plain.

Within that fastness nothing moves, either, though at times mists of light shimmer as they leak over from beyond the gates of dream. Shadows linger in corners. And way down inside the core of the place, in the feeblest throb of the heart of darkness, there is life of a sort.

37

No will. No identity.

Now no Smoke.

Now just pain. So much Smoke drifted away. Now just slavery to the memories.

Now at home in the house of pain.

38

There you are!

So here we are again. You were missed.

. . . faceless thing that, nevertheless, seems to be smiling, pleased with itself.

It has been a night full of adventures. Has it not? And the fun continues. Look. There. The Black Company and their auxiliaries have begun making life especially unpleasant for Shadowlanders so bold as to have taken up residence inside Dejagore's wall.

See how they use the doppelgangers and imaginary soldiers to lure the southerners into deadly traps, to get them to betray themselves.

Oh. And come back to the wall. This is a small thing but it could become the stuff of epics.

The fighting has all shifted to the east side of the city. Hardly anybody is over there now. A few men to watch from the ramparts is all. And some unenthusiastic Shadowlander scouts down there in the darkness, not really paying attention. Otherwise how could they miss this spidery little figure rappelling down the outside of the wall?

Why on earth would a two-hundred-year-old, fourth-rate sorcerer want to climb down a rope to go where very unfriendly little brown men might decide to dance on his head?

The wounded stallion of mysterious sorcerous breed has stopped screaming. At last. It is dead. Green misty stuff still rises from its death wound. The wound still glows at its edges.

Out there? Yes. Look at them. Two very devils they are, aren't they, cloaked in their pink mists? They don't seem to be coming to devour the city, though, do they?

What is that? The Shadowlanders out there are scattering like the fox is in the henhouse. Their cries are filled with pure terror. Amongst them something dark moves swiftly. Look. It pulled a man down there. Didn't it?

There is so little light now that the focus of battle has shifted. The old man is as black as the heart of the night itself. Think any mortal eye will notice him sneaking around among the dead? Where is he headed? Shadowspinner's dead horse?

Who would expect that? It's the act of a madman.

The creeping darkness is moving toward the dead horse, too. See how its eyes flash red when the fires in the city flare up. Look at that fool, running toward it instead of away. There go his guts. Stupidity can be fatal.

The little black man has vanished because he has stopped moving. There he is. He heard something. There he goes, trotting toward the dead stallion. He wants his spear back. And maybe that does make some crazy sense. He worked hard making it.

He has stopped again, eye huge as he sniffs the night and catches an almost-forgotten odor. At the same moment the deadly darkness catches wind of him.

A pantherine roar of triumph stills hearts all across the plain. The darkness begins moving faster and faster.

The little black man grabs his spear and runs for the wall. Will he make it? Can two stubby, ancient legs carry him there fast enough to escape the death racing toward him?

The thing is huge. And it is filled with joy.

The little man reaches the rope. But he is still eighty feet down from safety. And he is old and winded. He whirls. His timing is perfect. The head of his spear reaches out just as the monster leaps. The beast twists in the air, evading the killing thrust but taking a cruel wound from its snout back through its left ear. It howls. Green mist boils off its redly-glowing wound. The beast loses all interest in the old man, who begins his long climb to the ramparts. That bizarrely carved spear is slung across his back now, held there by a mundane length of cotton string.

No one notices. No one cares. The fighting has gone elsewhere.

39

The southerners seem to have just closed their eyes and shoved their heads into a beehive, don't they?

What? Why so reluctant? Come see. This is amusing.

Everywhere you look the southerners are falling back. Sometimes they are running, sometimes just slinking away through the shadows before death overhauls them.

Look there. Shadowspinner, the king enemy himself, all but crippled, paying no attention to anyone or anything but those two pink-limned archetypes come out of the hills to devour him.

And Mogaba? Watch him be the master tactician. Watch him be the ultimate warrior exploiting the enemy's every weakness—now that there is no chance to accomplish the deviltry that moved him earlier in the evening. See that? No southerner, however great his reputation, dares come near Mogaba. Even their great heroes are like novice children when he steps forward himself.

He is way bigger than life, this Mogaba.

He is the triumphant centerpiece of his own imagined saga.

Something has gone out of the southerners.

They wanted to conquer. They knew they had to conquer because their master Shadowspinner would not tolerate anything less. He has a particular lack of understanding when it comes to failure. His followers are established solidly inside the city. Mild stubbornness will give them success.

But they are on the run.

Something has grabbed hold of them and convinced them that it is not possible for even their souls to survive if they stay inside Dejagore.

40

"Y ou all right, Murgen?"

I shook my head. I felt like a kid who had spun around about twenty times, intentionally trying to make himself dizzy before jumping into some silly competition.

I was in an alley. Runt boy Goblin was beside me, looking

extremely concerned. "I'm fine," I told him.

Then I fell to my knees, stuck my hands out to grab the alley walls so I would not spin around anymore. I insisted, "I'm all right."

"Of course you are. Candles. Keep an eye on this dork. He tries to take over, get deaf. He's got too tender a heart."

I tried not to let my ego become engaged. Maybe I *was* too tender, too much a sucker. The world sure isn't kind to the man who tries to be gentle and thoughtful.

Its spin slowed down till I no longer had to hold on.

A scuffle broke out behind us. Someone cursed in a nasal, liquid tongue. Somebody else growled, "This asshole is fast!"

"Whoa whoa whoa!" I yelled. "Let the man alone! Let him come up here."

Candles didn't knock me over the head or contradict me. The short, wide Nyueng Bao guy who had shown me to Ky Dam's hideout marched up to me. The fingers of his right hand rubbed his right cheek. He seemed utterly astonished that somebody had laid a hand on him. His ego suffered again when he spoke in Nyueng Bao and I said, "Sorry, old-timer. No speakee. Gonna got to be Taglian or Groghor with me." In Groghor, which my maternal grandmother spoke because Grandpa captured her from those people, I asked, "What's happening?" I knew maybe twenty words in Groghor, but that was twenty more than anyone else within seven thousand miles.

"The Speaker sends me to lead you to where the invader is most vulnerable. We have watched closely and know."

"Thank you. We appreciate it. Lead on." Shifting languages, I observed, "Marvellous how these guys suddenly talk the lingo when they want something."

Candles grunted.

Goblin, who had sneaked forward for a look around, returned just in time to offer me directions to the same weak point the Nyueng Bao had in mind. The squat man seemed a little surprised we could find our butts with our hands, maybe even a touch disgruntled.

"You got a name, short and wide?" I asked. "If you don't have one you prefer I guarantee you these guys will hang one on you and I promise you won't like it."

"Hear hear," Goblin agreed, chuckling.

"I am Doj. All Nyueng Bao call me Uncle Doj."

"All right, Uncle. You going up there with us? Or did you just come over to direct traffic?" Already Goblin was whispering instructions to the guys creeping up behind us. No doubt he had left a few soft spells of sleepiness or confusion amongst the southerners as he was scouting.

Little discussion was needed. We would drive into their soft spot, kill anything that moved, split them in half, butcher anybody who didn't run away, then we would back away before Mogaba began feeling too confident.

"I will accompany you although that stretches the Speaker's instructions to extremes. You Bone Warriors surprise us continually. I wish to watch you at your work."

I never considered killing people to be my profession but did not care to argue. "You speak Taglian very well, Uncle."

He smiled. "I am forgetful, though, Stone Soldier. I may not remember a word after tonight." Unless the Speaker jogged his memory, I supposed.

Uncle Doj did a great deal more than watch us hack and stab southerners. He turned into a one-man cyclone flailing around with a lightning sword. He was as sudden as the lightning but as graceful as a dancer. Each time he moved another Shadowlander fell.

"Damn," I told Goblin a while later. "Remind me not to get into a quarrel with that character."

"I'll remind you to bring a crossbow and let him have it in the back from thirty feet is what I'll do. After I put a deafness and a stupidity spell on him to even things up a little."

"Don't be surprised if it's me distracting you someday when One-Eye sneaks up and offers you a cactus suppository."

"Speaking of the runt. Tell me. Who's being conspicuously absent without leave lately?"

I sent messages to the various units suggesting that we had done our part to relieve Mogaba's troops. We should all go back to our part of town, patch ourselves up, take naps, like that. I told the Nyueng Bao elder, "Uncle Doj, please inform the Speaker that the Black Company extends its gratitude and friendship. Tell him he is free to call upon that at any time. We will extend ourselves as much as possible."

The short, wide man bowed far enough that his movement had to mean something. I bowed back, almost as deeply. That must have been the right move because he smiled slightly, bowed shallowly for himself, hustled off.

"Runs like a duck," Candles observed.

"I'm glad that duck was on our side, though."

"You can say that again."

"I'm glad that duck . . . Argh!" Candles had me by the throat.

"Somebody help me shut him up."

That was just the start of what became a wild night of blowing off tensions. I got no chance to participate myself but I heard it was a banner night for the Jaicuri whores.

41

"Where the hell have you been?" I snarled at One-Eye. "The Company just fought through its nastiest episode in, oh, just *days*, and you were obviously absent every stinking second." Not that his presence would have made any difference.

One-Eye grinned. My displeasure did not bother him a bit. He had outlived or outstubborned a parade of snotnoses like me. "Shit, Kid, I had to get my Shadowmaster sticker back, didn't I? I've got a lot of work in that thing. . . . What's the matter?"

"Huh?" For a moment I saw a little black louse scuttling

across a grey landscape from a height unattainable anywhere in Dejagore, even atop the citadel, where Old Crew guys were not welcome anymore. "Never mind, runt. I'd like to kick your ass but it wouldn't do any good now. So you were out there. What became of Widowmaker and Lifetaker?" While I was arranging a quieter life for our leader those two vanished without a trace.

I wondered how Mogaba would write all this if he was keeping the Annals.

"One-Eye?"

"What?" Now he sounded irritated.

"You want to answer me? What happened to Widowmaker and Lifetaker?"

"You know something, Kid? I don't have the faintest freaking idea. And I don't care. I only had one thing on my mind. I wanted my spear back so I could use it next time that sucker ain't looking. Then I had to worry about dodging a gang of raggedyass Shadowlanders who tried to jump me. They went away somewhere. All right?"

And none of us could fathom that. Because they vanished just when the Shadowlander confidence was rockiest. Shadowspinner had his tail between his legs and his boys could have been broken.

I grumbled, "If that *was* the Old Man and Lady they would've kept coming till they broke the whole show wide open. Wouldn't they?"

I glared at an albino crow perched not twenty feet away. Its head was cocked. It stared at me with malign intelligence.

There were a lot of crows tonight.

Other agendas were being pursued. I was just one pawn caught up in tides of intrigue. But if we were careful the Company need not get swept away.

Mogaba and the Nar and their Taglian troops stayed busy for days. Maybe the Shadowmasters decided to make Mogaba pay for his failure to fulfill his end of the implicit bargain.

Which was just one more example of the way people down here go bugfuck when they are involved with the Black Company.

It could make a guy nervous if he thought about everybody within a thousand miles seeming to wish he'd never been born.

My guys enjoyed Mogaba's situation. And he could not squawk about their attitudes. We gave him exactly what he asked. We saved his ass and set him up so all he had to do was chase a few Shadowlanders out of town.

I had to see him almost every day at staff meetings. Again and again we showed ourselves to the soldiers, pretending to be brothers marching shoulder to shoulder against our evil foe.

Not once was anybody fooled except maybe Mogaba.

I never took it personal. I took a stance I believed the Annalists of the past would approve, just picturing Mogaba as not one of us.

We are the Black Company. We have no friends. All others are the enemy, or at best not to be trusted. That relationship with the world does not require hatred or any other emotion. It requires wariness.

Perhaps our refusal to remonstrate, or even to acknowledge Mogaba's treachery, was the final straw, or perhaps the backbreaker was his awareness that even his Nar compatriots now believed the real Captain might still live. Whatever, the ultimate and perfect warrior drifted across a boundary from beyond which he could not return. And we did not discover the truth until we had paid in treasures of pain.

It took ten days for Dejagore to return to normal—if normal was our state before the great attack. Both sides had suffered terribly. I believed Shadowspinner would now just lick his wounds and let us get hungry for a while.

42

"Got something for you, Kid."

I started awake. "What . . . ?" What happened? I don't drift off that way.

One-Eye had a big shit-eating grin on but it evaporated when he looked at me closer. He darted in, grabbed my chin, turned my head right and left. "You just have one of your spells?"

"Spells?"

"You know what I mean."

Not exactly. I just had their word for the fact that I went spooky sometimes.

"You've got a kind of psychic shimmer. Maybe I caught you just in time."

He and Goblin kept talking about doing experiments to find out what is happening but there never seemed to be time to actually do anything. "What do you have?"

"The work parties broke into the old catacombs this morning."

"Longo told me."

"Everybody's charging around in there, all excited."

"I can imagine. Find any treasure yet?"

One-Eye looked put-upon. For such a blackhearted toad he can manage a truly impressive show of self-righteous injury.

"I take it not."

"We found some books. A whole pile. All sealed up neat and everything. Looks like they've been there since the Shadow-masters first came."

"Makes sense since they always burned the books and the priests. You find any priests lurking down there?"

"Not hardly. Look, I got to get back." Before somebody grabbed a treasure out from under him, no doubt. "I got a couple guys lugging them books up for you."

"Gods forfend you should have lifted anything yourself."

"You got a serious attitude problem, Kid. I'm an old man."
One-Eye did a fade. He has that knack when he is about to find
himself in an indefensible position.

A city seldom is buttoned up so tight that no news gets in from
outside. Sometimes it seems almost mystical but the word does
come through. In Dejagore rumor seldom brought in anything
Mogaba wanted to hear.

I was studying the discovered books, so intrigued I was letting duties slide. They were written in Jaicuri but the written
form thereof is almost identical to written Taglian.

Goblin stepped in. "You doing all right? No more dizziness?"

"No. You guys worry too much."

"No, we don't. Look, some new rumors are going around.
There's supposedly a relief column headed our way. Blade, of all
people, is in charge."

"Blade? He isn't. . . . He's never run anything bigger than a
reduced company. Before we ever got here. Fighting guerrilla
style against amateurs."

"I don't make them up, I just report them. He did do well."

"So did Willow Swan and Cordy Mather. But that was accident and luck and Shadowlander stupidity more than anything those three actually did. Why on earth is he command-
ing an army?"

"He's supposedly Lady's second in command. Not much
doubt anymore that she survived. She's also pissed off. And
putting together a new army."

"Bet Mogaba's jumping for joy. Running around hollering,
'We're saved! We're saved!' "

"You might say he's jumping."

Over the following few days we heard a thousand wild stories. If a tenth were true some really bizarre changes were un-
derway out there in the world.

"You heard the latest?" Goblin asked me one night when I
took a rare break from the books to examine that outer world
from the wall. "Lady ain't Lady after all. She's the incarnation

of some goddess named Kina. A real badass, too, apparently."

"She would be. Thai Dei. You know Kina, don't you? Tell us about her." Thai Dei wasn't allowed into our warrens but he always turned up whenever I came up for air.

He forgot all three words of Taglian he had admitted to knowing. The name of that goddess scrubbed his brain clean.

I said, "That's what happens when you mention Kina to any of these people. I can't even get our prisoners to talk about her. You would think she belonged to the Black Company."

"Must be a real charmer," Bucket opined.

"Oh, she is. She is. There's one." I meant a shooting star. We were keeping count. Also of enemy watchfires. The southerners had scattered in small unit encampments around the plain recently. I guess they were afraid we might sneak away.

"You know something about her, then?" Goblin asked.

"From those books you guys found." The men were bitter. The books and some sealed jars filled with grain were the only treasures they unearthed. The Gunni were the majority religion in Jaicur and the Gunni do not bury their dead. They burn them. The minority Vehdna do bury their dead but do not include any grave goods. Where their dead are bound they have no need of luggage. In paradise everything is provided. In hell, too. "One was a compilation of Gunni myths, in variants from all over. The guy who recorded them was a religious scholar. His book wasn't meant to get out where it might confuse ordinary people."

"I'm confused and there ain't nothing ordinary about me," Bucket observed.

"So what's the scoop, Murgen? How come they won't tell us about this bitch? Whoa! Did you see that one? It exploded."

"All right," I told them. "The Gunni religion is the most common one around here."

"I think we know that, Murgen," Goblin said.

"Just making the point. Most people down here believe in Kina. Even if they're not Gunni, they believe. Here's the story.

The Gunni have Lords of Light and Lords of Darkness. They've been doing their lording since the beginning of time."

"Sounds like standard stuff."

"It is. Only the value systems are different from what we knew back home. The balance between darkness and light is more dynamic here, and isn't weighted the same emotionally as our struggle between good and evil. Moreover, Kina is a sort of self-elevated outside agency of decay and corruption that attacks both darkness and light. She was created by the Lords of Light to help defeat a horde of really nasty demons they couldn't handle any other way. She helped by eating the demons. Naturally, she got fat. And apparently wanted dessert because she tried to eat everybody else, too."

"She was stronger than the gods who created her?"

"Guys, I didn't make this stuff up. Don't ask me to rationalize it. Goblin, you've been everywhere. You ever seen a religion that can't be picked to shreds by any nonbeliever with brains enough to tie his own bootlaces?"

Goblin shrugged. "You're as cynical as Croaker was."

"Yeah? Good for me. Anyway, there's a lot of typically murky mythological stuff about mothers and fathers and vicious, hideous, probably incestuous carryings-on amongst the other gods while Kina kept getting stronger. She was real sneaky. That's one of her attributes. Deceit. But then her main creator, or father, tricked her and put a sleep spell on her. She's still snoring away somewhere but she can touch our world through her dreams.

"She's got her worshippers. All Gunni deities do. Big, little, good, bad, indifferent, they all have their temples and priesthoods. I can't find out much about Kina's followers. They're called Deceivers. The soldiers won't talk about them. They flat refuse, like naming Kina might actually waken her. Which, I gather, is the holy mission of her worshippers."

"Too weird for me," Bucket grumbled.

Goblin said, "That explains why Lady scares the shit out of

everybody whenever she dresses up. If they really think she's turned into this goddess."

"I figure we should find out everything we can about this Kina."

"Crack plan, Murgen. How? If nobody will talk?"

Yeah. Even the boldest Taglians threatened to get the vapors if I pressed. It was obvious that they were not just terrified of this goddess. They were scared of me, too.

One-Eye brought heartening news. "This stuff about the relief force is gold, boss. Every night now Spinner is sneaking troops out through the hills like he don't think we can see them go if it's dark."

"Could he be giving up the siege?"

"The troops are all headed north. Home ain't north."

I did not offer another alternative. One-Eye would not have come if he was not sure.

Of course, One-Eye being sure never meant that One-Eye was right. He was One-Eye.

I thanked him, sent him to do a small chore, found Goblin and asked him what he thought. The little wizard seemed surprised I would bother. "Did One-Eye stutter or something?"

"No. But he's One-Eye."

Goblin could not contain his big frog grin. That made perfect sense to him.

Nobody relayed the news to Mogaba. I thought it would go easier for everybody if he didn't know. But Mogaba heard rumors, too.

Dejagore was a nightmare town filled with factions only loosely united in defiance of the besiegers. Mogaba's forces were the strongest. The Jaicuri were most numerous. We Old Crew, with our auxiliaries, were less numerous and less powerful. But boy were we strong in our righteousness.

And then there were the Nyueng Bao. The Nyueng Bao remained an enigma.

43

Ky Dam's family occupied the same dismal, filthy, smoky, pungent hole until the deluge drove them out. The perquisites of power did not appeal to the Speaker. He had a place to get out of the rain. That was enough.

Maybe that was more than he had had back in the swamp. He did share with a troop of descendants who stopped bickering only when the outsider came around. And then the children restrained themselves only for a while.

On successive afternoons Ky Dam summoned me to consult on trivial matters. We faced each other over tea served by the beautiful granddaughter while the children quickly lost their awe of me and resumed brawling. We traded information on friends and enemies. That fevered character in the shadows moaned and groaned.

I did not like that. He was dying. But he was taking a long, long time getting it done. Every time he cried out the beautiful one went to him. I ached in sympathy. She was so haggard.

Second visit I said something to indicate sympathy, one of those things you toss off without much thought. Ky Dam's wife, whom I now knew to be named Hong Tray, glanced up from her tea, startled. She said three soft words to Ky Dam.

The old man nodded. "Thank you for your concern, Stone Soldier, but it is misplaced. Danh welcomed a devil into his soul. Now he pays the due."

A burst of rapid, liquid Nyueng Bao erupted from the shadows. A squat old woman waddled into the light. She was bowlegged, ugly as a warthog, in a vicious humor. She barked at me. She was Ky Gota, the Speaker's daughter and my shadow Thai Dei's mother. She was a dark legend among her own people. I have no idea what she was on about but I got the feeling that she laid all the ills of the world squarely at my feet.

Ky Dam said something gently. It did not get through. Hong

Tray repeated his words, more gently, in a whisper. Silence fell instantly. Ky Gota scurried into the shadows.

The Speaker offered, "In all our lives we enjoy successes and failures. My great sorrow is my daughter Gota. She has within her a cancer of agony she cannot conquer. She insists on sharing it with the rest of us." A tiny smile touched his lips. This was self-deprecating humor, meant to inform me that he was speaking metaphorically. "*Her* great failure, the wellspring of heartbreak for all of us, was her hasty choice of Sam Danh Qu as the husband for her daughter." He indicated the beautiful flower. The flower betrayed a blush as she knelt to refill our cups.

There was no doubt that all these people understood Taglian perfectly.

Ky Dam added, "That is the one great error that Gota cannot deny, a culmination of deficiencies that is like a brand. She was widowed young. She arranged the marriage hoping to enjoy her elder years luxuriating on the wealth of the Sams." The Speaker showed me that little smile again, probably sensing my incredulity. Wealth and Nyueng Bao are contradictory concepts.

The old man continued, "Danh was clever. He concealed the fact that he had been disinherited because of his cruelty and wickedness and treachery. Gota was too much in a hurry to investigate harsh rumors. And Danh's evil only grew worse after the nuptials. But that is enough about me and mine. I asked you here because I wish to keep an eye on the character of the leader of the Bone Warriors."

I had to ask. "Why do you call us that? Does it mean anything?"

Ky Dam traded looks with his wife. I sighed. "I get it. It's more of the Black Company claptrap everybody does. You think we're something our predecessors were supposed to have been four hundred years ago, only probably weren't because oral history exaggerates ridiculously. Speaker, listen. The Black Company is just a gang of outcasts. Really. We're plain old mercenary soldiers caught up in circumstances we don't understand and really don't like. We're just passing through. We came this way because our Captain has a bug up his ass about the Company's history. Most of the rest of us couldn't think of anything else we wanted to do more." I told him about Silent and Darling and others who had parted with the brotherhood rather than hazard the long journey south. "I promise you, whatever scares everybody—and I wish somebody would tell me what that is—it would have to involve way more work than I'm willing to put into anything."

The old man eyed, me, glanced at his wife. She said and did nothing but something passed between them. Ky Dam nodded.

Uncle Doj materialized. The Speaker told me, "Perhaps we misjudge you. Even I allow prejudice to guide me at times. There is a chance I will know better when next we speak."

Uncle Doj made a small gesture. Time for me to leave.

44

Goblin caught me hitting the Jaicuri books. "Murgen!"

I started. "Huh?"

"About goddamn time."

"What? What're you talking about?"

"I been standing here watching you for ten minutes. You never turned a page. You never blinked an eye. I couldn't tell if you was breathing."

I started to make an excuse.

"Won't sell. I had to yell four times and slap you on the back of the head to get your attention."

"So I was thinking." Only I could not recall even one thought.

"Yeah. Right. Mogaba wants your scrawny ass over to the citadel."

"A lot of southerners have sneaked off to meet this relief column," I told Mogaba. "At first I thought they were trying to trick us. Pull back and hit us when we tried to take advantage. But Goblin and One-Eye promise me they've just kept going. There can't be a relief army, though. Where would the soldiers come from? Who would lead them?" Would Mogaba believe that I had not heard the more interesting rumors? He heard more than I did. And Croaker's survival probably figured in a lot of those.

What would he do if the Old Man turned up alive?

I was pretty sure Mogaba thought about that a lot.

I was thanked and told to return to my people with no other comment. I did not find out why he sent for me.

Mogaba did just what I feared. He launched a recon in force, maybe trying to find new weak spots. He employed only his own most trustworthy men. And I was content to sit atop my part of the wall, watching. And wondering why Mogaba was so sure we would desert if we got outside.

I tend to ignore Mogaba here. He was a much greater part of everyday life than I show. He was misery on the hoof. My dislike makes it impossible to write about the man rationally so I discuss him only when I must.

Of all the Nar, in those days, only Sindawe ever made the effort to be civil.

Anyway, Mogaba thought he had a chance to hurt the Shadowmaster but the planners outside were getting the hang of how his head worked. He did not let a lack of success discourage him. There was that about Mogaba. He never became discouraged. No setback ever shook his conviction that he was invincible. If his plans fizzled he just recalculated.

Mogaba's soldiers began to desert without benefit of escape from the city, coming to hide out with friends among our Taglians. They complained that Mogaba was too profligate with soldiers' lives.

Mogaba responded by ordering special rations and preferential access to prostitutes for his most dedicated men.

We found those sealed jars of grain left over from the Shadowmasters' first siege. Whether to share generated considerable debate. One-Eye insisted that Mogaba would not be satisfied just to share. He would want to know all about our find. He would want to see for himself. Did we want him wandering around our warrens?

No.

So what does the little shit do? He turns right around and starts selling fresh-baked bread for twenty times what a loaf cost before the siege.

I found a nice quiet spot for just One-Eye and me, atop the wall on a lazy afternoon. There were fresh rumors of a battle up north but that was not our topic. I asked, "What did you tell me about why we shouldn't let Mogaba share the stores we found?"

"Huh?" This was not the hassle he expected.

"You were extremely persuasive. All that stuff about not letting the man get into our hideout."

He grinned, proud of himself. "So?"

"You stand by what you said?"

"Sure."

"Then what the fuck are you doing selling his men bread when we're not supposed to have no grain to grind for flour?"

He frowned. The connection eluded him. "Making a profit?"

"You really figure Mogaba is so stupid he won't notice that bread? You really figure he won't ask questions?"

"You got too rigid a way of looking at things, Kid."

"You keep up your crap you're really going to think rigid. You get me killed I'm going to haunt your ass forever."

"You probably would. There's times I think you're halfway a haunt already."

"What's that supposed to mean?"

"These spells you have. When you have them it's like there's somebody else looking out from behind your eyes. It's like there's some other soul swirling around you."

"I never noticed." Would I notice?

"If we had us a skilled necromancer or a spirit talker we might be surprise what we found. You wasn't born twins, was you?" His stare was fierce.

A chill stalked my spine. The hairs on my neck stirred. I did feel spooky, sometimes. But he was just trying to change the subject.

Goblin joined us uninvited. "There's something going on with the Shadowlanders, Murgen."

A crow nearby made a sound like laughter.

I asked, "They aren't setting up for another big attack? I thought Mogaba screwed their main ramp."

"I couldn't get close enough to catch any details. Mogaba is staying out where people can see him. But I think there *was* a battle. And I think Shadowspinner's creeps got whipped. We may have friends out there ready to bust us out."

"Calm down. Don't start packing your gear."

One-Eye snickered. "That's the runt all over, counting his chickens when he ain't even stole no eggs yet."

I grumbled, "You remember what we were just discussing? Stupid moves? And you'd dare get down on Goblin?"

Of course he would. That was his great mission.

"What's going on?" Goblin demanded.

Uncle Doj materialized. His presence ended the discussion. That man could be spookier than any shade, he moved so fast and quiet. "Speaker says tell you southerners carrying tools instead of weapons are assembling south of the city."

"And what's that over there?" From our perch most of the activity was hidden behind the curve of the wall but it looked like a big engineering party had begun to gather north of the city as well. "You see any prisoners or slaves out there . . . ? Huh? What's that?"

That was the sparkle of sunlight off metal in the hills. The sparkle repeated itself. People were moving out there, not carefully enough.

Shadowspinner's men had no need to sneak. I told Goblin, "Pass the word. Full alert come sundown."

Uncle Doj considered the hills. "You have good eyes, Bone Warrior."

"Know something, Stubby? I'd a whole lot rather be called Murgen."

The squat man smiled thinly. "As you wish, Murgen. I have come on behalf of the Speaker. He says tell you hard times are coming. He says prepare your hearts and minds."

"Hard times?"

One-Eye laughed. "The party is over, Kid. Now we got to pay for loafing around and getting fat while the houris slithered all over us."

"Keep it in mind next time you're tempted to do some profiteering."

"Huh?"

"You can't eat money, One-Eye."

"Killjoy."

"That's me all over. Tell Wheezer to hike over to the citadel and tell Sindawe the southerners are up to something." Sindawe might be all right. I could talk to him without having to conquer an urge to squeeze his throat. And this would cover me on keeping Mogaba informed.

What would happen if the Shadowmaster just up and walked away, leaving us to sort ourselves out?

Sounded like the smart thing for him to do.

45

Wheezer barely made it to the top. Then he spent five minutes hacking and wheezing before he could talk. That old man had no business soldiering at his age. He ought to be off living off his grandchildren. But like the rest of us he had nothing outside the Company. He would die under the deathshead standard. Under what passed for a standard today.

It was sad. Pathetic, even.

Wheezer was an anomaly. Usually the mercenary life is brutal and short, pain and fear and misery only occasionally interrupted by a fleeting moment of pleasure. What keeps you sane is the unfailing comradeship of your brethren. In this company.

In lesser bands. . . . But they are not the Black Company.

Croaker and I both put a lot of effort into sustaining that brotherhood. In fact, it looked like time to resurrect Croaker's habit of readings from the Annals so the men would remember that they were part of something more enduring than most kingdoms.

I told Wheezer, "You better take a couple hours off."

He shook his head. He would go on the best he could until he could go on no more. "The Nar lieutenant. Sindawe. Sends greetings. He said . . . we better . . . look out tonight."

"He mention why?"

"He sort of hinted . . . that Mogaba might try . . . some big stunt after . . . dark."

Mogaba was always trying some big stunt. Shadowspinner ought to let him set himself up. One raid too many, at the wrong time, and Mogaba would find out personally why Spinner was called a Shadowmaster.

Wheezer said something in his native tongue. Only One-Eye understood him. Sounded like a question. One-Eye muttered a few clicky syllables in reply. I figured the old man wanted to know if it was all right to talk in front of the Nyueng Bao. One-Eye gave him the go ahead.

Wheezer said, "Sindawe said tell you guys the rumors about a big battle are probably true."

"We owe Sindawe, guys," I said. "That sounds to me like him telling us he won't back Mogaba a hundred percent anymore."

Thai Dei and Uncle Doj sucked up our conversation like Nyueng Bao sponges.

Tension built for hours. With no real evidence we began to feel this night would be critical. Mostly the guys worried about new nastinesses from Mogaba. We didn't expect trouble from the Shadowmaster any time soon.

I kept an eye on the hills.

One-Eye snapped, "There it is!" He shared my anticipations. Pinkish light flared. Lightning crackled around a bizarre rider.

"She's back," somebody said. "Where's the other one?"

I did not see a Widowmaker right away.

Panic swept the plain. The apparition had taken the scattered Shadowlander camps unawares. Sergeants shrieked orders. Messengers galloped around. Soldiers stumbled into one another.

"There he is!" Bucket yelled.

"There who is?"

"Widowmaker." He pointed. "The Old Man."

The Widowmaker figure shimmered back in the hills, larger than life.

Goblin grabbed my arm. I don't know where he came from. "Look over there." He indicated the Shadowlander main camp. We could not see the camp itself but a pale, gangrenous glow rose from its approximate location. The light intensified steadily.

"Spinner wants to play," I observed.

"Yeah. He's sending a big one."

"A big what? Do we need to get our heads down?"

"Wait and see."

I waited. And I saw. A nasty ball of green fire streaked toward the hills. It hit near where Lifetaker first showed herself. Earth flew. Stone burned. All to no avail. Lifetaker was long gone.

"He missed."

"What an eye!"

"Lifetaker didn't play fair. She didn't stand still."

"He made a stupid choice of tools," One-Eye sneered. "You can't expect somebody to just hang around and wait for you."

"Maybe that was his best go. He hasn't been healthy."

I sidled away. In a few minutes Goblin and One-Eye would start bickering.

The confusion on the plain worsened. The southerners were more rattled than seemed reasonable. What I could get from their chatter suggested that they had been caught just starting something big of their own and their disarray left them virtually unable to defend themselves. In hushed tones, too, I heard Kina mentioned.

Lifetaker, who resembled that goddess of corruption, vanished. Maybe she lost interest. She did not reappear. Shadowspinner pasted the hills with any sorcery he could slap together. Other than starting a few brush fires he had no obvious impact.

The fox was in the henyard. Southerners scooted all over, their panic feeding on the panic of others. When one got close my guys took turns sniping. Goblin said, "They keep cussing about their feet getting wet." I heard that, too. It made no sense.

"Holy shit!"

I don't know who said it but I could not have agreed more.

Scores of brilliant white fireballs erupted straight up above the Shadowlander main camp. They obliterated the darkness completely. They seemed a tool of more use to a Shadowmaster's enemies than to the villain himself.

A huge uproar followed.

Uncle Doj vanished. One moment he was beside me, the next a shadow running through the street below, then gone.

One-Eye told me, "This time I'm sure it's Lady."

His tone alerted me. "But what?"

"But the other one ain't the Captain."

Widowmaker had been visible for less than one minute. "Tell me it ain't so," I muttered.

"What?"

"That we got two sets. Each one only half the real thing."

A crow nearby cackled.

I asked, "What kind of sorcery would do that? Split them in two?"

"I wish I could tell you something you want to hear, Kid. But I've got a very bad feeling there's stuff going on we don't even want to know about."

46

One-Eye was a prophet. Although I did want to know. And thanks to the Nyueng Bao I heard a story.

The light across town faded. The attendant racket subsided. Part of that drifted toward the hills. The rest fell back toward Mogaba's part of town.

The crackle of small sorceries rippled across the plain. The whole expanse glistened silver. "That was a strange one. One-Eye, what say we build a watchtower on top of one of the enfilading towers? That way we could get high enough to see what Mogaba and Spinner are doing."

"You got Nyueng Bao to spy for you over there."

"Suppose I don't ask you to do any work yourself?"

"The idea sounds a lot better already. But I still think the Nyueng Bao could be your eyes, you play it right. You don't need to get as paranoid as Croaker. Just look at what they bring you so you see whose purpose it might serve. Consider what might be missing the same way."

"Sometimes I'm as lazy as you are," I told One-Eye. "Only with me it's mental. That sounds like a lot of thinking. And I'd rather see stuff with my own eyes anyway."

"Just like the Old Man," he grumbled. "You got to read them Annals all the time, how about you read some that was written by somebody besides Croaker? I *was* looking forward to a little relief from his righteousness."

So we were back to the black-market bread scheme.

Goblin turned up. "Pretty exciting stuff happening over there."

"Yeah? Like what?"

"I got up on the wall over there. For a while. Mogaba's guys weren't worried about getting caught letting me peek. He led this raid in person."

"Just tell us about it," One-Eye grumbled. "You all the time got to flap on about stuff that . . . Awk!" A huge bug landed in One-Eye's mouth. Goblin's smirk hinted that he might have been involved in the insect's errant navigation.

"That Doj character can tell you more than me. Some of his guys snuck out there behind Mogaba's gang."

"Why?"

"I think Mogaba was trying to bushwhack Spinner. But he stumbled into Lady instead."

"You're shitting me."

"When that bunch of flareballs went up? There she was. Her and about fifteen guys. They were right outside the camp gate, practically crawling over Mogaba's mob. Least that's what I heard. I didn't see it myself."

"So where's Uncle Doj?"

"Probably checking in with the Speaker."

Probably. "Yeah? Look, we've got a bunch of deserters from the First. See if some will sneak back to find out more."

"Here comes chunky boy now."

We talked right in front of Thai Dei, like he was deaf. Or like we didn't care squat what he heard.

Uncle Doj brought a couple other Nyueng Bao. They surrounded another chunky boy, this one a wide little Taglian. He seemed more prisoner than companion though no weapons were in evidence.

It amazed me that Uncle Doj could climb to the ramparts without breathing hard. Maybe he used some wild sorcerery that stole Wheezer's breath.

That sounded like something out of the Gunni myth book.

"What have you got, Uncle?" I stared at the squat Taglian. He was indifferent to my gaze.

"An outsider. The Speaker sent Banh and Binh to watch the black men, who wanted to attack the Shadowmaster himself. But they ran into others from the outside pursuing a similar goal. This one left his party and joined those running for the wall when the flares went up. The outsider group may have been betrayed intentionally so this one could become separated in the confusion."

I continued to study the outsider. He was a Gunni, more stockily built than anyone in these parts. Maybe he worked at that. He seemed possessed of a powerful arrogance.

I asked, "Is there anything special about him?" Uncle Doj seemed strongly interested in him, too.

"He bears the mark of Khadi."

That took a moment. Oh. Yeah. In the books from the catacombs. Khadi was an alternate or regional name for Kina. There were quite a few of those. "If you say so. I don't see it myself. Point it out."

Uncle Doj's eyes narrowed. He drew a deep breath, exasperated. "Even now you refuse to reveal yourself, Soldier of Darkness?"

"Even now I don't have any fucking idea what you're raving about. I *am* tired of hearing it." I was developing suspicions, though. "Instead of sputtering and fussing and offering cryptic grumbles why don't you say something I can understand? Pretend I'm what I say I am and can't call down the lightning to part your hair. Who is this guy? Who do you think I am? Come on, Uncle. Talk to me."

"He is a slave of Khadi." Uncle Doj glared at me, daring me not to understand that. He did not want to be more explicit.

That made no sense to me. But I am not a superstitious man. Did he believe his one mouth had the power to raise the she-devil alone? "Kina must be one badass bitch," I told One-Eye. "She's got Uncle drizzling down his leg. You. You got a name?"

"I am Sindhu. I am of the staff of the warrior woman you call Lady. I was sent to observe the situation here." He continued to meet my gaze. His eyes were colder than any lizard's.

"Sounds reasonable enough." If taken with a block of salt. "Lady? This is the Lady who was second in command in the Black Company?"

"That Lady. The goddess has smiled upon her."

I asked Uncle Doj, "Is he a liaison man, then? Between us and Lady?"

"He may tell you so. But he is a spy for the *toog*. He will not speak truth when a lie will do."

"Uncle, old buddy, you and me and the old man need to sit down and try to talk the same language for a while. What do you think?"

Uncle Doj grunted. Which could mean anything. "The *toog* will not speak truth when a lie will do."

Sindhu was amused.

The man struck me as a complete false face. I said, "Goblin, find this guy some place to sleep." I shifted languages. "And don't let him out of your sight."

"I have chores enough already."

"Somebody's sight. All right? I don't like him at all. I don't think I'm going to like him even this much tomorrow morning. He smells like trouble."

One-Eye agreed. "Big trouble."

"Why don't we just chuck his hairy ass off the wall, then?" Goblin can be pragmatic in the extreme.

"Because I want to find out more about him. I think we've crawled right up to the edge of the mystery that has hung us up ever since we got here. Let him run free. We'll play dumb and keep track of every breath he takes." I was sure I could count on the Speaker's help with that.

My two wizards scowled and grumbled. Hard to blame them. They always end up carrying the load.

47

I was snoring heroically down deep in our warrens, having gone to Nod confident I could sleep in. Tomorrow nobody would have the ambition to get up to any mischief.

I was down there so far and so far out of the way that not

five people knew where to find me. I was on a mission to catch up on my sleep. If the end of the world came the guys could celebrate without me.

Somebody shook me.

I refused to believe it. It had to be a bad dream.

"Murgen. Come on. You got to come see this."

No I didn't.

"Murgen!"

I cracked an eyelid. "I'm trying to get some sleep here, Bucket. Go away."

"You ain't got time. You got to come see."

"I got to come see what?"

"You'll see. Come on."

There would be no winning this. He would pester me till I lost my temper, then get his feelings hurt. But the long climb to the sunshine was not an inducement to rise.

"All right. All right." I got up and got myself together.

They didn't need to drag me out but I understood the impulse. Things had changed. Radically.

I stared at the plain, mouth open. Only, what plain? Dejagore was surrounded by a shallow lake that featured the tops of burial mounds as small islands. Each mound boasted its handful of disconsolate animals. "How deep is it?" I asked. And, "There any chance we can catch some of those critters for the pot?" With all that water down there no southerner would be guarding against sorties.

"Right now, five feet," Goblin said. "I had men go down and measure."

"Is it still coming up? Where is it coming from? Where is Shadowspinner?"

Goblin pointed. "I don't know about Spinner, but there's the water. Still coming in."

I have good eyes. I made out the water boiling and foaming as it roared out of the hills. "The old aqueduct came down there, didn't it?" Two major canals had irrigated the hill farms and fed aqueducts to Dejagore before the fighting started. The Company cut those when the southerners were on the inside. Now the city survived on rainwater and the contents of large, deep, very stagnant cisterns we knew nothing about back then.

"Exactly. Clete and his brothers figure they diverted the entire river into the canal. Same thing south of town."

Dejagore sits on a plain below the level of the country beyond the hills. Modest rivers run both west and southeast of the hills.

"I presume the boys are studying the engineering aspects?" I asked.

"Them and three dozen Taglians who had some skills the guys could use."

"Any conclusions yet?"

"Like?"

"Like how high will the water get? Are we going to drown?" If that was Shadowspinner's plan it indicated major changes in his thinking. Before, he wanted Dejagore recovered intact. This seemed a more practical and final answer to his problems, though more destructive of property—which, of course, was more valuable than any number of lives.

"They're trying to figure that out right now."

I grunted. "I take it Spinner pulled out after Lady left."

"No," One-Eye responded. "They hung around to swim. They don't get to a lot of beach parties where they come from."

"Man's not as stupid as we thought," I mused.

"Huh?"

"He floods the plain, even if he don't drown us he locks us up so tight he don't have to use hardly any men to keep us under control. He can chase Lady all he wants. We can't help her and she can't help us. For him it's better than getting reinforcements out of the Shadowlands. Longshadow's soldiers couldn't be trusted behind his back."

Thai Dei showed up. He always turned up soon after I came

out, which indicated how closely we were being watched.

Thai Dei was a waste of manpower. He didn't carry many messages. He didn't understand any of our languages well enough to be a good spy for the Speaker. But he was always, always just a few steps away.

There would be a reason. The Speaker would do nothing without consideration. I just did not grasp his view of the world.

The longer I stared at the flood the more questions I came up with that needed answers soon. Most critical? How high would the water rise? How long would it take to do so? The rate of rise would slow down substantially as each vertical foot required more water volume because of the fall back of the hills, evaporation from the larger surface area, and absorption by more covered soil.

I told Goblin and One-Eye, "Dig up every educated man in town and give him to the brothers." I thought about building boats and heightening towers and securing stores. I thought about our vast and wonderful warrens and the likelihood that thousands of manhours would go for naught. I thought about how we would have to prepare ourselves mentally for lots worse if we were going to survive. I thought about Ky Dam and his talk of hard times to come.

Thai Dei stepped over when nobody else was near. "Grandfather would speak with you. Soon, if possible." His manners were impeccable. He did not call me Stone Soldier even once.

The old man must want something badly. "As you wish." I noticed the outsider Sindhu on the battlements off toward the Western gate. I could feel him watching me. "One-Eye."

"What?"

"You don't need to bark. If you want to bark I'll see if I can't have the Shadowmaster turn you into a dog."

One-Eye was startled. "Huh?"

"You guys keeping an eye on our guest?"

"Geek and Freak are taking turns. He ain't done much yet. Wandered around town. Talked to people. Tried visiting with the Taglians, here and over with Mogaba. Ours wouldn't have anything to do with him. The al-Khul Company ran him off with their swords drawn."

"Would anybody talk about him?"

One-Eye shook his head. "It's the same old shit. Maybe even worse. You better make it clear him being here wasn't your idea."

Thai Dei, listening, murmured something that sounded cabalistic. He followed with a gesture resembling that meant to avert the evil eye.

"Hey," One-Eye said. "Something can bother these guys after all."

"I'm going to go listen to their boss talk. You're in charge, but only because everybody else around here is less trustworthy than you."

"Thanks a shitload, Kid. You make a guy feel like he's on top of the world."

"Try to have something left when I get back."

48

The vertigo hit me in the same alleyway as before—just yesterday? I remembered it as the darkness closed in. This was more of a sneaking, gentle, enveloping blackness than the thunderbolts that got me before.

My thoughts scrambled but I did recall several minimal episodes since the big blackout, just moments when I was out of my head and I came back as soon as somebody said something.

This one was stronger. Thai Dei's hands closed on my left bicep. He spoke but his words were sounds that had no meaning. The light faded. My knees went watery. Then there was no sensation at all.

There was a place that was brighter than day, although it was daytime. Huge mirrors gathered sunlight and splashed it onto one tall, gaunt individual in black. The gaunt man stood upon a windswept parapet high above a darkening land.

A scream ripped through the air. A dark rectangle slanted toward the tower from high above and far away.

The gaunt figure fitted a stylized mask to its face. Its breathing increased pace, as though it needed more air to face visitors.

Another scream tore the air.

The gaunt man muttered, "Someday . . . !"

The ragged flying carpet settled a short distance away. The masked man remained motionless, glaring at every hint of shadow around the device. The wind tugged at his robe.

Three persons rode the flying carpet. One was a tiny thing bundled in dark, stinking rags crumbling with mildew. He was masked, too, and shook continuously. He could not control the occasional scream. He was the Howler, one of the world's oldest and most wicked sorcerers. The carpet was his creation. The gaunt man hated him.

The gaunt man hated everybody. He had little love for himself. He mastered his hatreds for short periods only, entirely through the implacable exercise of will. He had a powerful will—as long as he was not threatened physically.

The ragball gurgled as it stifled a scream.

Howler's nearest companion was a short, skinny, filthy little man in a ragged loincloth and grubby turban. He was frightened. His name was Narayan Singh, living saint of the Deceiver cult, alive only because of Howler's intercession.

Longshadow considered Singh less than a flop of buffalo dung. Nevertheless, he had potential as a tool. The reach of his cult was long and lethal.

Singh's opinion of his own new ally was of no supreme elevation, either.

Beyond Singh was a child, a pretty little thing, though filthier than the *jamadar*. She had huge brown eyes. Eyes like the windows of hell. Eyes that knew all evil of old and would revel in it now and forever more.

Those eyes troubled even Longshadow.

They were whirlpools of darkness that pulled, pulled, twisted, hypnotized. . . .

A sudden, sharp pain in my left knee sent wires of agony searing through my flesh. I groaned. I shook my head. The stink of an alleyway penetrated my awareness. I seemed blind. But my eyes, apparently, were adapted to brilliant sunlight. Hands gripped my left arm, pulling, lifting. My vision began to return. I looked up.

A gaunt face looked back, startling me. I retained a legacy of fear from my vision, though what that had been was fading already. I tried to hang on but the pain in my knee and Thai Dei talking shattered my concentration.

"I'm all right," I said. "Just hurt my knee." I tried to stand. When I took a step the knee almost folded. "I'll manage, damn it!" I pushed his hands away.

The vision was gone except for a memory that it had happened.

Had it been the same with my other blackouts? Were there visions that flew away so thoroughly that I could not recall having had them? Did they have any connection with reality? Vaguely, I recalled seeing lots of familiar faces.

I would discuss it with Goblin and One-Eye. They ought to know what to make of it. They picked up a little loose change interpreting dreams.

Thai Dei started gabbling the moment we entered the Speaker's presence. Ky Dam considered me speculatively, his expression deepening oddly as Thai Dei chattered.

The old man appeared to be alone when we walked in but as Thai Dei talked and Ky Dam became unusually attentive other Nyueng Bao came out of the shadows to study me. Hong Tray and Ky Gota were the first. The old woman settled by her husband. Ky Dam said, "I hope you do not mind. Sometimes she is able to part the veil of time."

Gota said nothing. I suspected that that was unusual.

The beautiful woman appeared. She got right onto the tea

service business. Tea is a big thing with the Nyueng Bao. Did she serve any other function in the family?

The guy in the shadows wasn't moaning and groaning today. Had he left us?

"Not yet," the Speaker said, reading my glance. "But soon." Again, he sensed a question. "We sustain our share of the marriage vow even though he betrayed his. We will stand before the Judges of Time without stain on our karma."

I had a notion what he meant only because I was studying the Jaicuri scriptures. "You are a good people."

Ky Dam was amused. "Some might argue. We do strive to be an honorable folk."

"I understand." We so strive in the Black Company.

"Excellent."

"I came because Thai Dei said you want to talk."

"I did."

I waited. My gaze kept straying to the woman making tea. "Standardbearer."

I started. . . . "No," I said softly, unaware that I was speaking aloud. I had not fallen into one of those black fugues. I'd just become distracted momentarily. Couldn't blame a man for that. Not with a woman like that to distract him.

I said, "Thank you, Speaker. For not labelling me with one of those unappealing names you tend to employ."

I could not resist a small smile that told him I knew he wanted something badly enough to keep me in a generous mood.

He nodded in turn, acknowledging my awareness.

Damn. I was turning into an old man myself. Maybe we could sit here grinning and grunting and nodding and arrange the whole future of the world. "Thank you," I said when the pretty woman presented my tea.

That surprised her. She looked me in the eye for a moment, startling me. Her eyes were green. She neither smiled nor acknowledged me in any other way.

"Remarkable," I said, to nobody in particular. "Green eyes." Then I controlled myself and waited while the Speaker sipped some tea before he started circling in on his problem.

He told me, "Green eyes are rare and greatly admired among Nyueng Bao." He took a ritual sip. "Hong Tray may part the veil occasionally but her visions are not always true, or not always fixed. Or they may be visions that have not yet come to pass. She does not see recognizable people so it is hard to determine when the visions might be taking place."

"Uhm?" The woman in question sat with eyes downcast, slowly turning a jade bracelet that hung loose upon her left wrist. Her eyes were green, too.

"She foresaw the flood. We believed that would prove to be a false vision because we could imagine no way so much water could be brought to Jaicur."

"But we're in the middle of a lake now. The world's widest moat. The Shadowlanders won't bother us anymore."

It took the old man a minute to understand that I was not serious. "Oh." He chuckled. Hong Tray looked up and smiled. She had gotten the joke first. "I see. Yes. But it will serve the Shadowmaster, not us. Any attempt to leave will require rafts or boats, easily spotted, which cannot move enough men to force a breakthrough."

The old boy was a general, too.

"You got it." Shadowspinner had found an ingenious solution to his manpower problem. Now he could challenge Lady confident that we would not jump on his back.

"The reason I wished to confer is that in her vision Hong Tray saw the water rise to within ten feet of the battlements."

"That would make seventy feet of water." I glanced at the old woman. She seemed to be studying me in a way that had nothing to do with curiosity. "That's a shitload."

"There is another problem."

"Which is?"

"We tried to calculate how many structures will rise above the waterline."

"Oh-oh. I see." I saw. Dejagore enjoyed a vertically oriented architecture, as walled cities do, but not many buildings overtopped the wall. And most surviving structures, even many that were partially burned, were occupied by someone. There would not be much housing available if the city flooded.

Luckily for us Old Crew our quarter boasted a lot of tall tenements.

"Oh-oh indeed. In this area there are enough such structures to house our few pilgrims. But elsewhere it will go hard for the Jaicuri when the black men and their soldiers finally understand how much space they will need."

"No doubt." I thought a moment. Hell. People could camp out on the wall. Them getting in the way would not be a problem militarily.

Still, whatever we did, life would become pure hell if the water rose that high. "Presents a dilemma, doesn't it?"

"Possibly a larger dilemma than you suspect."

"How so?"

"If preparations are not initiated immediately much that might prove useful will be lost. But if you tell Mogaba this then it is likely the strong will rob the weak and leave them to suffer. There is now no need to exercise restraint because of potential attack."

"I see." Actually, I had foreseen the scramble for stores and high ground. But I did overlook the fact that Shadowspinner extricating himself also freed Mogaba to manage internal frictions in a manner more to his liking. "You have something in mind?"

"I wish to examine the possibility of a temporary alliance. Until Jaicur is relieved."

"Has Hong Tray foreseen that as well?"

"No."

I was surprised by the black despair that collapsed upon me.

"She has seen nothing one way or the other."

I brightened. A very little.

"I am reluctant to undertake such an obligation," Ky Dam confessed. "It was not my idea. It was Sahra's." He indicated the beautiful tea server. "But she trusts you for no reason she will explain and, moreover, her arguments make sense."

Hong Tray wore a bemused expression. There was, in the way she looked at me, a hint that she foresaw much that she did not share.

I shivered.

Ky Dam continued, "We have no hope if we assume a traditional Nyueng Bao stance and depend upon ourselves alone. You have little hope if your Mogaba does not feel he needs your arms anymore."

I stared at the beautiful one, though that was bad manners. She blushed. The attraction was so powerful, suddenly, that I gasped. I felt as though I had known her several lifetimes already.

What the . . . ? This did not happen to me. Not anymore, anyway. I was no sixteen-year-old. . . . Hell, I never felt like this when I was sixteen.

My soul was trying to tell me I knew this woman as well as a man ever knew any woman when, in truth, I had only just heard her name spoken for the first time.

There was something else over there, with her. That was more than one lovely daydream. I knew another one just like her, somewhen else. . . .

The darkness came.

It was sudden and absolute and I had no time to decide if I was running away or being pulled down.

49

There was a long, long time in the dreamless dark. A time without an I. A time neither warm nor cold, a time with no happiness or fear or pain in a place no tortured soul would want to leave. But a pin pricked a hole in the envelope. The tiniest thread of light found its way in and fell upon an imaginary eye.

Movement.

A rush toward a point, which swelled and became a passageway into a world of time and matter and pain.

I knew who I was. I staggered under the crushing weight of a host of congruent memories surfacing all at once.

A Voice spoke to me but I could not comprehend its words. I floated like gossamer through golden caverns where old men sat beside the way, frozen in time, immortal but unable to move an eyelid. Madmen, they, some were covered with fairy webs of ice as though a thousand winter spiders had spun threads of frozen water. Above, an enchanted forest of icicles grew downward from the cavern ceiling.

Because I had memories of memories within memories I recalled having read words very much like those somewhere in something I did not believe had yet been written.

"Come!"

The power of the call was like the punch of a thunderbolt.

Darkness came. I tumbled away, ceased being I. Nevertheless, before I faded from that cavern I sensed a startled presence coming alert and striving to direct its attention my way.

Somehow I had gone somewhere where no mortal was welcome to travel and still come away.

Memory fled. But pain went along on the journey.

50

Light in the darkness, again. I began to be I, though without a name. I shied from the light. The light was not a pleasant place. The pain would be waiting. But something farther beneath my surface turned to the light like a drowning man fighting toward lifesaving air.

I became aware that I was flesh. I felt my muscles, tightened till some were cramped. My throat was painfully dry. I tried to talk. "Speaker . . ." I rasped.

Someone stirred but no one replied.

I was slumped in a chair.

The Nyueng Bao had no furniture in their place, which was little more than an animal den. Had they returned me to my own people?

I forced an eye open.

What the hell? What was this place? A dungeon? A torture chamber? Had Mogaba snatched me? There was a skinny little Taglian over there, tied into a chair just like mine, and another man was strapped onto a table.

That was Smoke, the Taglian royal wizard!

I levered myself up. That hurt. A lot. The prisoner in the chair watched me warily.

"Where am I?" I asked.

His wariness redoubled. His lips pursed. He said nothing. I looked around. I was in a dusty, almost barren chamber—but the nature of the stone answered my question. I was in Taglios. This was the Royal Palace. There is no stone like this stone anywhere else.

How?

Ever seen paint run down a wall? That is what happened to reality. Right in front of my eyes it ran and dribbled and streaked. The man in the chair squeaked. He shook. I have no idea what he thought he saw. But reality drifted away and I was in a grey place, confused, filled with memories of things never experienced or seen. Then the confusion began to sort itself out and the grey washed away and in a short time I was in a room somewhere in the Palace at Trogo Taglios. Smoke lay on his table breathing slowly and shallowly as always. The Deceiver was in his seat. He earned a narrow-eyed glare because of the way he was sweating. What was he up to now?

His eyes bugged. What did he see when he looked at me?

I rose, aware that I had to be recovering from one of my spells. But there was no one here who could have brought me back. Didn't it take Croaker or One-Eye to drag me up out of the depths of darkness?

Hints of memory stirred in the deeps of my mind. I snatched at them, tried desperately to hang on. Something in a cavern. A song of shadow. Waking up once in a past long ago but still only a moment earlier in this time.

I was weak. This business was debilitating. And thirst was becoming a rage within me.

I could do something about that. A pitcher and metal cup stood on the table beside Smoke's head. Beneath the cup I found a scrap of paper torn from a larger sheet. It carried a message in Croaker's tight script. *No time to coddle you now, Murgen. If you wake up on your own drink this water. There is food in the box. One-Eye or I will be back as soon as possible.*

The scrap might have come from a procurement request. The Old Man hates to waste any fragment of blank paper. Paper is too damned dear.

I checked the tin box on the other side of Smoke's head. It was filled with heavy, unleavened cakes of the sort my mother-in-law bakes despite all pleas to desist. In fact, on closer examination, I knew no one else could have baked them. If I survived here I would owe Croaker a swift kick in the slats.

P.S. Check the Strangler's bonds. He nearly got away once already.

So that was what he was doing when I woke up. He wanted to worm out so he could murder me and my pal Smoke and then make a run for it.

I drank from the pitcher. The Deceiver looked at me with a longing you could almost smell. "Want a sip?" I asked. "Just tell me what's going on."

The man was not yet ready to sell his soul for a drink of water.

Soon after I wolfed down one of Mother Gota's sinkers I felt my strength returning. "Let's get you cinched up good and tight," I told my companion. "Wouldn't want you wandering off and getting hurt."

He stared at me in silence while I fixed him up. He didn't need to speak to let me know what was on his mind. I told him,

"This is the risk you took when you signed on with the bad guys."

He would not argue but he refused to agree. I was confused. I was the bad guy because I wasn't blazing hot on the effort to bring Kina back into the world. I patted his head. "You could be right, brother. But I hope not. Here." I snatched up the cloth and drew it back over him, where it belonged. Then I drank some more water and ate part of a roll and when I got to feeling frisky I decided to return to my apartment. It was subjective as hell but it was an age since I had seen my wife. In reality it could not have been more than a few hours.

I got lost.

51

Of course I got lost. It was inevitable. The future me within me did not recall anything else but it did remember that I was going to get lost, then find my way to someplace I was not trying to go. That much came to me just after I realized that I did not have a clue how to get back to any familiar part of the Palace. I stopped to take stock.

At that moment I had enough near-current memories of other Murgens from other times that I was ready to trust any memory from any time, though it came with no supporting context whatsoever.

This memory of getting lost carried flavors of the excitement of unexpected discovery and powerful overtones of pain. An echo told me I did not want to find my way again.

Somewhere, while still stubbornly trying to get out, I came upon a gloomy hallway that seemed to smell of old magic. A few yards away a shattered door hung precariously upon a single hinge.

Discovery beckoned.

I went forward unafraid.

One look inside told me I had found Smoke's secret library, the place where the only surviving copies of the first several Annals had been gathered and sealed away so there would be no chance we Black Company types would ever chance upon them.

I wanted to read them so badly. But I had not come to read. I did not have time to sort the wheat from the chaff of a hundred other books. I had to get back to my family.

I strove valiantly but could not get there. Head spinning, I tried to retrace my steps. It looked like I would have to wait with Smoke until One-Eye or the Old Man turned up. They could lead me out the easy way—and maybe tell me why I did not want to go, because that part would not come to mind clearly.

I got back to Smoke easily, with no misturns. I had begun to suspect that there were spells webbed into that part of the Palace, cast so no intruder could find his way around the maze without One-Eye's blessing. It might be that all paths led to the same destination. Or maybe they all led away if you did not start out with Smoke to begin.

That would not surprise me, though I had no idea if One-Eye had the skill and power to manage it. Nor would it surprise me to find out that he did not remember casting the spell in the first place, so had made no provision for me to get around it.

The Deceiver was wiggling when I returned, my step so soft he did not sense my presence immediately. He froze when he did. Give that man credit for determination.

I settled into the empty chair. I waited. Nobody came. It seemed hours passed but probably it was just a few long minutes. I got up and tramped around, back and forth. I tormented the Strangler some but that just made me feel bad, too. I covered him up and sat down again.

I stared at Smoke. I thought about the Black Company and its tribulations. I remembered what Smoke could do.

Why not? Just to kill time? But where to go? What to see? When?

Why not the great enemy again?

It was easy this time. Nothing to it. Like closing my eyes and drifting off into a reverie.

I did not go without some reluctance. I was spending way too much time beyond the normal pale, against my will. Why add to my confusion by going wandering on my own, too?

With almost a snap and pop I found myself adrift outside fortress Overlook. The mad sorcerer Longshadow stood atop one of his tall towers, amidst reflected light, less than ten feet away. I suffered a mild panic. He was looking right at me.

Right through me.

Behind him, stance mocking, was that wretch Narayan Singh, with Croaker's kid, the mortal flesh of Kinda, the Daughter of Night, the One Foretold who would bring on the Deceivers' Year of the Skulls, which will end with the awakening of their goddess. Singh never let the child out of his sight.

Singh was a dangerous tool but Longshadow needed every ally willing to join him.

Quite a few folks seemed willing to sign on against the Black Company.

A figure emerged from a hatchway apparently dark only because of the intensity of the light surrounding the mad wizard. This man was tall, ebony, lithe as a panther. No anger touched me because emotions turn pale in Smoke's domain, although this was Mogaba, the most dangerous of the Shadowlander generals.

I suspect Longshadow appreciated Mogaba less for his abilities than because he could be trusted. Mogaba has nowhere to run. The Company stands astride every road to safety.

I cannot understand why Croaker does not hate Mogaba. Hell, he makes excuses for the man, even feels sorry for him. He takes his feud with Blade much more to heart.

Mogaba said, "Howler brought news. The storm system no longer works."

Longshadow grunted. "I saw. My small shadows remain useful. I recall that I predicted they would catch on quickly. Have you any thoughts on how the woman Senjak could regain her powers when, by the nature of these things, she ought to be at the mercy of anyone who knows her True Name?"

I had a feeling he really wanted to know how Howler could survive a Lady with her powers restored and her old, wicked knowledge intact. Longshadow viewed the world through a lens of paranoia.

I wondered myself. About Lady's powers. Croaker guessed it had something to do with crossing the equator. That did not sound plausible. Neither One-Eye nor Goblin would hazard a guess. Lady herself refused to discuss it. I had no idea what she believed. Nobody pressed. That was not something you did if you wanted to stay friendly with somebody like Lady. She can get real unpleasant if she doesn't like you.

"No ideas," Mogaba said. "It isn't something I understand." There were many things Mogaba did not understand, including any languages native to that region. He communicated with Longshadow using his improved but still flawed Taglian. "Maybe she changed her name."

Could they do that?

I realized the remark was Mogaba's attempt at a joke. But Longshadow did mull it over as though it was possible in some subjective fashion.

The moment passed. Longshadow faced Singh. "Deceiver. Why are you here? What machinations has the Howler involved you in now?"

Mogaba answered for Narayan. "The Black Company jumped them in their holy grove and killed everyone but him and the girl. Your shadowweavers barely had time to call for Howler before they died. Howler found these two hiding a few miles away and got them out only yards ahead of the pursuit."

So. This was only a short while after our raid. And here was a surprise. I believed Narayan had gotten warning from the Shadowmaster. But he had not. So how had he shaken the sleep spell?

Mention of the shadowweavers rocked Longshadow. I

thought he would fly into one of his famed foamy-mouthed rages. Those strange little old men were a resource he dared not squander. It took a lifetime to train them. And we have taken care of a bunch of them over the years.

Longshadow sucked in a deep breath, held it, restrained his insanity. "My error. I should not have sent them. Have you any idea how our enemies could appear at a time so propitious to their cause?"

Nobody volunteered the news that we could hover over his shoulder any time the urge hit.

Longshadow observed, "This is not good. Each day they develop new resources. Each day ours dwindle." He glared at Singh. "What are we getting from these Deceivers?"

Mogaba replied. "They spy. Before long they will undertake selected assassinations. The enemy shows no awareness of that program. If their assassinations succeed the results will be of more value that anything but a decisive encounter on the battlefield."

Mogaba invited comment from Singh with his glance but Narayan held his tongue.

Mogaba said, "Unfortunately, the intelligence the Deceivers gather grows less reliable with each report. The enemy have enjoyed considerable success in their efforts to eliminate the cult."

Still no one else spoke.

Mogaba continued, "Lady and Croaker have become very aggressive against spies. I believe that indicates a major move is imminent."

"It's winter," Longshadow said. "And my enemies are in no hurry. They are content to nibble me to death. This so-called Liberator will never be satisfied that he has men and weapons enough."

He was right about that. Croaker never stopped going after more.

The Howler joined the group, stifling a scream as he did so. He husked, "The enemy labor battalions have completed the paved road linking Taglios and Stormgard. A similar road is almost complete from Stormgard to Shadowlight."

Shadowlight lies near the heart of the most populous and prosperous region of the Shadowlands. Shadowspinner had been overlord there. Nominally, the city and its environs still owed allegiance to Longshadow. Yet our soldiers were building a road in the area untroubled.

I wondered why. Croaker's strategic plan did not require it. He had no intention of besieging Shadowlight. That would tie up too many men for far too long.

Mogaba grumbled, "They press us everywhere. No day passes but that we hear of the fall of another town or village. Many places the locals no longer resist at all. And it would be folly to assume that Croaker and Lady will respect the season."

Longshadow turned his dread mask toward Mogaba, who flinched. "Have you done anything to make it difficult to sustain a major campaign, General?"

An army *must* live off the land if it ventures far from home. You cannot carry enough food and fodder to sustain it any length of time.

"Very little." Mogaba didn't show an ounce of contrition. "I have my orders. And our enemies know what those orders are."

"What?" Now Longshadow was testy.

"They expect me to sit still." Mogaba indicated Singh, who nodded agreement reluctantly. "Their strategy assumes that I will defend one fixed point. Because your orders constrain me to do just that they scatter their forces and attack everywhere. Blade cannot blunt their sword alone. The villages will not resist because the people know no help will come. I could defeat the fools in detail, in a short while, if our strategy changed suddenly."

I don't think so, I thought, floating there smug in the knowledge that we had Smoke.

"No!" Longshadow forced his quaking flesh to face southward. He glared at the plain of glittering stone. "We will discuss military matters in private only, General."

Howler delivered a horrible scream edged with mockery. Singh practically dove through the hatchway. His contempt for the Shadowmaster was obvious to everyone but Longshadow himself—though it was likely Longshadow would not have cared. To the Shadowmaster the Strangler was little more than a useful termite. In his mind none of us were much more than pesky insects.

The child left last. She considered Longshadow coldly. Her eyes seemed as old and wicked as time itself. She was a scary little thing for sure.

I wondered what the Old Man thought when he saw her. Or if he even dared look.

Longshadow said, "They don't think I know what I'm doing."

"My soldiers are wasted where they are," Mogaba replied. "They're losing what edge they had."

"You may be right. But to attack in any direction you will have to leave what protection I am able to afford you. Without my lost comrades I cannot reach nearly as far as once I did. Will you risk their sorcery without mine to support you?"

Mogaba grunted. He glared at the glittering plain.

"You believe I am a coward for fearing that, General?"

"I stipulate the danger. I grant the value of your protection. But there is much that I could do anyway. Blade has been allowed to act on a limited scale and has accomplished great things. For certain he has demonstrated repeatedly how these Taglians will collapse if you attack their weaknesses."

"You trust Blade?"

"More than most. Like me, he has nowhere else to run. But I trust no one completely. Our allies least of all. Neither Howler nor the Deceiver joined us out of love for our cause."

"Indeed." Apparently amused, Longshadow seemed to relax. "I must explain, General." Mogaba's surprise told me that this was an extraordinary eventuality. "I do not stay bottled up here because of the plain. I can leave Overlook for short periods. I will if I must. The Shadowgate wards are fresh and strong and reliable and entirely under my control. But if I do venture out I will have to so do by stealth."

Mogaba grunted again.

"The reason I stay here is that there are some less obvious players in this game."

Mogaba frowned. Sounded like a crock to me, too.

"Howler springs from that clan once known as The Ten Who Were Taken."

"I know."

"Stormshadow matriculated from that slave school as well. Another graduate was Senjak's sister. They called her Soul-catcher."

"I believe we've met."

"Yes. She embarrassed you at Stormgard." Actually, that was Lady that time. Wasn't it?

Mogaba nodded. I was surprised. Time seemed to have given him the ability to manage his temper.

"Some years ago circumstances deceived Howler and I. We took Soulcatcher prisoner under the impression that we had captured her sister. She was masquerading as Senjak at the time so the mistake was more her fault than ours. She escaped during some confusion that arose later. Although we did not treat her severely she bears us a unreasonable ill will. She has done us mischief before now and awaits the opportunity to do us major harm."

"You think if you left Overlook she might invite herself inside and forget to leave the door unlocked?"

"Exactly."

Ha! Imagine hijacking that incredible fortress.

Mogaba sighed. "So whether I like it or not it will have to be decided on the Plain of Charandaprash."

"Yes. Will you win?"

"Yes." Mogaba never did lack confidence. "As long as Croaker remains the man I knew, scarred by that streak of soft-ness."

"If?"

"He hides behind a hundred masks. His soft streak may be another of those."

"So this man concerns you despite your desire to discount him."

"We continue to play to his strengths, not to attack his weaknesses. We allow him time to think, to plan, to maneuver, so he does not need to be subtle. His forces advance everywhere. Along the frontier the people are more afraid of the Black Company than of you. For pure viciousness there is nothing to match his war against Singh's kind. The Croaker I remember would have taken prisoners. He would have pardoned Stranglers willing to abandon their religion."

Right, I thought sarcastically. Then I reconsidered. Mogaba might be correct. Croaker *had* been forgiving, once upon a time.

"Maybe Senjak wants the example made."

"Possibly. She is that hard. But her influence doesn't explain Croaker's having spent seven thousand lives trying to get Blade."

What? This was news.

"Blade deserted him."

"I deserted him. And I was Company. Blade was only an adventurer, not a brother. He hasn't come after me that way. With Blade he's fighting a personal war."

The falling out with Blade and Blade's subsequent flight and defection baffled a lot of people, especially his buddies Cordy and Willow. And my name can go to the top of the list. Whispers were that Croaker stumbled onto something real going on between Lady and Blade. Whatever, it was certain that he was as obsessive about Blade as he was about Narayan Singh.

Lady did not interfere in Croaker's vendetta. Neither did she help.

"That troubles you?"

"Croaker confuses me. In some ways he has become dangerously unpredictable. At the same time he becomes more and more the high priest of the Black Company legend, admitting no other gods before his precious Annals."

That was not true. Croaker grew less interested all the time. But allow Mogaba his hyperbole. He wanted to sell something.

Mogaba continued, "I fear he may become so skewed he'll attack in a way so novel we won't recognize it until it's too late."

"As long as he comes. Only disaster awaits him."

"He'll come. But is the overall outcome so certain?" I got the feeling both men nurtured major doubts, but each mostly about the other.

"You circle back upon my constraints. Desist. You fear him?"

"I dread him. More than I dread Lady. Lady is straightforward in her enmity. She comes right at you with everything she has. Croaker is determined to flim-flam you into looking somewhere else while he sticks a knife in your back. He will come at you with everything he has, too, but how will he use it? He is not a man of honor."

Mogaba didn't really mean that Croaker was dishonorable but that he was not a gentleman in the sense that meant so much to Mogaba—who could not be considered a cavalier himself anymore.

Mogaba continued, "He is no longer sane. I do not believe he is sure what he is doing himself. These days he has to face much for which there is no precedent in his Annals."

Wrong again, chappie. After four hundred years there is a precedent for everything in the Annals somewhere. The trick is knowing how to look.

"He has limits, General."

"Of course. Those Taglians are factious and divisive."

"And that could be his undoing. Politically he will have no option but to try his luck at Charandaprash soon. Where we will crush him."

"And if I do? We should consider the possibilities of life unplagued by this disease called the Black Company."

"Oh?"

"Winning one battle will not be enough. If even one of them survives and maintains possession of the Lance of Passion new armies will rise against us. Lady proved that."

"Then you will have the pleasure of crushing them again."

Mogaba wanted to argue but elected not to bark into the wind.

"Once Overlook is complete you can hare off on any adventure you like, with my approval *and* with my total support."

"Adventure?"

"I understand you better than you suppose. You were Gea-Xle's greatest warrior but you could not prove that to yourself. In the Black Company you were overshadowed by your captain and Senjak. It was necessary for you to have command in order to demonstrate your scope and genius. When you did have an opportunity all your efforts were sabotaged and suborned. You came to me because the Black Company would not allow you the opportunity you need."

Mogaba nodded. He did not seem pleased with himself, though. And that surprised me. I had thought him too self-centered to entertain moral doubts.

"Go. Conquer the world, General. I'll enjoy helping you. But you have to crush the Black Company first. You have to stop the Taglians. Because you will have nothing if I fall. Will the Strangler be much help, really?"

"He could be. He talks big about his goddess getting involved but I won't count on that. I've never seen the gods actually take a hand in mortal affairs."

Odd. Mogaba's god was Narayan's goddess, more or less. Had Mogaba lost his faith? Maybe Dejagore had scarred him deeply, too.

"Use them up. Leave none over to turn on us later."

In my imagination the Shadowmaster was always this huge stinking devil incarnate, a colorful lunatic the magnitude of the worst Taken back in the north. But the real Longshadow was just a mean-spirited old man blessed with too much power.

He told Mogaba, "If this becomes the Year of the Skulls I want it to be *our* year. Not theirs."

"Understood. What do you think of the child?"

Longshadow grunted uncomfortably.

"Spooky, right? A thousand years old. Her mother in miniature, only worse. More intense, with a deeper darkness inside."

He could be right. The kid definitely looked weird and evil from my ghost's eye view.

The Shadowmaster mused, "We may have to hurry her into the embrace of her goddess."

Mogaba shrugged. He turned to go. "Anyone else you want to see alone?"

"Howler. Wait!"

"What?"

"Where is the Lance of Passion?"

"Wherever Croaker is, I imagine. Or the Standardbearer. That's still that serpent Murgen, I believe."

I love you too, Mogaba.

"We must take possession. Might that not be a task for the Deceivers? Even destroying the Black Company may not be enough in the long run. And one other thing for the Deceivers. Have them find out why Senjak wants all that bamboo."

"Bamboo?"

Was there an echo?

"She has been stripping the Taglian territories for months. Wherever her soldiers go they loot bamboo."

"That is curious. I will find out." I followed Mogaba for a moment. Once he was clear of the parapet he muttered, "Bamboo. I have to humor a lunatic."

I tried to travel south of Overlook. Smoke went only a short way before he balked. Well.

I would find out sooner than I wanted, I supposed. After we settled Longshadow and Overlook the plain was next on the list of obstacles blocking our path to Khatovar.

52

I returned to the chamber with Smoke and our stinky pet Strangler. I was hungry and thirsty but also so excited I shook. I had not uncovered much of resounding import, but, gods! The potential!

I drank from the pitcher, cleared my throat, lifted the corner of the cloth covering the prisoner. "You in there? Want a drink? Want to tell me . . . ?" He was asleep. "Be that way."

So what now? Help had not arrived. I gnawed on one of Mother Gota's stones. That eased my hunger. That was all I wanted at the moment.

What now? Keep going out until somebody came to reclaim me? See Lady? Look for Goblin? Hunt for Blade? How about finding out where Soulcatcher was hiding? She had to be out there somewhere, though we had not stubbed our toes on her lately. No place was free of crows if a member of the Company was around.

Soulcatcher is patient. That is her scariest trait.

It was kid-in-the-candy-shop time.

I decided to look for Soulcatcher. She was the oldest mystery going right now.

Smoke jumped right out, but then he stalled. His soul, or ka, or whatever, became more agitated as I grew more insistent. "All right! She always was more trouble than I want to deal with, anyway. Let's find her goofy sister."

Lady did not intimidate Smoke at all.

I found her in the citadel at Dejagore, in the conference chamber with four men, leaning over a map. The frontier markings on the map lay far south of Dejagore. Earlier boundaries were noted and identified by date.

She needed a new map. Her old one was too busy. She had won too many skirmishes.

Lady is a beauty even fresh from the field. She looks way too young for Croaker although she is far older than One-Eye. One-Eye never mastered any youth sorcery.

Two of Lady's companions were Company men, Gea-Xle Nar anxious to show the world that Mogaba and his traitors were mutants, that their like would not be seen again. I did not buy that. Neither did Lady or the Old Man. We were confident that Mogaba had left somebody behind. Croaker once told me, "Watch out for somebody to start pointing fingers. That'll be the traitor."

A third man was the Prahbrindrah Drah, the ruling Prince of Taglios. He was about as nondescript, for a Taglian, as a man could be and still be breathing. He put in the last four years learning the arts of war. He commanded a full division now, the right wing of the field army. Lady and the Old Man took pains to entangle him deeply in their war machine so he had a personal stake to maintain there.

The last man was the improbable Willow Swan. When I focused on him Smoke became agitated, which proved to me Smoke's self was partially aware on some plane. He and Swan had gotten on like rats and mice.

These days Swan is the captain of the Royal Guards detachment assigned to Dejagore.

Swan wears his cornsilk hair longer than Lady does her shoulder-length black hair. Sometimes Willow braids his but at the moment it was pulled back into a ponytail. Lady's hair was back in a tail, too. Usually she lets it hang free. She did keep it combed and clean when she could.

A soldier by accident, Swan did not want to be a hero. His Guards existed outside the army and functioned mainly as military police. He and they owed their allegiance directly to the Prince and his sister.

Lady said, "Howler has quit attacking outposts."

"You said he ain't stupid," Swan replied.

"I got too close when I missed him. That scared him off for good."

One of the Nar observed, "Our raids must trouble them."

"They trouble me, Isi. And I authorized them." Lady shivered momentarily.

"They are effective."

"Beyond a doubt."

The Prince asked, "But would the Liberator approve?"

Lady's smile revealed glistening white teeth that were almost too perfect. She had mastered the cosmetic sorceries early. "He doesn't approve. Definitely. But he won't interfere. I'm the one who is here and I'm relying on my own experience."

The Prince asked, "Will Longshadow unleash Mogaba?"

The Nar brigadiers tensed. Mogaba shamed them greatly by letting pride and vanity seduce him away from the ancient ideals of the Nar. Not to mention he was going to be blue-assed hell in a fight.

Swan asked, "You take any prisoners down there?"

"Yes. And what they knew would fit into a thimble with room left for a stork's nest. Nobody responsible down there ever sits around the campfire swapping secrets with the troops."

Swan stared at her while her gaze was directed elsewhere. He saw a woman five and a half feet tall, blue-eyed, 110 perfectly arranged pounds. She was big for this part of the world. She looked like she might turn twenty soon.

That old black magic.

Swan was transparent.

Lady is cold and hard and committed and deadlier than a sword with a will of its own, but these guys just can't seem to help themselves. It started with the Old Man way back but the parade goes on. The fever cost Blade big.

Despite what may have happened with Blade I am convinced that Lady is the Captain's woman absolutely. Whatever happened, Croaker took it to heart. He drove a good man over to the enemy and became something as cold as Lady himself. Half the time, anymore, Croaker is this living wargod so fierce that when he barks even the Prince and the Radisha jump.

Aloud, Lady wondered what Howler's raids were meant to

accomplish. Swan blurted Bucket's answer. "He wanted to pick off Black Company guys. That's obvious."

"Isi?" Lady asked. "Is there more?"

One of the Nar replied, "Mogaba wouldn't test himself against lesser men. Longshadow might want to remove those so he can better manipulate Mogaba's obsessions. Or he might be trying to initiate the final battle by being a continuous irritant."

The Prince nodded to himself. Now *he* was watching Lady with that gleam in his eye.

Was it the fatal lure of evil?

"Perhaps he does want to bring Croaker to the front."

How many times over the centuries has Lady stood like that, about to loose fire and sword? She said, "We do need to move this headquarters nearer to the action. The communications lag has become unacceptable. Swan. Hand me that map there."

Swan plucked a map off a sideboard cluttered with mystic paraphernalia. His caution indicated that he found that stuff obscure and wanted it to stay that way.

The map portrayed the far south. A large blank space on its left was labelled Shindai Kus, which was a desert. Beyond the unmapped nether edge of the desert was additional blank space labeled Ocean.

Beginning in the Shindai Kus, running east and curving northward, are mountains generically refered to as the Dandha Presh. They become rougher and rougher as they swerve around to form, eventually, the eastern limits of the Taglian territories. The range changes its local name frequently. It is supposed to be impassable east of the Shindai Kus except through the high pass at Charandaprash.

Longshadow, Shadowcatch and Overlook lie on the far side of the Dandha Presh. Mogaba's army was the cork in the pass bottlenecking the road south. For ages a common subject when officers were not listening was how badly would we get whipped if we took a crack at Mogaba.

A racket apparently arose outside because Swan jumped to the window. "A courier," he announced. I could hear no sound from outside that room. In fact, when I did glance out the window I could see nothing but greyness. Strange.

Lady elbowed Swan aside. "Can't be good news. Get him before he talks too much."

Swan returned quickly. "It's not *too* bad. Seems a really huge mob of Shadar and Vehdna fanatics were chasing Blade and had the bad luck to catch him."

What? That wasn't news. I knew about it. The Shadowmaster knew about it. . . . Of course. Lady did not have a Smoke or a screaming-nut sidekick with a flying carpet. And I had known for just a little while. Maybe it seemed longer because I learned it so far away.

"What are you babbling?" Lady demanded.

"Blade wiped out over five thousand religious goofs who were after him to punish him for his religious excesses." Blade was pretty hard on temples and priests when he had the opportunity.

His religious attitude had a lot to do with his running away, too. He had made thorough, blood-bitter enemies of all Taglian priests long before his falling out with the Old Man. The devout considered his fall from favor a blessing from heaven.

I was confident that the priests secretly looked forward to all of our fates becoming gifts from the angels.

"Five thousand?"

"Maybe more. Maybe up to seven thousand."

"Loose on their own? How could that happen?" Neither the ruling family nor we liked having huge groups of armed men not under our control blundering around righting wrongs. "Out. All of you, out of here. Come back in two hours."

Lady started murmuring the instant she was alone. "That damned Croaker." She grabbed stuff off the sideboard. "He's out of his mind."

I learned that you got damned focused out there with Smoke. Time could rush past if you let yourself become introspective.

Fragments of all that was happening to me came to me in no rational order and I almost got lost trying to piece the puzzle together.

Realization, and resulting terror, feeble as it was out there, brought me back to the present in the place I was watching when I lost my concentration. Hours had passed.

Lady was still grumbling about the Old Man. "What's the matter with him? How could he *believe* those damned rumors?"

She was angry. She had managed some mystic scrying of the distant battlefield as it appeared after the event. All that carnage had left her more upset. "Damned fool!" It was the worst disaster for Taglian arms since Dejagore.

From some hidden recess in the sideboard she produced a piece of black cloth. I was startled, despite having studied her Annals closely. That was the silk rumel of a master Strangler. She began exercising with the killing scarf.

Maybe that helped her relax.

She was upset because she had been left out of something. Usually she was the Captain's partner.

Got you a clue, woman, I thought. Lately he is cutting everybody out.

Lady's scarf flashed. She was good. I wondered. Was there still some connection with Kina?

Did Croaker fear there might be?

They were not called Deceivers for nothing.

She calmed herself. She sent for her council. Once they gathered she said, "There were survivors from that battle. Some are still there burying the dead. Catch me a few."

53

Croaker never came to the hidden room. Neither did One-Eye, nor even the Radisha to torment our prisoner. Nobody wakened me.

I drifted back there almost without design, perhaps summoned by my body. I had been gone a long time. Longer than the subjective time spent out there. My stretch of introspection must have extended farther than it had seemed.

My stomach was roaring. But Mother Gota's baked rocks were all gone.

The Strangler had gotten the cloth off himself again. He watched me wide-eyed. I got the feeling he had been about to do something that I would regret.

I discovered that he had managed to work one hand free. "You naughty boy." I took a long pull off the pitcher of water, then fixed him up again. Then I tried to decide whether to risk the labyrinth once more, in an effort to get to some of Mother Gota's lethal chow, or to stay and take yet another look at the wide world through Smoke's eyes while I awaited help.

"Water."

"Sorry, pal. I don't think so. Unless maybe you want to tell me what your buddies are up to." My belly grumbled again.

The Strangler did not answer. Weak as he was, his will remained firm. Even ignoring my own presence it seemed somebody should have come to feed him.

It was late. Maybe Mother Gota was asleep and Sarie would handle my meal. She did not cook like she was out for vengeance.

I was at the doorway, trying to make up my mind. Was there some way to mark my passage? Some way to follow footprints in the dust? But there was no light. This part of the Palace was not in regular use. No one maintained any candles or torches. The lamp in the chamber behind me would be the only light available. Unless I waited till daylight, when the sun would steal in through random cracks and tiny windows.

I glanced back at the lamp. It had been burning a long time. No one had been by to fuel it. I ought to see about refilling it before I did anything else.

There was a metallic sound from far, far away, come around a hundred corners and down the rambling halls. It chilled me despite Taglios's natural heat and humidity.

"Water."

"Shut up." I found a beaker of lamp oil, cocked my head while I worked. The metallic sound did not repeat itself.

I had not covered the Strangler again. When I glanced at him I discovered his deathshead face stretched in a grin. It was the grin of Death.

Spilling oil, I flung myself out of there.

I got lost again. Fast.

54

Lost in the Palace was not a matter for panic so I didn't. I confess to a certain amount of frustration, though.

You would think my situation vulnerable to the application of common sense. I sure thought so.

One good rule proved to be not to enter any corridor dustier than the one I was using. Another was to avoid apparent short-cuts religiously. They never led anywhere I wanted to go. Most important was, don't yield to emotion or frustration.

The Palace is the only place in the world where you can step through a doorway and end up on a different floor. I found out the hard way. And it was not any sort of elf magic. It came from the place being a conglomeration of ages and ages of add-ons built upon very uneven ground.

My anxiety reached the point where I elected to pursue what seemed the wimp route. I decided to go down to ground level, find one of the Palace's thousand postern doors, which can be opened only from the inside, and get out into the street. Out there I would know where I was. I would walk around to the entrance I used regularly. Then I would be home.

It is really dark in there in the middle of the night. I found that out after I stumbled descending a stair and dropped my lamp.

It broke, of course. And for a while there was a lot of light down below. But soon the fire burned out.

Oh, well. It was a certainty that there would be a door to the street below. The stairwell curved down against an exterior wall. I had leaned out a window to make sure before I ever entered it.

Descending an ancient stair that spirals isn't easy when there are no handrails and you cannot see what you are doing. Nevertheless, I got to the bottom without breaking any bones, although I did slip a couple of times and endured one long spell of vertigo after passing through the smoke from the burned lamp fuel.

Eventually the stair ended. I felt around for a door. As I did so I frowned. What was I doing? Took me a moment to reach back into my head and bring up the answer.

I found the door, felt around for a release. I found an old fashioned wooden latch bar, which was not what I expected at all.

I yanked, pushed. The door swung outward.

Wrong answer to your problem, Murgen.

Within that fastness nothing moves, though at times mists of light shimmer as they leak over from beyond the gates of dream. Shadows linger in corners. And way down inside the core of the place, in the feeblest throb of the heart of darkness, there is life of a sort.

A massive wooden throne stands upon a dais at the heart of a chamber so vast only a sun could light it all. Upon that throne a body sprawls, veiled by shoals of shadow, pinioned by silver knives driven through its feet and hands. Sometimes that body sighs softly in its sleep, impelled by bitter dreams acrawl behind its sightless eyes.

This is survival of a sort.

In the night, when the wind no longer licks through its unglazed windows, nor prances along its untenanted halls, nor whispers to its million creeping shadows, that fortress is filled with the silence of stone.

55

No will.
No identity.
At home in the house of pain.

56

There you are! Where have you been? Welcome back to . . .
The house of pain?

57

The house of pain.
I went there but do not remember the journey or the visit.

I was on hands and knees on broken pavement. My palms and knees hurt. I lifted a hand. My palm was torn. Blood oozed from a dozen abrasions. My mind was numb. I raised my other hand, began picking out bits of paving brick.

Fifty yards away the side of a building glowed olive, pulsating. A circle of masonry blew outward. Shadows sprang out of the darkness. With weapons bare they scrambled through the hole. Shouts and the clang of metal came from inside.

I got up and wandered that direction, vaguely interested but not sure why, not even thinking definable thoughts.

"Hey!" A shadow at that hole stared at me. I did not yell so that must have been the shadow. "That you, Murgen?"

I kept walking, head spinning. My course curved to the right. I banged into the side of a building. After that I had a sure means of navigation. Like a drunk I steered by keeping one hand on the wall.

"Here he is!" The shadow pointed at me.

"Candles?"

"Yeah. You all right? What did they do to you?"

I had little pains everywhere. I felt like I had been stabbed and cut and burned. "Who? Nobody did anything? . . ." Did they? "Where am I? When?"

"Huh?"

A man leaned through the side of the building. He wore a scarf wrapped around his face. Only his eyes were visible. He studied me momentarily, popped back inside. Somebody in there yelled.

People jumped into the street. Some carried bloody weapons. All were masked. A couple grabbed my arms and took off.

We scurried through darkened streets in a nighted city and no one would answer my panted questions so for a while I had no idea when I was, or where. Then we crossed an open space from which I glimpsed the citadel of Dejagore.

That answered my most immediate questions.

But a new crop sprouted. Why were we outside the Company's part of town? How had I gotten there? Why didn't I have any memories of this? I recalled sitting with Ky Dam, secretly lusting after his granddaughter. . . .

The men accompanying me removed their wraps and masks. They were Company. Plus Uncle Doj and a couple of Nyueng Bao sprites. We ducked into an alleyway that led to Nyueng Bao territory. "Slow down," I gasped. "What's going on?"

"Somebody snatched you," Candles explained. "At first we thought Mogaba did it."

"Huh?"

"Shadowspinner's taken his whole army off after Lady. We could walk away if we wanted. We thought he decided to take a hostage."

I did not believe Spinner was gone. "Uncle Doj. The last

thing I remember was sipping tea with the Speaker."

"You began to behave oddly, Stone Soldier."

I growled. He did not apologize.

"The Speaker thought perhaps you had been drinking before you arrived. He instructed Thai Dei to take you home. He was offended. You proved to be such a burden that Thai Dei was unable to defend himself when you were attacked. He was beaten badly but managed to get home with word. Your friends began looking for you as soon as we informed them." His tone suggested that he wondered why they had bothered. "They seem more skilled than they pretend. They pinpointed you quickly. You were not in the citadel, which is where Mogaba would have confined you."

"How did I get clear across town?" I winced. In addition to the other pains I had a hangover-type headache. I had been drugged.

Nobody had an answer for me.

"Is this the same night, Uncle?"

"Yes. But many hours later."

"And it definitely wasn't Mogaba that grabbed me?"

"No. There were no Nar in that place. In fact, soon after you were taken someone attacked Mogaba, too. They may have planned to murder him."

"Jaicuri?" Maybe the locals wanted to get to the heart of the problem.

"Perhaps." He did not sound convinced. Maybe he should have taken prisoners.

"Where's One-Eye?" Only One-Eye could have ripped that hole in the wall back there.

Candles told me, "Covering our backtrail."

"Good." I was near normal now. Which meant I was as confused as ever, I guess. Whoever grabbed me had done some slick work to sneak through Nyueng Bao territory unnoticed.

Uncle Doj divined my thoughts. "We have not determined how the villains managed to ambush you, nor how the others got so close to Mogaba. Those four did pay in blood."

"He killed them?"

"By all reports it was an epic battle, four against one."

"Goody for Mogaba. Even he deserves a little happiness in life." We were approaching the tenement that masqueraded as Company headquarters. I invited everybody in. The boys got a fire going. When One-Eye showed up I suggested he see if he could not scare up some beer, that I had heard there was some floating around and we sure could use a drink.

Grumbling, One-Eye returned to the night. Before long he and Goblin turned up lugging a barrel. "On me," I told everybody. One-Eye made a whining noise.

I stripped down and flopped onto a table. Which is why the fire. To take the edge off the chill. "How do I look, One-Eye?"

His tone was that of a man responding to a stupid question. "Like a guy that's been tortured. You don't know how you ended up in the street?"

"My guess is they heard you coming and tossed me out to distract you while they got away."

"Didn't work. Roll onto your side."

I spotted a face outside the open door. "Come in here. Have a beer with us."

The outsider Sindhu joined us. He accepted a mug but appeared to be very uncomfortable.

I noted how closely Uncle Doj watched him.

58

It was still that same adventurous night. I was still disoriented, still hurting and definitely still exhausted but here I was wrapping a rope around me so I could rappel down the outside of the wall. "You sure the Nar can't see us from the gate tower?"

"Damn it, Kid, will you just go? You fuss worse than a mother-in-law."

One-Eye might know. He has had several.

I started down. Why did I let Goblin and One-Eye con me into this?

Two Taglian soldiers were waiting when I reached the crude raft. They helped me board. I asked, "How deep is the water?"

"Seven feet," the taller man replied. "We can pole across."

The rope stirred. I held it. Soon the outsider Sindhu dropped onto the raft. Mine was the only help he got. The Taglians wouldn't even acknowledge his existence. I tugged the rope three times hard to let the top end know we were going. "Start poling."

The Taglians were volunteers chosen in part because they were well rested. They were quite happy to be leaving the city—and depressed because they would not get to stay gone.

They considered this crossing an experiment. If we made it over, slipped through the southerners, then got back to Dejagore tomorrow night or the next soon whole fleets would hazard the crossing.

If we got back. If Shadowspinner's men did not intercept us. If we found Lady at all, which the soldiers did not know to be part of the mission. . . .

One-Eye and Goblin browbeat me into looking for Lady. Never mind them injuries, Kid. They ain't shit. Sindhu was along because Ky Dam thought it was a good idea to get him out of Dejagore. Sindhu's opinion had not been asked. The Taglians were supposed to guard me and provide strong backs. Uncle Doj had wanted to come but had failed to convince the Speaker.

The crossing was uneventful. Once we stepped ashore I retrieved a tiny green wooden box from my pocket and released the moth inside. It would fly back to Goblin, its arrival announcing my safe arrival.

I had several more boxes, each a different color and each containing a moth to be released in a particular circumstance.

As we started to move up a ravine Sindhu quietly volunteered to take the point. "I am experienced at this sort of thing," he told me. And I believed him within minutes. He moved very slowly, very carefully, making no sound.

I did all right but not as well. The two Taglians might as well have worn cowbells.

We had not gone far before Sindhu hissed a warning. We froze while grumbling Shadowlanders filed across our track twenty yards uphill. I caught only enough conversation to understand that they prefered a warm blanket to a night patrol through the hills. Surprise. You would think things would be different in somebody else's army.

We encountered another patrol an hour later. It, too, passed without detecting our presence.

We were past the ridgeline when dawn began creeping in from the east, extending visibility to the point where it was too dangerous to keep moving. Sindhu told me, "We must find a place of concealment."

Standard procedure in unfriendly territory. And it was no problem. The ravines out there were choked with brush. A man could disappear underneath easily as long as he remembered not to wear his orange nightshirt.

We disappeared. I started snoring seconds after we went to ground. And I did not go anywhere else, or anywhen.

The smell of smoke wakened me. I sat up. Sindhu rose at almost the same instant. I found a crow studying me from so close I had to cross my eyes to focus on him. The Taglian who was supposed to be keeping watch was sleeping. So much for well-rested. I said nothing. Neither did Sindhu.

In moments my fears were confirmed.

A southern voice called out. Another answered. Crows laughed. Sindhu whispered, "They know we are here?" It sounded like he had trouble believing that.

I lifted a finger, requesting silence. I listened, picked out a few words. "They know somebody is here. They don't know who. They're unhappy because they can't just kill us. The Shadowmaster wants prisoners."

"They aren't trying to lure us out?"

"They don't know any of us can understand some of their dialect." The albino crow in front of me cawed and flapped its way up out of the brush. About twenty others joined it.

"If we cannot evade them we must surrender. We must not fight." Sindhu was an unhappy young man.

I agreed. I was an unhappy young man myself. The Taglian soldiers were two more unhappy young men.

We evaded nothing and no one. The crows found our efforts amusing.

59

Time had no meaning. The Shadowmaster's camp lay somewhere north of Dejagore. We four were among the earliest prisoners taken but more soon joined us in our pen. Lots of Mogaba's guys wanted to leave town.

He would have less trouble feeding the ones who stayed behind.

One-Eye and Goblin seemed to hold our part of town together. Nobody I knew became a prisoner.

I did not send any more moths so they knew I had found trouble instead of Lady.

Even our guards had no notion how Spinner meant to use us. We were happier not knowing, probably.

I spent uncounted days in total misery. Piglets in a feed lot live better than we did. More and more prisoners arrived. The food was inadequate. After a few meals everybody got the runs. There were no sewage provisions, not even a simple slit trench. They would not let us dig our own. Maybe they did not want us getting too comfortable.

In fact our life was not much worse than that of the Shadowlander private soldiers. They had nothing anymore and could expect only nothing. They indulged in a ferocious desertion rate despite the Shadowmaster's reputation. They hated Shadowspinner for putting them into such an awful state. They took their anger out on us.

I do not know how long we were there. I lost track. I was busy trying to die from dysentery. I noticed only that there was a sudden absence of crows one day. I was so used to having crows around that anymore I noticed them only when they were not there.

I faded in and out. I suffered a bunch of my spells. They were more frequent now and left me emotionally drained. The shits left me physically drained.

If I could only get some sleep . . .

Sindhu wakened me. I recoiled from his touch. It was astonishingly cold and seemed vaguely reptilian. I was the only man in the pen he knew so he wanted to be my pal. I was willing to do without a friend. He offered me a cup of water. It was a rather nice tin cup. Where did he get that? "Drink," he said. "It's clean water." All around us prisoners lay in the mud twitching endlessly in haunted sleep. Some cried out. Sindhu continued, "Something is going to happen."

"What?"

"I felt the breath of the goddess."

For an instant I smelled something that was not the stink of vomit or unwashed bodies or dead men or pools of liquid shit, too.

"Ah," Sindhu whispered. "It's happening now." I looked where he pointed.

The happening something was going on inside the big tent belonging to the Shadowmaster. Lights of strange color flickered and flared. "Maybe he's getting something special ready for somebody." Maybe he had Lady spotted.

Sindhu snorted. He seemed to thrive in these conditions.

The something went on a long time but attracted no attention. I became suspicious. I had Goblin's ward against sleep spells set on me. Oh . . . ? I dragged myself to the compound fence. When nobody smashed me back with the butt of a spear

I was sure. The camp was under an enchantment.

Sindhu's water gave me strength quickly and started my brain perking. It occurred to me that if no one was inclined to stop me this might be the perfect time to take leave of the Shadowmaster's hospitality. I started worming my way between the fence rails.

My stomach rumbled in protest. I ignored it. Sindhu grabbed my arm. His grip was iron. He said, "Wait."

I waited. What the hell? That was one of my favorite arms. I didn't want to deprive myself of its company.

The moon began to rise, a big old squashed orange egg in the east. Sindhu continued to restrain me and continued to stare at the big tent.

A shriek drifted down from high above.

"Holy shit," I muttered. "Not him."

Sindhu cursed, too. He was so startled that he let me go. He glared upward.

"That's the Howler," I told him. "Really bad news. Shadowspinner could take advanced cruelty lessons from him."

The side of Spinner's tent opened. Out rushed a bunch of people carrying what proved to be human body parts. I recognized some of them. The people, that is. Who could mistake Willow Swan with his wild yellow mane? Or Lady, who carried a severed head by its mangy hair? And Blade was only a step behind her, his ebony skin shiny in the moonlight. I did not recognize any of the others.

The sleep spell on the camp, laid rather poorly, unravelled. Southerners jumped up to ask what was happening. Metal clanged and jingled as weapons and mail were located.

One of Lady's companions, a huge Shadar, started bellowing something about bowing down to the true Daughter of Night.

Sindhu chuckled. Nothing bothered him, it seemed. He could take anything.

He was not holding on to me but I no longer had the strength or inclination to go anywhere.

60

They pulled it off, Lady and her damnfool gang. Audacity pays. They slipped into the camp, murdered Shadowspinner, and when they got caught they convinced the southerners that it was all fated and they should not go doing anything because of that. I could not be much of a witness to their mass conversion. My bowels overruled my desire to observe. I spent most of my time making a worse mess of myself.

At some point our former guards decided to bring us to Lady's attention in an effort to curry favor.

Blade recognized us as they brought us out of the pen.

Blade looks like he might have been born Nar. Like them he is tall, black and muscular, without an ounce of fat on him. He says little but has a strong presence. His background is shadowy. He ran with Willow Swan and Cordy Mather, who saved him from crocodiles several thousand miles north of Taglios. What everyone knew for sure, what Blade made no effort to hide, was that he hated priests, singly, collectively, and without any prejudice whatsoever where belief system was concerned. Once I thought he was an atheist who hated the whole idea of gods and religion, but after further exposure I decided it was only the retailers of religion he detested. That suggested sharp incidents in his past.

No matter now. Blade took Sindhu and I away from our guards. "Standardbearer, you stink."

"Call out the ladies in waiting. Let them give me a bath." I could not remember my last bath. In Dejagore we did not waste water on trivialities.

Of course, now we could bathe all we wanted—although the water would be unclean.

Blade obtained fresh clothing by the expedient of robbing some southern officers, had us clean up and visit the inadequate field physicians Croaker had tried to train for the Taglian forces.

They knew less about stopping the drizzling shits than I did.

It was daylight when Lady saw me. She already knew the prisoners were deserters from the city. She was blunt. "Why did you run out, Murgen?"

"I didn't. We decided somebody had to come find you. I lost the election. . . . Uh." She was in a bleak mood, apparently pretty sick herself. Never mind the humor, Murgen. "One-Eye and Goblin figured I was the only trustworthy guy who had any chance of getting through. They couldn't leave. I didn't make it, though."

"Why did you feel the need to send someone?"

"Mogaba elected himself god. With the water around us, keeping the southerners back, he doesn't need to get along with anybody who doesn't agree."

Sindhu said, "The black men believe they serve the goddess, mistress. But their heresies are grotesque. They have become worse than unbelievers."

I pricked up my ears. Maybe I would learn something about Sindhu's bunch. I had bones to pick with them. I had not yet found any evidence to suggest that it was not them who kidnapped me and took a crack at murdering Mogaba.

Still, I could not imagine why they would bother.

Sindhu and Lady talked. Her questions sounded vaguely doctrinal. Sindhu's replies made no sense.

Once Lady interrupted the interview to be sick. A skinny little gink named Narayan, who kept hanging around, seemed inordinately pleased. I noted that Sindhu showed him considerable deference.

I was not happy. The little I knew of their cult assured me that I did not want them influencing my captains.

The interview ended. Blade's cronies took me away. I got to hang out with Swan and Mather, meaning I had somebody to speak a reasonable language with for a while, but soon I felt like a forgotten man.

"What are we doing?" I asked Swan.

"I don't know. Cordy and I just tag along behind Her Lordship pretending not to be watching her for the Prabrindrah Drah and Radisha."

"Pretending?"

"Ain't much good being a spy if everybody knows it, is there? Anyway, Cordy gets to do all the worrying. He's the one playing pattycake with the Woman."

"You mean that ain't just a vicious rumor? He's really plooking the Radisha?"

"Hard to believe, ain't it? She's got a face like . . . Hey! Cordy! Where's them cards? We got us a pigeon here thinks he can play tonk."

"Thinks? Swan, you're gonna think I invented the game if you get into it with me."

Mather was a nondescript character of average height with ginger hair who stood out only because he was white in a land where nobody but harem girls, kept out of the sun from birth, had fair skin. He asked, "Willow's mouth running away with him again?"

"Maybe, I've made a career of playing tonk. Hell, they boot you out of the Black Company if you don't make journeyman player."

Mather shrugged. "Then you'll twist Willow's head back around straight for him. Here. Deal. I'll see if the mighty general Blade wants to sit in."

Swan grumbled, "That would take him out of sight of Lady." Sounded like some sour grapes there. Mather showed him a smirk that confirmed my guess.

"What *is* it about her?" I asked. "Every damned guy that walks on his hind legs gets near her for five minutes, he starts floating around with his tongue hanging down, banging into things. But I've been around her for years. I can see she's got the right stuff in the right places put together about as good as you could want but I don't think I could get excited even if she didn't used to be the Lady and she wasn't married to the Old Man." Not that that was literally true. They had not even bothered to jump over a sword.

Swan shuffled. "Cut?"

I cut. I always cut. One-Eye taught me that.

Swan asked, "You really don't feel it? Man, she comes around me and my brain goes south. And she's a widow now, so . . ."

"I don't think so."

"What?"

"She ain't no widow. Croaker is still alive."

"Shit. That'd be my luck, too. You want to stack Cordy a hand, make him think he's got a winner, then skunk him?" As soon as I shook my head he wanted to know how come I thought Croaker was alive. I evaded a definitive answer for the few moments it took Mather to return.

"Blade's too busy looking for an angle to use while he's close to the magic. You load me up again, Willow? No? Bullshit. Let's just pick them up and deal them over."

"Ain't this the story of my life?" I grumbled. "Look here." I had two aces, a pair of deuces and a trey. An automatic winner, damned near couldn't be beat. "And that's a true natural, no help."

Swan snickered. "Don't matter. You don't got anything to do anyway."

"You got a point. Why don't you guys come over to Dejagore? I'll buy you a mug of One-Eye's home brew."

"Ha! Competition, huh?" Swan and Mather had gone into the brewing business back when they first came to Taglios. They were out of the racket now, among their reasons the fact that the priests of all the native religions condemned the use of alcohol.

"I doubt it. The only thing good about their brew is it gets you skunked."

"That was the only good thing about the rat piss we made," Mather said. "My dear old daddy the brewmaster rolled over every time we tapped another keg."

"We never laid any beer up," Swan countered. "Soon as it

was ripe we skimmed the scum off and poured it down Taglian throats. And don't buy that shit about his daddy, neither. Old Man Mather was a tax assessor who was so dumb he didn't take bribes."

"Shut up and deal." Mather snatched up his cards. "He did brew his own beer. And Swan's old man was a hod carrier."

"But a handsome one, Cordy. And a lover. I inherited his good looks."

"You take after your mother. And if you don't do something about that hair pretty soon you're going to wind up in somebody's harem."

This was a side of these guys I had not seen before. But I had not spent much time loafing with them. They were not Company. I kept my mouth shut and concentrated on my cards and let them tell me about who they used to be before the wander-dust settled on their shoes and set them roving against all odds.

"What about you, Murgen?" Swan asked after he noticed that I was winning more than my share of hands. "Where did you come from?"

I told them about growing up on a farm. There wasn't anything exciting about my life until I decided that farming wasn't what I wanted to do. I joined one of Lady's armies, found out I didn't like the way things were done there, deserted and joined up with the Black Company, which was the only place I could hide with the provost after me.

Mather asked, "You ever regret leaving home?"

"Every goddamned day, Mather. Every goddamned day. It was boring raising potatoes but not one time did I ever did have a spud try to stick a knife in me. I was hardly ever hungry and almost never cold and the landlord was all right. He made sure his tenants had enough before he took his share. He didn't live much better than we did. Oh, and the only magic we ever saw was the kind your wandering conjurers perform at town fairs."

"So why not go home?"

"Can't."

"If you're careful and don't look prosperous and don't go around pissing people off you can travel almost anywhere safely. We did."

"I can't go home because home ain't there no more. A Rebel army came through a couple years after I left." The Company passed through later still, marching from somewhere unpleasant to somewhere where we would be unhappy. The whole country had been turned desert in the name of freedom from the tyranny of the Lady's empire.

61

Lady sent for me after six days. I had shaken the runs and had eaten well enough to regain a few of the pounds I lost in the pen. I still looked like a refugee from hell. And I was. I was indeed.

Lady did not look good. Tired, pale, under severe pressure, apparently still fighting the sickness that had her puking the other day. She wasted no time on small talk. "I'm sending you back to Dejagore, Murgen. We're getting disturbing reports about Mogaba."

I nodded. I had heard some of them. Every night more rafts crossed the lake. The deserters and refugees always were astonished to learn that Shadowspinner was dead and Lady controlled his army—though that was evaporating through desertion, too.

Lady was a hard one. My guess was she meant to let the problem posed by Mogaba solve itself—despite what that would cost Taglios and the Black Company.

"Why?" That was not smart. All those Taglians in there had relatives back home. Many were people of place and substance, for it was that sort who had volunteered to defend Taglios.

"I need you to just go back and be yourself. But write things

down. Hone your skills. Keep the Company together. Be prepared for anything."

I grunted. That wasn't something I wanted to hear, knowing that the siege could be ended right now.

Lady sensed my reservations. She smiled wanly, made a sudden gesture. "Sleep, Murgen."

I collapsed on the spot.

She was her nasty old self.

My mind would not clear. The Taglians who had helped me
leave Dejagore were like zombies. They did not talk and seemed
almost blind. "Down!" I muttered. "Patrol coming." They did
what I said but like men heavily drugged.

Patrols were few by day. It was easy to elude them. It was
not their mission to keep people out, anyway. We reached lake-
side without any trouble.

"Rest," I ordered. "Wait for dark." I was not sure why we had
crossed the hills by day. I did not recall starting. "Have I been
acting real weird?" I asked.

The taller Taglian shook his head slowly, not quite sure. He
was more confused than I was.

I said, "I feel like I walked out of a fog a couple hours ago. I
remember getting captured. I remember them keeping us in a
nasty pen. I know there was a fight or something. But I don't
remember how we got away."

"Nor do I, sir," the shorter soldier said. "I do have a very
strong feeling that we need to get back to our comrades quickly.
But I don't know why."

"How about you?"

The taller man nodded, frowning. He was going to bust a
vein trying to remember.

I said, "Maybe Shadowspinner did something to us and let
us go. That's worth keeping in mind—especially if you have
urges that really surprise you."

After dark we stole along the shoreline till we found a raft, jumped aboard and headed for Dejagore. And discovered immediately that we were going to get nowhere using poles. The water was too deep. We ended up using poles and broken boards as inefficient paddles. It took us half the night to make the crossing. And then, naturally, everything went to hell.

One-Eye was on watch and had been passing the time making love to a keg of beer. He heard water splash and people ask for a hand up and concluded that the evil hordes were upon him, whereupon he flung fireballs hither and yon so any handy archers could plink us.

One-Eye recognized me before more than three or four arrows whizzed past. He yelled for a ceasefire. But the damage had been done. The Nar at the North Gate saw us.

We were far enough away that they should not recognize faces. But the possibility that the Old Crew might have outside contacts would get Mogaba's interest.

"Hey, Kid, good to see you," One-Eye said as I clambered to the top of the wall. "We thought you was dead. We was going to have a funeral in a few more days if we got time. I been stalling it, account of if you was officially dead then I'd have to start keeping the Annals." Generously, he offered me a drink from his very own unwashed for a fortnight mug. I declined the honor. "You all right, Kid?"

"I don't know. Maybe you can tell me." I told him what I could remember.

"You have another spell?"

"If I did these guys had it with me."

"Interesting. Come around and see me about it tomorrow."

"Tomorrow?"

"I'm gonna be off watch in ten minutes and I intend to hit the sack. And you need some sleep yourself."

My pal. Don't know what I would do if I didn't have One-Eye to worry about me.

62

Bucket wakened me. "One of Mogaba's guys is here, Murgen. Says His Majesty wants to see you."

I groaned. "Does it have to be so bright out there?" I had not bothered to go down into the warrens.

"He's pissed off. We've been pretending you were here but couldn't talk to him. Goblin and One-Eye put doubles of you on the wall sometimes so the Nar could see you."

"And now you have the real Murgen back you want to throw him to the wolf."

"Uh . . . Well . . . He didn't ask for nobody else." Meaning he did not want Goblin or One-Eye. He wanted to stay away from those two.

"Find my bitty buddies and tell them I need them. Now."

The wizards turned up at their own leisure, of course. I told them, "Put me in a litter and lug me over to the citadel. We're going to admit that you've been lying about me but only because I was totally sick. What we were doing on that raft last night was taking baths. You thought it would be cute to pop off a few fireballs while I had my pants down."

One-Eye started to complain but before he could start I growled, "I'm not face Mogaba without backup. He don't have any reason to be nice anymore."

"He won't be in a good mood," Goblin predicted. "There's been rioting. Food shortages are getting really bad. He won't turn one grain of rice loose. Even his handpicked Taglian sergeants have started to desert."

"It's all falling apart for him," I said. "He was going to take over and show the world wonders but his followers can't match his iron will."

"And we're some kind of philanthropic brotherhood?" One-Eye muttered.

"We never kill nobody who don't ask for it. Come on. Let's

do it. And be ready for anything. Both of you."

But first we went up to the battlements, both so I could see this world by daylight and so the Nar at the North Gate could see me looking sick before I presented myself that way.

The water level was just eight feet below the ramparts, higher than Hong Tray's prediction. "Any flooding inside?"

"Mogaba sealed the gates somehow. He has Jaicuri working parties bucket-brigading what seepage there is."

"Good for him. How about down below?"

"There's some seepage in the catacombs. Not a lot. We could keep up by hauling it up in buckets."

I grunted. I stared at Shadowspinner's lake. I saw more corpses than I could count. "Those didn't float up from the mounds, did they?"

Goblin told me, "Mogaba threw people off the wall during the riots. And some might be from rafts that turned over or broke up."

I squinted. I could just make out a mounted patrol beyond the water. A raft with Jaicuri piled high had been caught by daylight. The people aboard were trying to move away from the waiting patrol by paddling with their hands.

Thai Dei turned up so we knew his people were watching. I figured he would want me to visit the Speaker. But he said nothing. I told my bearers, "Take me to his worship."

As we approached I observed, "The citadel looks like something out of a spook story." And it did, with the sky overcast behind it and crows swarming around. Dejagore was a paradise for crows. They were going to get too fat to fly. Maybe we would get fat eating them.

The Nar at the entrance would not let One-Eye and Goblin inside. "So take me home," I told them.

"Wait!"

"Stick it, buddy. I got no need to put up with Mogaba's crap. The Lieutenant is alive. So is the Captain, probably. Mogaba ain't shit nowhere but inside his own head anymore."

"You could have at least argued until we were rested up."

One-Eye started shuffling sideways so he could turn and head back down the steps.

Ochiba caught us before we reached street level. He was cast in the same mold as all Nar. His face remained neutral. "Apologies, Standardbearer. Won't you reconsider?"

"Reconsider what? I don't especially want to see Mogaba. He's been eating magic mushrooms or chewing lucky weed or something. I been shitting my guts out for over a week. I ain't in no shape to play games with no homicidal lunatic."

Something fluttered behind Ochiba's dark eyes. Maybe he agreed. Maybe there was another war going on inside him, a struggle between keeping faith with Gea-Xle's greatest Nar ever and keeping faith with his own humanity.

I was not going to pursue it. Any hint of outside interest would push waverers in the direction of "That's the way it's always been."

That was the top two, then, quietly questioning Mogaba's way. If these guys doubted him things were probably worse than I thought.

"As you wish." Ochiba told the sentries, "Let the litter-bearers in."

Nobody missed the significance of who my litterbearers were. It was a pretty direct statement.

I felt comfortably confrontational.

63

Was Mogaba happy to see Goblin and One-Eye, and them looking so fit? You better believe he wasn't. But he did not pursue his displeasure. He just ticked something on his mental get-even slate. He would make me even more unhappy than he had planned. Later.

"Can you sit up?" he asked, almost like he cared.

"Yeah. I made sure. That's partly why I took so long. That

and I wanted to make sure I'd stay rational."

"Oh?"

"I've been suffering severe fevers and dysentery for over a week. Last night they took me out and threw me in the water to cool me down. That worked."

"I see. Come to the table, please."

Goblin and One-Eye helped me into a chair. They put on a fine show.

There were just six people in the conference chamber, us three and Mogaba, Ochiba and Sindawe. Through the window behind Mogaba I saw water and hills. And crows. They squabbled over space on the window sill, though none would come inside. An albino turned an especially baleful pink eye my way.

I suppose we looked too hungry.

For one instant I saw that same room in another time, with Lady and some of the same faces around the same table. Mogaba was not among them. The window behind *them* opened on greyness.

One-Eye pinched my earlobe. "Kid, now ain't the time."

Mogaba watched intently.

"Less recovered than I thought," I explained. I wondered what the vision meant. And vision it was because it was too fully realized for imagination.

Mogaba settled into a chair opposite me. He pretended solicituousness, avoided his usual assertiveness.

"We face numerous grave problems, Standardbearer. They are out there and indifferent to whatever animosities we have developed amongst ourselves."

Goddamn! Was he going to turn reasonable on me?

"They will be there whether or not we want to believe the Lieutenant or Captain survived. We will have to face them because I do not expect to be relieved any time soon."

I would not argue with that.

"We would be better off had Lady not interfered this last time. We are isolated and trapped now because the Shadowmaster was forced to find a solution for managing two fronts."

I nodded. We *were* in a worse situation. On the other hand, we would not have yowling hordes piling over the wall every few nights anymore. Nor would Mogaba be flinging men hither and yon without regard for their lives, just trying to irritate the Southerners into doing something stupid.

Mogaba glanced out the window. We could see two Shadowlander patrols raising dust in the hills. "He can starve us out now."

"Maybe."

Mogaba grimaced but controlled his anger. "Yes?"

"For no rational reason I feel confident that our friends will break us out."

"I must confess that I remain a stranger to that sort of faith. Although I concede the importance of maintaining an optimistic aspect in front of the soldiers."

Was I going to argue? No. He was more right than I could be.

"So, Standardbearer, how do we survive a protracted siege when most of our food stores are exhausted? How do we recover the standard once we do get out of these straits?"

"I don't have any answers. Although I think the standard is in friendly hands already." Why was he interested? Almost every time we talked he asked something about the standard. Did he believe possessing it would legitimize him?

"How so?" He was surprised.

"The Widowmaker that was here the first time carried the real standard."

"You're sure?"

"I know it," I promised.

"Then share your thoughts about food."

"We could try fishing."

Wisecracking was not a good idea with Mogaba. It just made Mogaba angry.

"Ain't no joke," Goblin snapped. "That water comes down here from regular rivers. There's got to be fish."

The little shit wasn't as stupid as he acted sometimes.

Mogaba frowned. "Do we have anyone who knows anything about fishing?" he asked Sindawe.

"I doubt it." They meant among their Taglian soldiers, of course. Nar are warriors, back for a dozen generations. They do not sully themselves doing unheroic work.

I was negligent. I failed to mention that the Nyueng Bao came from country where fishing was, probably, a way of life.

"It's a thought," Mogaba told me. "And there is always baked crow." He glanced back at the window. "But most Taglians won't eat flesh."

"A conundrum," I agreed.

"I will not surrender."

No reply seemed adequate.

"You have no resources either?"

"Less than you," I lied. We still had a little rice from the catacombs. But not much. We were stretching ourselves every way possible, in accordance with hints recorded in the Annals. We did not look like famine victims. Not quite yet.

We looked, I noted, less well fed than did the Nar.

"Suggestions for reducing the number of unproductive mouths?"

"I'm letting my worn-out Taglians and any locals who want build rafts and go. But I don't let them take anything with them."

He controlled his anger again. "That does consume valuable timber. But it is another thought worth consideration."

I studied Sindawe and Ochiba. They remained jet statues. They were not even breathing, it seemed. They expressed no opinions.

Mogaba glared at me. "I feared this meeting would be this nonproductive. You haven't even thrown the Annals in my face."

"The Annals aren't magic. What they say about sieges is plain common-sense stuff: Be stubborn. Ration. Don't support the nonproductive. Control the spread of plague. Don't exhaust your enemy's patience if there is no hope of outlasting him. If surrender is inevitable do it while your enemy is still amenable to terms."

"This enemy never offered."

I wondered about that, although the Shadowmasters did have a tendency to think like gods.

"Thank you, Standardbearer. We will examine our options and keep you informed of what we mean to do."

Goblin and One-Eye helped me ease my chair back. They settled me into the litter. Mogaba said nothing else and I could think of nothing I wanted to tell him. The other Nar just stood there awkwardly and watched us go.

"What was that in aid of?" I asked once we were clear. "I expected yelling and threats."

"He wanted to pick your brains," Goblin said.

"While he made up his mind if he was going to kill you," One-Eye added cheerfully.

"Oh, that's real encouraging."

"He did decide, Murgen. And he didn't pick the option you want to hear. It's time to start being real careful."

We did make it home unharmed.

64

"Don't bother dragging me up there till we find out what Uncle wants." Goblin and One-Eye were at the foot of steps leading to the battlements. Doj was up top, looking down.

"I wasn't planning to carry your dead ass anywhere anyhow anymore," One-Eye told me. "Far as I'm concerned this exercise was for camouflage."

Uncle Doj started downward.

I stared at the wall. Tiny beads of sweat covered it, but that was because the stone was cooler than the air, not because water had begun seeping through from outside.

The Shadowmasters were good builders.

"Stone Soldier. You are well?"

"Not bad for a guy with the runs. Ready to dance on your grave, Stubby. We got business?"

"The Speaker wishes to see you. Your excursion was not successful?" He moved his head to indicate my trip outside.

"If you call spending two weeks as a guest of the Shadowmaster a success I tore them up, Uncle. Otherwise, all I did was get sick, lose some weight, then have barely enough sense left to run for it when some Taglians hit Shadowspinner's camp with a nuisance raid. That's all right. I can walk that far." Just don't let me fall down any rabbit holes.

I could walk to the Speaker's place easily but why give up the pretense of weakness if it might be useful?

Nothing changed with the Speaker's crew. Except that this time one smell was absent. I noticed that as soon as I stepped inside. I could not identify the missing odor, though.

The Speaker was ready. Hong Tray was in place. The beautiful one had tea brewing.

Ky Dam smiled. "Thai Dei ran ahead." He read my curiosity from my glance and flaring nostrils. "Danh has gone to his judgment. At last. A bleak season has ended for this house."

I could not help myself. I looked at the young woman. I found her looking at me. Her gaze shifted immediately, but not so fast that I did not feel guilty when I returned attention to the Speaker.

The old man missed nothing. Neither did he get excited about something best left ignored. He was wise, was Ky Dam.

I had come to respect that frail oldster a lot.

"The hard times have come, Standardbearer, and will lead to more terrible tomorrows." He reviewed my discussion with Mogaba well enough to convince me that someone had watched us.

"Why tell me this?"

"To support my claim when I tell you we spy on the black

men. After your departure they spoke only their native tongue until they sent messengers to the tribunes of the cohorts and other senior Taglians. They are to gather at suppertime."

"Sounds big."

The old man bowed slightly. "I would like you to see something for yourself. You know these men more certainly than do I. You can determine if my suspicions are well-founded."

"You want me to spy on that meeting?"

"Something of the sort." The old man did not tell me the whole story. Not then. He wanted me walking into it cold. "Doj will conduct you."

65

Doj conducted me. The way led through cellars as intricately connected as ours but less care had been used in the tunneling. The people who did this just wanted to be able to sneak away. They had had no intention of hiding. They must have been Jaicuri collaborators in Stormshadow's administration, acting for her. She would have wanted an emergency exit.

"I'm surprised at you," I told Uncle Doj. "I wouldn't think underground would occur to swamp people. I don't suppose there are a lot of tunnels in the delta."

"Not many." He smiled.

My guess is they found the escape route through sheer blind luck, maybe coupled with an informed suspicion about how Stormshadow's mind worked.

Getting into the citadel, then, was no problem, though it required some crawling. The architects had not been concerned with Stormshadow's dignity. It was tough for me. I was not yet back to my best.

We came to a small open space beneath a ladder. That rose straight up into infinity, so far as I could see by the light of one feeble candle. I had a feeling the candle was a luxury laid on for me, that the Nyueng Bao made this journey entirely in darkness.

I could not have endured that. I dislike enclosed places intensely despite having lived in them. Close places, darkness, recurring spells and visions were not a combination I wanted to tempt.

I did seem more stable lately, I reflected.

I set a hand and foot on the ladder.

Uncle Doj grabbed my wrist, shook his head.

"What? Isn't that the way to the council chamber?" My whisper rattled off like the scurry of mice.

"Not what the Speaker wants you to see." Doj used almost no air when he whispered. "Come."

There was no crawling now, just a lot of easing along sideways in an airspace almost too narrow for Uncle. His belly was going to ache from rubbing against stone.

I learned that there was a lot more to Stormshadow's citadel than I had seen in the little time I spent there these past few months. Down below there, beneath the surrounding plazas, were countless unsuspected storerooms and prison cells, armories and barracks rooms, cisterns and smithies. I whispered, "They have supplies down here to hold out for years." Meaning the Nar and their favorites, holed up inside the citadel. Stormshadow had laid in a great store against the evil day.

Mogaba had lied to me, just trying to find out how well off we Old Crew were.

Was that what the old man wanted me to know?

Was this why the Nyueng Bao had seemed to prosper while everyone else became gaunt? Were they nibbling at these stores like mice, taking just a little here and there so their predations would go unnoticed?

Uncle Doj beckoned. "Hurry."

Soon I began to hear a distant chanting. "We may not be in time, Bone Warrior. Hurry."

I didn't slug him mostly because the racket would have alerted the singing men.

I knew they were Nar before I saw a thing. I had heard the rhythms and style before, though not these particular lyrics. Always before, though, there had been joy in their work songs and celebrations. This song was cold and grim.

Uncle Doj left the candle, tugged my elbow. We continued to step sideways until, suddenly, we were in an ordinary passageway, not some tight, secret squeeze behind a wall. Nothing concealed the entrance to the hidden ways. That was just a shadowed corner unlikely to entice a closer look.

There was light out there, from candles in sconces widely spaced. The people in charge were frugal despite their wealth.

Uncle Doj placed a finger to his lips. We were near dangerous people who might detect us in an instant. He dropped to his knees and led me right into a large chamber where most of the Nar had gathered. Lighting was nonexistent except down where they were. Doj got behind a pillar. I squatted behind a low, dusty table just inside the doorway. I wished I was as dark as the Nar. My forehead must be shining like a little half moon.

This life hardens you. Too soon you have seen so much that when you encounter another something terrible you don't howl and run in circles, snapping at your tail. But most of us still appreciate horror if horror is there.

Horror was there.

There was an altar. Mogaba and Ochiba were involved in something ceremonial. Above the altar stood a small statue of dark stone, a four-armed woman dancing. I was too far away to make out details but I was pretty sure sure she had vampire fangs and six teats. She might be wearing a necklace of baby skulls. The Nar might give her another name but she was Kina. The worship offered by the Nar was not that described in the Jaicuri scriptures, though.

The Deceivers do not want to spill blood. That is why they are called Stranglers.

The Nar not only spilled blood on behalf of their goddess,

they drank it. And it looked like they had been doing so for some time down there. Drained corpses hung to one side. Their latest sacrifice, a hapless Jaicuri, got hoisted up with those soon after I arrived.

The Nar were practical in their religion. After the grim ceremony ended they began butchering one of the bodies.

I got down and crawled out of there. I did not give one rat's ass what Uncle Doj thought.

I have seen a lot with the Company, including tortures and cruelties almost beyond comprehension and inhumanities I do not have the capacity to fathom, but never had I encountered socially-sanctioned cannibalism.

I did not puke or boil over in outrage. That would be silly. I just put distance between me and that till I could speak without worrying about who might overhear. "I have seen enough. Let's get out of here."

Uncle Doj responded with a thin smile and lifted eyebrow.

"I have to relay this. I have to write it down. We may not survive this siege. They will. Word of what they are has to survive, too." He watched me closely. Was he wondering if the rest of us also enjoyed the occasional long-pig roast as well?

Probably.

This sort of thing might go some toward explaining our ambiguous reception in these parts.

Mogaba could not read. If it did not occur to him that the dark side of the Nar was no secret anymore I could leave word in my Annals, to be salvaged by Lady or the Old Man.

"They are all down there," Uncle said. "So we will return by a swifter path." By which he meant we would stroll through regular passageways just like we belonged there.

"What's that noise?" I asked.

Uncle gestured for silence. We stole forward.

We discovered a group of Taglian soldiers bricking up a sallyport we could have used to leave. Why were they doing that? That door could not be broken open from the outside. It still had Stormshadow's spells protecting it.

Uncle pulled me back, headed another direction. Obviously, he knew the citadel quite well. And I had no difficulty imgaining him roaming around in there all the time, just for the hell of it. He seemed like that kind of guy.

66

Y ou look like somebody ate your favorite puppy," Goblin told me. Cracks like that could be heard all the time now that there were no more dogs. There were just two sources of meat left. The Nar exploited both. We restricted ourselves to stupid crows.

I told Goblin and One-Eye what I had seen. Uncle Doj stood behind me, quietly disgruntled because I wanted to see my own people before I visited the Speaker. I was barely halfway through it when One-Eye interrupted. "You got to tell the whole Company this one, Kid." For once he was as serious as a spear through the gut.

And for once Goblin agreed with One-Eye without any big groan and moan about the unfairness of it all. "You need to get this word out exactly the way you want it known to everybody. There's going to be a lot of talk. You don't want anybody building it up worse than it is when they pass it along."

"Get them together, then. While I'm waiting I'm going to skim those Jaicuri books. There may be something else I need to tell them."

"May I join you?" Uncle Doj asked.

"No. Go tell the old man that I'll be there as soon as I can. This is family."

"As you will." He said something to Thai Dei, stalked away.

Bucket interrupted my reading. "Got them together, Murgen. All but Clete. He's off somewhere whoring and even his brothers don't know where to find him."

"All right."

"It something bad? You got that look."

"Yeah."

"It can get worse than it already is?"

"You're going to hear all about it in just a little bit."

In five minutes I got up in front of sixty men and told my tale, marvelling as I did that a band so frail and few could be so feared. More, I marvelled that there were so many of us when, hardly more than two years ago, there were just seven of us pretending to be the Black Company.

"You guys want to keep it down until I'm done?" The news had them excited in a grim way. "Listen up. That is the word. They're making human sacrifices and eating the corpses. But that ain't the whole story. Ever since they joined us at Gea-Xle they've been hinting and even saying right out that us northern guys are heretics. That means they think the whole Company used to do things their way."

That started everybody talking and yelling.

I pounded a mason's hammer on a block of wood. "Shut up, you morons! It *ain't* the way the Company ever was. The Nar never kept any Annals. They would know that if they had. But they can't even read."

I could not be absolutely sure that human sacrifice was never a Company rite. We were missing several early volumes of the Annals and I now suspected strongly that our earliest forebrethren did follow a dark and hungry god with breath so foul and cruel that even oral histories were enough to keep the native people terrified.

Most of the guys did not care about the implications. They were just angry because the Nar were going to make life harder for them.

I told them, "This is one more thing to make trouble between us and them. I want you all to realize that we might have to fight them before we get out of here.

"Tonight I'm bringing back some traditional business that

we have let slide since Croaker got to be Captain. We are going to have regular readings from the Annals so you all know what you have become part of. This first reading is from the Book of Kette, this part probably set down by the Annalist Agrip when the Company was in service to the Paingod of Cho'n Delor." Our forebrethren endured a long and bitter siege then, though there had been a lot more of them to suffer. Additionally, I planned readings from books Croaker recorded on the Plain of Fear, when the Company lived underground for so long.

I dismissed the men to supper. "One-Eye. No more groaning when I announce a reading. All right? These guys didn't live through that stuff."

"Cho'n Delor was way before my time, too."

"Then you need to hear about it."

"Kid, I been hearing about it for two hundred years. Every damned Annalist that ever was wallowed in the horrors of Cho'n Delor. I wish I could get my hands on those guys who did the Book of Kette. You know Kette wasn't even the Annalist? He was the . . ."

"Goblin. Grab Otto and Hagop. I want a little confab with the oldest Old Crew."

We five put our heads together, conjured a little something for the meanness. Once we had a scheme I said, "I'll see what the Speaker thinks."

67

Ky Dam listened patiently, as an adult will to a bright child with an ingenious but impractical idea. He told me, "You are aware this could spark fighting?"

"Sure. But that's inevitable. Doj says Mogaba decided that at our meeting. Goblin and One-Eye agree." So did Hagop and Otto. None of us favored a get-along effort. "There are more of

us than there are Nar." But their Taglians way outnumbered ours
and there was no way to guess how the Taglians with either
group would jump.

The old man turned to Hong Tray. A quizzical expression
accentuated the lines at the corners of his eyes.

Ky Sahra knelt beside me, presenting tea. This was a step
beyond anything previous. She met my wondering gaze. I don't
think I slobbered.

Hong Tray observed without reaction. That made her far
calmer than I was. She focused on her husband, nodded. He
said, "There will be fighting. Soon. The Jaicuri will revolt."

That was not what I wanted to hear. I asked, "Will they
bother your people or mine?" I should not have shoved in. I
apologized immediately.

Ky Sahra poured more tea for me, before even she served her
grandparents.

Ky Gota manifested like a demon conjured for its serrated
tongue. She barked at her daughter in a harsh, lilting gale.

The old man looked up, said one word sharply. Hong Tray
supported him with a complete sentence in what I would have
to call a sharp whisper. It seemed she could speak no other way.

Ky Gota withdrew. There were well-defined limits and absolute hierarchy inside the Ky family.

I glanced at the beautiful woman. She met my eye again,
rocked back and rose. Flushing.

Was something going on? They would not try to manipulate me, would they?

It would not work. No woman, not even this woman, was
that special. And Ky Dam had seen enough of me to guess that
about me.

If he wanted to manipulate me he would have better luck
trading me the straight poop on why the hell everybody pissed
blue when the Company got mentioned.

He and the old woman batted whispers back and forth in
flurries. Suddenly, he told me, "We will join you in this enter-
prise, Standardbearer. Provisionally. Hong believes that fight-

ing between the Jaicuri and the soldiers of the black men is imminent. It will be fierce but might not touch the rest of us. That would provide sufficient distraction. But I must insist that Doj has the option to end it if it risks calling unfriendly attention to our people."

"Excellent. Of course. Done. Though I would have tried it without you."

Ky Dam permitted himself a small smile, either at my enthusiasm or at the prospect of adding a little more misery to Mogaba's life.

After dark, assuming the riots got started, we were going to steal Mogaba's food stores.

68

It started like a well-rehearsed play where Mogaba's characters were desperate to please their audience. The rioting, that is. Uncle Doj and I formed work parties to take advantage. We got into the storage chambers without challenge, ten Old Crew and ten Nyueng Bao. We started dragging off sacks of rice and flour, sugar and beans. The riots were nasty from the start. They swamped the whole southern half of Dejagore. Every man Mogaba controlled was out there helping crush the rebellion. And every Jaicuri man and boy seemed to want to get at the Nar, even if they had to exterminate the whole First Legion to reach them.

My people went on the alert, established in strong positions, long before nightfall. Likewise the Nyueng Bao, who had no immediate trouble. We ambushed one mob. A shower of missiles from front, sides, and above swiftly changed their minds.

Mogaba's men had more problems. They were not ready. Worse, they were scattered, often in isolated work parties and patrols.

For a while everybody joked and cracked wise and speculated on Mogaba's first words after the fighting ended and he found his cellars plundered.

I ran into Bucket my second trip back. "Beans," I told him, dropping a huge sack. "The change of diet will do us good."

"It's real bloody out there this time, Murgen. Mogaba has asked for support twice. We told him we couldn't find you."

"Well, keep on not being able. Unless it looks like we would end up worse off if we didn't help."

"That's not likely. He has most of the weapons. His men have been throwing people off the wall by the hundreds, just anybody, whether or not they're rebelling, men, women and children."

"That's Mogaba's way. What about those fires?" There were a few. Whenever there is disorder somebody starts burning things down.

"They're burning themselves out."

"Everything is going fine, then. But keep an eye out."

I went back to my looting happy as the proverbial clam. This might be the end of Mogaba as a royal pain in the ass.

Uncle Doj caught me in the storage chamber later. "Some Taglian soldiers are abandoning their posts for the safety of the citadel. If we continue this raiding we will get caught."

"Yeah. If we don't get spotted Mogaba will blame it on natives who knew about the passageways." This raid was going to cost us our opportunity to spy on any more staff meetings.

It was worth it.

Would I feel the same way tomorrow, when Mogaba began looking for his stores? When I had a full belly?

"There is a small problem, Standardbearer," Uncle Doj said a while later. Each of us staggered under a last sack of rice. We were the last brigands out.

"What's that?"

"News of our success is sure to leak."

"Why? Only a few people know. It's in all their interests to stay clammed."

"Someone talked about what I showed you earlier."

"Huh?"

"The dark ceremonies. Someone talked. The rumors sparked tonight's riots."

"I don't believe that. They were too organized."

"There was an organized cadre, naturally, but this uprising was more widespread. It is also out of control."

"Whatever you say." He had spent his evening with me. He had had no chance to observe any riots.

Before he could respond Thai Dei popped out of the darkness. He gobbled away, becoming too animated for the space. If he killed my candle I was going to choke him. As soon as I found him. "What's happening?"

"The black men are trying to break open the north gate and flood the city."

"They're what?" That would take care of the riots, all right. But not even Mogaba would go that far. Would he?

Uncle Doj and I did our best to run carrying sacks of rice. I bet we looked silly.

69

Otto. Hagop. One-Eye. Goblin. Geek. Freak. Bucket and Candles. You guys come with me. The al-Khul company will help us. Wheezer went to get them. We'll go straight along the battlements. If the Nar get in the way we trample them. If they fight us, we kill them. That understood?"

Not even Goblin or One-Eye tried to lawyer. We were some of the people Mogaba meant to drown.

The Taglians arrived. They were Vehdna by religion and the best Taglians attached to the Company. They were reliable and almost friendly. Of six hundred who had come south from Taglios months ago only about sixty were left.

I explained what was happening, what I wanted to do about it and how they could help. They would overrun anyone trying to open the gate after Goblin and One-Eye softened them up. "Don't hurt anybody unless they just plain force you."

"Why not?" Candles demanded. "They're trying to hurt us."

"Mogaba is. These guys are just following orders. I'll bet you we don't find any Nar there when we get there. And I'll bet you that if they open the gate they get hurt as bad as anybody else. Mogaba doesn't need them anymore."

"Let's just do it," Goblin groused. "Or go back and catch a few beers."

I moved them out.

Maybe my blackouts gave me the gift of prophecy. There were no Nar at the North Gate. The fighting was so brief and desultory it almost did not take place. The Taglians working there fled. Damn! Mogaba would find out who foiled his latest nastiness. I told One-Eye, "This will mean no more pretending we're buddies."

"Yeah. Show me how to sneak into the citadel. I'll put a sleep spell on him, then leave pieces of him all over his crazy temple."

That did not sound like a bad idea.

We had no opportunity to implement it.

Somebody yelled up at me. I peered down into the gloom. It was Uncle Doj. I had not included any Nyueng Bao in this. I had not seen any need to put them onto Mogaba's bad side, too.

"What?"

He shouted, "This was a diversion! The real flooding will start at . . ."

"Oh, shit! Yeah." Mogaba did know me well enough to anticipate that I might interfere. "Come on!" I snapped. "Everyone!" I hustled down to the street. "Where?" I demanded of Doj.

"East Gate."

Would Mogaba also anticipate me crossing town to spoil his game, amidst the Jaicuri uprising?

He might. He might hope my crew would get trapped and

'overrun, or badly cut up. There was no guessing what he thought anymore. He was crazy.

One-Eye and Goblin eased us past bands of both Jaicuri and Taglians. We skirmished with the Jaicuri twice, our numbers and sorcery telling quickly. The light of scattered fires set scary shadows dancing everywhere.

What a time for the Shadowmaster to send his monsters out to play.

We encountered barricades erected to protect the soldiers trying to open the gate. This time we faced Nar as well as Taglians. A lot of shouting went back and forth. Some of their Gunni Taglians tried to run away when our Vehdna Taglians convinced them that Mogaba was trying to drown everybody. The Nar cut down several would-be deserters. I told Goblin and One-Eye, "You break up whatever they're doing to open the gate. The rest of you, let's chase them off. Go for the Nar first."

An instant later an arrow found the eye of a Nar named Endibo. Another of the Nar speared the Geek, an incredibly handsome youngster who joined the Company while we were crossing the savannah north of Gea-Xle, several years earlier. One-Eye hung the uncomplimentary name on him. He wore it with pride, refusing to be called anything else.

For the first time in its history, insofar as I was aware, Company brother slew sworn brother in willful combat.

Geek's blood brother Freak slew the Nar responsible for Geek's death but I never learned the Nar's name so I cannot remember him here.

Most of the First Legion Taglians took off then. Many of the al-Khul soldiers did not want to fight, either, although those other Taglians were Gunni. Still, quickly, a genuine small battle had friend hacking at supposed friend.

I happened to glance back and notice that armed Jaicuri had begun to gather to watch. Uncle Doj faced them alone, poised in an odd but apparently relaxed ready stance, long sword vertical.

"Oh, shit!" Goblin shrieked. "Gods damn it! Look out!"

"What?"

"We're too late. It's going to go."

Something began to grind and groan like the hinges of the world breaking loose. The masonry blocking the gateway bulged inward.

The fighting stopped fast. Everybody faced the gate.

A sudden spear of water shot through the bulge.

Every man there took off, Nar and Black Company, Gunni and Vehdna Taglian, Jaicuri and lone Nyueng Bao running side by side, splitting up, heading whatever direction felt safest but everybody always getting away from that gate.

The masonry gave one final, mighty groan. The water roared triumphantly and charged inside.

70

The water thundered through the gate but there was no evidence of it yet where I stood. I was in a good mood, considering. While passing the citadel I saw the Nar trying to shuffle their own kind inside without admitting any Taglians. I chuckled. Mogaba was going to bust a vein when he found the water coming in through his cellars.

I now understood why those soldiers had been bricking up. The flood was no spur of the moment plan. Mogaba must have nurtured the idea from the moment that Shadowspinner had used water to isolate Dejagore.

As we parted I told Uncle Doj, "Swim over and see me sometime." Fifteen minutes later I was discussing waterproofing. Our measures had begun the day we started our warrens but not in anticipation of anything like this. Enemies employing smoke and fire had been our real concern.

"Longo, you guys explored every part of those catacombs? They aren't open anywhere?" I was surprised that Stormshadow had not broken into them when she was building the citadel. Maybe she got her location advice from knowledgeable locals.

"I didn't see anything. There were plastered good way back when because they were below the level of the plain. But if you put seventy feet of water out there and thirty in the streets sooner or later it will find a way in. The best we can do really is fight a holding action."

"How about just sealing them off?"

"We could try. But I wouldn't bother until flooding became a threat. We close them off, spring a leak up here, we got no place for the water to drain."

I shrugged. "Is everything that could be damaged up high?" The guys started preparing for the worst back when the plain started flooding. We were not weighed down with a lot of possessions.

"We're all right. We can hold out for a long time yet. We might want to beef up our fortifications a little, though."

"Do what you can." Longo and his brothers always saw a little more that could be done.

71

Mogaba counterattacked while the water was still just ankle deep and the rest of the city was just starting to panic. He used all his Taglians and encouraged cruel behavior. The slaughter was terrible.

I may never discover the truth about the attack on the Nyueng Bao. It has been said that the Taglian tribune Pal Subhir misunderstood his orders. Others, like me, believe Mogaba was responsible, maybe because he suspected the Nyueng Bao of looting his stores.

I know he knew some had been plundered. He found out right away because he sent soldiers down to see if any water was getting inside. By questioning a few Jaicuri prisoners he discovered that no locals were crowing about snatching a ton of food. Too, somebody in my outfit might have shot off his mouth again.

Whatever, Pal Subhir's cohort, with transfer replacements to bring it to full strength, attacked the Nyueng Bao. The tribune cannot testify. He died early. In fact, a lot of Taglians died during the attack. But reinforcements kept turning up, which is why I believe Mogaba engineered the massacre.

I knew nothing about it at first. I had located no listening posts outside our perimeter. I had no way of making sure my people would be secure out there. And where we bordered the Nyueng Bao community there was no reason to doubt that we would receive ample warning.

Thai Dei was, as always, nearby. I had gone to the top of an enfilading tower to stare at the nighted hills and brood. Would help ever come? Lately no news at all came in from outside.

Plenty of people wanted to leave. I could hear some of them out there now, willing to take their chances with the Shadowmaster. Fickle folk. A little hunger and stress and they forgot all about liberty.

"What is that?" Thai Dei astonished me by asking a whole question. I was amazed. I looked where he pointed.

"Looks like a fire."

"That is near grandfather's house. I must go."

More curious than suspicious, I said, "I'll go with you."

He started to argue, shrugged, told me. "Do not suffer any spells. I cannot care for you."

So the Nyueng Bao knew about my blackouts. And apparently suspected they were epileptic. Interesting.

Thai Dei surely learned plenty just standing around with his ears flapping and his jaw tight shut. My guys hardly noticed him anymore.

Nowhere was the water yet deeper than halfway to my knees. But it grabbed my feet when I tried to run. And Thai Dei was in a hurry. He was sure something was wrong. And he was correct.

We ran through that alley where I had stumbled before and had plunged into hell. For a second I thought I had run from Dejagore into another nightmare.

Taglian soldiers were dragging Nyueng Bao women and children and old people out of the buildings and throwing them to soldiers in the street. Those soldiers hacked and slashed. Their faces were distorted with the horror of their actions but they were out of control, far past the point where they could stop. The flicker of firelight made everything seem more hellish and surreal.

I had seen this before. I had seen my own brothers this way, a few times, back in the north. The blood smell takes control and kills the mind and deadens the soul and there is nothing human left.

Thai Dei howled a tortured cry and flung himself toward the building the Ky family occupied, sword wheeling overhead. The place showed no obvious signs of having been invaded. I followed him, my own blade bare, unsure why, though I thought fleetingly of the woman Sahra. Probably my actions were as thoughtless as those of the Taglians.

Taglians got in our way. Thai Dei engaged in some sort of bobbing, weaving dance. Two soldiers fell, their throats spurting. I beat another around with my sword, leaving him a collection of bruises and a lesson about dueling a guy a foot taller and fifty pounds heavier.

Then there were Taglians everywhere, most paying no attention to us. I did not have much trouble defending myself. Those people were smaller and weaker and had a much shorter reach. And what I managed by brute power Thai Dei accomplished through maneuver. Hardly anyone was interested in us by the time we reached the Speaker's door.

I had guessed wrong before. Five or six Taglians had gotten inside. They just were not going to leave again. Not walking.

Thai Dei barked something in Nyueng Bao. A voice replied. I took a wild swing at one last particularly stupid Taglian, spending the rest of the edge of my blade on his helmet. Then I shoved the door shut and barred it. And looked around for something to pile against it. Unfortunately, the Kys were so poor their best furniture consisted of ragged reed mats.

A lamp's flame rose, then another and another. For the first time I saw the entire room the Kys occupied. I saw the mauled corpses of several invaders. They had become focused on exploiting the beautiful woman before they finished everyone else.

Ky Gota was still mutilating the Taglian corpses.

But not all the corpses were Taglian. Not even the majority were Taglian. Only a small percentage were Taglian.

Sahra was holding her children to her chest but neither would ever know fear again. Sahra's eyes were empty.

Thai Dei made a sound like a kitten's whimper. He threw himself onto a woman. The woman lay face downward upon two little ones she had attempted to shield with her body. Her effort had not been in vain. The youngest, less than a year old, was crying.

No Taglians seemed inclined to try the door. I dropped to my knees where I had sat talking to the Speaker so often. It appeared he and Hong Tray had watched death arrive and had engaged it in their places of honor. The old man was stretched out with his head and shoulders in Hong Tray's lap but his lower body remained almost as it had been when he was seated. His wife slumped forward over him.

The racket outside picked up. "Thai Dei!" I yelled. "Get your ass pulled together, man."

What? The old woman was still breathing, making a raspy, bubbly sound. Gently, I lifted her.

She was alive and even aware. Her eyes unglazed. She seemed unsurprised to see me. She smiled. She managed to whisper despite the blood in her throat. "Don't waste time on me. Take Sahra. Take the children." Her wound was a sword thrust that had gone in outside her right breast and downward through her lung. At her age it was a miracle she had lived this long.

She smiled again, whispered, "Be good to her, Standard-bearer."

"I will," I promised, not understanding what she meant.

Hong Tray managed a wink and a wince of pain. She leaned forward onto Ky Dam again.

The racket outside increased again. "Thai Dei!" I leapt over the bodies, flung a foot that glanced off Thai Dei's behind. "If you don't get your ass up and get organized we're not going to help anybody." I spotted a couple more kids cowering in the back. One of them had lighted the lamps. Other than Sahra and her mother no adults appeared to have survived. "Sahra!" I snapped. "Get up!" I slapped her. "Round up those kids back there." They were too terrified to trust me even if they knew me. I was still an outsider.

A little yelling was all Thai Dei and his sister needed. Their universe suddenly regained structure and direction, though they could not see its sense. They just needed somebody to get them started.

We found only one more living child and no more surviving adults.

"Thai Dei. Can you keep these kids together if we make a run for the alley?" The Taglians would cease to be a problem if we made it that far. In there one man could hold off a horde till help arrived.

He shook his head. "They are too frightened and too badly hurt."

I was afraid of that. "Then we'll carry them. Can you settle your mother down? She'll need to help. Sahra. Take the baby. I'll carry the girl. On my back. I want my hands free. Tell her to hang on tight but to keep her hands out of my face. If she don't think she can do that let me know now. We'll tie her wrists together."

Sahra nodded. She was past her hysteria. She knelt beside Hong Tray, held the old woman for a moment, then removed her jade bracelet. With a deep sigh and evident reluctance, she slipped the bracelet onto her own left wrist. Then she turned to Ky Gota and began trying to calm her.

Thai Dei talked to the children, translating my my instructions. I realized that Sahra never spoke at all, not even in a whisper.

The girl I was going to carry was about six years old. And she did not want to go.

"Tie her on, then, damn it!" I snapped. I had begun to shake. I did not know how much longer I would retain full control. "We're running out of time."

Only the baby was unhurt. A boy of about four looked like he would not make it. He for sure would not if I did not get him to One-Eye in a hurry.

Water splashed and a man shrieked right outside. A body slammed against the door, which creaked and gave a little. Sahra swatted the girl to calm her, fitted her onto my back. I asked, "How about your mother?"

Never mind. The Troll was with us now. She had a two-year-old of indeterminate sex riding her left hip and the business end of a broken spear clutched in her right hand. She was ready for Taglians.

Getting ready actually took less time than it requires to tell it.

Sahra carried the baby. Thai Dei tied the wounded boy onto his back, kept his sword in hand. He and I went to the door. I peeked through cracks between the mutilated timbers. A Taglian soldier lurched past outside. I asked, "You first? Or me? One to lead, one as rearguard."

"Me. From this day forward."

What?

"Back!" I snapped. But he glimpsed the hurtling shape at the same time. He slid to the right as I moved to the left of the doorway. We were out of the way when the door blew inward. We jumped at the intruder, recognized him barely in time.

"Uncle Doj?"

He was a lucky man. The weight of the children we carried

had slowed us just enough to allow us time to see who had blown in.

"Go," I told Thai Dei. We did not need to hold a conference.

Thai Dei encountered a pair of Taglians immediately. I jumped out and drove one away. Ky Gota wobbled out behind us. She stuck the tip of her spearhead into the throat of the nearest Taglian. Then she settled the child more comfortably on her hip, turned on the other soldier.

A white crow swooped past, laughing like a troop of monkeys.

The surviving Taglian was not a foolish young man. He headed for the nearest gang of his countrymen.

"Go! Go!" I barked at Thai Dei. "Gota. Sahra. Follow Thai Dei. Uncle! Where are you? We're gonna leave your ass here."

Uncle Doj stepped outside as the Taglian pointed us out to his comrades. "Take the child away, Standardbearer. Ash Wand will be your shield."

He put on an amazing display—though I glimpsed only a few furious moments. That funny little wide man took on the whole mob of Taglians and killed six of them in about as many seconds. The rest took off.

Then we splashed into the alley. We reached safety moments later. In minutes One-Eye was working on the wounded children, albeit not cheerfully. And I was deploying some of the Old Crew, with Goblin, for a limited counterattack.

72

That night was the final watershed. There was never any pretense of friendship with Mogaba again. I had no doubts myself that he would have come after us if the "mistaken" attack on the Nyueng Bao had been a success.

Fighting continued until the water got too deep.

Despite insistence by One-Eye and others that protecting the Nyueng Bao was not our mission I did salvage a third of the pilgrims, about six hundred people. The cost of the attack to Mogaba was bitter. The following morning most of the remaining Taglians found themselves in positions where they had to commit for or against Mogaba.

The Taglians who had been with us from the beginning stuck with us. So did those who had deserted to join us. More came over from Mogaba's side now but not a tenth as many as I expected. Tell the truth, I was disappointed. But Mogaba could make a hell of a speech to the troops when he wanted.

"It's that old-time curse again," Goblin told me. "Even now they're more afraid of yesterday than they are of now."

And the water kept rising.

I took the Nyueng Bao down into our warrens. Uncle Doj was amazed. "We never suspected."

"Good. Then neither do our enemies, whose brilliance is eclipsed by yours." I brought the Old Crew inside, too. We packed people in as comfortably as we could. The warrens were quite spacious for sixty men. Adding six hundred Nyueng Bao did cramp things some.

We had to learn to recognize one another, too. My men had been trained to strike instantly at any unfamiliar face encountered underground.

I went back outside after darkness fell. Thai Dei and Uncle Doj dogged me. I assembled the Taglian officers who had attached themselves to the Old Crew. I told them, "I believe that we have done all we can here. I believe it is time to begin evacuating everyone who wants to get out of this hellhole." I did not know why but was convinced that not much work would be required to evade or outwit the Shadowlander pickets ashore. "I will send one of my wizards to cover you."

They did not buy it. One captain wondered aloud if I intended to drive them into slavery so I could make it easier to feed my own men.

I had not thought this through, had not considered possible difficulties. I had forgotten that many of these men had attached themselves to us only because they believed that that was their best shot at staying alive. "Never mind. If you guys want to stay and die with us we'll be happy to have you. I was just trying to release you from your soldier's oaths so you would have *some* chance."

After dark, too, we let the Nyueng Bao men go back home to look for salvage and survivors and stores. They did not find much. Mogaba's soldiers had been thorough in their own search and the water had risen to cover everything.

Mogaba's men, using makeshift boats and rafts, began attacking Jaicuri-occupied buildings one by one, harvesting stores forced out of hiding by the rising water.

Mogaba had drowned his own supplies.

73

When I was sure nobody would notice I pulled all my brothers inside. We bolted up and locked up and left Dejagore to its misery. We took the Nyueng Bao survivors with us. Excepting a few men who kept watch from lookouts accessible only from inside we withdrew into the deepest, most hidden parts of the warrens, behind booby traps and secret doors and a web of confusion spells scattered by Goblin and One-Eye, who left only the occasional flicker of a doppelganger to mark our passing.

I started out sharing my quarters with eight guests. After just a few hours I told Uncle Doj, "Let's you and me take a walk."

With all those Nyueng Bao down there the air was stuffy and getting riper fast. Light was provided by candles so scattered you could get lost trekking from one to the next.

Uncle Doj was close to being spooked. "I hate it, too," I told him. "It keeps me riding the edge of a scream. But we'll manage. We lived this way for years once."

"No one can live like this. Not for long."

"The Company did, though. It was a terrible place. It was called the Plain of Fear, with good reason. It was filled with weird creatures and every one of them would kill you in a blink. We were hunted constantly by armies led by wizards way worse than Shadowspinner. But we gutted it out. And we came through it. Right here in these tunnels you have five survivors who can tell you about it."

The light was too bad to read him, though that was difficult in broad daylight. I told him, "I'm going to go crazy if all of you stay with me. I need room. Nobody can get around without stepping on somebody right now."

"I understand. But I do not know how to help."

"We have empty rooms. Thai Dei and his baby can have one. You could. Sahra could share one with her mother."

He smiled. "You are open and honest but pay too little attention to Nyueng Bao ways. Many things happened the night you helped Thai Dei rescue this family."

I snorted. "Some rescue."

"You saved all who could be saved."

"What a good boy am I."

"You had neither an obligation nor any cause of honor." In actuality he used honor and obligation in lieu of Nyueng Bao concepts of similar but not identical meaning which include overtones of free-will participation in a divine machination.

"I did what seemed like the right thing."

"Indeed. Without any appeal or obligation. Which caused your current predicament."

"I must be missing something."

"Because you are not Nyueng Bao. Thai Dei will not leave you now. He is the oldest male. He owes you six lives. His baby will not leave him. Sahra will not leave because she must remain under her brother's protection until she marries. And, as you can see, she may be a while getting through the horror. In this city, upon this pilgrimage she never wanted to make, she has lost everything that ever meant anything to her. Except her mother."

"A man might almost think the gods had it in for her," I said, then hoped that did not sound too much like a wisecrack.

"One might. Standardbearer, the only good thing she recalls about that hellnight is you. She will cling to you the way a desperate swimmer will cling to a rock in a rushing stream."

It was time to be careful. A big part of me wished her clinging was more than metaphorical. "How about Ky Gota and those other kids?"

"The children can be adopted into the families of their mothers. Gota, surely, can move." Doj continued muttering under his breath, which was uncharacteristic. Sounded like something about wanting to move her a couple thousand miles. "Though she will not take it well."

"Don't tell me you're less than enchanted with Ky Gota too?"

"No one is enchanted with that ill-tempered lizard."

"And I once thought that you two were married."

He stopped cold, stunned. "You're mad!"

"I changed my mind, didn't I?"

"Hong Tray, old witch, what hast thou wished upon me?"

"What?"

"Talking to myself, Standardbearer. Engaging in the debate I cannot lose. That woman, Hong Tray, my mother's cousin, was a witch. She could see into the future sometimes and if what she saw failed to please her she wanted it changed. And she had some strange ideas about that."

"I trust you know what you're talking about."

He did not get it. "Not entirely. The witch toyed with all our destinies but never explained. Perhaps she was blind to her own fate."

I let myself be distracted. "What will your people do now?"

"We will survive, Standardbearer. Like you Soldiers of Darkness, that is what we do."

"If you really think you owe me for stumbling in there with Thai Dei, tell me what that means. Soldiers of Darkness. Stone Soldier. Bone Warrior. What do they mean?"

"One might almost accept your protestations."

"Look at it this way. If I do know what you're talking about you have nothing to lose by telling me what I already know."

In that light it was hard to tell but I believe Uncle Doj smiled again. For the second time in one day. "Clever," he said. And did not explain a thing.

74

Uncle Doj relieved me of most of my guests. I ended up sharing quarters with Thai Dei and his son To Tan, plus Sahra. Sahra helped with the baby and struggled to put together meals, though the Company kitchen could serve everyone in the warrens. She needed to stay busy. Thai Dei followed me almost everywhere. Both he and Sahra were lethargic and uncommunicative and added up to about half a human being between them.

I began to worry. They belonged to a hardy people accustomed to surviving cruel disasters. They should show some signs of recovery.

I assembled the brains of the outfit: Cletus, Loftus, Longinus, Goblin and One-Eye, Otto and Hagop. "I got some questions, troops."

"He got to be here?" Goblin meant Thai Dei.

"He's all right. Ignore him."

"What kind of questions?" One-Eye demanded.

"So far we haven't had any major health problems in the Company. But there's cholera and typhoid out there, not to mention plenty of the old-fashioned drizzling shits. We all right?"

Goblin muttered something and passed gas loudly.

"Barbarian," One-Eye sneered. "We're all right because we follow Croaker's health rules like they was religious laws. Only we can't make the rules stick much longer. We're almost out of fuel. And these Nyueng Bao. They don't like to bother boiling water and keeping clean and not shitting where they live. We got them going along right now but it ain't going to last."

"It's been overcast and nasty for a few days, I hear. Are we collecting any rainwater?"

"Plenty for us," Loftus told me. "But not enough for us and them, let alone getting any put back into the cisterns."

"I was afraid of that. About the fuel, I mean. You guys know any way to fix rice or beans so you can digest them without cooking them?"

Nobody knew. Longinus suggested, "Maybe soaking them a long time in water might help. My mother did that."

"Damn. I really want us to get through this. But how?"

Goblin seemed to develop a small secret smile at that. like he had a definite idea. He exchanged glances with One-Eye.

"You guys got something?"

"Not yet," Goblin told me. "There's an experiment we still have to try."

"Get on with it."

"After the meeting. We need you to help."

"Wonderful. All right. Can anyone tell me what the rest of the city thinks about our disappearance?"

Hagop coughed, clearing his throat. He did not say much ordinarily so everybody paused to listen. "I been doing watches in the lookouts. Sometimes you can hear talk. I don't think we done our reputation any good. Also, I don't think we fooled anybody. They don't talk about us much but nobody figures we just cut out. They think we found some way to dig a hole and fill it up with wine, women and food and pulled it in after us and we ain't coming back out again till the rest of them are good and dead."

"Guys, I tried to get the wine, women and banquets but all I could come up with was the hole."

Out of nowhere, Otto said, "The water's going down."

"What?"

"It is, Murgen. It's down five feet already."

"Would flooding the city make that much difference? No? Why's that?"

Goblin and One-Eye exchanged significant looks.

"What?" I demanded.

"After we do our experiment."

"All right. The rest of you guys. You know the problems. Go see if there's anything we can do about them."

75

Talk to me," I told the runt wizards.

Goblin said, "We think something was done to you when you were out there." He jerked his head shoreward.

"What? Get serious! I . . ."

"We are. You were gone a long time. And you changed. How many disappearing spells have you had since you got back?"

I gave it an honest think. "Only one. Maybe. When I was kidnapped. I don't remember anything about it. I'm sure they drugged me. I was drinking tea with the Speaker, then I was in that street where you found me. I have no idea how I got there. I have vague recollections of smelling smoke and going out a door which put me somewhere that I did not expect to be when I got to the other side. I vaguely remember thinking something about being in the house of pain."

"They tortured you."

"They did." I still had the nicks and bruises to prove it. I had no idea what I might have been asked, if anything. I did suspect that Sindhu's pals were behind my abduction and the attempt on Mogaba.

If so, their life sure took an unpleasant turn when the Black Company found them.

"We've been watching you," Goblin said. "And you have been behaving pretty strange sometimes. What we want to do is put you to sleep and see if we can't reach the part of you that was there when things happened."

"I don't get you."

"You don't have to. You just have to cooperate."

"You're sure?"

"We're sure."

He did not sound sure.

I awakened on my own pallet. Not refreshed. Someone was wiping my hot face with a cold, wet cloth. I opened my eyes. In the light of one tiny candle Sahra looked more lovely than ever. She looked better than imagination. She continued to wipe my face.

I had another hangover-type headache. What had they done? I ought at least to get the enjoyment that came before the pain.

To Tan began to fuss. He slept in a basket of evil-smelling rags beneath my writing table. I reached over and took his hand. He stopped crying, content to have human contact. He did not cry for his mother much anymore.

I raised my other hand to take Sahra's. She pushed it back gently. She never spoke. I never did hear her speak, not even to her own children.

I looked around. Thai Dei was gone. Anymore it seemed I had a better chance of shaking my shadow. Thai Dei was there even in the dark.

I started to sit up. Sahra held me down with two fingers. I was too weak to do anything. And my head felt like it doubled in size just rising that foot.

Sahra offered me a hand-carved wooden cup filled with something that smelled so foul my eyes watered. Nyueng Bao swamp medicine. I drank. It tasted worse than it smelled.

She continued to mop my face. I shivered and shook. The pain went away. I began to relax, to feel both energetic and positive. That was good stuff. Maybe they made it smell and taste bad so people would not take it all the time.

We stared at one another a long time, saying nothing but reaching a decision our conscious minds did not entirely recognize at the moment. Hong Tray drifted across my thoughts with a smile and an admonition.

This time I managed a smile when I sat up. Unchallenged. "I have work to do."

Sahra shook her head. She fished under the table for To Tan, dug him out of his basket. He was in desperate need of changing. Sahra tugged my finger.

"I haven't done this in twenty years." Not since I was a kid myself and had baby brothers and sisters and cousins to change. "Stop wiggling, you little turd. You ought to know the drill by now." To Tan looked back at me with serious big eyes, not understanding my words but catching my tone.

We got him cleaned up and clothed again, in rags that would have embarrassed a beggar. I told Sahra, "I'll go kill somebody, get him something better to wear."

She laid a hand lightly on my forearm, restraining me.

"That was a joke, hon. You hang around with me, you're going to hear some dark stuff. I don't mean it literally. I'm going to work now."

I moved into the passageway slowly, my legs watery. Sahra followed, To Tan straddling her left hip. We ran into Bucket right away, looking groggy as he headed for his own pallet. I asked, "You seen Goblin and One-Eye?"

"They went upstairs with their magic junk. To the big lookout."

"Thanks."

Before we walked five feet, Bucket called, "Longo tell you the water is coming up in the catacombs?"

I sighed and shook my head, listened to the half-hearted rumble of my stomach, wondered if anybody had found a way to get some food cooked, wound my way through the maze to the ladders that would take me up to Goblin and One-Eye.

The light of day might do me good. If I had the strength to climb that far. I had not seen the sun for a long time.

76

I would not see the sun for a while longer.

Sahra handed To Tan up through the trapdoor. He was asleep again. I guess you do sleep a lot when you are a baby starving to death.

It was daytime but a driving rain was falling. Hagop sat astride a chair turned backwards, forearms on the chair's back, staring into the rain morosely. "How long has this been going on?" I asked.

"Day or three."

"We getting any fresh water out of it?"

"About as much as we can being as we're hiding out."

"What're those two doing?" Goblin and One-Eye were on the floor in the middle of the room, crosslegged, farthest from the moisture blowing inside. They did not look up.

"Wizard stuff. Don't bother them. They'll bite your leg off."

One-Eye grumbled, "And somebody's gonna lose a set of ears if he don't stop yakking."

Hagop and I each spent one of our diminishing supply of single-finger salutes. One-Eye did not acknowledge the accolade.

The lookout had a window facing each direction. I went to the biggest.

This rain was not what we called a gullywasher back home but it was strong and steady. I could barely sense the vague loom of the surrounding hills. Nearer at hand I could make out the surface of the water. It was down despite the rain. It was a grey that spoke of sickness.

I saw a Jaicuri raft out there, so loaded with people that it was awash. Men using short boards as paddles labored carefully to drive it toward shore.

I made the rounds of the other windows, studied the city. I was pleased to see our Taglians at their posts the way they had been taught.

"They've been doing it by the numbers," Hagop agreed. "And that gets them left alone."

"By Mogaba?"

"By everybody. The fighting is almost constant."

The streets and alleys were now canals. I saw bodies floating everywhere. The stench was overwhelming. The water level, though, was lower than I had expected. I could see the citadel from the east window. There were Nar up top there, ignoring the weather. They moved around the parapet, studying our part of town.

Hagop noticed me watching them. "They're worried about us. They think we might come sort them out sometime."

"Sure we will."

"They're superstitious about guys like Goblin and One-Eye."

"Which shows you how dangerous a little ignorance can be."

"I heard that," One-Eye grumbled. He and Goblin could have been playing some obscure dice game for all I could tell. I liked it better when they conjured big lights that went around smashing things and burning them up. Destruction I can understand.

Sahra seemed tired of lugging To Tan so I took him. She offered a grateful smile. It lit up the lookout.

One-Eye and Goblin paused to exchange glances amongst themselves and with Hagop.

"What are you guys doing?" I demanded.

"We found out we were right."

"Yeah? That might be a first. You were right about what?"

"About your head having been tampered with."

I shuddered to a sudden chill. That is not something anyone welcomes. "Who did it? How?"

"How we haven't been able to figure out for sure. It might have been managed several ways. Who and what are more interesting, anyway."

"So give."

"*Who* was Lady. And *what* was knowledge of the fact that she is out there."

"Excuse me?"

"It's a little hard to tell from here, especially when we got tourists and their girlfriends traipsing through the workplace, but it looks like Lady and the Taglians are in charge out there. Their camp is on the other side of the hills, up the north road. The southerners we see patrolling are auxiliaries who report back to Lady."

"Run through that again."

Goblin did so.

I said, "You guys go ahead. I'm just going to sit over here in the corner and think."

77

Uncle Doj and Thai Dei were back from wherever they had gone. They scowled at Sahra and me when we returned but neither said a word. Hong Tray still had her hold on the Kys. Thai Dei took his son. The little guy brightened immediately.

Uncle Doj told me, "My people are not mushrooms, Standardbearer. They cannot endure this much longer. You Stone Soldiers have been generous to a fault and have given no provocation but even so there will be trouble eventually. A wounded animal will strike out at even the most loving master."

"We'll be out of here sooner than I planned." I was not in a good mood. I wanted to drag Lady across my lap and paddle her. "I've already given orders to start the process."

"You sound angry."

"I am angry." Lady used me in a political game with Mogaba with never a thought for the Company's welfare. She was no more real Company than he was.

Longo leaned in the doorway. "You get the word about the catacombs flooding, Murgen?"

"Bucket told me. How soon is it going to be a problem?"

"Four or five days. Maybe more. Unless the leak gets a lot worse."

"We'll be gone. Your brothers and One-Eye are up in the big lookout. Go find out what's up."

Longo shrugged and went, grumbling about the climb.

I asked, "Who speaks for the Nyueng Bao now?"

"We have not yet chosen," Uncle Doj replied.

"Could you? Quickly? A Taglian general name of Lanore Bonharj—the guy who's in charge of the freed slaves and friendly Taglians and Jaicuri right now—is going to come by. We'll need somebody Nyueng Bao to join us in planning our evacuation." He started to say something. I rolled on. "It seems that the Shadowmaster isn't a problem anymore, only nobody bothered to tell *us*. Our own so-called friends have been jobbing us for political reasons. We could leave any time—I don't know for how long now."

I put all the blame for our ignorance on Goblin and One-Eye. You can blame a wizard for anything and people will believe you.

Sahra tried to make a meal from what we had. I touched her hand as she passed. She smiled. I told her, "This should be the last time we'll need to do this."

I hoped.

I was wrong.

Everything takes time.

Lanore Bonharj followed me down into the warrens. He was both amazed and appalled. He was high-caste Gunni. It was bad up top but this squalor down below was beyond his imagination. We talked. Uncle Doj spoke for the Nyueng Bao. Bargains were struck, agreements agreed, plans quickly laid. Preparations began in earnest.

78

In the dark of night, in the rain, the Black Company stole forth, crossed a rickety makeshift bridge to stairs to the battlements, joined the Taglians of the al-Khul company. With Goblin at the point we sneaked along the wall, seized the North Gate and barbican from the Nar and their Taglians. Goblin's sleep spell made that easy. Nobody got hurt. In our gang.

Before the last body splashed into the water outside Goblin and I and the Company cadre headed back to grab the West Gate and its barbican.

With the gates in our hands we could proceed unobserved by Mogaba's men.

Loftus and his brothers got to work inside the central of the three towers between the gates. While the wall itself was stone with a rubble fill the towers were not solid. They had to be hollow to allow crossbowmen inside to pepper the wall faces with missiles. The boys got to work opening a hole to the outside from the floor nearest the present water level.

The Nyueng Bao brought our remaining food stores to the surface. The women would use the last of the Taglians' fuel to cook for everyone. I wanted everybody to build strength. A lot of us were little more than stick figures now.

When the sun rose next morning the Nar atop the citadel saw nothing they had not seen the day before, except less rain. They got no signals from the north or west barbicans but did not seem concerned.

"Aren't many crows around anymore," Goblin noted as daylight began to fade.

"Maybe we ate them all."

Night returned. Everybody went back to work. The hammering and pounding and the collapse of masonry into water had to be audible all over town but nobody could see what we were doing and nothing was evident when the sun rose except that several derelict buildings were missing.

The lake continued its slow fall. The weather continued damp.

The rafts the carpenters were building floated outside, against the wall. Everything capable of offering flotation went into their construction. Even the occasional empty beer barrel.

That afternoon we acquired some useful lumber when Mogaba sent three rafts to the North Gate to find out why his signals were not being answered.

We could not keep the ambush from being seen from the citadel. Mogaba wasted no more men or materials.

Loftus and his brothers said the best raft would be built long and thin so more people could paddle against less front-end water resistance. Working in three feet of water the three brothers and a few skilled Taglians assembled one raft after another, each able to carry ten or more adults. By using everything they could find they built forty-one craft. They guessed that fleet could carry seven hundred people, more than five hundred of whom could be put ashore while the rest brought the rafts back, reloaded them and got under way again before dawn.

So about twelve hundred could get away overnight. Enough to establish a modestly solid beachhead on what we did not know for certain would be a friendly shore.

Problem. The numbers we needed to move undetected were greater than I had guessed. I had my forty Old Crew, more than six hundred Nyueng Bao, and a whole lot more Taglians, freed slaves and Jaicuri volunteers than I had thought.

Lanore Bonharj wanted to move nearly a thousand men and dependents. There was no way to get everyone out in one night.

"Here's what you do," One-Eye said. "You only take one load across the first night. Draw lots for the spots. That way we don't get people climbing over each other and nobody getting out in the panic. Figure the draw so a representative percentage goes from each group. Then nobody bitches. Dump the five hundred and some with orders to build a camp. Have the rafts come back and tie up, then finish up with two trips next night."

"The man is a genius," I said. "You or Goblin will have to go, just in case."

"Shouldn't be necessary."

"Why not?"

"Things aren't that dangerous anymore."

"Then we won't need to dig in. We can send the Nyueng Bao and dependents out first."

"That will go down great."

"Women and children and old people? That will work. I'll bet you. Include the Taglians' dependents. Hold up on the Jaicuri, though, or we'll have the whole damned city lining up. We figure how many that all is, then draw lots for the rest of the positions."

It worked out that thirty Taglians, five Black Company guys and fifteen Nyueng Bao warriors could be sent with the first group. We would have fifty swords on the beach.

Uncle Doj grumbled about the scheme because for one night he would not be able to keep his whole tribe together. "Clever, Soldier of Darkness." We were back to that? "You hold us warriors hostage."

"You want to go, go. There are more of you than there are of us. Take the rafts."

He scowled, his hand called.

"It's one night, Unc. And fifteen warriors will go with them. They'll be drawn by lot so one of them might even be you."

One-Eye and Goblin did not want to leave. "I'm not going over tonight," One-Eye told me.

"Me too neither," Goblin insisted.

They had that weasel look they get when they are dealing off the bottom of the deck. "Why not?" They looked like they could use a straight man.

"It ain't safe out there," One-Eye told me, after Goblin failed to convince me of his altruistic desire to protect the world by blunting Mogaba's wickedness. "That bitch from Juniper. Lisa

Daele Bowalk. She's laying for us out there."

"Who?" I heard no bells ringing.

"Lisa Bowalk. From Juniper. Nasty little bitch. Ran with Marron Shed. The corpse runner. Shifter took her as his apprentice after the Company went on the run. She was there when we skragged Shifter. The Old Man let her get away. Well, she's out there, prowling, waiting for a chance to get even. She's already tried a couple times."

"And you never bothered to tell me?" A healthy dose of skepticism is in order any time One-Eye waxes passionate on any subject.

"Wasn't no problem till now."

Why argue? The truth seemed evident. Those two had plunder stashed and did not want to leave it unguarded. Nor did either want the other left with it alone. I told them, "Take your chances with the rest of us."

Bonharj and Uncle Doj, Goblin and One-Eye all glowered at me. I told them, "I shouldn't have to take a turn."

One-Eye chuckled. "Maybe not. But *you* said we *all* had to take our chances."

I had not yet drawn. Trouble was, the outcome was not in doubt. There was only one stone left in the jar. Five black pebbles had been allocated to the Company and only four had been drawn.

I would go to the mainland with the first wave.

Why did my bitty buddies look so smug? "Pick your rock and pack your shit," Goblin said. They would not have rigged the draw, would they? Nah. Not those two. Paragons of virtue, they were.

"Anybody want to buy this?" I held up the expected black pebble.

"Stuff it, Kid," One-Eye said. "We'll manage without you. Again. What could go wrong in one day, anyway?"

"With you guys in charge?" It did not seem right, me going ashore before the last Black Company brother was out of the city.

"Just get your stuff together and go," Goblin snapped again. "It'll be dark in an hour."

It was still drizzling. Darkness would come early, though not early enough to complete two crossings and get the rafts back unseen. Damn it.

Sahra was burdened down with odds and ends and six pounds of rice and beans. I carried a pack containing a Nyueng Bao tent, blankets, various clutter useful in the field, plus I had To Tan perched on my hip. That kid was the least troublesome baby I ever saw.

Thai Dei had not drawn a black stone.

I meant to enjoy his absence.

We climbed out of the warren, descended steps, crossed to the wall, climbed up, walked the battlements, descended inside the middle tower. And that was about as much exercise as I wanted.

On my raft we were all Nyueng Bao except me and Red Rudy. The Nyueng Bao were patient about waiting their turns. The guys in the tower, operating by feeble lamplight, were patient too. Morale was good.

"Careful," Clete said as I stepped aboard. I accepted children as he started handing them across. "I picked you a good one, boss, but it will lean over if you don't keep the weight balanced. Ma'am." He helped Sahra. She acknowledged his courtesy with a dazzling smile.

"Thanks, Clete. See you tomorrow night."

"Right. Round up some cattle and dancing girls."

"I'll check around."

"Kneel down. You got to keep the center of gravity low so the damned thing don't tip."

I glanced around. We were ready to go.

Six Nyueng Bao men were aboard. They would paddle over. Five would bring the raft back. Other than them, Rudy and I and one gimp Nyueng Bao about fifty were the only adult males aboard. There were fifteen or sixteen kids and half as many women. We were crowded but Nyueng Bao make a light load. I volunteered to help paddle but the men on the job lost their capacity to understand Taglian.

Rudy said, "If they want to be dicks and bust their nuts, no sweat off our asses."

"You're right. But keep it down. We're doing a sneak here."

It turned out the Nyueng Bao were skilled boatmen. Which should have been no surprise considering their origins.

They remained as quiet as falling feathers. And made rapid headway. The rafts immediately ahead had Taglian paddlers who not only made a lot of noise, they were slow. With just a whispered word my paddlers swung right and began passing.

It was not much of a sneak, overall. Paddles splashed. People bumped, grunted, banged around and occasionally managed to collide with other rafts. But those were noises that came off the water every night and tonight the drizzle was deadening some of the racket. And, of course, we were headed straight away from the city. The light inside the opened tower served as a navigational beacon.

My paddle men maybe did not keep the best watch on the light. We drifted way off line and lost it altogether.

Somebody hissed.

Paddles stopped dipping. Even the murmur of the little ones stilled as mothers placed hands over their mouths or pulled lips to teats.

I heard nothing.

We waited.

Sahra rested her hand lightly upon my arm, sharing reassurance.

Then I heard the clumsy paddling. Somebody was farther off course than we were. . . . Only this raft was headed the other way.

It was too early for that.

The sounds grew louder.

The other raft came abreast, so close that it seemed they had to see us despite the darkness and rain.

A voice said something softly, just a few words edged with anger. In the language of Gea-Xle. I had picked up maybe twenty words, none of which I recognized now.

I did not need to know words. I knew the voice.

That was Mogaba.

He had not been spotted leaving during the day. From the north and west barbicans it was possible to watch most of the lake surface.

Which meant that he had been away at least since the previous night. Which, in turn, would explain why there had been no response to our capture of the barbicans.

What business could Mogaba possibly have over there?

The Nar paddled on into darkness. We resumed our journey. I remained lost in thought till the raft ran aground and tossed me forward.

Sahra and I took up To Tan and our burdens and marched ashore. The little guy was sleeping like his aunt's arms were a palace bed.

In moments I discovered that my companions, although utterly ignorant of the Taglian language, expected me to be in charge on this side, too. Uncle Doj's idea, no doubt, and in effect only till he arrived.

"Rudy. Take charge of getting camp set." We had swung back into the general course of the fleet and had made landfall where others joined us in savoring the miracle of life outside Dejagore's walls.

Hanging around in a rainstorm in the middle of the night did not seem much of an improvement to me.

"Let's go, people. We can't just stand here. Start putting up those shelters." We had the tents the Nyueng Bao had carried on pilgrimage. We had blankets, wrapped inside those same tents so they would stay dry. "Somebody collect some brush and get some fires going." Maybe easier said than done in this weather. "Bubba-do. Take some men and set a perimeter. You. Joro? That your name, sergeant?" I was talking to one of the Taglian soldiers. "Get patrols out. Come on! Come on! We don't know that there aren't people over here who want to kill us." But it gets hard to care when you are cold and wet and tired.

I was tired to the point of collapse but I made myself an example. Sahra followed and helped. While I barked at people we took turns caring for the baby. I had visions of some major historical asskicker like Khrombak the Terrible ordering his hordes about while he had a smelly baby tucked into the crook of his arm.

To Tan was a good kid but he always needed changing.

Soon everyone was bustling industriously. Shelters went up. Brush got cut. Small fires took life and spawned others until there were enough to heat water to cook rice. The water we gathered using some tents to collect rain into the pots. It was going to be difficult for any of us to get wetter than we were already.

We even sent several small loads of brush over to the city on returning rafts. Our friends might get to do a little cooking, too.

79

We had known so much misery for so long that night became just another sad chore. And in time there was poor shelter, bad food, and feeble warmth for all. But by then it was getting light and the rain was just an occasional sprinkle. Sahra and To Tan and I crept into our tent and bundled up. For a while I was almost happy.

That To Tan was remarkable. He was almost as quiet as Sahra most of the time, though he could get a good fuss going when he wanted. He was content to sleep right then. For the first time in a week his tummy was full.

Mine, too.

I got four hours of perfectly wonderful sleep before disaster interrupted.

First it took the shape of Ky Gota. I had not seen Sahra's mother since Uncle Doj cajoled her out of my quarters. I had not missed her, either.

Because I was asleep I did not witness the part where she ripped open the end of the tent. When I awoke she was spitting and howling in a mix of Nyueng Bao and really bad Taglian. Sahra was sitting up already, her mouth open and tears starting.

To Tan began to cry.

Ky Gota was not immune to baby tears. The soul of a granny did lurk behind all the ill temper. Way behind. She said something to the toddler. Gently!

Rudy hurried up. "You want I should throw this one back in the lake, Murgen?"

"What?"

"She crawled out of the water a while ago. Claimed somebody tried to murder her. Supposedly pushed her off the raft she was riding. Looks to me like maybe she asked for it."

"She probably did." Sahra looked at me in surprise. Despite her tears. "But I got to be nice. She's almost family."

"Man," Rudy said. He walked off shaking his head.

Sahra began gesturing exasperatedly at her mother. To Tan stared at his granny, sucked his thumb. I caught a whiff. "Go to Nana," I whispered. "Show her how good you can walk." He did not understand me but she did and held her arms out.

Near as I could tell To Tan was the only person in the world who cared for Ky Gota. He toddled and his granny forgot all about being wet and cold and cranky.

Sahra looked at me hard. I shrugged, grinned, mouthed, "He needs changing again."

Rudy found me staring at the city. Fresh smoke hung over our part of town. "Bubba-do just ambushed a patrol, Murgen."

"Shit. When they don't report . . ."

"He said they knew we were here. They were sneaking up. That Swan character is with them."

"One-Eye was right, then. Anybody get hurt?"

"Not yet."

"Good. Good. Did they get a look at the camp?" The Nyueng Bao had done a good job of camouflage, considering. You could tell where the camp was but not its extent.

"I think they just saw the smoke. They were real surprised to get jumped according to Bubba-do."

"They see him?"

"Yes."

"Unfortunate. Maybe they didn't recognize him." I shrugged. "Some things can't be helped. I'll deal with them. Hang on." I stomped over to Sahra and her mother. "Hush!" I snapped when the old woman opened her mouth to start. "We have trouble. Who can speak for the Nyueng Bao?" I did not know who else to ask. These strange people did what I said when I told them, if that improved our situation, but they did not talk.

The old woman put the baby down and rose. She squinted. Her eyesight was not good. "Tam Dak!" she barked.

A frail ancient turned. Despite his age he was carrying a huge bundle of brushwood. Ky Gota beckoned imperiously. The oldster headed our way at a high-speed shuffle.

I went to meet him. "Greetings, father. I am the one who dealt with the Speaker." I spoke both loudly and slowly.

"I'm not deaf yet, boy," he replied in Taglian better than mine. "And I know who you are."

"Good. Then I'll get to the point. The soldiers over here have found us. We don't know what their attitude toward your people might be. If they're in a bad temper I can't help much. Your warriors have scouted. Can you disappear?"

He looked at me for a dozen seconds. I looked back. Sahra came to stand beside me. Behind us, To Tan giggled as he played with his grandmother. The old man shifted his look to Sahra. For a moment he seemed to be staring into yesterday. He shivered. His expression grew more inscrutable. "We can."

"Good. Do it while I'm with them." I jerked a thumb uphill. "I'll get word to Doj. He'll find you."

Tam Dak continued to stare cooly. Not inimically at all, just without comprehension. I was not behaving like a proper foreigner.

"Good luck." I returned to Rudy. "Here's the deal. The Nyueng Bao need to take a powder. I'll go with Swan. I'll stall around when I get to his camp. You see that the Nyueng Bao get moved out, then make this mess look like we were setting up for the guys coming over tonight."

The old man overheard every word.

I continued, "As far as anybody around here goes, these people never existed."

"But . . ."

"Do it. And let them have most of the food. We can sponge off Lady's gang." I hoped.

Rudy looked at Sahra. Everybody seemed to think that she was the key. He shrugged. "You're the boss. I guess I don't need to understand. How are you going to explain her?"

"I don't have to." I headed toward where Swan's patrol was surrounded.

Sahra came right along after pausing to grab up To Tan.

"Stay here," I told her. She looked at me blankly, smitten by sudden deafness. I took a few steps. She matched them. "You need to stay with your own people."

A little smile teased her lips. She shook her head.

Hong Tray was not the only witch in this family.

"Ky Gota . . ."

Boom!

"You! Soldier of Darkness! You her ruin, now is not good enough for you? Cruel witch was my mother but . . ." She became incomprehensible but not the least bit quiet. I checked Tam Dak. He remained inscrutable but I would have bet my shot at heaven he wanted to laugh.

"Fuck this. Rudy! Find out what belongs to Sahra and see that it stays in our tent. Come on, woman."

80

H oly shit," Swan murmured when I stepped out where he
could see me. "No wonder you went back."

"Hands off, pretty boy. Ay, Nyueng Bao! If you are out there
go see Tam Dak. It's important. Taglians. See Rudy from the
Company." I turned back to Swan. "There. We're down to a few
snipers. Just in case."

He stopped staring at Sahra. "Sorry. You really stumbled
into the sweet shit, didn't you?" He did have the courtesy to
make his remarks in Forsberger.

"Yeah. I did. What's going on? I wake up the other day, after
my wizards did an experiment on me, and I find out that somebody has been inside my head, messing with my memories. I find
out I'm back over there in hell's kitchen hunting rats and fighting cannibals when all the time my so-called friends are sitting
around out here not even letting me know the Shadowmaster
is dead."

Swan gave me a dumb look. "But . . . You knew that, Murgen. You was over here when we killed the bastard. You was here
for a week after that."

"Killed him?"

It began to dawn. "You didn't insist on going back? She said
you. . . ."

"No. I didn't. When I found myself headed that way I
thought I was escaping from Shadowspinner. I really believed
that I hadn't gotten to you people. I think." It got more confused as I tried to figure it out.

Somebody called out something in Nyueng Bao. My troops
had not followed orders. Someone else, in Taglian, called, "Can
you come up here please, Mr. Murgen?"

I told Swan, "I don't know what's up. You better stand fast.
These guys are real touchy."

"I got nothing else to do with my life."

"I mean it. They're paranoid in a big way. If you had spent the last several months in there you'd understand." I clambered up a steep slope to where one Taglian knelt in some scraggly brush with a Nyueng Bao about fifteen years old.

The boy pointed, eager to be the first to deliver bad news.

Fresh smoke rose from Dejagore. From, near as I could tell, the north barbican. It looked like there was fighting there.

A mauve flash told me One-Eye or Goblin was involved. Mogaba must be trying to recover the barbican.

I spied flickers around the west gate, too.

"Damned Mogaba. Thanks, guys. Nothing we can do about it, though." I hoped One-Eye and Goblin carved Mogaba a new poop chute. "Get on back to camp, will you? There's stuff that's got to get done."

Lady was gone. Blade was in charge and just sitting around collecting refugees from the city, keeping them from reporting back with news about Shadowspinner. He admitted that. "That's what she wants done." He seemed indifferent to Sahra, unlike every other man in camp.

"She's lucky she's not here," I grumbled. "I'd turn her over my knee."

Since there was nothing else going on I sat around with him and Swan and Mather until it started to get dark. Somebody found a puppy for To Tan to play with. When it got late I said, "We'd better get back to our people. They'll be getting nervous."

"No can do, buddy," Mather told me.

Blade agreed. "She said no exceptions."

The warmth went out of the air. I gave each one what I thought of as the Nyueng Bao look. Swan and Mather averted their eyes. Blade took it but with a twitch.

Sahra seemed untroubled. I suppose, after Dejagore, it was hard to imagine a turn for the worse. She even smiled.

"I assume the prison pen is where I left it?" I remembered that part of my previous visit perfectly.

"We will keep you more comfortably," Blade promised.

Mather volunteered, "I'll show you where to bunk."

We were far enough away not to overhear, Swan thought. He told Blade, "You look at her good? That's one spooky woman."

I glanced at Sahra. I assumed she heard, too, but her expression told me nothing.

If Blade answered Swan he spoke more softly.

I continued to study Sahra, wondering what Swan had seen.

81

The tent was decent. It must have belonged to a middle-grade Shadowlander officer. We were not unhonored guests. And the tent came with a man assigned to make us comfortable and bring us our supper. Blade's troops were foraging successfully, it seemed. I ate better than I had for a long time.

"What I want more than anything in the world," I told our man, whose name I never learned, "is a bath." Sahra hit him with a smile guaranteed to melt armor plate. She was enthusiastic about that idea. "I'm so filthy my fleas have lice," I said.

Must have been a real ration of guilt going around at high levels. An hour later several soldiers showed up humping a looted stone horse trough. With them came guys lugging buckets of hot water. I told Sahra, "We must of died and come back as princes."

Our tent was big enough to contain the trough and water with room left over.

Swan turned up. "What do you think of that, eh?"

"If I didn't have friends over there fighting and dying I'd ask for a life sentence."

"Take it easy, Murgen. It'll all work out."

"I know that, Swan. I know that. But some of us aren't going to be happy how it does."

"Yeah, well. Good night."

It was. Beginning with the bath Sahra made it clear her definition of our relationship was exactly what others feared or suspected. She astounded me with her ability to communicate without spoken words, amazed me that in the midst of such unrelenting hell a flower of such beauty could bloom and defy the night.

I slept longer and better than I had for months. Maybe some part of me just resigned and let go.

Water in the face wakened me.

"What?" I cracked an eyelid. And popped upright. Sahra sat up as I did. "To Tan? What're you doing, kiddo?" The little guy was leaning over the edge of the horse trough, spanking the water. He looked at me and grinned, said something in Nyueng Bao baby talk that sounded like "Dada."

"What's going on?"

Sahra shrugged. To Tan said "Dada" again and headed out of the tent.

Things were happening outside. I grabbed my clothes, climbed in, stuck my head outside. "Holy shit! Where the freak did you guys come from?" Thai Dei and Uncle Doj were seated outside. Their swords lay across their laps. Sheathed, thankfully. Gangs of Taglians were coming by to check them out. I guessed they had not been there long nor had they asked permission to enter camp and assume their posts.

Swan and Mather appeared.

Uncle Doj told me, "Only one group made it out again last night. The black men attacked. Many men were injured. Numerous rafts were damaged. But their soldiers did not want to fight and many asked to join Bonharj."

"Who the hell are these guys?" Swan demanded. "How did they get here?"

"The rest of the family. I expect they sneaked. They're good at that. Obviously, your perimeter ain't what it should be."

Blade shouted something from the distance. "Crap," Swan grumbled. "Now what?" He jogged away.

Mather considered Thai Dei and Uncle Doj briefly, shrugged, followed Swan. Uncle Doj said something to Sahra. She nodded. I guess he wanted to know if she was all right.

To Tan climbed around on his father.

Doj told me, "You did well, and more than you were obliged, Standardbearer. Our people are safely away and these men know nothing about them."

"Yeah? Good. What about mine?"

"They would not come out. The wizards want to pursue their vendetta with Mogaba. They might come tonight."

82

They did not come that night. Nor did they come the next though they sent a lot of Taglians and Jaicuri out in place of the Company.

Two mornings later Mather finally let me in on what the excitement had been about when Blade interrupted our discussion over Uncle Doj and Thai Dei. He told me, "Croaker will be here in an hour or two, Murgen. You might put in a good word."

"What?"

It was not an hour and it was not just the Old Man. Croaker was travelling with the Prahbrindrah Drah himself. He looked like he had seen a lot of hard road. I moved toward him in fits and starts, unsure where we stood after all this time.

He jumped down, said, "It *is* me. I'm real."

"But I saw you die."

"No. You saw me get hit. I was still breathing when you cut out."

"Yeah? The shape you was in, there wasn't no way . . ."

"Shouldn't have been, either. It's a long story. We can chew on it over a few beers sometime." He waved. A soldier trotted up. Croaker grabbed his spear, which was almost long enough to be a pike, shoved it at me. "Here. You left this when you ran off to play Widowmaker."

I did not believe it. Not at first. It was the lance for the standard.

"You really need to hug it?"

"It's really it! I was almost sure it was lost." Despite what I had told Mogaba. "You got no idea how guilty I felt. Although I did think I saw it that one time. . . . It's really you?" I looked at him closely. Having seen what illusions One-Eye and Goblin could conjure I was not quite ready to accept the evidence of my own eyes.

"It's me. Really. Alive and in a mood to kick some ass. But that's not what I've got on my mind right now. Where's Lady?"

Poor boy. Blade gave him the bad news. His paramour had left more than a week ago, headed north. They missed each other on the road.

Swan and Mather were impressed by the presence of the Prince, their supposed boss.

Why was he out running around, anyway?

I noticed Croaker had a hard stare for Sindhu, who had stayed behind when Lady left.

The Old Man snapped, "Quit making love to that damned thing, Murgen. I need to catch up. I'm way out of touch. Will somebody take this damned butt-cruncher?"

A soldier grabbed his mount's reins.

"Let's get out of the sun."

"I want to hear your story," I said. "While it's fresh."

"Going to put it into the Annals? You been keeping them up?"

"I tried. Only I had to leave them in the city." I did not like that, either. One-Eye could promise the moon about taking care of them but would he deliver?

"I'll look forward to reading the Book of Murgen. If it's any good you've got the job for life."

Swan said something about Lady planning to write a book of her own when she got time. Croaker flung a stone at a crow. It was the first of those birds I had spotted since the albino in the night. Maybe he brought it with him. I sketched some of what had been happening in Dejagore.

"Guess it hasn't been fun for anybody. Seems Mogaba is the main problem. Better get right after him. How many people are still over there?"

"My guess is him and the Nar have a thousand to fifteen hundred men. I don't know how many people I have. Some come out every night but since I got elected prisoner here I can't keep track. Goblin and One-Eye and most of the Company are still over there." I hoped Uncle Doj and Thai Dei were using this distraction to get To Tan and Sahra and themselves on the road.

"Why would they stay?"

"They don't want to leave. They say they want to wait till Lady gets all her powers back. They say something is out here waiting for them."

"Powers back?"

"It's happening," Blade said.

"Hunh. So what are they afraid of, Murgen?"

"Shapeshifter's apprentice. That bitch from Juniper. She almost got One-Eye once already once. . . ." How come I believed the little rat now but had not when he had told me?

I had a momentary vision of One-Eye puffing through the night with fanged death closing in. It was as solid as actual memory.

"I remember her. She was a real piece of work. Marron Shed should have taken care of her when he had the chance."

"Evidently she wants to get even with us for doing Shifter. She may be locked into the forvalaka shape, too. Which would really piss anybody off, I guess. But if you was to ask my personal opinion I think she's only an excuse. They want to stay where they are because otherwise they might have to leave something behind."

"Like what?"

I shrugged. "They're Goblin and One-Eye. They've had months to pilfer and profiteer."

"Tell me about Mogaba."

Now we got down to the grim stuff.

Before the discussion ended even nasty Sindhu condemned the Nar.

"I'll put an end to that. You want to take a message to Mogaba?"

I looked over my shoulder. He could not be asking the guy behind me. There was nobody there. "You shitting me? Not unless it's an order. And maybe not then. Mogaba wants my head. Not to mention my heart and liver for breakfast. Crazy as he is right now he might go after me with you standing right behind me."

"I'll get somebody else."

"Good idea."

"I'll go," Swan volunteered. Then him and Mather got into an argument about that. Evidently Swan had something to prove to himself and Cordy did not believe he needed to bother.

83

My status in camp changed sharply. Suddenly I never was a prisoner, never had been unfree to do whatever served the common good.

Only problem was, my tent was cold. All I had left of Sahra and the Nyueng Bao was the jade amulet Sahra had taken from Hong Tray before we had carried the children out of the killing place.

"You done yet?" Croaker demanded, finding me seated in front of my tent, working on the standard.

I showed him what I was doing. "Good enough?"

"Perfect. You ready?"

"Ready as I'll ever get." I touched the jade amulet.

"She pretty special?"

"Very special."

"I want to hear all about her people."

"Someday."

We walked through the hills and down to the shore. A sizable boat was out on the lake already. Blade's soldiers had transported it overland after having failed to work it along the canal from the nearest river to the lake. Croaker and I took up position on a prominent hummock. I displayed the standard. They would be able to see that from the city even if they did not recognize me and the Old Man.

Mogaba wanted to know where the standard was? He could see for himself, now.

While the boat crossed over and returned Croaker and I speculated as to what made both Mogaba and Lady want to be in charge so badly.

"Looks like Swan is getting results. Can you see what's going on?"

"Looks like somebody black getting into the boat."

That somebody turned out to be Sindawe. I told the Old Man, "This guy was always as right with us as having Mogaba for a boss would allow. Ochiba and Isi and some of the others weren't too bad, either. But they wouldn't disobey orders."

Sindawe stepped ashore. Croaker saluted him. He responded uncertainly, looked to me for a clue. I shrugged. He was on his own. I had no idea where this was headed.

Sindawe made sure he was face to face with the real Captain. Once he was satisfied, he suggested, "Let us step out of sight and talk."

The Old Man made a small gesture that told me I should let them talk in complete privacy. They walked around behind the hummock and sat on a rock. They talked for a long time, voices never rising. Sindawe finally rose and walked back to the boat like a man borne down by an incredibly heavy burden.

"What's the story?" I asked Croaker. "He looks like he suddenly added twenty years on top of the wear and tear of the siege."

"Years of the heart, Murgen. Feeling morally compelled to betray somebody who has been your best friend since childhood will do that to you."

"What?"

He would say nothing more. "We're going over there. I'm going to meet Mogaba nose to nose."

I thought of a pile of arguments against. I did not bother. He would not listen. "Not me." I shuddered. My spine was shivering to that chill they say happens when somebody walks over your grave.

Croaker looked at me hard. I drove the butt of the standard into the earth, vigorously, meaning, "Here I stand." He grunted, turned and went down to the boat. The creature Sindhu snaked out of nowhere and joined the party. I wondered how much of Sindawe's and Croaker's conversation he had overheard. Not a word, probably. The Old Man would have used the Jewel Cities dialect.

Once the boat was well out onto the water I sat down beside the standard, clung to the pole and tried to figure out what made it impossible for me to go back over there.

84

I had suffered no big seizures for a while. I was not on guard anymore. This one began insidiously, like just losing focus and drifting into a lazy daydream. I stared at Dejagore but no longer really saw it, thought of the women who had entered my life and the ancient one who had left it. Already I missed Sahra and so-serious To Tan.

A white crow landed on the crossbar of the standard, cawed down at me. I paid no attention.

I stood at the edge of a shimmering wheatfield. A twisted, broken black stump rose thirty yards from me, in the field's center. Bickering crows surrounded it. The fairy towers of Overlook gleamed in the distance, days' walk away. I recognized them for what they were without understanding how I could know.

Suddenly the crows rose up and wheeled around, flew that direction in an uncrowlike flock. One white crow stayed behind, circling.

The stump shimmered darkly. A glamor faded away.

A woman stood there. She looked very much like Lady but was even more beautiful. She seemed to look right through me. Or at and into me. She smiled wickedly, playfully, seductively, perhaps insanely. In a moment the albino bird settled onto her shoulder.

"You are impossible."

Her smile shattered into shards of laughter.

Unless I was completely, inescapably mad there was only one person this could be. And she died long before I ever joined the Company.

Soulcatcher.

Croaker was there when she went down.

Soulcatcher.

That would explain a lot. That would illuminate a hundred mysteries. But how could that be?

A huge black beast that looked something like an ebony tiger padded past me, from behind, went and settled on its haunches near the woman. There was nothing servile in its manner.

I was frightened. If Soulcatcher was alive and in this end of the world and inclined to meddle she could become the greatest terror around. She was more powerful than Longshadow, Howler or Lady. But, unless she had changed since the old days, she preferred to use her talents in small ways, for spite or her own amusement.

She winked at me. Then she spun around and just seemed to disappear, leaving more laughter rippling in the air behind her. Her laughter became the mirth of the white crow.

The forvalaka became bored with the show, went off into the distance.

And I faded.

85

A crow cawed overhead.

A hand shook my shoulder, not gently. "Are you all right, sir? Is there a problem?"

"What?" I was seated on a stone step, clinging to the edge of a massive wooden door. An albino crow paced back and forth on the door's top edge. The man who held my shoulder tried to shoo the bird with his free hand and some pithy curses. He was huge and hairy.

It was the middle of the night. What light there was came from a lantern the man had set upon the cobblestones. It set eyes glowing across the street, at a low level. For an instant I thought I saw something huge and catlike slipping past.

The man was one of the Shadar patrolmen the Liberator had employed to roam the streets after dark, maintaining order and keeping a watch for outsiders of dubious provenance.

Laughter came from the darkness across the way. The patrolman was not doing a good job. I was supposed to be one of the good guys here. She was one of the dubious strangers.

I was in Taglios!

I smelled smoke. The lantern?

No. The odor came from the stairwell behind me.

I recalled dropping a lamp. Recalled a confused cacophony

of wheres and whens. "I'm all right. Just had a dizzy spell."

Laughter from across the street.

The Shadow glanced back but otherwise seemed indifferent. He did not want to believe my story. He wanted to find something wrong right here right now. He did not like foreigners. And us northerners were all madmen and drunks. But, unfortunately, we were also very much in favor with the Palace.

I got up. I had to get moving. My mind was clearing. The truth was coming back. I had a desperate need to get to the old familiar entrance to the Palace because I had to get to my apartment in a hurry.

The moon suddenly splashed its light down into the street. It had to be past midnight. I saw the woman watching from across the way. I started to say something to the Shadar but a sharp whistle came from the distance, in the direction the monster had seemed to be moving. Another patrolman needed assistance. He said, "Take care, foreigner." He jogged away.

I ran too, not pausing to take the elementary step of closing the sally door.

I reached my customary entrance. Something was wrong. Cordy Mather's Guards should have been on duty there.

I was unarmed except for a belt knife. I drew it, pretending I was a fierce commando. There was no way Mather's gang would leave an entrance uncovered. You could not bribe those guys to screw up.

I found the sentries in the guard room. They had been strangled.

No need to question the prisoner further, now. But who was the target? The Old Man? Almost certainly. The Radisha? Probably. And anyone else important that they could get.

I fought panic, managed to keep from haring off blindly. Thai Dei and Uncle Doj were up there, anyway.

I stripped the shirt off one dead guard, wrapped my throat. That should afford some protection against a Strangler's scarf. Then I bounded upstairs like a mountain goat who was long out of practice. I reached my own floor so winded I had to lean against the stairwell wall and strain to keep from puking. My legs were jelly.

Alarms banged everywhere now. It was happening as I stood there. I got some wind back, left the stairwell for the corridor—and tripped over a dead man.

He was filthy and undernourished. A blade had laid him open from left shoulder to right hip. His right hand lay ten feet away. It still clutched a black rumel. There was blood everywhere. Some still seeped from the corpse.

I stared at the scarf. The dead man had murdered many times. Now Kina had betrayed him.

Such treachery is one of the goddess's more endearing qualities.

Only Ash Wand could cut that clean and deep.

Another corpse lay near my apartment door. A third lay in the doorway itself, holding the door open.

All the blood was fresh. The corpses still bled. As yet few flies were in evidence.

Knowing I did not want to do so I entered my quarters ready to sink bare teeth into anything that moved.

I smelled something.

I spun and stabbed as someone skinny and brown and unwashed flew at me, hit me, threw me backwards. A black rumel spun around my neck but failed its function because of the shirt wrapping.

I hurtled backward into my worktable. There was a sharp pain in the back of my head. Inside I screamed, "Not again!"

Darkness closed down.

Pain awakened me. My arm was on fire.

My crash into the table had overturned a lamp. My papers, my Annals, were burning. I was burning. I leaped up shrieking, beating my arm, and when I had that extinguished I began jumping around trying to save the papers. I saw nothing else and thought of nothing else. This was my life, going up in smoke. And beyond the smoke there was only the house of pain, only the bleak seasons.

Way, way over there, like down a long, cruel tunnel, I saw Uncle Doj kneeling beside Thai Dei. Between them and me lay three dead men. The floor was invisible beneath their blood. Two of the dead showed Ash Wand's characteristic precision cuts. The other had fallen to a cross cut that betrayed a hint of raggedness. The swordsman had been in the grip of an uncontrolled rage.

Uncle Doj held Thai Dei's head against his chest. Thai Dei's left arm hung as though broken. His right surrounded To Tan on his lap. The five-year-old's head was tilted at a bizarre angle. Thai Dei's face was pale. His mind was not in this world.

Uncle Doj rose, came toward me, stared into my eyes, shook his head, then stepped close and wrapped powerful arms around me. "They were too many and too fast."

I collapsed.

This was the present. This was today. This was the new hell where I did not want to be.

. . . fragments . . .

. . . just blackened fragments, crumbling between my fingers.

Browned page corners that reveal half a dozen words in a crabbed hand, their context no longer known.

All that remains of two volumes of Annals. A thousand hours of labor. Four years of history. Gone forever.

Uncle Doj wants something. He is going to make me drink some strange Nyueng Bao philtre.

Fragments . . .

. . . all around, fragments of my work, my life, my love and my pain, scattered in this bleak season. . . .

Darkness. And in the darkness, shards of time.

Hey there! Welcome to the city of the dead. . . .

86

The apartment was overrun with guards.

What was going on? I was confused. Another fainting spell?

Smoke. Blood. The present. The hard present that breathed pain like a dragon breathes fire.

I became aware of the Captain's presence. He came from the back of the apartment shaking his head. He eyed Uncle Doj curiously.

Cordy Mather blew in looking like a man encountering the worst horror show of a long and unhappy lifetime. He went straight to the Old Man. I heard only ". . . dead men all over the place."

I could not catch Croaker's response.

". . . were after you?"

Croaker shrugged.

"You just moved out last. . . ."

A Guard rushed in. He whispered to Mather. Mather barked, "Listen up! We've still got some live ones out there. Be careful." He and the Old Man moved a little closer. "They're lost in the labyrinth. We'll need One-Eye to find them all."

"The excitement never ends, does it?" Croaker sounded really tired.

To no one special Uncle Doj announced, "They have only just begun to pay." His Taglian was excellent considering he had been unable to speak a word the day before.

Mother Gota came from the back, bent and moving slowly. Typically of Nyueng Bao women dealing with disaster she had brewed tea. This was quite possibly the worst day of her life. It would be a good pot.

The Captain gave Uncle Doj another searching look, then knelt beside me. "What happened here, Murgen?"

"I'm not sure. I walked in in the middle of it. Stabbed a guy. That one. Got thrown across a table. Tripped and fell through a hole in time. Maybe. Woke up on fire." I still had charred pages around me. My arm hurt like hell. "There were dead people all over. I lost it. Next thing I knew it was now."

Croaker caught Mather's eye. He used a rocking motion of his right hand to indicate Uncle Doj.

Cordy Mather asked Uncle for his story. He spoke perfect Nyueng Bao.

It was a night of a thousand surprises.

Uncle Doj said, "These Deceivers were skilled. They gave no warning. I wakened just an instant before two fell upon me." He explained how he had evaded death, breaking a neck and a spine in the process. He described his kills clinically, even critically.

He spoke harshly of both himself and Thai Dei. He was down on himself because he had allowed himself to be tempted into pursuing other Deceivers when they fled. Their flight proved to be a diversion. Thai Dei, who had not been drawn away, received criticism for showing the instant of hesitation that had cost him his broken arm.

"Cheap lesson for him," Croaker observed. Uncle Doj nodded, missing the Captain's sarcasm. He had to face the cruel cost of having allowed himself to be deceived.

There were fourteen corpses in my apartment, not including those of butchered Annals. Twelve had been Deceivers. One had been my wife and one my nephew. Six perished by Ash Wand, three at Thai Dei's hands. Mother Gota gutted two and I pigstuck one when I walked in.

Grasping my shoulder in what was meant to be a comforting gesture, Uncle Doj said, "A warrior does not slay women or children. That is the work of beasts. When beasts kill men all men are constrained to hunt and destroy them."

"Nice talk," Croaker said. "But the Deceivers never claimed to be warriors." He was not impressed by Uncle's speech.

Neither was Mather. "It's religion, Old Timer. Their Path. They are the priests of death. The sex or age of their sacrifices doesn't mean squat. Their victims all go straight to paradise and never have to take another turn around on the wheel of life, no matter how buggered up their karma was."

Uncle Doj's mood grew blacker by the minute. "I know *tooga,*" he muttered. "No more *tooga.*" Nobody was revealing any mysteries to him.

Cordy smiled wickedly at the swordmaster. "You guys probably won a high spot on their desirable victim list by killing so many of them. If you're a Deceiver there's big status to be gained by killing somebody who has killed a lot of people."

I heard Mather's blather but it did not register as sense. I muttered, "*Tooga* ain't no crazier than any other religion around here."

That seemed to offend everyone equally.

Good.

Mather turned to fuss at his Guards. They had failed their trust. My own disaster was just one of several. Others were still happening.

Numbly, I said, "You can't defend against this kind of thing, Mather. These guys weren't commandos." I swatted the nearest corpse with the charred sheets I was holding. "They came in here expecting to make it to paradise by midnight. Probably didn't even have an escape plan." In a softer voice, I said, "Captain, you might better check on Smoke."

Croaker frowned like I had given away everything but asked only, "You need anything? Want somebody to stay?" He understood what Sarie meant to me.

"This is where I came from. When I kept falling back. I got family with me, Captain. If I start to go bugfuck in the head they'll cool me down. You really want to help? Fix Thai Dei's arm. Then go do what you got to do."

Croaker nodded. He made a small gesture that, in normal times meant "Go!" but which meant a good deal more now. "Narayan Singh is going to wake up some morning and realize that he has reaped the whirlwind. There is no safe place for him anymore."

I rose. Grimly, I set out for my bedroom. Behind me, Thai

Dei groaned as Croaker set his arm. The Old Man paid him no other mind. He was busy issuing orders that meant a major intensification of the war.

Uncle Doj followed me.

The reality hurt less than the anticipation had. I indulged in the pointless gesture of removing the rumel from my wife's throat. I stood there with the scarf dangling, staring. This Strangler must have been a true master. Her neck was not broken, nor had her throat been bruised. She looked like she was sleeping. There was no pulse when I touched her, though. "Uncle Doj. Can I be alone?"

"Of course. But drink this first. It will help you to rest." He handed me something that smelled really nasty.

Did we do this already?

He went away. I laid down beside Sarie for the last time. I held her while the medicine began to course through me, calling forth sleep. I thought all the usual thoughts, nurtured the usual hatreds. I thought the unthinkable, that it might be best that this had happened before Sahra learned what it really meant to be Company.

I reminisced the great miracle. Ours was a match that never should have been. A match neither ever regretted for an instant, yet one created by a force so slight as the unspoken whim of an old woman cursed with hysterical, unreliable precognitive visions.

I thought both sanely and crazily—and commenced the process of beatification that is inevitable after any untimely death. I slept. But even in Nod I could not escape the pain. I dreamed cruel dreams I could not reclaim when I awakened. It was almost as if Kina herself were mocking me, telling me that triumph was a costly deception.

Sarie was gone when I awakened, my head throbbing with a medicinal hangover. I stumbled around until I ran into Mother Gota. The old woman was fussing over some tea and talking to herself exactly the way she talked to the rest of the world.

"Where is Sahra?" I asked. "Tea. Please. What happened to her?"

Gota looked at me like I was mad. "She is dead." No pulling punches for her.

"I know that. Her body is gone."

"They have taken her home."

"What? Who?" Anger began to rise within me. How dare they . . . ? Who was they?

"Doj. Thai Dei. Her cousins and uncles. They have taken Sahra and To Tan home. I am here to watch over you."

"She was my wife. I . . ."

"She was Nyueng Bao before she was your wife. She is Nyueng Bao now. She will be Nyueng Bao tomorrow. Hong Tray's fantasies cannot change that."

I gained control before I exploded completely. Gota was right, from a Nyueng Bao point of view.

Also, there was not a lot I could do about it right now. Not without coming up with a lot more ambition than I had this morning. All I really wanted to do was sit around feeling sorry for myself.

I went back to our room with my tea. I settled on our bed, picked up the jade amulet that had belonged to Hong Tray. It seemed very warm this morning, more alive than I. I had not worn it for a long time. I slipped it onto my wrist now.

I could work my anger out on Uncle Doj when he got back. If he came.

87

Not one Strangler attack team achieved its tactical objective, but even so their raid was successful psychologically. It stunned the city. It shocked the leadership. It generated terror out of all proportion to actual damages.

Croaker grabbed it and turned it around.

Next morning, while most of us were still wrestling with our emotions, he went to the Taglian mob and spoke in his old guise as Liberator. He announced a new and furious era of total, relentless warfare against the Shadowmaster and *tooga* although he divulged few real facts about the Palace raid. That set rumor running wild through the alleys and byways and fueled fresh anger. For years the war had been a long way away, in the old Shadowland, and so had become emotionally remote to most of the people. The Deceiver raid brought the war back home. The old enthusiasm resurfaced.

The Liberator told the crowd that the years of preparation were over. It was time to carry justice to the wicked.

But moving immediately meant a winter campaign. I asked the Old Man if he really intended that.

"Damned straight. More or less. They have their feet up down there. You know that. You've been riding Smoke. I mean, who would be crazy enough to take a crack at the Dandha Presh when the snow is flying?"

Who indeed? "It'll mean some major hardships for the soldiers."

"If an old fart like me can take it they all can take it."

Right. Only some of us can take it better than others. Some of us are obsessed.

Hell. Us Black Company guys have obsessions and hatreds enough for everybody.

Work became my all. I was past the evil time. No longer did I fall back into cruel yesterdays in order to escape crueler todays—that I could detect. But I did not sleep well. Hell still lurked beyond sleep's wall. I lost myself in the Annals, rerecording everything the fire had claimed. I ran away by riding Smoke out into the past, where and when I could, to check my recollections.

One-Eye's arsenal increased its production. The Old Man drove the ruling class crazy trying to get money to pay for everything.

Word of the new stage spread through the Taglian territories as fast as horses could run.

Lady began gathering her forces and training them to deal with the darknesses that had given the Shadowmasters their name.

I became aware that Goblin had dropped out of sight, completely, but that only weeks after the actual event. I feared that he had been murdered. But Croaker did not seem concerned.

One-Eye was fussed. He was desperate to get his sidekick connected with my mother-in-law but he could not unearth a trace of the little toad.

In the night when the wind no longer licks through its unglazed windows, nor prances along its untenanted halls, nor whispers to its million creeping shadows, the fortress is filled with the silence of stone.

Cold cruel dreams stir within the figure pinned to the throne so ancient that bits have given up to dry rot. A gleam from beyond flickers. The figure sighs, drawing in the light, exhaling a balloon of dream that somehow finds its way through the tortuous passages of the fastness and out into the world in search of a receptive mind. Upon the plain itself the shadows swirl like minnows sensing the passing of a huge predator.

The stars wink down in cold irony.

There is always a way.

88

House of pain?

Mocking laughter.

She is beautiful. Yes. Almost as beautiful as I. But she is not for you.

The woman tucked a child in for the night. Her slightest movement bespoke grace.

I . . . There was an I, suddenly.

NO! Not for you!

She is mine!

Nothing is yours but what I give you. And I give you pain. This is the house of pain.

No! Whatever you are . . .

GO!

89

"Ouch!" I opened my eyes. Uncle Doj and Thai Dei crouched beside me, one to either side, looking concerned. I rolled my head, surprised to see them back so soon.

I was on the floor in my workroom. But I was dressed for bed. "What am I doing here?"

"You walked in your sleep," Doj told me. "Also talked, which alerted us."

"Talked?" I never talk in my sleep. But I do not walk in my sleep, either. "Gods damn it! I was having another spell!" And this time I remembered. Some. "I have to get this down. Right now. Before I lose it." I scrambled across the room. In moments I was scratching away.

And when I was done I realized I did not have a clue about anything. I threw my pen down.

Mother Gota appeared. She carried a pot of tea. She poured for me, then for Doj and Thai Dei. Sahra's death had hurt her deeply. For the moment her normal, contentious character was submerged. She was an automaton.

This had been going on for days.

"What is the trouble?" Uncle Doj asked.

"There's nothing there. I remembered perfectly but can't find a clue toward an explanation."

"Then you must relax. Stop fighting yourself. Thai Dei. Get the practice swords."

I wanted to scream that this was not the time. But this was his answer to all stress. Come to the swords. Pursue the exercise rituals. Parade the stances. To do it right required total concentration. And it always worked, no matter how much I disbelieved.

Even Gota joined us, though she was less adept than I.

90

The night that I had tried to find my way back from Smoke's hideout I had wondered if One-Eye had cast some confusion spells around there. I learned that he had—and had scattered random pockets of confusion all through the disused parts of the Palace so the one critical area would not stand out. He gave me an amulet of charmed woolen strings, several colors twisted together, that I was supposed to wear on my wrist. It would let me pass through the spells no more confused than my usual state.

"Be careful," he told me. "I change these spells every day now that you're working Smoke regular. I don't want nobody stumbling in there while you're out of body. Especially not the Radisha."

That made sense. There was no calculating Smoke's value. No instrument for espionage this valuable had ever existed before. We did not dare risk compromising him.

The Old Man gave me a list of regular checks he wanted made. These included keeping a close watch on Blade. He did not use that information immediately, though. I supposed he was laying back, letting Blade gain confidence. And, occasionally, letting Blade deal with our religious problem children for us, too.

I did not ask but I am sure the policy was coolly deliberate. The priesthoods provided our main political challenges. Made sense to me, too, to use them up keeping Blade from getting too strong.

I had my personal list of investigations, too, some meant to satisfy my own curiosity, most to get straight events that needed to be recorded in the Annals. I spent about ten hours a day just working on the books.

I rise, write, eat, write, visit Smoke, write, sleep for a little while, then get up and do it all again. I do not sleep long or well because I do not care to tarry in the house of pain.

Uncle Doj has decided not to return to his swamp. Likewise, Mother Gota. They stay out of my way, mostly. But they are always here, always watching. They have expectations.

The new phase of the war is here. They have decided to play a part. They mean the cruelty of the Deceivers to be requited by the cruelty of the Nyueng Bao.

One of the big problems of espionage, I have discovered, is figuring out *where* to look for the information you want. When I need to know something for the Annals I usually have an idea when things happened, where and who was involved. It is a chance to flit off and double-check my memory, which I have found to be astonishingly unreliable.

Apparently none of us really remember anything exactly the way it happened. And often the divergence is proportional to the amount of ego and wishful thinking we have invested.

One-Eye has his ego problems, of course. Maybe they are why he will not let me wander through his arms factory. If it does not have something to do with guarding his ledgers from outside scrutiny. I will spy on him now that he plans to close down soon.

One-Eye carries a lot on his old shoulders. Among the things he does is he acts as a sort of Minister of Armaments. He has a whole fortified section of town where he oversees the manufacture of everything from arrowheads to monster siege engines.

Much of his production gets crated up and sent straight to the docks, to be loaded aboard barges and sent downriver to the delta where, via a series of crude canals, the barges are worked over into the Naghir River, which shares the delta. Then they travel up the Naghir and its tributaries to armories near the frontier. I have no doubt that some of the material fails to reach its destination. I expect that One-Eye somehow profits. I hope he has sense enough not to sell to the enemy. Croaker catches him doing that and One-Eye will think that Blade gets treated like a mischievous kid brother.

My first swoop into the arsenal was a quick psychic raid. One-Eye's compound consisted of a gaggle of once dissimilar and unrelated structures now interconnected in a mad maze. All windows and most doors had been bricked up. Men selected for their size, bad tempers and lack of imagination infested the few entrances. They allowed no one in and no one out. The street outside the freight entrance was crowded day and night. Files of wagons and carts, drawn by weary oxen, crept forward to be unloaded and loaded by weary workmen watched banefully by the unimaginative men, who foamed at the mouth if carters and laborers so much as made eye contact. Around and amongst the carts swarmed countless runners carrying long poles from which hung dozens of pails filled with hot food for the workers. The guards checked every pail. They even took turns checking on each other.

Taglios has a richly diverse, complex, and deeply specialized labor economy. Folks will make a living one way or another and other folks will give them room. Near the Palace is a bazaar devoted entirely to grooming services, catering mainly to Palace functionaries. One guy does nothing but trim nose hairs. Right beside him, operating in a space less than four feet wide, with oils and silver tools displayed on a tiny inlaid table, is an old character who will clean the wax from your ears. He does nothing else but retail gossip. This business has been in his family for generations. He is sad because he has no son to inherit.

When he goes his family will lose that space in the bazaar.

It is all symptomatic of horrid overpopulation and the desperate difficulty of surviving at the bottom. I would not want to be a Taglian of low caste.

Lucky me, I did not have to check in with One-Eye's thugs. There seemed to be no provision against magical espionage. I darted inside. I guess One-Eye did not worry because Longshadow could no longer send his pets snooping this far. But what about the Howler? He could sneak up on us any time he wanted.

Trying to track Howler was one of my regular duties.

The arsenal workers were doing ordinary things. Making arrowheads. Sharpening them. Making arrows. Fletching them. Building artillery pieces. Attempting to mass produce a light cotton body armor for the ordinary infantryman—who, no doubt, would discard it because it was hot and uncomfortable and a nuisance to lug around.

Only the glassblowers surprised me.

There were two dozen workers in that department and most were employed producing small, thin bottles. A platoon of apprentices tended fires, heated the silicates that became raw glass, carried off trays of bottles once they cooled. Those went to carpenters who placed them into crates with sawdust packing. A few of the crates went aboard big long-haul wagons but most went to the waterfront.

What the devil?

There was a big piece of slate in One-Eye's office. Upon it, in Forsberger, were chalked what appeared to be production targets. Fifty thousand bottles. Three million arrows. Five hundred thousand javelins. Ten thousand cavalry lances. Ten thousand sabers. Eight thousand saddles. One hundred fifty thousand infantry short swords.

Some of those numbers were absurd and there was no way any could be reached by One-Eye's arsenal alone. But production took place all over the Taglian territories—most often in one-man blacksmith shops. One-Eye's main job was to keep track. Which looked to me a lot like letting the fox do bedcheck at the chicken house.

The list also included animals and wagons and lumber by the hundred barge loads, much of which I did understand. But five thousand box kites, ready for assembly, twelve feet by three feet? Each with one thousand feet of string? One hundred thousand yards of silk in bolts six feet tall?

He was not going to get that one.

I went roving to see what else was being readied for Mogaba and his friends.

I saw training camps where commando teams prepared for every imaginable terrain and mission. Down south, Lady pursued her own programs, creating forces prepared to operate offensively on the sorcerous battlefield.

She had scoured the Taglian territories for every person possessed of even the slightest magical talent and had schooled them just enough to make them useful in a program I could not fathom no matter how I poked at it. As Longshadow had noted, she was stripping the Taglian territories of bamboo. That got cut into several standard lengths and had red-hot rods run through to burn out the joints. Lady had the resulting tubes packed with little spongy colored marbles created by her squads of hedge wizards.

Another game of baffle the Shadowmaster? Half of what we were doing was smoke and mirrors meant to confuse the opposition and make them waste resources or commit them in the wrong places. But I was more confused than Longshadow could possibly be.

Lady slept less than did the Captain. Croaker seldom slept more than five hours a night. If sheer drive could conquer Mogaba and the Shadowmaster we were surefire winners.

Both Lady and the Old Man hide so much inside themselves that even after all these years I have no sure grasp of how they think. They share a strong love but seldom demonstrate it.

They want to recover their daughter and avenge themselves upon the Deceivers but never speak of the child publicly. Croaker is determined to lead the Company back to mysterious Khatovar, to unearth its origins, but does not talk about that at all anymore.

On the surface it would seem those two live only for the war.

I drifted back to One-Eye's factory. I was reluctant to leave Smoke. I knew if I delayed much longer I would return to find my body exhausted, starved, and extremely thirsty. The smart way to use Smoke was to take short journeys mixed with lots of times out for snacks and drinks. But that was hard to recall out there, especially when there was so much pain waiting back in my own slice of reality.

This time I discovered a room I had overlooked earlier. In it Vehdna workers moved lazily amongst a dozen ceramic tubs. Some carried buckets from which they scooped fluid into the tubs a cup at a time. The fluid came from a vat a man kept stirring when he was not adding water or some white powder.

I saw little remarkable about those tubs. The solution got added at one end. At the other end fluid trickled down a glass tube into a large earthenware jug. Once filled each jug got stopped and carried carefully to storage on shelves well out of the way. Unlike wines, they were shelved upright. Curiously, the lamps in the room burned unusually bright.

I studied one tub, noted that small bubbles kept rising at the end where the workers added the fluid. At the far end, well below the surface, were dozens of short rods caked with a silvery-white substance. On the floor of the tub were several handleless glass cups. Using ceramic tools a gloved worker moved a cup under a rod, scraped stuff off into the cup. Once that settled he used wooden tongs to lift the cup from the tub. He carried it with considerable care but, nevertheless, managed to stumble.

The stuff off the rod blazed fiercely when exposed to the air.

I had to get back to my flesh. I had to eat. Soon enough I would have to pack because real soon all of us would be headed south. The war's next stage was gathering momentum.

91

Otto and Hagop were back, after innumerable frustrating delays on the last river leg, which should have been the easiest part of their journey. They were concealed in the same Shadar waterfront warehouse that I had used to hold the captives from the Grove of Doom. One-Eye collected me from my quarters. He and I and my brown shadow headed for the river.

The Old Man beat us there. He could drop everything when he really wanted. "You all right, Murgen?"

"I'm handling it."

"He's spending too much time with Smoke," One-Eye said. "That don't sound healthy. Would you look at these guys?" He meant Otto and Hagop, though the others of their expedition were confined to the warehouse, too, and were not enthusiastic about being kept away from their families.

It had been almost three years.

Neither Otto nor Hagop looked much different. I told Hagop, "I'd almost given up on you guys." We shook hands. I shook with Otto, too. "I thought your luck finally ran out."

"We came close, Murgen. We used up a lot."

"So," the Old Man said. "What took so long?"

"Actually, there ain't that much to tell." Hagop looked at Croaker oddly, as though to make sure he was talking to the real Old Man. Croaker was in his Shadar disguise. "We went, we did what we could, we came back." Like a fourteen-thousand-mile round trip was routine? In the Company we do not brag about the big stuff. "We didn't do a lot of sightseeing."

While Hagop talked Otto made a circuit of the doors and

windows. He asked, "We need to worry about spies?"

"This is Taglios," Croaker replied. By which he meant that everyone is always watching everyone else, looking for an edge.

"We figured you guys would have then all squared away by now."

"That's a lot of squaring. Shadowlander spies, yeah, they aren't a problem. Lady and Goblin and One-Eye took care of them."

I said, "We still have the priesthoods."

"And we've had a little Deceiver trouble lately."

Something in my face warned Hagop against pursuing that. Not now. "How goes the war, then?"

"Slowly," Croaker told him. "We can talk about that later. You do us any good up there?"

"Not much, to be honest."

"Damn!"

"We did get a bunch of stuff for the Annals. Murgen, you might want to work it in. It's stuff about what other people were doing that will help make better sense of what we did. I figure you could work it in between stuff that Croaker wrote. That way them that comes after us can see both sides. Huhm?"

"Maybe you ought to take over." Sourly.

"Learn me how to read and write. I'm too old for this other shit."

"Might do that," I glanced at Croaker. "Long as you don't edit me."

The Old Man grinned.

Hagop chuckled. "The gods forfend, Murgen. Not me. Hey. I found out all about what happened after we left up there, too. You wouldn't believe the excitement. The Limper came back one more time. Don't worry. It's all settled now. The empire is boring these days."

"Sounds like I wish I was back home."

Croaker asked, "Did you actually get into the Tower?"

"We spent six months there. Mainly getting the runaround at first."

"And?"

"We finally convinced them that Lady was getting her powers back. They got cooperative then. Folks in the Tower these days like not having her around."

"Gee. That'll break her heart," I said.

Hagop grinned. "Yeah. They won't send us any help. Say they don't want to make any new enemies. I think it's mostly because they don't want Lady getting nostalgic for her good old days and heading back north."

Croaker said, "We figured that. There's nothing in this for them but keeping Lady away. What did you get?"

"They opened their records. Lent us translators. Even opened graves when we asked."

"They would have an interest in who was buried there themselves."

"Damned if they didn't. They had to change their linens after we told them who all turned up alive down here. See, they had a major scare when the Limper came back and damned near took them apart."

I said, "That guy had a bigger boner for us than Soulcatcher does." No way did we need to add the Limper to our list of enemies. "What about my turnip seeds?"

Hagop said, "They made sure of Limper this time. Absolutely sure. I got your seeds. Turnips and parsnips and even some seed potatoes—if they haven't spoiled."

Croaker said, "They *would* make sure of Limper." He watched Otto prowl. Otto was restless, uncomfortable. "So they let you poke around and even gave you some help with it. What did you learn?" That had been the point. To see if they knew anything way up north that we could use here.

"Not much. It don't seem likely that Longshadow was ever one of the Taken."

I was confident of that. I was sure he would have betrayed himself to Howler by now if they had been allies in the past. "Those potatoes. Did you get the little kind like I . . ."

Hagop glowered at me, told the Old Man, "There is the remotest chance that he could be the Faceless Man, Moonbiter, or Nightcrawler—although everybody up there was sure those three really did bite the dust. It was just that we couldn't come up with any bodies."

"How about one of the later Taken?" Croaker mused.

"Five actually survived. Journey, Whisper, Blister, Creeper and Learned. But Lady stripped all five of their powers. In front of witnesses."

"But Lady has been getting her powers back," I argued.

"A point. On the other hand, we know the exact day when the Shadowmasters appeared. Even the hour, I gather. All the later Taken were still in business up north. In fact, most of them weren't even Taken yet."

I traded glances with the Old Man. He began pacing. He said, "When Soulcatcher held me captive she told me one of the Shadowmasters who died at Dejagore wasn't ever one of the Taken."

I added, "Neither was Shadowspinner."

Hagop said, "All they could tell us, really, was that they didn't have a clue if Longshadow used to be one of the old mob. The written record supported them."

Croaker kept pacing, narrowly avoided a collision with Otto, but stayed well away from the cluster of unhappy Taglians awaiting his blessing upon their desires to go home. After all this time could they recognize him through his Shadar disguise? Probably.

I was sure he was thinking that this war with the Shadowmasters was no ordinary struggle, that the stakes went far beyond simple survival. He said, "We've taken three of the bastards down. But Longshadow is the worst. He is the craziest. He's working on Overlook day and night. . . ."

"Still?"

"Still. The poor idiot is a living testimonial to the fact that everything takes longer and costs more. Even magic can't get you around that. But he's a lot closer to being finished than he was when you left. And if he does get done before we get him we can bend over and kiss our butts goodbye. It'll be the end of the world. His plan is to pull his hole in behind him and loose the dogs of hell—then come out later and collect up the pieces of whatever is left."

I grumbled, "I've heard this one before." I never took it entirely serious despite the characters involved. But it did sound like Croaker believed Longshadow was capable of doing it. Maybe his adventures with Smoke had shown him something I had missed so far.

So the end of the world was imminent, either at the hands of Kina and her Deceivers or at those of Longshadow. Either way, only the Black Company could prevent the tragedy.

Yeah. Sure.

I wanted to tell Croaker, old buddy, we're only the Black Company. We're just a gang of misfits who can't make it in life except as hired swords. Sure, we got ourselves into an asskicking contest with some bizarro creeps now but there ain't nobody going to care in a hundred years. We are entangled in an affair of honor because of promises we made and stuff like the Stranglers snatching your kid. But don't try to sell anybody on saving the world.

I was scared the Old Man might be developing a case of the big head, like Longshadow, Mogaba, the Howler, Kina, all the devils of our time. One of the Annalist's duties is to remind the Captain that he is not a demigod. But I was out of practice. Hell, I could not deflate Uncle Doj when he got going.

"I need an edge, Hagop," Croaker said. "I need it bad. Tell me you found something. Anything."

"I found Murgen's turnip seeds."

"Damnit. . . ."

"The best suggestion they had was that we might try to trace the survivors of the Circle of Eighteen."

Well. That was interesting.

Croaker stopped pacing. He looked at me as though I might be able to tell him something. I saw his focus fade. He was remembering the Battle at Charm.

The Circle of Eighteen raised huge rebel armies to pull Lady down. The culminating battle at Charm had been the bloodiest in recorded history.

The Circle did not win.

Croaker said, "We killed Harden and Raker. Lady turned Whisper to Taken. That accounts for three."

"A lot more just got lost when we whipped them," I observed. My "we" drew smiles from Otto, Hagop and the Old Man. I was maybe twelve at the time and had not yet even heard of the Black Company.

Hagop said, "We were too damned thorough back then, boss. We went out looking for and flat could not find any Rebel veterans to interrogate. We couldn't even find names for seven of the Eighteen. But there were people at the Tower who were junior officers then who claimed they had witnessed the deaths of all of the Eighteen except one called Trinket, those who became Taken, and one of the ones whose names we couldn't find out."

"Trinket." Croaker resumed pacing. He mused, "I remember Trinket. But just the name. We were at the Stair of Tear. We got word that Trinket was surrounded. In the east. We were busy with Harden. I don't know if I even mentioned it in the Annals."

Ha! A chance to show off. "You did. One sentence. That's it, though. You said Whisper had taken Rust and Trinket was surrounded."

"Whisper. Yes. She'd been Taken only a little while." He had been there to help set up the Taking. "That's one for Lady. She would know if there was anything between those two."

"Trinket was female," Hagop told us. "What's Longshadow?"

Croaker frowned.

I said, "He never gets all the way naked but I'm pretty sure Longshadow is a he. Physically."

The Old Man offered me a daggers look. Damn! But the Taglians were way off in a corner sulking. None of them caught my slip. Hagop was not on the list of three, either, though. I hastened to amend myself. "But Smoke is the only one who ever saw him in the flesh. And he ain't talking."

"He still alive?" Hagop asked.

"Barely," Croaker said. "We keep him alive. Men have come back from comas before. That's it, Hagop? All that time and travel. That's all you got me?"

"That's the way she goes sometimes, boss." He grinned. "Oh. I almost forgot. They did give me a coffin full of papers and stuff that night have belonged to some of the people who *maybe* could have turned into Longshadow—if he was ever one of the Eighteen. The stuff is all packaged and labeled in case some wizard decides he wants to use them."

Croaker's face lit up like a bonfire. "You shithead." Grinning, he yelled, "Otto, send them guys home, why don't you? Bonharj, the rest of you, what the hell are you doing hanging around here? Your people want to see you." He told me, "Guess we ought to ship that stuff down to Lady. She'll know what to do with it."

Otto hustled the Taglians out of the warehouse. They seemed baffled by the Liberator's sudden generosity. Me too.

Hagop said, "Now how about you guys telling what's been happening?"

I said, "A whole lot. But nothing big and dramatic. We keep nibbling them to death."

"Is Mogaba really the head honcho of Longshadow's army?"

"Absolutely. He's one kickass sonofabitch, too, only Longshadow won't let him run loose. He has to mess with us secondhand, mostly, letting Blade do his dirty work."

"Huh? Blade? Like in Blade of Blade and Mather and Swan?"

"Oh. Yeah." I glanced at the Old Man, whose expression had gone stony. "Yeah. Blade defected while you were gone."

"Let's get back to the Palace, Murgen," Croaker said. "We have work to do."

92

Croaker did not say much as we walked, though he did snarl at people who dared stare at the Shadar and his white-devil companion. We northerners are so few that even after years few of the commoners have yet seen any of us. And, of course, we have done very little to dispel our evil reputation.

Some intellectuals inside the priesthoods have argued that the friendship of today's Black Company is as deadly to Taglios as was the enmity of its remote forbears.

Their complaint may have merit.

We were coming up to the Palace. Croaker kept grumbling to himself, mostly because so little had come of the expedition. That had been his pet and his expectations had run away with him. He asked, "How long are your in-laws going to hang around?"

I was not going to make him happy. "For the duration. They want their slice of Narayan Singh." The Old Man still distrusted Uncle Doj.

"They know about Smoke?"

"Of course not! Damnit . . . !"

"Keep it that way. You find his library again yet?"

I had mentioned having stumbled onto that. "Not yet." Fact was, I had made no more than a token effort. I had too much else on my mind.

"Try a little harder." He knew. "Don't spend so much time with Smoke. And I think it might be useful to look at those old Annals before we head south."

"How come you never looked for the library yourself? You've had years."

"I heard it got destroyed the night that Smoke got mauled. Now it looks like that must have happened in some other room. The Radisha wouldn't mislead me about something like that. Would she? Nah."

We paused while a Vehdna cavalry regiment passed in review outside the Palace. It had come from upcountry somewhere and was just paying its respects before taking the field. The robes and turbans of the troopers were clean and gaudy. Their lances were all brightly pennoned. Their spearheads gleamed. Their mounts were beautiful, admirably trained and perfectly groomed.

"Too bad pretty don't win wars," I said. The Black Company is not pretty.

Croaker grunted. I glanced at him. And surprised what might have been a teardrop in the corner of his eye.

He knew what awaited all those brave young men.

We crossed behind the horsemen, stepping carefully.

One-Eye met us in the hall way outside Croaker's apartment. "What's the word?"

Croaker shook his head. "No magic answers."

"We always get to do it the hard way."

I told him, "I'm supposed to look for that library room I found the other night. You got something to help keep me from getting confused?"

He looked at me like that might be a tall order. "I already gave you something." He indicated the yarn on my wrist.

"That was for *your* spells. There's probably still a bunch of Smoke's left over, too."

The runt thought about that. "Could be. Give me that." His gaze fell on my amulet as I removed the yarn. "Jade?" He held my wrist momentarily.

"I think so. It belonged to Sarie's grandmother, Hong Tray. You never met her. She was the old Speaker's wife."

"You been wearing this all these years and I never noticed?"

"I never wore it till Sarie . . . Until the other night. Sarie wore it sometimes, though, when she wanted to dress up."

"Ah, yes. I recall." He frowned like he was trying to remember something, then shrugged, went off into a shadow and muttered to the yarn for a while. When he returned he said,

"That ought to get you through anybody's confusion spells. Except maybe your own."

"What?"

"You had any of your attacks lately?"

"No. Not that I remember." I offered the amendment because I had had them before without being aware of them. Apparently.

"You had any new ideas about what caused them? Or who you kept running into when you went back to Dejagore?"

"I was escaping from the pain of losing Sarie."

One-Eye laid one of his more intense stares upon me, just the way he had whenever he helped fish me out of the past. Evidently he was not convinced.

I asked, "Is it suddenly important again?"

"It never stopped being important, Murgen. There just hasn't been time to pursue it."

Nor was there now.

He said, "We just have to let you take charge of yourself, to watch out and do the right thing in a crunch."

One-Eye being totally serious? That was spooky.

Croaker had lost interest. He was back at his charts and figures. But he did reiterate, "I want to see those books before we hit the road."

I can take a hint, sometimes. "I'm on my way, Boss."

93

I stopped in to make sure Smoke was still breathing. I fed him while I was there. Keeping him fed and clean was now my cover for being there should someone like the Radisha ever penetrate One-Eye's network of spells, much augmented since I had begun working with the old wizard. Then I tried to recall the various twists and turns I had taken the night I found Smoke's library. My memories were not clear. That had been a time of stress and a lot had happened since.

I did know it was on this same level. I had not gone downstairs or up. And it was in an area apparently undisturbed since Smoke's own last visit. The dust and cobwebs were heavy and untouched.

It did not take me long to reach desert territory. It was almost as though the deep interior of the Palace became a vast and dusty maze, needing no spells of confusion to protect it.

I found the dead man only minutes after leaving Smoke. I smelled him first, of course, and heard the flies. That told me what would be coming up before I saw anything. Only the who was a mystery until the Strangler appeared at the limit of my lamplight. He had fled here to die of his wounds, trapped by darkness and confusing spells.

I shuddered. That touched my deepest fears, the wellspring of my nightmares, my crushing dread of tight, dark places underground.

I wondered if his fickle goddess had taken delight in his unhappy end.

I moved around the corpse carefully, averting my eyes and pinching my nose. In death he continued to serve Kina's corruption avatar.

Soon afterward I discovered evidence that at least one more Strangler had become entangled in the confusion of the Palace. I nearly stepped in it, being alerted only when my approach startled the attendant flies.

I paused. "Uh-oh." That looked fairly fresh. Maybe there was still a madman in here willing to dance for his goddess.

I started moving much slower and more carefully, one hand at my throat. I started imagining noises. All the ghost stories I ever heard came back to haunt me. Each few steps I paused, turned around completely, searching for the gleam of eyes betrayed by my lamp. Why did I decide to do this alone?

I began to see signs of recent traffic. I knelt, discovered what appeared to be my own previous footprints in the dust. Someone had been through since, armed with a battery of candles.

Drops of wax had fallen into the disturbed dust. And somebody had been through after that, possibly crawling, perhaps even eating what wax drops he could find.

I listened to the silence. This deep within the Palace even vermin were scarce. They could only eat each other.

Still cautious, I followed the trails of those who had come after me. My heart thumped like it was about to explode.

I started sneezing. And once I did the sneezes just kept coming. I could hold off for half a minute sometimes, but that only made the next sneeze worse.

Then I started hearing all sorts of sounds. And could not still myself long enough to reassure me that I was imagining these noises, too, or to get a fix on their source if they were genuine.

Maybe it would be better to do this some other time.

Then the broken door loomed out of the darkness. I stopped and studied it. I had a notion it was hanging a little differently. Disturbances in the dust suggested that someone had visited since I had done so myself.

Cautiously, touching nothing, I rounded the door, stepped into the room.

"Shit!"

It had been torn apart. Few of the books, bound or scroll, remained on their shelves or in their cubbies. The undisturbed items, where I could decipher titles, were prosaic inventories or tax records or irregular city histories of little interest. I wondered why Smoke would bother with those. Maybe just to hide the good stuff? Maybe because he was fire marshall as well as court wizard?

Whatever, the good stuff was gone. And by that I mean not only any long-missing volumes of the Annals that might have been lying around but also a number of what I had suspected to be magical texts when last I looked in.

"Damn it! Damn it!" I wanted to throw things, to break things, to bounce rocks off villains' heads, Even before I found the single fallen feather I had a good idea of what had happened.

I collected that feather.

On the way back I definitely heard sounds that did not spring from my imagination. I did not bother to investigate. The man tried to follow my light but could not keep up.

94

Croaker looked up, puzzled, when I laid the white feather in front of him and said, "The books are gone. And there are Deceivers lost in there. At least one dead one and one still alive."

"Gone?" He plucked the feather off the document he was studying.

"Somebody took them."

His distress was apparent only because his hand began to shake. "How?"

"They just walked in off the street and carried them away." I did not for a moment consider the possibility that someone inside the Palace had visited Smoke's books.

He said nothing for a while. "What perfect timing." Another silence. "What's this feather?"

"Maybe a message. Maybe just a lost feather. I found one like it when I discovered that the Widowmaker armor had disappeared from hiding in Dejagore."

"A white feather?"

"From an albino crow." I ran through my catalog of encounters, real and possibly imagined.

His hand shook again. "You never actually met her. But you recognized her? She was here the night the Deceivers struck? And you never said anything?"

"I forgot that. That was the worst night of my life, Captain. That night has twisted everything else around me. . . ."

He gestured for silence. He thought. I stared. He was noth-

ing like the Croaker who had been Company physician and Annalist when I joined up. After a while, he muttered, "That must
be it."

"What?"

"The voice you encountered whenever you were pulled back
to Dejagore. Think. Was it inconsistent?"

"I don't think I understand."

"Did it seem like it might be different people talking all the
time?"

Now I got it. "I don't think so. It did seem to have different
attitudes and styles sometimes."

"The bitch. The sneaking bitch. Always playing another
game. I won't swear this for sure, Murgen, but I think the root
mystery behind you tumbling all over time must have been
Soulcatcher playing."

Not a wholly original theory to me. Soulcatcher rated high
on my own suspects list. Motive was my big stumbling block. I
could not figure a "why Murgen?" for anybody, Soulcatcher included.

"Where is she now?" Croaker asked.

"I don't have the foggiest."

"Can you find out?"

"Smoke balks every time I try to head her way."

Croaker considered that. "Try again."

"You're the boss."

"As long as it suits everybody's convenience. You sure your
in-laws won't go home?"

"They're going wherever I go."

"Tell them we'll be on the road befor the end of the week."

"I look forward to that like a case of the piles." I took my
white feather and stomped off for a session with the fire marshall.

95

I did not go straight there. I stopped by the apartment, collected a flask of tea, a gallon of water, a basket of fried chicken and fried fish, rice and some of Mother Gota's special baked rocks. I expected a long session. There were things I wanted to do beyond my expected swift rebuff in a search for Soulcatcher.

Smoke seemed unchanged. As always. I wondered what he would remember if, as sometimes happened, one day he just woke up from his coma. I hear tell people have done that even after being under years longer than Smoke has.

I filled my stomach with water before I left the apartment. I took in more fluid when I reached Smoke. I went to work.

Drifting. Quick check of all the villains. Mogaba and Longshadow, Howler and Narayan Singh and the Daughter of Night were all acceptably located, either at Overlook or Charandaprash. Blade was skirting the Shindai Kus with maybe twelve hundred men, trying to get behind the Prahbrindrah Drah, but the Prince had a screen of light cavalry out far enough to give him plenty of warning.

The man had a knack.

Before I carried out my obligation to look for Soulcatcher I took Smoke back in time to see just how early I could find and spy upon some of the principals. I wanted to see what had happened that night I had been held captive and tortured. I wanted to unveil the details of Mogaba's defection.

I found that I could not go back that far.

I recalled that raft on the lake, Mogaba cursing in the darkness. That had to be it. He should not have been there. What honest mission could have taken him ashore? Had he changed allegiances while still holding Dejagore for the good guys? Was his deal already made when Croaker faced him down? Did he meet the Howler out there, far enough away that Goblin and One-Eye would not detect the sorcerer's flying carpet?

Maybe. And if he had that might explain why even Sindawe and Ochiba were willing to abandon him.

All of us would be dead already and the war long since lost had Longshadow been in a position to seize that moment.

The cold claws of death may have come closer than ever I had suspected.

I wish I could have had eyewitness evidence, though.

Smoke can be tricked. And he can be driven by a sufficiently-determined will.

From the frontiers of past time I raced toward the night of my despair. I did not drive him to the center of its evil, though. Instead, I slowed and drifted into an earlier hour, as the Stranglers first approached the Palace and in best Deceiver form used two of their number, disguised as holy prostitutes of Bashra out to perform their obligated random acts of joy, to get close to the Guards.

But that was not the history I wanted to review. I brought him forward to the moments of my own interlude upon the sallyport steps. I watched myself emerge from the Palace, vacantly settle to the stone. The seizure lasted scarcely a minute, for all the time I spent amongst the horrors of yesteryear.

Now the slick move. The focus upon the woman in the shadows across the way, behind the hairy Shadar. The lock onto her despite Smoke's increasing anxiety and spiritual wriggling.

I never got to know Smoke in full life but, by most accounts, he had been a pure chickenshit, inalterably opposed to anything that might involve even the most minor risk to anyone in the court wizard or fire marshal rackets. Cowardice must have run right down to the foundations of his being because he writhed like a worm on a fishhook the whole time I watched Soulcatcher loot his library.

She had no trouble with confusion spells. She had none with Stranglers, either, though she did encounter a band. They just gaped at her briefly, then decided their best interests ought to lead them elsewhere.

She seemed unaware of my scrutiny, unlike that time in the wheatfield. Could it be that even she was unaware of the secret of Smoke?

Wouldn't that be lovely?

I watched her for a long time, even after she departed the Palace. Smoke resisted every second.

Then I went back and had a drink and a snack before I tackled the more interesting business of tracking Goblin down and, to slake my own curiosity, having a look at the final falling out between Croaker and Blade. I had been unable to find witnesses to the actual explosion.

96

To track Goblin I went back to the last time I saw the runt myself, then followed him forward in time.

Soon after having helped me out of one of my plunges into yesterday Goblin walked out of his quarters carrying one modest bag, hiked to the waterfront, boarded a barge manned by trustworthy Taglians who had become professional soldiers, and drifted down the river. Right now—approximately today—he was in the heart of the delta, transferring the barge's cargo, himself and most of the Taglians, to a deep-sea vessel wearing flags and pennons entirely unknown to me. Off on the sodden shore flocks of Nyueng Bao children and a handful of lazy adults watched as though this business of outsiders was the greatest entertainment they had encountered in years. Despite my familiarity with the tribe they all looked inscrutably alien in their native context, more so than they had in Dejagore where we all had been out of place.

For no reason clear to me I had never visited Sahra's world. I just welcomed her into mine and savored the miracle.

Goblin's behavior was less interesting than his whereabouts, which I had now established. So why not see what life was like for the Nyueng Bao? Uncle Doj insisted that the delta was paradise.

Possibly, if you were of the mosquito clan. I swear. The fact that I was a disembodied point of view was all that kept me from being devoured. Goblin was candyass enough to protect himself and his crew with potent spells, augmented by bad smells. But the Nyueng Bao had to deal with bloodsucking buzzards able to carry off small children. I reminded myself that I had seen all the bugs I wanted coming south through One-Eye's home jungle and it was likely that Sarie's people could manage excellently without the presence of Sarie's husband.

I drifted through the area, curious about how she had lived before we met. Hamlet, rice paddies, water buffalo, fishing boats, the same yesterday, last year, last century and tomorrow. Everyone I saw looked like someone I might have met in Dejagore or among the Nyueng Bao serving with the Company now.

What?

I was sweeping along like a darting swallow. I glimpsed a face looking up in a hamlet miles back from the river where Goblin and his crew were sweating their guts out. My heart flipped. For the first time out there with Smoke I enjoyed a really strong emotion. If I had been in my body I would have wept crocodile tears.

Man-eating crocs adorn the delta, too.

I whipped back, around, hunting that face so much like Sahra's that it could have belonged to her twin. Down there somewhere, near that old temple.

No. I guess not. Wishful thinking, Murgen. Plain wishful thinking. Probably just another Nyueng Bao girl newly a woman, endowed with that incredible beauty they have for four or five years between childhood and the steep slope into despair.

I pressed in once more, wanting desperately to find even the simulacrum of Sahra. And, of course, I found nothing. The pain became so great I withdrew from that region entirely and went looking for a place and time where the gods held me in higher favor.

97

I had to fall backward in time, tumbling smugly toward the one era in my life when I was totally happy, when perfection was the order of the universe. I went to the hour that was my pole star, my center, my altar. I went to the moment every man who ever lived dreams of, that one instant when all wishes and fantasies have the potential to come true and you have only to recognize that and grab it within a heartbeat to make your life complete. For me that moment came almost a year after the end of the siege of Dejagore. And I almost wasted it.

Nyueng Bao were almost always a part of my life then. A scant three weeks following Croaker's showdown with Mogaba, and Mogaba's consequent flight, while us survivors were still creeping north toward Taglios, pretending to be triumphant heroes who had liberated a friendly city and rid the world of a bunch of villains, I awakened one morning to find myself under the dubious and permanent protection of Thai Dei. He was no more talkative than ever but in a few words he insisted that he owed me big and he was going to stick to me forever. I thought that was just hyperbole.

Boy, was I thrilled. I was not in a mood to cut his throat so I let him hang on. And he did have a sister I wanted to see a lot more than I wanted to see him, though I never found the nerve to tell him that.

Even so . . .

Back in the city, established in the Palace, in my tiny room with my papers and books and Thai Dei sleeping on a reed mat outside my door, him insisting that To Tan was in good hands with his grandmother, I lived a life of confusion, trying to figure out what had happened to us all and to make sense of Lady's writings. I was not thinking with absolute clarity when I received a gentleman name of Bahn Do Trang, who was a relative of one of the pilgrims of Dejagore. He had a message for me. It was so cryptic it could have qualified as one of the great goofball sybilline pronouncements of all time.

"Eleven hills, over the edge, he kissed her," brother Bahn told me, all splashed up with a huge and un-Nyueng Bao grin. "But the others were not for hire."

To which I offered this countersign, "Six blue birds in a peppermint tree, warbling limericks of apathy."

Death of the grin. "What?"

"That's my line, Pop. You told the guys downstairs you had a critical message for me. Against my better judgment I let you come up here and right away you start spouting nonsense. Tamal!" I yelled at the orderly who assisted me and several others who worked out of rooms nearby. "Show this clown the way to the street."

Do Trang wanted to argue, looked at my sidekick, thought better of making a fuss. Thai Dei watched the old boy closely but did not look like he wanted the honor of flinging him out on his enigmatic ass personally.

Poor Bahn. It must have been important to him. He seemed stricken.

Tamal was a huge Shadar man-bear, all hair and growl and bad breath. He would have liked nothing better than to pummel a Nyueng Bao all the way to the street and thence to the edge of the city. Bahn went without protest.

Less than a week later I received the identical message as a handwritten note that looked like it had been inscribed by a six-year-old. One of Cordy Mather's Guards brought it up. I read it, told him, "Give the old fool a beating and tell him not to bother me again."

The Guard gave me a funny look. He glanced at Thai Dei, then whispered, "Ain't old, ain't a him, but probably is a fool,

Standardbearer. Was I you I'd take the time."

I got it. At last. "I'll just box his ears myself, then. Thai Dei, try to keep the bad guys out. I'll be back in a few minutes."

He did not listen, of course, because he could not bodyguard me from a distance, but I did confuse him long enough to get a headstart. I got down there and got my hands on Sahra before he caught up or got ahead of me. After that he had little say. And my clever lady had brought To Tan to distract him.

Thai Dei did not talk much but that did not make him stupid. He knew he could not win with the cards he held right now.

"Clever," I told Sahra. "I thought I'd never see you again. Hi, kiddo," I said to To Tan, who did not remember me. "Sahra, honey, you gotta promise me. No more of that cryptic stuff like Grandpa Dam. I'm just a simpleminded soldier."

I led Sahra inside and up to my little hole in the wall. For the next three years I marvelled every morning when I wakened to find her beside me and almost every time I saw her during the day. She became the center of my life, my anchor, my rock, my goddess, and every damned one of my brothers envied me almost to the borders of hatred—though Sahra converted them all into devoted friends. She could give Lady lessons on softening the hearts of hard men.

Not till Uncle Doj and Mother Gota came to visit did I find out that Sahra had done more than just defy the customs of the Nyueng Bao. She had ignored the express orders of her tribal elders to come make herself the wife of a Soldier of Darkness. Confident little witch.

Those toothless old men put no value on the wishes of the "witch" Ky Hong Tray.

I think I have a realistic picture of who and what I am so I am amazed that Sahra ever thought as much of me as I thought of her.

98

I sipped water, ate, and reflected that this was one time when I had no trouble leaving Smoke's world. There was no attenuation of the pain if I went out there to see Sarie.

What was I doing here?

There was one mystery yet to be illuminated before I allowed Croaker to drag me off into the next fun phase of our great adventure. I wanted to know what had happened between him and Blade.

Smoke and I zigzagged back and forth through time, quartering the temporal reaches, tacking into the winds of time, following a search pattern, looking for anomalies in the relationship between Blade and my boss. I knew about when the blowup happened so, instead, for the time being, I sought contributory evidence.

You can cover a lot of time fast riding Smoke. It did not take long to establish, beyond a doubt, that Blade's relationship with Lady was never anything but proper, however charged with wishful thinking on his end. Lady never acknowledged Blade's mooneyes—nor those of anyone else. She seemed too accustomed to them to pay them any mind.

So what did happen?

I worried it like a wild dog trying to dig a rodent out of its hole. Smoke was no help at all. There were places, times, angles that he just refused to go see. I tried tricking him several ways, just to find out why he could not or would not go where I wanted him to go. None of that did any good.

Maybe I was baying down the wrong trail.

The actual headbutting had been less than wildly explosive and made only marginal sense when viewed from another point in time. All I could find out that made sense was that Blade and

Croaker were sipping some potent home brew before they started getting crazy.

Verbal sniping turned into angry implications which became threats on the Old Man's part. And the beer continued to flow.

I have to say that Croaker was definitely the bad guy. Or fool. He kept on and on while Blade did his best not to let himself be baited.

That only infuriated Croaker. He spouted threats that left Blade no choice but to run.

I backed away, embarrassed for my Captain. I had not thought that he could be such a complete asshole. I did not understand why he was so insecure about Lady. I felt for Blade, deeply, and had to think less of one of my heroes.

Now that I reflected on it, I recalled occasional bestowals of unpleasantries upon Willow Swan that had *not* gotten out of hand. And Croaker had even exchanged cross words with the Prahbrindrah Drah once.

I sensed a pattern. It was not one I wanted to see. But it was obvious if you looked for it.

Croaker was obsessed with his woman. He would alienate anyone who offered her too much attention, however costly that might be.

Shit. Why? She was not Sarie.

We had lost Blade already. I do not have a lot of use for Willow Swan, who is much too pretty and too blond, but I would really hate to have the Company on the wrong side of the Prince just because one man could not be sure of his woman.

More scales fell from my eyes, leaving disappointment behind.

I needed to take this up with the brain trust, the oldest of the old, One-Eye, Otto and Hagop. Goblin was too far away and Lady both too far and disqualified by being too intimately involved. A Captain who thought with his balls instead of his brains could get a lot of people killed.

I do not worship any gods myself, though I guess some are real in their own ways. I have to believe that all of them get regular belly-laughs because one of them was ingenious enough to create human sexuality. Even greed and lust for power do not come close to generating the stupidities that us being male and female do.

But by giving it half a thought I can think of as many glories that spring from the same dichotomy.

Say, Ky Sahra.

Gods, Murgen. You need to get away from this half-dead old man. You are a hired sword. A soldier. You should not be playing philosophical games. Not even with yourself.

99

I popped out of contact with Smoke. "It's time, One-Eye. She's gone."

The little wizard tossed a friendly miniature owl into the darkened hallway. Untouched by confusion spells it headed for that part of town where it imagined it nested. It did not look for any particular human. That was not its mission. But plenty of humans looked for it. When it fluttered past them two dozen Black Company veterans and their Nyueng Bao bodyguards rushed a building that had deserved razing a generation before the Shadowmasters entered this quarter of the world.

I had tracked Soulcatcher back to that building from her raid on Smoke's library. She felt so safe there she was almost contemptuous of security precautions. She had managed to get by undisturbed there for years.

She was going to be one unhappy player when she discovered that she was less in control than she imagined.

I watched, pleased, while Black Company soldiers took the building by the numbers and in a manner so professional that not one Captain ever would have found cause for complaint.

The men now even had the knack of getting their jobs done
without stumbling over the Nyueng Bao, who were worse than
a herd of cats when it came to getting underfoot. You just had
to use them like they were your shadows.

Hardly anyone not directly involved noticed my guys. They
got inside, spread out, dug deep, found what I wanted, gathered
it up and got back out long before Soulcatcher discovered that
she had been outmaneuvered.

Otto and Hagop directed the raid. Putting them in charge was
my way of bringing them back into the family. Good soldiers
they, they carried out my suggestions, not just cleaning out
Soulcatcher's hideout but grabbing her favorite white crow.
They plucked a couple of his feathers and left them in place of
the books, tied together with a strand of hair taken from the
head of a much younger Soulcatcher, a long time back, and
come south with the plunder brought by Otto and Hagop.

That ought to rattle her.

Maybe I should have let Croaker and Lady in on my scheme.
In a way, I was making a statement in their names. But this had
become personal. I had a statement to make for Murgen. And
there was no time for consultations and conferences.

Smoke and I swooped over the guys as they lugged their plunder toward the Palace. I meant to give the books to Croaker as
soon as they arrived. He could do whatever he wanted with
them. Which probably meant that they would bounce once
and land back in my lap, to be disappeared from the ken of all
villains and villainesses—probably no better than I had hidden
the Widowmaker armor.

I wondered if I was going to get too intimate with the meaning of hubris. Soulcatcher would know who done her wrong. She
was maybe only a year younger than Lady, which left her an age-
less amount trickier and nastier than me.

But what did I have to lose? The only thing I ever loved was
gone. I could dance with disaster and grin to the end. Soul-

catcher could not do anything that would hurt more than losing Sahra had.

Really?

Sometimes you bullshit yourself.

100

An hour before sunset four days before the winter solstice, consulting neither the convenience of mortal man, nor sorcerer, nor god or goddess, the earth shifted and shook. In Taglios dishes tumbled off shelves, sleepers awakened in confused panic, dogs howled and cracks appeared in old walls whose foundations had been set with incomplete diligence or without forethought for the possibility of earthquake. It was a half-hour sensation.

In Dejagore structures weakened by former high water or hidden structural defects yielded to the relentless seduction of gravity. Farther south the impact was more severe. Beyond the Dandha Presh, where mountains descended upon valleys with ferocious roars of triumph, the quake left epic horror. Kiaulune was devastated. Even Overlook suffered, though the masonry shrugged off the earth's worst. Longshadow was in a panic for hours, until it became obvious that the earth's convulsions had not broken his shadowgates and shadowtraps. Then he began to rage because the destruction and loss of life in Shadowcatch would delay his construction efforts by months. Perhaps even by years.

101

I had the vague feeling that somebody was looking over my shoulder, though how anybody could get behind me when I was nothing but a floating viewpoint I did not know. The voice was not there but otherwise the feeling of presence was the same as it was during my earliest plunges into the horrors of Dejagore with the taunting spirit that must have been Soulcatcher.

Only a smell accompanied this presence. An odor like. . . .

Like the smell of the dead Strangler I had found in the deeps of the Palace, like the stench that had become so much a part of life in Dejagore that eventually you noticed it only when it was gone. It was the smell of death.

I had felt a full measure of pain in the delta, imagining that I saw Sahra alive among the Nyueng Bao, despite being out in the numb with Smoke. Now I enjoyed a full measure of terror despite being out there.

I began doing what, in flesh, would have been a full turn-around, slowly. I turned a second time and a third and a fourth, each time faster than the last and each time less in control. And each time around, as I faced what I suspected was southward, I glimpsed something vast and dark and, horribly, each time more clearly, till the last time around I saw a black woman as tall as the sky. She was bare-ass naked. She had four arms and six teats and fangs like a vampire. The stench was her breath. Her eyes burned like windows into hell yet looked into my own and held them and spoke to me with a blistering compulsion and promise—a ferocious eroticism beyond anything I had known with Sahra.

I screamed.

I popped out of Smoke's universe.

Smoke had wanted to scream, too. I think he came close to being terrified awake.

One-Eye laughed. "Cold enough, Kid?"

I was soaked. With *very* cold water. "What the hell?"

"You try staying out there forever again, I'll freeze your ass for good."

I began to shake. "Oh, shit, that's cold." I did not tell him what I had seen, why I was shaking really. Probably just my imagination running away with me again, anyway. "You dog turd, what the hell are you trying to do, give me a heart attack or something?"

"No. Just trying to keep you from getting lost. You won't look out for yourself."

"I think I'm lost already, old timer."

The stars wink down in cold irony.

There is always a way.

The wind whines and howls with bitter breath, through fangs of ice. Lightning snarls and barks upon the plain of glittering stone. Rage is a red, near-animate force, as bloated with compassion as a starving serpent. Few shadows frisk among the stellae. Many have been summoned, there or yon.

At its heart the plain is disfigured by the scars of cataclysm. A jagged lightning bolt of a fissure has ripped across the face of the plain. Nowhere is that fissure so wide that a child could not step across but it seems bottomless. Trailers of mist drift forth. Some bear a hint of color when they emerge.

Cracks mar the surface of the great grey stronghold. A tower has collapsed across the fissure. From the fastness comes a deep great slow beat like that of a grumbling world-heart, disturbing the silence of stone.

The wooden throne has shifted sideways. It has tilted a little. The figure nailed thereon has changed its sprawl. Its face is drawn in agony. Its eyelids flutter as though it is about to awaken.

This is immortality of a sort but the price is paid in silver of pain.

And even time may have a stop.

GLITTERING STONE
will continue in *She Is The Darkness*.

TOR
BOOKS The Best in Fantasy

TOR
fantasy

ELVENBANE • Andre Norton and Mercedes Lackey
"A richly detailed, complex fantasy collaboration."—Marion Zimmer Bradley

SUMMER KING, WINTER FOOL • Lisa Goldstein
"Possesses all of Goldstein's virtues to the highest degree."—*Chicago Sun-Times*

JACK OF KINROWAN • Charles de Lint
Jack the Giant Killer and *Drink Down the Moon* reprinted in one volume.

THE MAGIC ENGINEER • L.E. Modesitt, Jr.
The tale of Dorrin the blacksmith in the enormously popular continuing saga of Recluce.

SISTER LIGHT, SISTER DARK • Jane Yolen
"The Hans Christian Andersen of America."—*Newsweek*

THE GIRL WHO HEARD DRAGONS • Anne McCaffrey
"A treat for McCaffrey fans."—*Locus*

GEIS OF THE GARGOYLE • Piers Anthony
Join Gary Gar, a guileless young gargoyle disguised as a human, on a perilous pilgrimage in pursuit of a philter to rescue the magical land of Xanth from an ancient evil.

TOR
BOOKS The Best in Fantasy

LORD OF CHAOS • Robert Jordan
Book Six of *The Wheel of Time.* "For those who like to keep themselves in a fantasy world, it's hard to beat the complex, detailed world created here....A great read."—*Locus*

STONE OF TEARS • Terry Goodkind
The sequel to the epic fantasy bestseller *Wizard's First Rule.*

SPEAR OF HEAVEN • Judith Tarr
"The kind of accomplished fantasy—featuring sound characterization, superior world-building, and more than competent prose—that has won Tarr a large audience."—*Booklist*

MEMORY AND DREAM • Charles de Lint
A major novel of art, magic, and transformation, by the modern master of urban fantasy.

NEVERNEVER • Will Shetterly
The sequel to *Elsewhere.* "With a single book, Will Shetterly has redrawn the boundaries of young adult fantasy. This is a remarkable work."—*Bruce Coville*

TALES FROM THE GREAT TURTLE • Edited by Piers Anthony and Richard Gilliam
"A tribute to the wealth of pre-Columbian history and lore."—*Library Journal*
